THE SPARKS OF SAINTS

CORA GRAY

Content Warning

Though these topics are not the focus of the story please note that this book includes the following:

-Hand to hand combat/violence

-Crude language

-Open door mature content

-Mention of off-screen suicide

-Loss of a parent

-Loss of a child

CONTENTS

PART I

"OUR WILLS AND FATES DO SO CONTRARY RUN, THAT OUR DEVICES STILL ARE OVERTHROWN; OUR THOUGHTS ARE OURS, THEIR ENDS NONE OF OUR OWN."

WILLIAM SHAKESPEARE

CHAPTER 1

*S*ilence.

On any given day, it was the companion I craved. The incessant beeping of monitors, infinite conversations of strangers, and buzzing of fluorescent lights combined to create an overstimulating nightmare. It drove me to seek solace at the end of each day. I would drive in an isolated trance until I crossed the threshold of my townhouse and fell into my bed, ensuring that the blackout curtains were closed against the sunlight. It was then, with a blanket of comforting quiet, that I would finally be able to find peace as I fell asleep.

That was what I longed for most days.

The same could not be said for today.

Silence on a night like this might as well have been a blaring siren for all to hear. Whether they were involved in the situation or not, all my coworkers would eventually know a generic version of what had happened, and it wouldn't be long before the details came to light. I had no doubts that the whispers in the halls would spread faster than wildfire during a dry summer. They always did with situations like this. Their murmurs would not end tonight, of course. No, they would be the start to a new day, carrying on into next week, as the story was told again and again for the benefit of those not present. Small details would be changed or forgotten altogether, leaving only the ending to remain consistent: the boy died.

It was just one more noise to add to the pandemonium that would await me when I inevitably had to return to work in the weeks to follow.

The beginning of the tragedy was marked by a very distinct sound. That specific alarm signified a bad omen to anyone who had spent time in the hospital. It was a shrill tone, activated by a button we prayed we wouldn't have to use at the start of every shift. It was never to be taken lightly.

And I'm the one who had to push it.

The second the code button was pressed, the unit came alive. Echoes of pounding feet and voices rose above the choir of ventilators and IV pumps beeping away to their unorganized nightly song. Half a dozen people appeared within seconds, looking into the room that had desperately signaled for help. My room—well, my patient's room.

I realized that was my cue. They were waiting for me to make the next move. After all, I was the only one in this room who knew anything about the kid lying in the bed. Without thought, I began delegating roles to fellow nurses. I found myself mentally summarizing the essential information, starting with who the kid was and moving on to IV access, medications, and whatever else was necessary as I compiled a list of what the team would need to know. It was like muscle memory, and I was thankful for the chance to let my brain slip into a state of natural instinct and automatic thought. It wasn't just a tool that helped me do my job; it was mental armor, too. It was a headspace that allowed me to detach from the situation staring me in the face.

Four years ago, I couldn't imagine being able to disconnect and still maintain confidence in the care I was providing, in a dire moment like this. Gone were the days of constantly feeling uncertain about my abilities, and I did not long for them.

"What happened, Kiara?" Dr. McCormick asked as he entered the room. To an outsider, his tone may have seemed cold as he took in the scene before him, but the rest of us understood it as a tone of neutrality. We all had different ways of donning internal protection, and the manifestations were hard to spot if you didn't know what to look for.

"James McCarthy, 16-year-old male, 63.7 kilos, brought in for extensive injuries due to a car accident."

I heard myself list off the information like I was reading back a coffee order; robotic and empty of any feeling. In the back of my mind, I was becoming increasingly aware that this night was heading south—and all too quickly at that. I knew it meant there was zero room for emotion to seep through if I wanted to be efficient. Especially when kids were involved, it never took much to break.

Though the code alarm was no longer screaming for help, the air buzzed more than ever. The monitor attached to the boy on the bed continued to belt its horrendous chorus as we all worked over him. The uproar was only drowned out by the stern voice of the doctor as he called out medications. Orders were repeated as staff drew them up and stated once again as I confirmed what had been pushed into the IV at specific times. Others were performing CPR, stopping only to check pulses when instructed to. I couldn't see them, but I knew social workers would be outside the room, waiting to speak with the parents who would be here any minute.

There was so much going on and too many people in a small space. But we were all needed, and we did our best to work in tandem. Conversations continued to layer on top of one another, and somehow, we all remained coordinated, never missing our cues, never stepping outside of our specified roles. To anyone looking in, it would look like pure madness. To all of us, though, it was a dance in organized chaos.

I chanced a glance through the glass doors. Outside, I could see James' parents. It was a mistake to look. His mom's expression was hidden, only the shuddering of her body visible as she cried into her husband's chest. His dad fought the tears, but the red rings around his eyes were undeniable. The couple clung to one another, every piece of them begging for something we could not promise:

Please save him. Please tell me he will come out of this alive.

I pulled my eyes back to the room. *Idiot. You know better than to look at them. Especially in the middle of this.* My emotions bubbled to the surface and threatened to break through before they had been given permission. Dutifully, I shoved them back down, locking them in a box tucked into the dark. Emotions rarely saved anyone.

We worked for what felt like an eternity. We pushed medication, took blood, compressed, and checked pulses. Then it started all over again. And again.

And again.

We continued like this until it was apparent nothing was going to change.

An hour into the code, the physician called for a pulse check. We waited, still slightly hopeful but mostly defeated. We were met with a flat line on the monitor. It was a single ear-piercing, gut-wrenching note that held and held until we could no longer stand it. What a cacophonous blare. I switched off the monitor to put an end to it all and mark the start of our collective heartbreak. And in the quiet—

"Time of death: 2230."

A heavy cloud weighed down all those present, dragging us to the center of the Earth. The world outside these doors seemed to fade away as it was drained of both color and sound. Even the adjacent rooms were suddenly mute. It was as if sound and time were tied together and neither could move forward. We would all be stuck in this moment forever, ready to leave but unable to propel the present onward without breaking the fragile, glass-like silence.

And then all hell broke loose.

I could never put into words the cries of a grieving parent. All I knew was that somewhere in those cries, I heard their hearts permanently shatter. It was the epitome of true misery. My humanity came crashing back into my body before I was ready, but I needed to stay strong for his parents. I was not allowed to mourn this loss. Not yet.

With a practiced ability, I slammed the fracturing box that held my emotions, mentally soldering it shut for good measure. I went back into overdrive, going through the motions once more. Many people came to discuss various things with the devastated couple. I checked on them often while they were forced to make difficult choices, ones I could only imagine in my nightmares. They dismissed me for the final time as they said their goodbyes before leaving their son for the last time. How they were able to walk out of that room on their own two feet was a mystery to me, and I was truly in awe of them.

I was sent home after they left, thanks to a low patient census. It was a rare occasion when anyone was sent home early, and I wasn't going to question the universe for gifting me this small reprieve. Without hesitation, I packed up my stuff and prepared for the trek through my unit and to my car. I didn't get very far before I was stopped in my tracks.

In a room three doors down, there was a man sprawled out on a bed. He was snoring loudly, his bed riddled with trash from the numerous snacks and drinks he had consumed in the short time he had been there. He had a small bandage over his forehead, and I could smell the alcohol that seeped out of his pores and into the hallway. I felt the last bit of resolve crack heavily in my chest, anger flooding my veins like a lethal poison.

This man was the reason why James would never see his seventeenth birthday. He was the reason the young boy with big dreams would never cross the stage to graduate. He was the reason those parents would go home to an empty house and prepare for a new, bleak future.

And he was fast asleep, not giving two shits about the life he had so recklessly taken.

I all but bolted out of the unit, leaving the hospital like a bat out of hell. It was a crisp fall night, and the cold air hit me as I stepped out. I breathed it in ravenously. It was as if I had been holding my breath underwater for too long and had finally been allowed to surface at the last minute. By the time I got to my car, my lungs were burning. I leaned against my door, hyperventilating. In an effort not to sob, my breathing had started to compensate. I tried to get a handle on it, but with no great success, so I crawled into my car and sat behind my steering wheel, gripping it tighter and tighter until my fingers turned bone white. I felt the ache in my hands as I squeezed with all my strength. It was only when I could not squeeze any harder that I let the scream escape me.

Everything I had been containing since the last pulse check came pouring out of me. Screams turned into sobs until sobs became silent tears. Barely a whimper slipped between my lips as I drowned in the emotions that my mental box could no longer contain.

"Fuck! God dammit!" A slew of unintelligible swears flooded the small space as my sadness ebbed and anger flooded my vision. The headrest of my passenger seat fell victim to my escalating outburst as

I hit it while continuing to swear and cry until I had nothing left. All that remained was the sound of my hyperventilation once more. It felt akin to purging the alcohol in your stomach until all that was left was bile. The exhaustion felt the same; I had tired myself out and probably bruised my hands in the process.

I forced myself to take control of my breathing once again. *Breathe in. Hold. Breathe out. Again. In. Hold. Out. You might as well be another accident waiting to happen if you try to drive in this state.*

I got my breathing back into a normal rhythm, and I was once again seated in the soundlessness of sorrow.

These were the times I wanted anything but silence. At the moment, I wanted to be overstimulated. I wanted a distraction. I needed to focus on anything other than my thoughts and feelings. I craved something surface-level to pass the rest of the night away. It would be the best way to kill time, even if it wasn't the healthiest way to cope with my feelings.

I briefly scanned my phone and hit play on the first angry playlist I came across. Pulling out of the parking lot, I headed for home as the bass of the drums vibrated the speakers in my car. I allowed myself the first ten minutes of my drive to reflect on everything that had happened what suddenly felt like a lifetime ago.

In those moments, I realized that, despite how I constantly sought peace, maybe that wasn't where I functioned best. The calm was something beautiful that could be turned lethal in the blink of an eye. My small solace turned into my own nightmare. No, the chaos, the constant action—that was where I existed best. In the eye of the storm, I was confident and steady-handed. I knew what to expect in madness. It never changed.

Silence was a fickle thing. The false sense of security it brought was only ever just that: false. It was never consistent. One day, it was pillows as soft as clouds and a cup of tea that carried me off to sleep. It wrapped me up in blankets, big and warm. The next day, it was a creature that preyed on my mind. It used its sharp talons, and as it tore into my thoughts, it replaced them with words that dripped venom and malice. It lived only to serve its own whims.

Chaos was constant. The severity of a situation may differ, but no matter what, I knew how it would affect me each time. I could face it head-on, shoulders back, and know that it would not feed me self-destructive lies.

To be able to find peace in the silence was never a promised reprieve. Perhaps it would be better for me to find comfort in the chaos instead.

CHAPTER 2

I walked into my house, flipping on lights as I went. The kitchen was untouched, the gray countertops and the island free of clutter. If someone were to walk in, their initial impression would be that no one had been here in days. The only small sign of my existence that they would find was the empty containers I had used for lunch, stacked up in the deep sink. Dishes were a problem for after the work week.

The open plan of the bottom level connected the kitchen to the living room. A blanket lay crumpled up on one of the couches, right where I had left it. Sometimes making it up the stairs to my bed was more effort than I felt like exerting, and tonight was no exception. I briefly thought about whether there was any ice cream left in my freezer. It would be easy to curl up under that blanket and watch some trash TV on one of the many streaming services I paid for yet rarely used. But the gray-scaled house with hints of blues and greens felt suddenly foreign to me. It was not the place I wanted to be tonight.

I took the steps up to the second level and opened up the door to the master bedroom. When I first moved in, I was in the other room. A girl in my cohort named Lainey had needed another roommate, and my studio had been on a month-to-month basis. We lived together well.

Most of our study groups were the same, so we were able to co-host study nights. We had the occasional party, too. Having a house that was far enough away from campus allowed for more casual kickbacks rather than the typical big party filled with a number of random, drunk freshmen who managed to stumble in through the front door.

Lainey and I became good friends. As we progressed through our program, we shared laughs, tears, and experiences with one another. There was a certain level of trauma bonding that came with nursing school, and I think each of us needed the other to get through those three years.

We helped one another relax through mandatory reality TV show nights. I showed her the stores with the biggest cheap wine selections, and she always picked the best discounted movies to go see. We would share all the hidden places we had found to eat at during our freshman year, and we spent the summer finding new ones to add to the list when she decided she wasn't going to go home for the break.

The start of our junior year, we were going to throw a party to kick off Fall term.

We were standing in the kitchen looking at our handiwork. The island was full of the liquor we decided to provide, along with whatever additional bottles were brought by those in attendance. Two of the other girls in our cohort had made a 'special punch' they were now placing in the center of the island. The sea foam green liquid and various fruits sloshed around in the massive bowl, but managed to remain from spilling over. One of the girls looked up at me with an expression that almost seemed to say, 'that would have been bad,' then smiled as she walked off with her roommate.

Around us, people were enjoying themselves. Some were laughing and talking in the kitchen or on the couches. Others were standing, playing various drinking games on folded tables set up in the hallway. Some people were even dancing to music playing from Lainey's soundbar, though I doubted either of our phones were connected anymore. There were faces I recognized, some who were merely friends of friends, but everyone was comfortable. There was no trouble, and the happiness of reuniting after a summer spent apart was thick in the air.

Lainey turned to me. "This was a great idea. It makes the start of the year almost feel exciting. I'm glad I let you talk me into this!" She was beaming now. Whether she would admit it or not, she loved to play host. A successful party for her was almost always going to end up as a core memory.

"We don't need to start stressing about school until we actually go to class. Everyone here deserves one more night of being careless."

"You're not wrong. Speaking of being careless..." She turned her back briefly, only to face me again, this time holding two cups full of the punch. "Should we head to our usual spot?"

I took my drink from her hand, sipping the sweet liquid. If there was alcohol in there, I couldn't tell. "Lead the way."

I followed Lainey as we weaved through the people and around the games of beer pong. As we walked by, Lainey's long caramel brown hair, a few shades brighter and several inches longer than my own, nearly ended up in one of the full cups. I almost reached out to stop it, but as if she knew her hair was about to be dipped in beer, she tossed it over to the other side of her head. I had always wondered how she could manage such long hair; I never allowed mine to grow just below my shoulders because it was always such a hassle to me.

We went out the back door and to the side of the house. There sat a makeshift set of steps we had put together last year. By using the steps, we were able to reach higher, thicker branches on the tree, which, in turn, gave us roof access. It was a questionable climb at best. With only one hand to climb, the other occupied with my cup, and a slight buzz already threading through my thoughts, it was likely not the safest thing to do.

However, we had done it several times before, scaling it to lay in the sun or watch fireworks, and we had yet to have anything bad happen. It offered a great view when you were looking for a change of scenery close to home.

Campus was great in the summer. It was quieter, and I was always ready for the pace of my life to slow down. But the start of Fall term was always something of a welcome gift. By the time it came around, I was grateful to switch back from the idle mindset. I was happy to see everyone coming back from vacations, too. It was one of the reasons I wanted to throw the party tonight.

We sat in comfortable silence, watching as people came and went. If they noticed us, they smiled and waved before going on their way. For the first time in a long time, my chest swelled with contentment. If I could freeze time—if I could stop anything from ruining this moment––I would've traded anything to do it. But I had nothing the heavens would be willing to bargain for in exchange for such a gift.

I took a big drink from my cup. Paused. Took another, and this time, it was big enough that Lainey noticed.

"You okay over there?" she asked, playful concern in her green eyes. "You're not suddenly afraid of heights, are you?"

I laughed, but it was half-hearted, and I knew it was plain on my face that something was on my mind. I lifted my head in hopes of holding her gaze, but unable to bring myself to watch her face, I dropped my head to look at the tiles of the roof under my crisscrossed legs. Seeking distraction in anything I could, I picked up a random leaf and began to twirl it between two of my fingers.

"Kai, are you okay?" Genuine worry was threaded in her voice now.

"You know, I grew up with my aunt. She was really great and welcomed everyone into our home. All she ever cared about was if I—or anyone, really—was a kind person. Nothing else mattered, and she never made a big deal out of anything, you know?" I continued to stare at the roof and wondered if she knew where I was going with this. Did I even know where I was going with this?

"Erica, right?" Lainey asked as her tone relaxed some, though apprehension still lingered. "Every time you mention her, she sounds more amazing, Kai. I bet it was a great childhood."

It really had been. We did so many things. She took me to parks, museums, zoos, oceans, and everything in between. To this day, I have such a variety of hobbies and interests, and I attribute that all to her. She was a saint among sinners, and judgment was not something she ever tolerated.

"I don't think I could have asked for anything better. I never really knew what it was like to be afraid of her. Worry about making a poor decision that broke her trust, sure, but what teenager doesn't make stupid mistakes? In the end, though, I always knew that nothing would ever be so terrible that she would hate me for it."

We sat in silence for a minute, Lainey ever the picture of patience as I tried to form my thoughts into clearer sentences.

I sighed. "When I—" My voice caught, and I cleared it. "When I brought home my first crush, which my aunt knew, she introduced herself and asked if she should set a third plate for dinner. Insisted, even, that there was plenty of food. And that was it. It didn't matter that the person next to me was a girl from my math class."

The breeze came in, blowing away the warm air to make way for the chill of fall. I sighed again, the weight of the small silence too much to bear. "I guess I never had to do this." I gestured wildly to the general space around us. "The whole coming out thing, I mean. I lived on my own after she passed, so I never had to explain anything to a roommate. And last year, with our courses, I wasn't really trying to date anyone. Maybe some coffee or dinner here and there, but nothing serious. I...I just..." Words started to fail me.

"Kai?"

"I just wanted you to know that I like women, and I didn't want to keep that from you anymore. Not that I was keeping it from you—shit. What I mean is it started to feel like a secret even though it never was meant to be. I hope you don't feel like I was trying to lie to you and that we can still be...you know..."

"Kiara"—her use of my full name startled me— "did you think that this would ever change anything about our friendship? I don't feel like you lied to me whatsoever. If anything, I'm sorry I never asked. I just assumed you were so dedicated to school, and that was why you never brought a guy around."

"You're sure?"

"Of course! Are you kidding me? You are my best friend. That doesn't change." She scooted closer to me, and I chanced looking at her once again. I could tell by the look on her face that she meant it. Everything was going to be alright. I grinned back at her as the tightness in my chest vanished and I felt myself releasing a breath I didn't know I was holding.

Lainey put her head on my shoulder as we took in the view once more. The silence, comfortable as it always was, lingered between us.

"Well, one thing might change." Lainey sat up quickly. My stomach churned suddenly, waiting for her to say she had changed her mind, but she followed it up with, "Can we finally talk about your dating life?"

I couldn't help myself—I burst out laughing.

I stood in the room that had been Lainey's during those three years. She had chosen to take a job a few hours away from here after graduation and got married last year. We tried to stay in touch, and we always made plans to see each other when we knew we would be in the same vicinity, but a tale as old as time is that of college friends trying to make time for one another as real life begins. It was doable, but hard and inconsistent.

Nights like these were when I wished, more than ever, that she was still here. We could go out, dance, and drink until our eyes were heavy and the world was light. Lainey was the closest thing I had to family since my aunt had passed. I thought back to the memory of that night on the roof and remembered how scared I was to tell her such an intimate detail about my life. The relief that flooded my body when she had accepted me without hesitation was immediate.

Acceptance from strangers was never something I concerned myself with. If the most interesting thing in their day was to condemn me, then so be it. They could think whatever they wanted about me, so long as they left me out of it. Acceptance from loved ones, though... That was another story. The two people I was closest to didn't shy away from who I was. They normalized it and understood that I was just existing on this planet, looking for a soul who mirrored my own. I was no different from them. Not in their eyes.

Shaking my head, I pulled myself away from my thoughts, ready to move on from the past and forward with my night.

I walked to my closet and stared at the options before me. The clothes hanging in there were a fraction of what I had to choose from. A four-drawer black dresser sat up against a wall that it shared with my headboard. I could start there, but looking around the room, I knew the drawers would be bare. There were various places in the room where folded laundry had been left in stacks.

One of my biggest flaws was that I could never get my laundry put away. It was something that had always been a topic of discussion with girlfriends in the past. I tried to be better about putting them away, and I had been somewhat successful. But with how organized my professional life required me to be, I allowed myself this little bit of disarray when it was needed.

I tried on several shirts, all in various colors, but continued to be unsuccessful in finding something to wear. I started to eye my sweatpants and oversized hoodies. This was usually the point when my plans of going out started to die. Once I became fed up with trying things on, I tended to end up in something extremely cozy, and I inevitably would spend my night inside. Tonight, however, I would not be so easily discouraged.

After a few more attempts, I settled for a simple long-sleeved black V-neck. I slid into black jeans and dark gray high-top shoes that were easy to slip on and off. My wardrobe lacked color, it was true, but black on black was never a bad look.

I stepped back to look at my full reflection. My dark brown hair fell just below my shoulders in waves of loose, mahogany curls. The shirt hugged my frame, its neckline coming to an end with the cinching of the fabric, dipping just low enough to intrigue the imagination. The material was thin enough that I should have been less worried about sweating in the club and more concerned with the chill of an early autumn night. The rips in my jeans that ran up and down the legs would not lend me any extra warmth, either.

I barely had any makeup on. Blue eyes with mascara and a touch of eyeliner stared back at me, the redness from earlier no longer visible. I put on a face of bored disinterest to complete the look. This would do just fine.

Fake it till you make it, Kai.

CHAPTER 3

If you want to be surrounded by consistency in an overwhelming quantity, there is no better place than a club.

Saying that out loud might make people think I'm unwell, but it's true. Coast to coast, every nightclub has the same basic blueprint. There are always walls of alcohol seated behind a bartender who has probably already been harassed despite being only a few hours into their night. Anything from shots to dark amber liquid to tropical drinks line the bar as orders are taken. I personally loved to play the guessing game of who bought what drink as I watched servers take them to tables.

There are always bodies on the dance floor. Groups of girls dance with their friends while the guys watch from the bar. Couples are dotted throughout the dance floor. Some have been together for a while. You can see it in the way they move together as one. Others move less flawlessly with their partner, but both convey the same message of desire. Singles looking for the distractions and pleasures of a night out wander about until something catches their interest. The music flows through all of them, the bass replacing their heartbeats.

It drowns out any words not spoken directly into the ear. So loud that even outside the club, it dully reverberates through the streets.

Another constant? There is always a line.

I stood outside with the crowd, waiting to be granted entrance into *The Arcane Club.* Some groups were fresh-eyed and seemed to just be starting out the night. Others were heavy-lidded, words slurring together as they swayed in their spots. If I had to guess, this would be their last club. I cast my eyes past those in line and out onto the sidewalk. People flocked to food carts, crawled into cars, and spoke loudly to one another about what the rest of the night looked like. One girl was telling her friend that she had lost her phone and started scanning the ground frantically for it. Ironically, the friend she was talking to was on the other end of a phone call. I almost wanted to point it out to her, but before I could, her laughter filled the air.

"That's so silly," she said loudly, though no one paid any attention to her. "I'm ordering the car now!" Within minutes, she was gone.

The flow of the line was a steady crawl, and I made it through the door 15 minutes later.

Inside *Arcane*, there was warmth. The packed club was dark, only illuminated by the flashing of multicolored lights. Red lights lit the shelves of the bar, the paneled dance floor, and underneath the edges of the bar top. To my left was the dance floor, and at the front, on a raised platform, a DJ. The platform had been barred off to keep away any drunk idiots who might decide they wanted to take a turn mixing music. To my right was the bar. The shelves holding liquor bottles rose nearly to the ceiling, and so far out of reach, that I wondered if those bottles furthest up had anything in them.

From where I stood, I started to debate what I wanted to do next. *Drink, dance, drink, dance.* The idea of going out alone used to be scary. But in the last handful of years, I found how great it could be when done safely. You get to go out when you want, go home when you want, and choose to go wherever you want. The freedom is amazing. *But when you're indecisive-*

"You look like you could use a drink."

I spun around to find the owner of the deep voice. He was standing just behind my right shoulder, as if he had just come inside as well. I took in the man before me. I suppose he was good-looking in the most general way. He was taller, 6'2" if I had to guess, and that was being generous. The stranger was dressed in a black button-down, short-sleeved shirt with one too many of those buttons undone. Stark white pants covered his legs. He had sandy blonde hair that had been styled into a perfect, natural-looking mess, but the gel flakes he had missed gave it away. He had sharp cheekbones that made someone look twice, and green eyes that surely had enticed most women with empty pro mises.

Most women.

"Please let me buy you a drink. It has been a shitty excuse of a night, and I worry that if I don't turn it around soon, it will be a loss." He flashed a charming smile then, showing immaculate white teeth.

"I appreciate it, but you should know that I'm not—"

"I'm not looking for anything other than a reason to throw some money around. You were just the first person I saw who happened to look like decent company."

The stranger looked at me with innocent eagerness and something like hope. He wasn't going to take no for an answer. In order to save *my* night, I was better off just appeasing him with one drink before disappearing into the crowd. He seemed harmless, maybe a bit arrogant, if anything. Surely one drink wouldn't hurt anyone.

He wants to show off his money, and I want to drink. We both win, even if it means I have to drink with this guy. I bet his name is Chad.

I smiled and nodded in acceptance. "What the hell, why not?"

The man held out his hand. "My name is Brad." *Dammit.*

"Kai." I grabbed his hand and shook it once. A brief look of surprise crossed his face when his gentle grip was met with the business-like vice of my own. But as quickly as it was there, it disappeared. I dropped my hand, and he turned and gestured towards the bar. "Shall we?"

I wove my way through the crowd with Brad on my heels. The line for drinks had no obvious beginning, so I paved a way up to the red glow of the bar top and waited to make eye contact with a bartender.

"We should take a shot too," Brad said loudly in my ear. "What do you want?"

I knew that what I wanted to shoot would not mix well with whatever drink I had. But I was willing to chance the hangover and let future me deal with the consequences. I told Brad my poison of choice, and he quickly relayed the order to the first bartender he saw. He made quick work of them and was back before either Brad or I could utter another word to the other. The bartender took extra care to hand my shot and drink directly to me before he attended to the next person in line.

The poster child for fraternity recruitments held up his shot. "Cheers to shitty nights and good booze."

And bad decisions

I tapped my glass to his, tapped the countertop, and threw back the clear liquid. I was instantly warmed to my core. I had no need to chase, lick the salt, or bite a lime. I just followed the shot with more liquor. The vodka and tequila mixed as they ran together in my stomach. *I am going to pay for this tomorrow.*

Brad was still choking on his shot. He was staring wide-eyed at me as I waited while he collected himself. I sipped on my lemonade patiently, giving him no sign that I saw how surprised he was at my ability to drink. *I doubt the female company he keeps is old enough to know what the inside of a bar looks like, let alone how to hold their liquor.* I couldn't hold it against him, though. Most of the guys in the college town had a fake ID and were in the bars the second week into their freshman year. *I wonder how old he really is.*

"Did that bartender give you water because I don't think I have ever seen someone drink like that."

"What can I say, when you've had a rough week, sometimes you gotta let the demons come out to play."

"I'll do my best to keep up with them."

He tapped his can to my half-empty drink and downed it. Before I could stop him, he was already in the process of flagging down another bartender for a second round, so I finished the rest of my drink as well. Another shot, chased with another drink. We made small talk in between, and it was almost a comfortable rhythm. I wasn't entirely paying attention, though.

If I'm being honest, I would ask him questions about himself that I knew he would expand on. People often have no issues with talking about themselves. I gave appropriate nods and other signs of acknowledgement as he bragged about his travels, athletic ability, or whatever else he might have raved about. In reality, though, I was sipping my drink as I glanced around the club. People-watching was always a favorite pastime.

I caught something in the peripheral of my vision as I scanned the room. It was quick. The smirk of a stranger who had also been observing club-goers. She had been standing there mere moments ago. Had she seen how we stood at an awkward distance from one another? Could she see how emphatically this man was talking to me and how uninterested I truly was? I had scanned past her so fast that when I looked back, she had vanished into the crowd. Based on the fleeting smirk, I felt this stranger would have been amused by my current situation. But no matter how hard I looked, she was nowhere to be seen.

"How old are you?" I asked, pulling my thoughts away from the stranger in the crowd.

"Well, it depends on who's asking," he said with a grin. "If the bar asks, I'm twenty-three, according to my ID."

"And if I'm asking?"

He paused for a minute, deciding if it was in his best interest or not to tell me the truth. His eyes had a slight glaze to them now. We were three rounds in, and the vodka was already getting to him. Not that I was entirely sober, either, but I wasn't slow to respond in the way he was.

Whatever war Brad was fighting internally seemed to end. His shoulders slumped a little, and he looked down at his shoes as he quietly said, "I'm 19." All of the proud bravado he previously had faded away with the admission. "I just thought that, coming in here, there wouldn't be anyone who would want much to do with me, knowing I was so young. So, I've been trying to seem like I've been around for a bit. I was hoping you wouldn't ask. I thought maybe this would go somewhere. I thought we were having fun even...but I didn't want to continue with a lie." There was a slur in his words that suggested this was more of a drunken confession rather than a morally driven one. Either way, the boy in front of me could no longer bring himself to look me fully in the eyes.

"Hey, I appreciate the honesty." I smiled at him softly. "And we are having a nice time. Really, you aren't the worst drinking buddy a girl could have." He looked at me then, hope lighting up his face. "I just want to be clear, though. This is not going to go anywhere."

"I knew it. I knew I shouldn't have said anything. It's because I lied and now—"

"It's because I like women, Brad."

There it was, in the open. What I had tried to tell him when we first entered the club, before he insisted on spending all his money on drinks. He watched me as what I said slowly processed through his intoxicated state. I let him have the time he needed, calculating what his next words would be, how he would handle it. Words were formed in his mind but erased before they escaped his lips.

We stood there, letting the music of the club fill the space until finally he graced me with a response. "Oh."

No judgment but not quite understanding either. The meaning was just as simple as the word itself. For the first time that night, he was speechless.

"I'm sorry. I tried to tell you before. I should have tried harder. I had hoped that we both understood this was just drinks between friends."

He held up his hand and shook his head to stop me from going on. "I cut you off earlier. Let me apologize for it with another round. If you're interested in still being drinking buddies, that is?"

I laughed, "Another round it is."

The 19-year-old version of Brad was less flashy in all the best ways possible. We drank and chatted. I listened to him for real now. We talked about school, and he asked me for advice, though he was more interested in areas of study like foreign policy and business of one kind or another. He asked if I knew of places to eat around campus, and I shared the list Lainey and I had made years ago. We discussed movies, books, and whatever else came up as the conversation evolved.

"Now that the cat is out of the bag, how old are you?"

"Don't you know it's impolite to ask a lady her age?" I said with heavy sarcasm. I sipped my drink for a second. "Twenty-four."

"Twenty-four isn't bad at all."

"I can't help but think"—I had started to slur a bit by now— "that the most out of place, and in between, I'll ever feel is going to be in my mid-to-late twenties."

As I said this, his eyes started to trail further down the bar to where a group of girls stood, giggling after taking their shots. *Typical boy. But can you blame him?* "When you talk to them," I said, dragging his attention back to me, "show them this version of you, not the one who 'summered in the Hamptons' or 'spent a month in Europe.' They will appreciate the authenticity more than your bolstering alternate ego."

He went to protest. Whether it was to say he wasn't planning on talking to them, or that he hadn't sounded *that* bad, I didn't know. I simply held up my hand. Instead, I insisted that he let me split the bill with him.

"It's the least I could do. After all, you have already saved me money for the night." I added, "If it makes you feel better, you can buy my drinks and I'll buy yours." He laughed but agreed that it was an acceptable idea.

"One more shot for the road?"

We threw back one more before going our separate ways, he to the girls at the end of the bar, and I to the dance floor. I was feeling warm and happy. My night at work was temporarily erased, and my mind was free of worries. I was light and airy and, more than anything, I wanted to dance.

So, I did.

I made my way into the middle of the packed dance floor on the other side of the club. The red lights on the floor outlined everyone around me. Some were dancing in couples, some in big groups with their friends. A handful of others were dancing alone, content to do so. Occasionally, more defined features were highlighted as the beams of moving, multicolored lights lit their faces. Just as quickly as they appeared, they vanished back into their silhouetted form. I briefly felt as if someone was watching me, but the feeling was fleeting, and I didn't have the ability to care. *You're in a packed club. Someone is always watching.*

I stopped thinking. The music flowed into my ears and throughout my body. I could feel the bass in my chest trying to replace the beat of my heart. Its speed took my breath away. I was often dancing by myself, but other times, I was caught up with a stranger. Girls would join me whether they were behind me or in front of me. Sometimes we were looking at one another, dancing nearly face to face. For some, it was innocent fun. Dancing was something they did with their group of friends all the time. With others, we were grinding up against each other. There was more tension, more heat. I was never one to initiate contact. They would always set the tone, and I would follow their lead.

One stranger had been facing me. She placed one arm on my shoulder when she first approached. We watched one another, gauging the rhythm that the other moved to. She ran her hands down my sides, gripping my hips, as she pulled us together, effectively removing the space that had just separated us. I felt her heat as she moved with me, but also against me. I moved my hands to her waist as one of hers moved to the small of my back while the other found its way behind my head and into my hair. She brought her forehead to mine, and we stayed there until the music ended.

As the song transitioned, I watched her look over her shoulder subtly, in the general direction of a group of guys. She looked at me once more, catching that my gaze had followed hers. She seemed to think that at that moment we were on the same page. *She is doing this for them.* Without warning, she kissed me. It was fast and lacked any meaning behind it. But it was enough to hold the attention of the men behind her.

She pulled away, giggling, clearly inebriated. With a squeeze of my hand as if to say thanks, and one last look back over her shoulder, she wandered into the crowd. I knew she meant nothing by it. I was a stranger to her. Just a girl at the club dancing with whoever was around. I knew I was straight passing. Without the ability to notice the little things that would suggest anything different, most people would have never guessed.

It was something I had explained to Lainey when we went out once. She had wondered at how things like that had never angered me. In truth, it was never the girls who made me mad. It was the perversion of men that promoted these actions, promising extra attention to women if they acted in this way. It had set the tone for the club culture, and anyone with enough liquor in their system was willing to turn almost anything into a game. Especially if they thought I wanted the attention of these guys the same way they did. I had learned to not take it personally.

After all, it's not like you're here to find your wife.

And I wasn't. I was here to be heavily distracted. I wanted to tire myself out. I wanted to make it so the demons in my head would let me sleep tonight. I wanted to feel anything but my sadness and anger at the world. It wasn't a healthy way to cope, but it worked.

I danced with everyone, even the men who came my way. I never allowed them to get too handsy. There were boundaries on where I allowed them to place their hands or how close I would let our bodies get. Most were fine with it, just happy to be dancing. Others, who continued to try to challenge those boundaries, I would move on from. They were usually too drunk to care and didn't want to expend the effort to follow me. It was easier to find someone else to dance with who was a more willing participant.

I was running out of steam. My core no longer felt warm from the drinks I had earlier, and I had started to feel my head clear as images of blood and sobbing parents and death floated to the surface. *Another drink it is.* I started to make my way to the edge of the group dancing around me. I hadn't realized just how close to the far end of the dance floor I had gotten until I was trying to find the bar through the throng of people. The sea of bodies was never-ending.

After what felt like 20 minutes of bobbing and weaving through drunken strangers, I had made it to the outer perimeter of the dance floor. As the last few people in my path cleared the way, I stopped in my tracks. *That smirk, I knew I had seen it earlier.*

In my direct line of sight, as a beam of white light illuminated the bar, I saw the stranger from earlier that I had given up on finding long ago. She had long blonde hair swept over to one side. She was dressed in a short-sleeved olive-green button-up, not entirely unlike the one Brad had on earlier. Her sleeves were rolled twice, taking away some of the excess material and accenting well-toned, tanned arms. The buttons were undone just far enough to tease the mind. Suddenly, my head was swimming again, but not from the alcohol.

She was seated on a bar stool, one foot flat on the floor, the other heel resting on a rung of the chair. Her back was against the bar where she had one elbow resting, perfectly at ease in the chaos of the club. In her right hand, decked with silver rings on her middle finger and thumb, she held half a glass of amber liquid.

She was probably the most perfect woman I had ever seen.

And she was making direct eye contact with me. Smoothly, she brought her cup up with a wink, as if inviting me over, before bringing the cup to her lips and taking a drink. Her gaze went right back to me, an amused half smile dancing on her face.

I was suddenly aware of how disastrous I looked. I had been dancing and sweating with strangers. My hair was likely knotted and flat, the effects of the liquor clear on my face. *Of course, this is when I would be noticed by someone as attractive as her. I don't even know what to say. She's just sitting there, looking so cool, so put together. Fuck. Why did I think another drink was a good idea?*

"Maybe because you had a feeling it would bring you over to me," a silky voice said, "and you knew I couldn't resist offering to buy you another."

Without any conscious permission from my brain, my body had closed the gap between us as I walked to the open seat at her side.

"I...I'm sorry?"

"You asked why you thought you needed another drink." She shrugged nonchalantly, a faint accent threaded in her words. "I only offered you an answer to your question."

"Did I say that out loud?" I put my hand to my mouth, not trusting any of my voluntary movements to work properly now.

She laughed a soundless laugh, looking down at her glass. When she looked up, amusement was burned in her blue-gray eyes.

Fuck me. My hand, which still covered my mouth in order to assure myself I didn't speak out loud, fell back to my side. I shook my head, not caring to hide my embarrassment.

"So how about that drink?"

"I guess one more couldn't hurt."

I watched as she downed her glass. Her tan skin was perfectly contrasted by the color of her shirt. As she tilted her chin up, exposing her neck, she revealed a thin silver chain. My eyes continued to move of their own volition. They drifted away from the chain, moving lower and lower until—

"Another whiskey for me and..."

"A cucumber lemonade for me, please." I waited until the bartender left, barely able to conceal my giggling in my inebriated daze. The beautiful stranger looked as if she wanted to be let in on the joke.

It only made me laugh harder.

I had her full attention, her body facing towards me now. "I must ask, what did I miss? Or do you just find ordering drinks to be *that* amusing?"

"I'm so sorry," I said, trying to gain my composure. If I were sober, I would have played it off much better. "I just can't take you seriously."

Whatever she had thought I was laughing at, it hadn't crossed her mind that I was laughing at *her*. She was stunned and, for half a second, it seemed like she was going to flounder. However, she swiftly composed herself. She picked up her fresh drink and took a smooth pull from it. Leaning her elbow on the bar, she shrugged. "Just as well, I hardly ever take myself seriously. But do tell." She flashed a brilliant smile then, showing off her perfect white teeth.

"The cool guy act, drinking straight whiskey," I sipped on my own drink, "even the silver chain! You are just the perfect blueprint, aren't you?"

"Perfect is my middle name. But what is it, exactly, that I am so flawlessly imitating?"

"To put it bluntly?"

"Please, I am begging you," she said, feigning exasperation.

"You are the poster child of a fuck boy."

The silence hung between us. I tried to read her face, worried that my teasing had crossed a line now. One I hadn't seen until I was already far past it. *You couldn't have just flirted with her like a normal person, could you? No, you had to be an asshole.*

There was laughter again, and this time, it wasn't mine. Her blonde hair concealed her as she doubled over laughing, nearly spilling her drink. When she sat upright, her eyes were sparkling, stunning.

"Is that so? But you're only basing this judgment on looks and what I chose to drink. Is my winning personality not enough for redemption?"

"Your personality is the basis of it all. You're charming, attractive, and you know it."

"So, you think I'm attractive?" she asked with a wry grin.

I ignored the question, not allowing myself to get distracted despite the heat I felt flush my cheeks at the accidental admission. "You are articulate and smooth and seem completely unbothered by anything. You flash that smile and offer to buy girls drinks, something I'm sure you have perfected to a science. In your mind, the world is your playground, and we are all just waiting to be invited to play with you in the sandbox." I shrugged and took another sip of my drink.

She was staring at the glass she clutched in her hand; half the liquid remained. When she looked up, all she said was, "This science you claim I have mastered..." Her eyes scanned my face, my posture, looking for any signs of genuine annoyance in my body language. "Is it working?"

"Typically, I like to know the name of the person I'm drinking with. I think that is where you failed."

"Well, allow me to remedy that." She stood, moving herself into the space my barstool occupied. It was only then that I realized the music and other sounds of the club still surrounded us. We were not, in fact, in our own room. I didn't have time to process much of this thought before she leaned her head down. I froze, not exactly sure what was going to happen.

Half a second later, her lips were at my ear. I fought the chill that went through me as her shoulder met mine. "I'm Sterling," she said softly. Her accent, from somewhere I couldn't place, was a little heavier than when we had been talking earlier. She pulled away, slightly extending her hand for me to take. As I did, she pulled me to a stand.

We were so close now that not much would fit between us. Her grip was warm and gentle yet strong and secure.

She was taller than me by a few inches. It was enough that, when I leaned forward to tell her my name, I had to incline my head. I glimpsed a small, fine line tattoo behind her ear. It was a symbol I had never seen before. Sharp lines forming a backwards capital 'N' were intersected in half by a horizontal line. "Kiara, but most people call me Kai."

I pulled back to look at her once again. *Sterling.* It was fitting. An uncommon name for someone who was already surrounded by a unique aura. "Now, would you allow me the pleasure of buying you a drink, Kai? Given that we are better acquainted?"

"Does this normally work?" I teased.

"Whatever do you mean?" she asked rakishly.

"The suave demeanor, loosening the hold on that silky accent of yours just enough to intrigue those around you. Does it work on most women?"

Sterling laughed into her empty glass, suddenly fascinated with studying the remaining ice. "Honestly? Yes, yes it does. Flawlessly, in fact." She gave me a wry grin, "Admittedly, I almost never have to work this hard."

I scoffed at her, rolling my eyes. Deep down, though, I believed it. She was beautiful and she knew it.

"Usually," she continued as she bent her lips to my ear again, "we don't get to names until *much* later in the night." I blushed as the shiver that ran through me was more evident than I would have liked. Sterling stood straighter once more. "But for you, Kai, I'd be willing to mix it up a little."

I realized we were still holding hands from when she had helped me stand earlier. Most women with her attitude would have left a while ago, given up. I looked up at her and let a small smile spread across my face, "I suppose we could try to start over, now that I know your name."

Sterling let go of my hand, and a small part of me was disappointed. I took my seat once more. As I sat, she turned her back and stepped away from me, heading away from the bar. My heart sank. *Is she leaving?* But she turned around just as quickly and sauntered the few steps back over to where she had just been standing. It dawned on me then that she was pretending to reset the scene.

"Kai, would you allow me the great pleasure of buying you a drink?" she repeated once more.

"A little dramatic, and corny if I am being honest, but I guess I'll allow it." I couldn't help but smile as she waved down the bartender for another round.

CHAPTER 4

I switched to something lighter, knowing that any more alcohol in my system would likely lead to further embarrassment. More importantly, the night would soon come to a close, and I didn't want to cross the line into forgetfulness. I didn't want to forget meeting *her*.

Sterling finished the last of her drink. "Do you want to get out of here?"

I looked at her, my eyes widening. I hadn't considered what would happen after the drinks were done. *What was the endgame here?*

My thoughts must have been clear on my face because she quickly clarified, "Oh no, that's not what I meant. I wasn't—how did you put it earlier? Inviting you to play in the sandbox?" Her eyes lit up, "I know a few places that are quieter than here. No alcohol, coffee is subpar, but it's within walking distance and generally lacks drunk idiots." As if on cue, someone stumbled into me from behind, nearly knocking me off my chair.

Sterling shot him a look that could cut through steel. She reached for me, catching me before I stumbled. He was too intoxicated to notice what he had done, much less the annoyance that radiated from the two of us.

Without another word, we left the club.

Within a short time, we arrived at a small diner. The coffee was cheap, as Sterling had promised. However, it was a fresh pot and, after a walk in the cold, its warmth was extremely welcomed.

"What do you do for work, Kai?" Sterling sat across from me, nursing her coffee.

"I work in the ER."

"I can imagine that's a stressful line of work. What made you choose to do that?"

"Most people go into healthcare because they want to help people. That was my reason at first, in some ways. I wanted to help those who needed compassion. Those who the world didn't entirely understand, or ever really forgive for their sins."

"You enjoy caring for lost souls."

"I suppose you could say that, though I have never thought about it quite like that before." I turned her words over in my head, feeling seen in a way I hadn't when talking about my career. "Even in medicine, we have our biases. But when I learned what it was to have empathy for those who others may have never spared a second thought, that was what made me pursue the field. At least in the beginning."

"In the beginning? So, has it changed then?"

I nodded.

"What is it now?"

"Honestly? It's stressful at times, like you said. But that's what I like. I enjoy being in the middle of it all. Not having time to sec-ond-guess myself, just letting my abilities, my knowledge, work for me. Oddly enough, it's when I feel most sure about myself."

Sterling watched me, processing what I had just said. Something behind those steel eyes flashed, like she could relate to the feeling.

"Most of the time, anyway," I continued, more to myself than to her, "usually things go well, or are predictable at any rate. Other times..." I trail off, unsure of how to finish what I was saying.

My face gave me away. "Other times you leave the situation doubting yourself more than ever before," Sterling finished.

I gave her a sad half smile that didn't reach my eyes. "You can't save them all."

Her gaze dropped, and she nodded as she measured her thoughts. Immediately, I was aware of the fact we were not the only ones at the diner. No one was paying attention to us, but I felt as if the whole room was watching. My heart was heavy in my chest, weighed down by the too-honest truth that left my lips. Words that only ever plagued my mind had now been given life as I spilled my trauma to the stranger in front of me. My nerves were on fire as my face flushed. I felt bare, vulnerable. It was uncomfortable. *Well done, taking a lighthearted night and dragging it down.*

"I think that, as hard as it might be," Sterling said, still not looking at me, "going back after feeling so uncertain of yourself, being able to face that and remember that you are capable is no small thing. I admire you for being able to conquer yourself. I have found that our inner demons are stronger than our physical enemies, more often than not."

She reached her hand over to where mine rested on the table and began tracing swirls on the back of my hand. Looking back at me once more, she said, "Though I don't know how a pretty thing like yourself could have enemies."

It took everything in me not to watch her hand on mine. With the trail of her finger followed a small electric sensation. My nerves were hyper aware of where she had been, anticipating where she would go next. I let her continue her slow, endless pathways. I appreciated her flirting, bringing us back to lighter conversation. "Where is that accent from?"

"Some small, unheard-of country. Probably long forgotten by anyone who wasn't born there."

"Is that so?"

"That it is. What I do remember is from the rose-colored lenses of childhood. I haven't been back there in over a decade."

I hadn't expected such a candid answer.

"Sounds like someone is due for a trip back to their mysterious land."

"Perhaps one day," she glanced down at our hands as if it was the first time she had noticed what she was doing. Deep in thought, she focused on the patterns she traced. "I may have grown up there, but I have created memories of home far from that place. It has always been a spot I intend to return to one day, but I keep pushing it off."

I didn't want to pry. An elusive response usually meant there was no desire to answer the question at hand. I decided to take a different route.

"Where are your friends tonight?"

"I felt it wasn't fair to them if I remained with the group all night. Seeing as how I am, understandably, a distraction," I rolled my eyes, feigning incredulousness. "So, I let them go on without me. Which, fortunately for you, brought me into that bar."

"Oh, how my luck has turned. Though I wish it would have manifested as a winning lottery ticket," I say with a shrug.

"You hurt me, Kai, valuing monetary success over our time together," Sterling grinned, "My friends are, to their credit, very social people. I'm afraid that if they had been around, we would never have been able to talk, which would have been a true tragedy."

"Has anyone ever told you that your dramatics rival those of Hollywood stars, Sterling?"

"What can I say? Every fuck boy has a flair for theatrics, no matter how small. How do you think pick-up lines are born? Certainly not out of mundane sentiments."

"So, you admit to it then?"

"Admit what?"

"That you are, in fact, a player?"

"Oh, Kai, a player suggests that there are others involved who stand a chance," she leaned back into her booth, taking her hand with her. Draping both arms over the back of her seat, she tilted her head, chin angling up ever so slightly. "I have found my biggest competition has only ever been myself."

"Sounds like a red flag to me."

"Some would say it sounds more like self-confidence, which I have been told is sexy. A word I also hear used interchangeably with my own name."

"You're terribly in love with yourself, aren't you?"

"I'm afraid so, but our relationship fluctuates and there is always room for another."

She flashed me a wicked grin, and I felt my face heat up as my core twisted with something a little more sinful than butterflies. My breath caught, but I wouldn't cave that easily.

"I'm not a fan of sharing, so it's probably best for me to leave you two to figure it out on your own."

"A pity. But an honest and respectable decision nonetheless." Amusement was still there in her eyes, but it was innocent now. *Just witty banter between strangers who shared a few drinks.*

Our cups had both run dry, and no one had been by to fill them for some time. I took it as a sign that, unless we planned on ordering something off the menu, we had outstayed our welcome.

"Can I order your car back?" Sterling asked politely as we stood to leave.

"Oh, you don't have to do that."

"Really, I don't mind. I'll take the same one once you make it home. One car for two trips. Consider it carpooling." I knew I wasn't going to talk her out of the idea, so I agreed.

She handed her phone to me so that I could put in my address. Within minutes, the ride had been accepted, and a bright red mid-level sports car zoomed up to the curb we were now standing on. The bass was vibrating the space around it, much like the music of the club from earlier in the night.

We hardly closed the door before the boy, who couldn't have been more than 18, sped away quicker than we could put our seatbelts on. He took a corner much faster than he should have and sent me flying into the door. While I slammed into the window, Sterling crashed into me, pinning me in place.

Nose to nose, both of our eyes widened with surprise. I could feel the movement of her chest against mine as she caught her breath, the smell of whiskey still tangible. The warmth radiating off of her was so palpable, I was surprised the driver didn't notice the temperature change in his car. She was so close, and the smell of sandalwood and vanilla wafted off of her skin as blonde strands of hair tickled my face. If I were to turn my head just a little, I could—

Sterling righted herself in her seat, throwing on her seatbelt, and I followed suit. I looked out the window briefly so that I could compose myself, hiding any trace of the disappointment I was feeling. I glanced back over to Sterling, who was watching me. She shook her head in mock horror. I couldn't hear the words she said, but I was able to make out the words 'no tip.' I laughed and shook my head along with her.

We didn't try to talk for the rest of the short drive. There was no point in making the attempt; the music was unbearably loud. And if that wasn't bad enough, the driver was now singing off-key to *his own* music. It was the worst ride I think I had ever taken.

Mercifully, we pulled up to my house. But the relief was short-lived as I remained in my seat, unsure of what I should do next. I continued to stay in place, overthinking the next few moments. Sterling analyzed me, only guessing at my thoughts.

I could ask her in. It would be the ultimate distraction, which was precisely what I had intended to find when I had walked into the club tonight. On the other hand, I wasn't sure that one night of meaningless sex was worth potentially ending something before it had a chance to begin. Especially if this had, in fact, been her plan all along.

One-night stands had never been a problem for me. As long as we both knew what the other was expecting, there was nothing wrong with it. This, however, felt different. I was already unsure if I could handle the fact that I may possibly never see her again. If I were to spend the night with Sterling, and that still be the reality, deep down a part of me knew that I could never come back from that. Even if we had only just met.

I sighed before I made my exit. I felt Sterling watch everything I did, trying to anticipate my next move. I stood from the car and rolled down the window before shutting the door. Standing outside the car, I bent down to look in the backseat. Sterling slid over to where I had been sitting seconds ago, a quizzical look on her face. The driver's playlist started at the beginning once more, causing Sterling to put her head out the window so she could hear me.

"I had a nice night, and I thought about inviting you in," I told her honestly, "Seriously considered it, actually."

"And I'm guessing I won't like the verdict?" she asked playfully.

"Honestly?"

"Have we been anything less than honest with one another tonight?"

"You should know I'm not normally like this. Casual usually works better for me," I took a deep breath. "For whatever reason, that isn't the case here. I could see you being someone I was destined to find, desperate to keep, and I'd drive myself crazy with delusions instead of acknowledging what this really was."

She nodded, not contradicting what I had said. *So, I was right after all. It was always going to be a single night.* Despite this fact and despite my best efforts, I couldn't bring myself to walk away. "Do you have a pen?"

It would have made it easier to walk away if she had said no. I could have chalked it up to a sign from the universe to leave her in that car and never look back. But surprisingly enough...

"I must have kept it after signing the bill at the diner," she noted as she passed a pen through the window. I took it from her, grabbing her hand before she could pull it away. After quickly writing down my number, I handed her the pen back. She examined her hand before looking back at me with a small smile.

"Destiny isn't necessarily set in stone," she offered.

"Be that as it may, I'm not one to tempt fate when I know my limits. Take care, Sterling." I stood, taking a step back from the car.

"Have a wonderful day, Kai." She offered me one last dazzling smile.

I walked away from the car, feeling her eyes on me. Dawn painted the world gray, proving that the night was, in fact, transitioning into a new day. As I unlocked and opened my door, I heard the car pull away, taking the booming bass and Sterling with it.

I felt her absence almost immediately. It was as if some part of me had cleaved from the whole and remained in the car with her.

I forced my feet up the stairs for the second time, ready to pour myself into bed for the duration of the day. As I made my way into my bathroom, I peeled off my clothes, leaving a trail behind me. Despite being tired, the need to rinse off the sweat from both myself and that of strangers would not be stifled. The water steamed around me, filling the bathroom, fogging the windows. It was relaxing to just stand in here, processing the events of the night. I played moments in my head over and over again. How her hand felt on mine, the cold look she had given the man who ran into me, the cab ride home.

I couldn't help but wonder if I had made the wrong decision.

My exhaustion hit me hard, and suddenly, standing under the running water became more draining than it was relaxing. I turned off the shower and wrapped myself in a towel, not bothering to mess with my hair. It would be a mess when I woke up, but I wasn't planning on leaving my house anytime soon.

I crawled into bed, curling up under the blankets. Depleted of any reserved energy, my body finally relaxed, and I felt my eyelids grow heavier by the second. I didn't even have time to form a thought before I let the fatigue wash over me. I slipped seamlessly into sleep as a pair of steel blue eyes followed me into my dreams.

CHAPTER 5

Everything was a blur, nothing remotely identifiable. Colors swirled around me, making me feel nauseous as if I was in motion with them, tumbling and rolling through a rainbow of nothingness. I shut my eyes as tightly as possible, though I still felt as if I were falling.

It felt like ages before the sensation stopped. Warily, I opened my eyes, worried that the colors that surrounded me were still spinning through the air. There were no mixtures of colors now. Instead, I was sitting in a field. The air was crisp and cool, like the grass I found myself sitting in. The sky above was the dreamy shade of blue one always thinks of after a long winter, and it was dotted with the fluffiest white clouds I had ever seen.

The quiet was so serene, and I lay back into the grass, content to take it all in. It felt like the perfect spring day. The only things missing were a blanket and a book. I closed my eyes, poised to take the best afternoon nap of my life.

It doesn't get better than this, does it?

I took in the sound of the trees that surrounded the field as the breeze wove through their branches. Birds were high in the boughs, chirping musically to one another. Insects buzzed in the distance. All the sounds of nature were accounted for. And then something new sounded in the distance. It was the sound of twigs breaking underneath soft footsteps as the owner cleared the trees. Leaves were disrupted as the newcomer came into view.

I suddenly realized how much better this could be as my eyes met a pair of gray-blue irises. They were unforgettable eyes. *Her* eyes.

I scrambled to my feet. Sterling was wearing the green shirt from the club. As she walked towards me, I let myself gape at her grace. She moved effortlessly, as if she were floating. I focused on her more intently the closer she got. I was entranced as the sun rays danced through her blonde hair. Her tanned skin almost seemed to glow in the lazy afternoon light. I was completely gawking at her, and she noticed. Her head dipped, while a smile spread across her face. A small laugh, like music to my ears, escaped as she looked back up at me.

Sterling had closed the distance in no time and was now standing before me. We stared at each other for what felt like an eternity. Neither of us moved nor dared to utter a word. It was as if we were both worried we might scare the other.

She took a step towards me. Then another. And another. She was inches away from me now, a tropical scent, as if vanilla had been carried on a fresh sea breeze, wafted from her skin. The heat radiating from her made me suddenly aware of the chill in the air, and all I wanted to do was be closer to her.

A slim hand reached out. Her long fingers were adorned with silver rings, I briefly registered, before she brushed a strand of dark hair away from my face. It took all of my power not to let the shiver run down my spine as she lightly grazed the shell of my ear. The moment seemed to stretch on and on until, rather than withdraw her hand, she let it rest on the side of my face. Her thumb lightly ran over my cheek, causing heat to follow her touch.

I was frozen in place.

We didn't break eye contact as she gauged my response, and I continued to try to control my breathing. It was no small task as the anticipation built in my chest.

Sterling took another half a step to close the space between us. She leaned towards me. The hitch in my breath was audible, and Sterling, head tilted and very close, smiled as her eyes lit up. She was clearly pleased with my reaction and continued to move closer.

I closed my eyes, waiting for what came next. For something I had somehow wanted forever. Her lips were barely a whisper away from mine. I could feel the smile still on her face.

Then the sky tore open.

The crack that sounded through the clearing was enough to startle both of us, causing us to separate from our near embrace too early on. The breeze was now a severe wind that started to pick up leaves and viciously shake the trees. Gray clouds had emerged and covered the sky, no longer allowing the sun to show.

The ground below our feet began to shake, and terror was evident on my face as I looked at Sterling. She had paled slightly, too, and as she tried to come to me, the earth split, effectively separating us from one another. Above us, a black cloud began to gather. It was darker than those that had come before it, and for the briefest moment, I wondered if it would be possible to see anything should someone become trapped inside.

A heavy sense of dread descended in the same instance that Sterling looked from the sky and back at me.

"Get behind that tree," she said as she pointed directly behind me. The relaxed, flirtatious tone I had associated with her was long gone, replaced by an assertive and apprehensive timbre. I began to protest. The ominous atmosphere surrounding us already had my stomach in tightly coiled knots. The possibility that something could make Sterling, self-assured and bright, feel such a sense of urgency set my teeth on edge. To her, this wasn't just bad weather. Something was coming. The idea of hiding while she faced it alone made me want to throw up the coiled ball of anxiety; I didn't want to be separated. But before I could form a sentence, a violet-blue light descended from the cloud above, striking like lightning.

When I looked back, Sterling was holding a sword with the confidence and ease of someone who often did so. Her back was to me as she watched the light that had descended. Slowly, shadows erupted from the light and began to swirl and take the shape of a person. There was nothing human about it, aside from the silhouette. The shape still whirled in smoke and night, while that same violet-blue light took place where eyes would have been. The shadow began to walk slowly towards Sterling.

Sterling wheeled back around to me. "Listen to what I am saying. Go! Now!" she commanded with a tone I would have never thought her capable of. There was no familiarity, only ice and direction. It was the voice of someone who could command legions.

But it was not the tone in her voice that shocked me. As she looked at me, her eyes seemed to change. Where they normally shone a steely blue, they were now ablaze. Her irises were shimmering as if they were made of melted gold. She looked inhuman.

Without waiting to see if I listened, she spun her sword around in her hand before walking a few paces to meet the shadow in the center of the field.

The fear I felt drove me to do as I was told. I made for the tree, reaching it as Sterling came face to face with the creation I had no name for. I peered from my spot as they seemed to converse. Though I wasn't sure if it was possible for the shadow to speak, I could see the tension in Sterling's jaw, the set of her shoulders, and it told me that whatever was going on was not something to be taken lightly.

In a flash of silver, the shadow produced a curved blade that was swiftly angled for Sterling's throat. Any normal person would not have had enough time to defend themselves, but Sterling moved impossibly fast and got her blade up quick enough to defend herself. The impact of steel on steel echoed louder than what should have been possible. A blinding white light flashed, and a wave of energy erupted from where they stood, rippling over the clearing.

I was sent flying further into the woods behind me, where I hit a tree and crumpled to the ground.

I woke suddenly from the dream. I was in my bed, in my home...but when I got up to open my curtains, I realized I was covered in sweat. The sun was out, and if I had to guess, it was probably around nine in the morning.

It was preferable to the times I had woken up at four in the morning from the nightmare—and on a day off, no less. At least I was able to make up a couple hours of sleep this time around.

I sat on my floor and considered what had just happened. It had been a month since I met Sterling at the club. One month since I had given her my number, hoping luck would be on my side. One month of telling myself I wasn't waiting for her call. But deep down, I knew that wasn't true. Even now, I felt just as empty as when the car pulled away that night.

I'd had this same dream seven times since that night at the club. It always started and ended the same way. I was always in the field, and Sterling and the shadowed figure always showed up. The only difference was how close Sterling and I were able to get to one another.

The first time, we had simply smiled at each other before the ground cracked and separated us. By the third time, we had finally been able to brush hands before it all went downhill. I was sure that this last time, I would have at least gotten to kiss her.

Apparently, it was not meant to happen, whether in reality or my dreams. Despite my best efforts.

I'd be lying if I said I didn't go to *The Arcane Club* after the first week or two with the hope of running into Sterling. I told myself I could play it off casually if I saw her, act aloof. After all, it had only been drinks.

But when I went to the club, she was nowhere to be seen. I had the first dream the following night. In the weeks to come, I allowed myself one night at the club, knowing that it was unlikely I would see her again, but still unable to fully give up hope.

By the fourth week, though, I was drained of hope and had given up. It didn't help that I was not pleased with myself for letting this woman, a stranger, take up so much real estate in my mind. I was ready to continue life as it was before, though there was a new sense of discontentment I could not shake. One that I didn't fully attribute to Sterling's absence.

The dreams did not help. Wanting something you can't have in real life was torturous. Not being allowed the satisfaction even in your dreams was maddening. It takes a special kind of masochist to create a mental hellscape like that.

I had hoped that not going to the club would stop the dreams. But instead, I got closer than ever to Sterling. I felt real fear when the sky darkened, and the shadows appeared. In my lack of pursuing her, it seemed as if the dreams had become more tangible than before.

I stood and stretched. The sweat that was stuck to my skin reminded me that, before I do anything else today, I need to shower. I went into the bathroom, where I stood under the steaming hot water for longer than necessary, as if it would rid me of the dreams for good. I closed my eyes as water hit my face and made myself a promise that Sterling would no longer be present in my thoughts.

CHAPTER 6

I spent three days going through the motions of my normal routine. By the morning of my fourth day off, there was nothing left to do. I had checked off everything on my to-do list. From dishes to cleaning the floors to wiping the counters, it was all done. I had even done my laundry. *All* my laundry. My hamper was devoid of clothes—dirty or clean—and every article was in its rightful place. The floor of my room was bare, and the loose clutter on my dressers had been put away. My room no longer needed attention, so I did the only thing I could do, which was to make my bed and head downstairs.

The living room and kitchen were immaculate. I wasn't able to sit idle over the weekend as the intensity of my nightmares had gotten worse. Cleaning had been an easy distraction and a great way to stay busy. I was exhausted by the end of the day. So much so that I would fall into a deep sleep and would rarely dream.

In the midst of staying busy, I had failed to make sure that I had left some sort of project for today.

I lit the candle that sat on my table in the middle of the living room before grabbing a blanket and curling up on the couch. I turned on the TV and searched through every streaming service imaginable before settling on the newest reality TV show. As the mindless entertainment played in the background, I scrolled through the social media accounts that I hadn't touched in the last three days.

I had thought about trying to find Sterling online in those first weeks. I was sure it wouldn't be a hard thing to do, but as I considered it, I realized I wouldn't have any idea what to do if I had actually found her. That was when I started my cleaning spiral, only allowing myself to touch my phone to change the music that played as I worked my way through the house.

Now, as I sat scrolling, I wasn't tempted by the idea. It was merely an afterthought at this point as I considered how crazy I had been. The feelings from the past month were gone. Though I still felt something was amiss, it was easy to ignore. The lack of dreams helped to dissipate...whatever I had been feeling. My life was finally returning to normal.

Content with this realization, I grabbed my book to pick up where I left off. I allowed myself to be consumed. Time stood still as the words before me painted a picture in my mind's eye. There was something soothing about allowing myself to become someone else as I was consumed more and more with every turn of the page.

I was vaguely aware that the light streaming through my windows transitioned into the burning beams that only come in the fall, when the early evening is the hottest part of the day. I savored the warmth that enveloped me as I went from reading words to watching scenes behind my eyelids.

I woke up feeling as if I had been falling. I sat up quickly and took in my surroundings. I was still on my gray couch, covered in my blanket. On the floor lay my book, face down to a random page. It was likely what had startled me awake. The sun was no longer out. My living room was bathed in what moonlight was able to find its way through the window. The only other light came from the soft glow of the TV screen, which inquired if I was still watching.

I closed the curtains to my main window and hit *continue* on the screen despite not knowing anything that had happened already. That was the beauty of reality TV. You could never completely pay attention and would still be able to figure out the big takeaways of each episode.

Sound filled the room once again as I meandered into the kitchen, searching for a light switch. After opening my refrigerator to find nothing but disappointment, it dawned on me I still had ice cream in the freezer. Dessert in hand, I took up my place on the couch once more, content to end my weekend this way.

I looked at the clock on my phone—10:30. Thanks to my early evening nap, I wasn't the least bit tired. That wasn't a problem, though. I liked to try and stay up as late as possible in order to swing back to my night schedule. Luckily, there were two more seasons left in this show.

The last episode of the first season was starting to wrap up. I could already sense the cliffhanger the producers were setting up, and I was thankful for the fact that I would not have to wait a year to find out what the outcome would be. I didn't let the credits roll, didn't allow the recap to play, as I made my way to the start of the next episode.

The brunette on TV was about to make her choice when I was startled by a rapid pounding on my door. I paused the show and waited, debating on whether I had really heard someone. I couldn't think of anyone who would be knocking on my door so late.

It was likely an accident. Or a prank. There were teenagers in the area, and it wouldn't be the first time the neighborhood had fallen victim to a game of ding-dong ditch. I started to settle back onto the couch, ready to hit play, when the knocking came once again. This time, it was insistent, emergent, and went on for a beat longer than before.

I slowly walked around the couch to my door as the knocking subsided again, and I couldn't help but be thankful that I had locked it earlier. Cautiously, I peered through the peephole, my pulse picking up with each second. I got my eye up to the door and I saw——

Oh hell no.

Their back was to me, and all I could see was a head of blonde hair. Hair I was sure I would recognize almost anywhere. I pulled back from the door, my mind suddenly a mess of thoughts.

The sheer audacity of this woman. Who does she think she is?! A month with no calls or texts, and she shows up at almost 11 o'clock at night with no warning?

I collected myself, aware that I was in sweats and my hair was a mess. I grabbed the handle, fully ready to deliver a lecture filled with all the feelings that came rushing back. There was no time for thoughts about what I would say or do after I was done yelling, and I frankly didn't care how she would react. I paused for one more second to take a deep breath as if that would help to steady me, and then I threw the door open. The words started to come out before I could even fully see her.

"You have some nerve to just—" But my train of thought rapidly derailed as I took in the scene in front of me.

Sterling was there, wearing black pants and a gray patterned shirt. She had turned back to face me, her hand in the air, about to knock on the door that was no longer there. I met her eyes and, in my core, I knew that something was terribly wrong. Her eyes were glassy, panic doing its best to come to the surface. Were it not for adrenaline, the tension in her face suggested she would have been in tears as her jaw worked, grinding her teeth, in an effort to keep it together. It was a face I saw frequently in my line of work. It was a face I had seen in the mirror the night James had died.

"Please," she asked quietly, the small quiver in her voice matching the slight shake of her hands, "I need your help."

I was distracted by a splash of color on her hand that was still raised to knock. I realized then what I was looking at. Her shirt wasn't a patterned material. It was a solid gray shirt.

And it was covered in blood.

"What happened to you?! You're bleeding!" The words came out in a torrent. Immediately, I started searching for the source of the bleeding. My hands gripped her shoulders and started to work their way down, gently seeking to staunch the bleeding—wherever it came from. I scanned her body, unable to find the wound, and my movements became more frantic in my desperation to find *something*.

Sterling grabbed my wrists and held them between us, bringing my focus back to what she was saying. "Kai, it's not mine. I'm okay, I'm not hurt," she reassured, words short and succinct, "but my friend is.

He needs help. Please, I didn't know where else to go. This was the first place I thought of. *You* were the first person I thought of."

In the time it took me to register what she was saying, her voice had become steady, but an undertone of worry still lingered. Now that I was sure Sterling was okay, my tunnel vision was receding. In the periphery, I spotted a whisper of a movement, and I glanced over her shoulder. What I hadn't noticed before was the two men at the bottom of my steps. One was kneeling on the ground, talking softly to the other. Though his tone was gentle, his posture suggested he was ready and willing to cut down anyone who got too close to his friend. He had a head of jet-black hair that was cut uniformly, and his pale skin looked silver in the moonlight. His lithe frame remained bent over, the angle obscuring his face, but I could glimpse the tension in his shoulders. He was a spring wound tightly, ready to uncoil at a moment's notice.

I could not see the man lying at the foot of the steps. I could only hear the groans of pain that came from him. If the sound was any indication of the extent of his injuries, I wasn't sure how much help I could be.

My eyes went back to Sterling. "Please," she begged. It was one word, but it was full of pleading and pain. She was desperate.

"Bring him in."

Sterling squeezed my arm briefly, a small acknowledgement of thanks, before she hopped over the small steps down to her friends. Getting low to the ground, she helped the one with black hair lift their friend to a stand and walked across the threshold of my home.

Despite the grotesque scene before me, I was impressed. Sterling's friends were tall and possibly double her size. Yet she was able to bear the weight of her injured companion as the man with the black hair made room by pushing my couch to the side, against my TV stand.

I walked over to where the other two stood and helped ease the near-limp man to the floor, not caring that my area rug was on the verge of ruin. Sitting on my knees, I assessed the damage before me.

He was dressed in light blue distressed jeans and a white V-neck t-shirt that was fitted to accentuate the corded muscles in his arms. The light-colored palette made the blood stand out garishly. Flecks of red were on his pants, and trails of blood ran down his face and onto his shirt. There were dried smear marks from places where the others had attempted to keep the gore out of his eyes, but their attempts had been in vain.

His face was contorted in pain, eyes closed as he grit his teeth together in order to try to keep the agony at bay. There was blood, both new and dried, clinging to the dark skin under his nose and on his chin. One eye was swollen and already beginning to change color, while the other eyebrow had a deep gash that had not yet clotted. It would likely need stitches. Given the amount of blood that was on Sterling's shirt, these injuries surely weren't the worst of it. But I couldn't see anything else.

The black-haired boy sat across from me on the other side of his friend, rolling him so that he was propped up on his right side. I looked at his face. He had inconspicuous laugh lines, suggesting that any other day, he was usually a happy guy. At the moment, though, there was no trace of humor as his emerald eyes glanced at me, serious, laser-focused. While he repositioned the battered man, Sterling came over to kneel beside me.

"I need you to not ask any questions right now," she said, her tone grave. "I will do my best to explain everything, but the amount of time that that will require greatly exceeds the time we have right now."

I watched as the man coughed, blood dripping from his mouth onto the floor. It was clear that the extent of his injuries were more serious than anything I could help him with here.

"Sterling, why did you bring him here? He needs serious medical attention."

"We can't go to a hospital. But we needed to get off the street, and we couldn't get the bleeding to stop."

"I understand that the facial bleeding isn't ideal. But Sterling, the bleeding from the gash on his eye is the least of his problems. I'm more concerned with what's going on *inside* his head. And given that he is starting to cough up blood, staunching the wound should be—" My thoughts evaporated when I finally saw the source of Sterling's concern. The whole back of his white shirt was a deep maroon, and a bright crimson stamped the floor, marking the place where his back had been.

Sterling saw the realization cross my face as I stood. My brain kicked into overdrive as my medical experience kicked in. "I'll see what I can find. I need his shirt off. It may hurt if any of that blood has dried it to his skin. Ball it up and hold pressure on the wound while I find supplies."

I took the stairs two at a time and came to a stop in front of my hall closet. Inside was my emergency bag. It was filled with various wound care items, and it was the most likely place to find anything I could possibly need. I grabbed the bag and was kneeling at his side once more, dumping the contents out around me.

They had cut the front of his shirt up the middle, along with the sleeves, so that it could be used to apply pressure on his back. There wasn't much white fabric left as blood continued to seep into the fabric and drip onto the floor. I quickly assessed his bare torso now that it was exposed. His chest was black and blue in various places, and as my living room transformed into a trauma bay, I knew I was in over my head.

"He is likely bleeding internally. Multiple broken ribs, potentially even one that could puncture his lung. He needs a doctor, equipment, and treatment that can only be provided at a hospital. That would be the best—"

"No. Hospitals," the dark-haired man across from me growled. His eyes were hard, and there was a cold edge to him that suggested he was unafraid to stop anyone with malintent. I couldn't help but cower slightly as I suddenly became aware of how small I was compared to him. It wasn't the first time I had dealt with hostile family members. In my line of work, it was a constant, and it rarely distracted me from doing my job. And yet, as his green eyes bore into me, I felt myself hesitate.

"Callen, bring it down a notch, okay? Intimidating her is neither helpful nor necessary," Sterling snapped, some of the commanding tone from my dreams lacing her words. She turned to me, her voice softening again, "We need him patched up, just so that we can move on to somewhere he can get the help he needs. I knew the true extent was beyond your control before we showed up at your door."

"Okay...I can't promise... I mean, I can't guarantee that he..."
Sterling nodded, not needing me to finish the thought.

"What is his name?"

"Mal," Callen murmured. He looked down at his friend, sadness in his eyes.

"Alright, Mal, your friends are going to hold you while I pull this shirt away. It may hurt, but you just have to breathe through it, okay?" I barely saw him nod as Callen and I traded spots. I pulled away the shirt, feeling it catch, and feeling Mal flinch, before it came free.

Just under the base of Mal's shoulder blades were two long, deep craters. They were about six inches in length, one on each side of his spine. Blood poured freely from them, now that there was nothing to stop it, and pooled on the floor. I put the shirt back over the wound once again. If there hadn't been so much blood, we would have been able to see the severed muscles in his shoulders.

"Sterling, what the hell happened to him?"

"Ask questions later, Kai, remember? He doesn't have time for—"

"I need to know what I'm becoming involved in. What are you mixed up in?" What I didn't say was that the last kid I had taken care of who looked this bad from an assault had been involved in a gang initiation gone wrong. It resulted in the entire department being locked down.

"Kiara!" Sterling exclaimed, the use of my full name taking me by surprise. She closed her eyes tightly and, in a more composed voice, said, "I swear on everything that is living and breathing, I will tell you every excruciating detail if you do the damn thing and help him."

I went numb at her tone. I nodded as I shoved my hesitation and curiosity into their box and got to work. I tried to place sutures where I could, but the wounds were wide and deep. I settled for the next best thing as I soaked packs of gauze in sterile water and packed them into the spaces. More soaked gauze layered on top, flat against Mal's back. Dry ones followed, padding layer after layer to help absorb, hopefully long enough to get them wherever they needed to go. Two big wound pads, one on each side, were then taped down to hold it all together before I gently wrapped gauze around the upper portion of his torso with help from the others.

No one spoke as I worked, and at some point, Mal had fallen unconscious, most likely from the pain. I bandaged up the cut over his eye as best as I could for good measure. "That's the best I can do.

These injuries are too great for anything within my skillset, let alone everything that could be going on internally. That should buy you maybe thirty minutes before he needs new dressings. Regardless of whatever happened, he needs a *doctor*."

I stood, blood now covering various places on me, and looked down at Sterling. Words weren't needed for her to know what I was thinking.

We aren't done here.

I walked to the kitchen to wash my hands, thinking about how I would have to clean my house again. *Of all the things to think about, this is what you're focused on? Unbelievable.*

I heard the whispers behind me, but I couldn't make out the words. Callen's tone became more insistent, defiant even. Whatever Sterling had said, he disagreed with her. However, her tone was firm and final. A decision had been made.

She walked over to me while Callen stood to make a phone call. "I need to make sure the boys are squared away. But I promise we will talk. Go change, and I will be up soon."

"How do I know you won't leave with them?"

"You don't. You have to trust me and, honestly, it will take more trust than that for you to believe what I'm about to tell you."

I nodded, feeling somewhat defeated. *What other choice do you have?* I made my way upstairs, where I scrubbed my hands a second time before I found a new pair of sweats and a hoodie. I felt the minutes drag on, still waiting to hear the sound of my door open. Doubt began to creep in as I considered the possibility that she might have left, after all.

I lay back on my bed, exhausted. I knew I should give up and try to sleep now, rather than stare at my ceiling. *It was a foolish thought to believe she would tell you anything. Maybe it's for the best, not involving yourself too much with the situation. Ignorance is bliss, after all.*

I heard the creak of my door as it opened and shut gently. I didn't need to look up at her to know it was Sterling; her presence filled the room the second she walked in. I sat up and pointed to the corner of my bed where a set of folded clothes waited. "For you. I figured you wouldn't want to talk in blood-soaked clothes. And if I'm being honest, I'd rather not have it on my bed, either."

"I can't say I blame you. Is there somewhere I can change?"

I pointed to the bathroom door, and she walked towards it with my clothes in hand. As she reached for the doorknob, she paused. "Thank you. For everything." She seemed to be searching for words, but came up short.

I gave her a nod, dismissing the need for her to speak further, and she disappeared behind the door. I could hear the water running a few minutes later. She was likely scrubbing her hands and arms clean with the washcloth I had laid out for her.

The door opened, and she stood there looking as refreshed as one could, given the circumstances. Sterling took a seat in my office chair and wheeled it over so that she was sitting directly in front of me, her elbows on her thighs. She had her hands clasped and her face pushed into them as if she were experiencing a bad headache.

"You have to trust me for this to work. Do you understand that?"

I nodded, grabbing the cup of water from my nightstand to take a drink.

She sighed and shook her head. "Are you religious?"

"I have my beliefs."

"I suppose that's somewhat helpful, though it doesn't matter in the grand scheme of things. Everyone practices religion differently, after all."

"You are only confusing me more."

"I'm building up to it, okay? This is hard for me to do, but I am trying to make good on my promise to you." Sterling's voice was wobbly, agitation slowly creeping into her words. It only amplified my anger.

"This is hard for *you*? I haven't heard from you in a month. You then bring a bleeding stranger into my house and beg for my help? And now, after I have helped God knows who, and have become a potential accomplice, you can't give me an answer to anything because it's '*hard for you*.'"

"Well, God definitely knows Mal if that helps any." Sarcasm seeped into her tone. She stood up and began pacing back and forth. "And you aren't going to be on *America's Most Wanted*, I can assure you of that."

"I swear to God—"

"From what I've been told, he doesn't take well to that if there is no follow-through. Something about how he considers it a broken promise or something along those lines."

"Sterling, I'm exhausted. This comedy act is getting us nowhere, and I am about to lose my ever-loving mind if you don't tell me—"

"You won't believe me. I know you won't. You aren't ready to know."

"Try me."

Her cold steel eyes bore into mine, refusing to be the first to look away. I was too defiant to give up ground.

"You don't know what you're asking me to do, Kai."

"I didn't know what you were asking me to do when you showed up here, but I still helped you. You promised, Sterling."

"Fine." I could see the muscles in her jaw working as she ran a worried hand through her long blonde hair. "Malachi is an angel."

CHAPTER 7

We sat in silence until I could no longer take it; I burst out in a fit of laughter. Sterling groaned audibly as she threw herself back into the chair. Her distress was so dramatic, it only made me laugh harder and stoked my own sarcasm to the surface.

"I mean, he was unconscious when I met him, but I'm sure that anyone who could provoke that kind of attack is a standup guy."

She stared at me, and I could only imagine what she saw. If how I felt was remotely reflected in my face, she probably thought I was on the verge of a mental breakdown.

"You wanted the truth," she said in an even tone. "But we won't get through this if you get hysterical every single time I add to the story. I'm not referring to his personality, though he is, in fact, pleasant company most days."

"So, what you're saying is you believe your friend is literally an angel?"

"I *know* he is, but yes, that's the gist of it."

"An angel? As in the thing with wings and a halo, who lives in the clouds and plays the harp?"

"Angels don't have halos and, unless they are inclined to learn, they don't play the harp either. Malachi's interests lie more in the realm of combat rather than the arts. As for the wings, well..." she dropped her eyes from mine as a look of sadness clouded her features.

I looked down at my hands, giving her the privacy to work through her emotions without my staring. Whatever the truth may be, it pained her greatly.

"What about the wings?" I prompted without looking up.

Sterling cleared her throat. "He lost them. Well, they were taken from him. That's why he was in such terrible shape when we brought him here. You see, Mal has fallen, and what you saw tonight are the consequences of being cast out."

I glanced up to see she was leaning forward on her elbows again, trying to gauge my reaction. "Are you going to tell me you and Callen are angels, too?"

"No, but I will tell you how we fit into all of this if you promise to let me get through everything without interrupting me."

I nodded once, sipping from my water.

"Okay. Callen and I are what some know as Nephilim. Depending on what texts you read, the stories tend to vary about our purpose, what we represent, and so on. But one thing that is universally agreed upon is that we are the children of angels and humans.

"Somewhere, long, long ago, in our family lines, angels and humans had crossed paths, giving life to children who were mortal yet possessed certain abilities that were not of Earth. Because of our abilities, we serve as an in-between in some sense. Ambassadors of Heaven and barriers to Hell, if you will.

"Our dealings are discreet, rarely ever close enough to be witnessed within the mortal world. And that is how we like to keep it. We prefer to stay invisible. That is why we couldn't take Mal to a hospital. I mean, could you imagine me explaining this to the authorities?" She stood and resumed her pacing once more, deep in thought about what to say next. "Callen and I decided to go out tonight. Mal was also planning to come with, and as far as we knew, we were supposed to meet him at the first club."

"Angels are allowed to drink?"

The joke was not well received, and the look Sterling gave me was the only reminder I needed to stay quiet.

"When we got to the club, Malachi wasn't there. We hadn't heard from him either, but we had just assumed that he was running behind. We made our way inside, ordered a few drinks, and waited. As time went on, Callen and I decided we should just go on with our night and let Mal know where we were. So, we made our way to *Arcane...*" She paused briefly, and I could see the memories of the night we met flash behind her eyes. "Only we didn't make it there. Instead, we stumbled on Malachi's body in an alley. Though we don't know *why* it happened, there was no mistaking what *had* happened. The Hosts of Heaven show no mercy, especially in regard to their own, and Mal was always a little different from most."

"Hosts of Heaven?"

"Angels," Sterling shrugged, "You'll hear them termed in different ways. Typically, the Host will refer to both Archangels and the angels below them as a whole. Anyway, if we hadn't found Malachi there, he would have died.

"The travel required to make it home would have exerted him too much. We couldn't find supplies to pack the wounds. I panicked, something that isn't normal for me, and the only plan I could think of—kept coming back to—was to bring him here. I was selfish and didn't think of how it would affect you. It was wrong. But if you expect me to apologize, you will be disappointed. I'm not sorry I did what I did, Kai, because it saved his life. *You* saved his life."

The last couple of sentences left her in a rush, like she had to get the words out before she could no longer speak. Sitting once more, she took my hand in both of hers. They were warm, and my skin came alive where we connected. Her touch was soft, but I could feel where calluses had developed in identical places on both hands. "I could never thank you enough for what you did tonight, and I will owe you a steep debt."

I stared into the deep pools that were her eyes, searching for any sign that she was lying. *How could she* not *be? None of this is real.*

"Sterling," I said quietly, removing my hand, "if you are going to spin me some delusional fairytale, rather than tell me the truth, then we are wasting each other's time. I'm glad I could help your friend if it means one less death today, but aside from the truth, I want nothing else from you."

Something like hurt flashed across her face. But just as quickly as it was there, it was gone. We sat in a silence that stretched out before us, both staring at the ground rather than one another. I finished the rest of my water and began toying with the glass in my hands. Minutes passed before Sterling spoke up.

"Would you mind if I got some water myself? I can refill yours, too."

I couldn't fully place why I wasn't more annoyed with the request. I should be telling her to leave, never bother me again. But my hand was still singing with the buzz from her touch and, despite the lies, I wasn't entirely ready for her to leave. "Cups are in the upper cupboard to the right of the sink." I handed her my glass, and she nodded her thanks as she disappeared down to the kitchen.

I heard the cupboard open and close. The sound of my refrigerator dispensing water for one glass, a second, then gentle footsteps coming back up the stairs. Sterling appeared in my room once more, hand outstretched with my newly filled glass. She took up a seat next to me on the bed. A small, half-hearted grin spread across her face as she raised her glass.

"To one hell of a night."

I ruefully shook my head, but tapped my glass to hers. I drank deeply from my glass, as if it had been filled with something stronger than water, and then looked at Sterling once more. Despite having been covered in blood an hour ago, she looked beautiful.

Her hair was a golden curtain over her left shoulder, waving more at the ends. I realized they were wet. She had probably scrubbed away blood from there as well. She was studying the glass she held in her lap, lost deep in thought. The sight of her in my clothes elicited thoughts that were immediately dismissed with great effort. Now was not the time, and yet...

I waited for her to give me something, some shred of honesty that showed she trusted me. I believed she was waiting for the ability to do the same thing. She just couldn't find the words or the air to do it.

"Before," Sterling said, "I told you that you would have to trust me. But it only just occurred to me that maybe you couldn't do that. I haven't given you much reason to think that it would be smart to, have I?"

I breathed out a humorless laugh, "That would be one way to put it."

Sterling faced me as I finished the last bit of my water. Her posture sank as if the weight of the evening was starting to make her weary. Her eyes shone bright, however. It was not the expression of someone who had never seen blood and pain and near death, only to come across it tonight. The normal signs of shock did not touch her.

There was exhaustion there that had started to set in slowly. The brightness in her eyes held more emotions than I could decipher, but I couldn't help but feel that anxiety was one of them. Not anxiety brought on by tonight's events, though. No, this was due to the present. Our conversation, now of all things, was causing Sterling obvious unease.

"Do you, or at least *did* you, ever trust me?"

"I wanted to," I quietly muttered, "I *still* want to, but all of this storytelling has made it hard to believe much of anything that you say."

She nodded in understanding. "Would you like me to leave?"

"No."

"I'm sorry?"

"Despite everything that has happened tonight, no, Sterling, I don't want you to leave."

Shock erupted before a small smile escaped her lips. Grabbing my hand once more, "What if you could see everything?" she asked, suddenly reenergized. It had a bit of urgency to it, emphasizing her accent, "Words are just words, but what if I showed you the truth?"

"They say seeing is believing," I was focused on our hands, how perfectly hers encased mine. I had started to feel my own exhaustion, and the physical contact was the only thing that seemed to be stopping me from crawling into bed. I focused hard on our hands, hoping it would keep me conscious long enough for whatever she was trying to ask me.

"Is that a yes?" Her tone was pressing. I couldn't fathom anything that would require so much energy right now.

A big yawn escaped from me, and I couldn't be bothered to be embarrassed. My eyelids started to droop, heavier than I could ever remember them being. Suddenly, my room started to fall around me. The surroundings blurred and shifted, and it was only when I heard

Sterling's voice once again that I realized it was actually me who had fallen.

I was on the floor. Sterling guarded my head and shoulders as if she were protecting me from a hard landing. I must have fallen into her first. I would apologize later, but I was so tired. It was the most relaxed I had felt in a long time.

"Kai..." She shook my shoulders gently. "I will show you everything, tell you any secret. Just say the word, or if you want to forget about me and this night entirely, I'll respect that too. Please, tell me what you want." I opened one eye to find I was staring up at her, my head cradled in her lap.

"Oh, Sterling," I laughed softly, mostly to myself, "don't be ridiculous." I closed my eyes once more. "I want you to show me everything. Tell me every secret, in this world and the next." It sounded silly coming from my lips, but deep down I knew I meant it. I felt some tension in Sterling release as I let myself drift into darkness.

CHAPTER 8

I was submerged in darkness. Heat danced along my skin as it chased after the mild chill that preceded it in a paradoxical sensation that wasn't entirely unpleasant. The kiss of clouds was the only thing surrounding me. I let out a sigh of contentment. It was as if I was floating here, wherever that may be, without a care in the world. It was relaxing. But it was brief.

Where am I? I tried to survey my environment, only to find that vast empty darkness.

Then the realization hit. It was apparent that I could feel the exterior environment around me. If anything, my nerves were heightened by the fluctuating temperatures running up and down my body. I tried to force my eyes open, only to come to a terrifying conclusion. My eyes *were* open——I just couldn't see. I tried to rein in my surmounting panic, but it only continued to build up as I re-assessed my body from head to toe. The natural internal awareness had been completely stripped from me. I was no longer aware of my mouth. I couldn't feel the weight of my limbs. If my muscles were contracting, I was none the wiser. All I had were my thoughts and the hot-cold buzz of God knows what.

Fear flooded me.

My thoughts exploded. What little calm I had been able to salvage evaporated as possibilities reeled in my mind. *Did someone drug me? Am I paralyzed? Oh my God, am I* dead? *If this is eternity, it's—*

I wasn't going to let myself fall that far off the deep end. I needed to be reasonable and think through this. Panicking would get me nowhere, and I needed viable options as to what had happened. I worked through the possibilities, eliminating the more far-fetched theories. The options still weren't great, but at least I was able to rule out being dead. If I knew more about the situation—

What was the situation?

I realized I had no idea what had happened. Try as I might, I couldn't conjure a single image in my mind. I couldn't even remember falling asleep, let alone anything that happened before.

Ouch! What the hell was that?

There was a jolt of discomfort. First in my arms and then my legs. It started out mild, feeling as if my hands and feet had fallen asleep. I felt the tingling as it started to spread, encompassing every limb. Then it was blinding. Tingling turned to burning. Burning became white hot pain. It was as if lightning had struck, jump-starting my nerves, only to set them ablaze.

Gritting my teeth, I slowly flexed and extended my fingers, trying to flush out the agony. The movement was useless. Aside from proving that I wasn't maimed or paralyzed, it did nothing to ease the fire coursing through me. I tried to make bigger movements, move my whole arm, roll to my side, anything. Everything felt so heavy, and the pain only made it harder. It wasn't worth it to move.

I felt like this was going to kill me. I was starting to hope that it would, if it went on much longer, when, at last, the constant blaze slowly started to relent. From my shoulders, down to my fingertips, it seeped away, followed by relief in my legs. Finally, it was gone.

My arms and legs were still filled with lead and felt impossible to move. As I lay wherever I was, it occurred to me that if my limbs were this heavy, perhaps I had never actually opened my eyes before. Maybe they were also weighed down.

I tried to open them again, willing my eyelids to obey. It proved to be impossible with sheer willpower alone. Using all the strength I could muster, I brought one hand up to my face. I began gently rubbing my eyes, coaxing them into working as they should. It took several minutes, and multiple attempts were made, but eventually they opened. My vision was initially blurred, as if I had been sleeping for days. As I blinked away the bleariness, the world finally came into fo cus.

I was in a bedroom. It was slightly bigger than my room, but still somehow modest.

Slowly, I forced myself to sit up and take in my new surroundings.

Multiple windows lined the light blue walls. The two that were over a bench seat were open slightly, allowing a cool breeze to mix with the sun before falling over my exposed arms. The floorboards had a gray-white stain to them, and the room smelled of sandalwood and vanilla. In the distance, there was the distinguishable crash of waves as they rolled towards the shore.

I looked down. The cloud I had been on was actually a king-sized bed. A sea foam green feather down duvet covered me up to my waist. Surrounded by the softest of pillows, I surveyed my body. There were no signs of harm. I was still in my sweats. I vaguely recalled having to change into them, but I couldn't remember why.

"What happened?" I murmured to myself again. My voice was raspy thanks to the coating of sandpaper on my throat.

My head was foggy. I could see shards of my memory flashing in my mind, but nothing was piecing together. I remembered the TV being on. There had been a lot of cleaning, but I didn't remember expecting company. I continued to stare into my lap, frowning, as I tried to dredge up a sliver of something substantial that would make this make sense. I looked once more at the windows, curtains billowing in the breeze, the sweet smell of the room vaguely familiar. The pale colors in the room made it feel bright and clear. The light blue paint tugged at something. Pulling a pair of blue eyes, filled with worry, to the forefront of my mind. But who was––

Oh shit.

It all came roaring back then. A man on the floor, crying in pain, while his friends knelt beside him. Malachi, that was his name. Yes, and Callen was there, the serious one... But his eyes weren't blue. No, those could only belong to one person.

Sterling.

It all came crashing back to me. I remembered Sterling as she sat beside me and begged me to help him. She told me that I needed to stop the bleeding or he'd die. I remembered Sterling as we sat in my room talking. She had given me some insane excuse for what had been going on. Something to do with angels and something else. What was that word?

Nephilim.

I remembered Sterling getting us water in the middle of our conversation, before I had fallen––

"Son of a bitch!" I seethed. With renewed strength courtesy of my newfound anger, I shoved down the covers and stalked to the door. I threw it open, unflinching as it slammed into the wall and stalked into the hallway. I was determined to find her, even if it meant opening every door in this place.

I passed two doors that proved to be nothing more than coat closets before I heard voices just down the hall. They were too quiet for me to tell if one of them belonged to Sterling, but that didn't stop me. It didn't even occur to me that I was in a strange place with possibly dangerous people as I crossed the threshold like a bat out of hell.

Sterling was sitting on the edge of a big oak desk. Her posture was relaxed, and one tanned hand rested on each of her thighs as another woman stood in front of her. Her silvery-white hair cascaded down to her waist in a flawless, silky curtain. She was standing between Sterling's knees and had shifted closer. They were too close to be casual, and there was no mistaking the intimacy between the two as the stranger slowly ran her hands up Sterling's thighs before resting them higher than appropriate in such an open area. I caught a glimpse of the look on Sterling's face. It was flirtatious, but slightly bored, as a small devious grin appeared on her face.

Neither one of them had noticed my presence.

"You fucking drugged me, you asshole!" Acid dripped from every word. If there hadn't been a living obstacle between us, I may have resorted to physical violence.

The two paused in the middle of whatever conversation they were having. The light in Sterling's eyes changed as the stranger in front of her whirled around. Though one hand had remained on Sterling's leg, the other now fell away from whatever exploration it was about to begin. It was clear in this beautiful stranger's bright green eyes that I had interrupted something.

I didn't acknowledge the fresh wave of anger that flared through me.

"I'm sorry," her tone suggested she was anything but, "who are you?"

Maybe physical violence is still on the table.

I briefly surveyed her. Her hair was perfect, not a strand out of place. Green eyes, popping against porcelain skin, stared back at me with a look that could cut glass. Her clothes fit her in a way that accentuated and emphasized her curves perfectly. Her subtle eyeliner and touches of other makeup I could only imagine knowing how to use allowed her to walk a line between angelic and lethal. She was devastatingly beautiful. And the attitude that emitted from her suggested that she knew it too.

I shifted my gaze back to Sterling, refusing to dignify her question with an answer. "You and I have unfinished business. We need to talk," I paused, taking petty satisfaction in the growing agitation from the other girl as I added, "Privately."

Sterling was mentally reeling as if she were trying to catch up to the situation at hand. Whatever *activities* her thoughts were previously fixated on seemed to require an extra minute or two to vacate her mind. At last, she nodded, acknowledging that she knew what was to come.

"I don't foresee Kai letting me off the hook without an explanation. And I fear the explanation cannot wait. Please, Eliza, could you give us a minute?" Sterling pulled her eyes away from mine to look at the girl still standing between her legs, black painted nails now slightly digging into her thigh. She looked between the two of us, incredulous that *she* was the one being sent away.

"Fine," she huffed out, "but don't be too long. *We* have some unfinished business, of sorts, as well." Without hesitating, she gripped under Sterling's chin, tilting it so that she could kiss her roughly, as if to accentuate what she meant for my benefit.

She pulled away, turning on her heels to walk towards me and the door. Each sway of her hips was intentional as she moved to my side and stopped. Though I didn't look away from Sterling on the desk, I could feel Eliza's eyes boring into the side of my head. The warmth of her breath caressed my face as she said to Sterling, "I'll be waiting in your room." With that, she strode out into the hallway.

"Well, now you've met Eliza."

"Are you serious right now?"

"I don't know how that could have possibly been a joke."

"No, that's not what I meant," I exclaimed, exasperated by this conversation already. "Cut the shit, Sterling. You *drugged* me."

She flinched as I emphasized my initial statement once more.

"Yes." One solemn, severe word. Then silence. She wasn't even going to deny it.

Good. It's about time for her to be honest. I paused a beat longer, waiting to see if she would go on trying to explain herself, but she did no such thing.

"'Yes'?" I repeated, "That's all you have to say is 'yes'? I woke up, first paralyzed, then in severe pain. I was in a room, in a house, that I know nothing about. *Alone.*"

She was leaning against the desk now. Her arms were crossed, and she was staring at her shoes. Confusion furrowed her brow. "Paralysis? Pain? You shouldn't have felt any of that," she murmured.

"Well, I did." This only deepened her frown, but I kept going. "When I could finally move enough to seek you out, where do I find you? In this..." I paused to gesture to the room. It was only now that I realized it was an expansive library. The desk suggested that it also may have served as a study. "In this room, *entertaining* some woman."

"It sounds as if the drugging isn't the only transgression you seem to be upset with," Sterling suggested, attempting to lighten the mood with a beautiful half-smile on her face.

"What I'm angry about," I seethed, "is that while you were trying to fuck someone, I was left to panic alone. In a place that *you* brought me to without my consent." I put as much bite into the words as I could muster, but my anger was slowly leaving me. I was tired and, as much as I hated to admit it, I was scared.

Still not looking at me, Sterling said tightly, "Not without your consent. The magic would not have let me leave with you if you had refused me."

"What the hell are you talking about?"

She sighed, running a hand through her hair. Her eyes suggested she was just as tired as I was, if not more. They were more gray than blue, some of their light dimmed, and faint bags were starting to appear under her eyes.

She hasn't slept.

And then—

She is still wearing the clothes I gave her. The thought that she was in my clothes—being touched by *someone else* in my clothes—sent a weird feeling like fluttering envy through my core. I filed it away to deal with later.

Sterling's voice came out as if she were explaining something very simple to a child for the hundredth time. "Do you remember before you fell asleep? I kept asking what you wanted?"

She let me have time to think, no doubt understanding there were still pieces of the night that were foggy.

'Words are just words, but what if I showed you the truth?'

'I want you to show me everything. Tell me every secret in this world and the next.'

"Yes, I... Vaguely, yes, I remember."

Her eyes locked with mine, unflinching. The sincerity in them showed no signs of deception or falsehood. "From the moment I brought Mal to your doorstep, I have not lied to you. I have not uttered any half-truths, either. And I promise to keep being honest with you.

"I put something in your water last night when I filled your cup. The magic in it was meant to protect us both in a way. It would consider you first and what your choice was. If you had said you wanted nothing more to do with me, if you wanted to forget it all, you would have woken up at home with no memory of the night we met, or any subsequent moments involving me after. Well, you would've remembered the whole night *except* for the parts with me in it, I suppose. I gave it to you because I thought you were ready to send me away. But then you said… You told me you didn't want me to leave. That you wanted to be able to trust me. So I had to push for option two, before the effects kicked in and you had forgotten everything."

"And option two was what exactly?"

"You could choose to let me show you my world. If you were to opt to allow me the chance to prove to you that I was being honest, the magic needed a verbal confirmation. That's why I kept asking you to tell me what you wanted. It had to be specific. You see, magic can be really particular at times."

"I'm glad it can be so considerate of my choices in the grand scheme of *kidnapping*. You said it was to protect both of us. How would it protect you?"

"It's simple, really." Her tone had shifted to something casual as her posture relaxed ever so slightly. "If you didn't voice a desire to see I was telling the truth, then everything I had told you, the big secret, would be forgotten. Saves my ass from being in a lot of trouble having a Child of Adam running around, knowing about the reality of the world.

"But if by some miracle you decided to come with me, well," she flashed a coy smile, "it would allow me to continue to have a reputation of always being right."

"Meaning?"

"I just couldn't bear the thought of you being out in the world, thinking I was a psycho who lied my way out of a situation. Even if you wouldn't have remembered, I would have always known your last thoughts of me before I was nothing to you at all. And I couldn't stomach that, Kai."

It was my turn to sigh heavily. I leaned against the wall behind me and briefly closed my eyes.

"If it's any consolation," Sterling broke the silence, her voice soft, "it really wasn't supposed to hurt you the way it did. And my...*preoccupations* leading up to you waking up were not appropriate. In that, you have every right to be angry with me. I had assumed I had more time before you were supposed to wake up, and I didn't want to be some psychopath who sat in the corner watching you sleep."

She stood straight from the desk, dropping her arms to her sides. She took a small step towards me. Sincerity burned in those eyes, and her stance was open, vulnerable. "I truly had planned to be there for you when you woke up. And I'm so sorry that I wasn't."

I cleared my throat. "I appreciate that. Really, I do. But," I huffed a humorless laugh, "I have to go back. I have a life, a job. One that I am actually supposed to be at tonight."

"That has already been taken care of, I promise. You will still have a job. As far as they are concerned, you are on vacation. Just taking time for yourself, nothing out of the ordinary. No questions asked upon your return."

"What about when people ask how my 'vacation' was?"

"Worst-case scenario, you can say you spent time by the ocean. That won't be a lie."

I had heard waves earlier. I looked at her skeptically. "You know, it doesn't ease any of my concerns that you were able to make me disappear from work so quickly."

I expected some witty retort. Instead, she said quietly, "Please, Kai. Just give me some time to show you that I haven't been lying."

The look in her eyes was one of pleading, and not dissimilar to the one she wore last night. I gave her a small nod.

"How is he?" I asked without thinking. It was as if whatever feelings she was experiencing had also pulled her back to the horrors of last night. She didn't need me to clarify to know who I was asking about.

"Physically, he is almost as good as new." Skepticism was obvious on my face as she continued, her tone more hushed now. "Mal has been through a lot in his life. Nothing *this* traumatic that I know of...but he made it back here thanks to you. And we are all hopeful he will be back to himself in no time."

"I'm glad he was able to get back to where he could get adequate help."

We were quiet as we let everything that had transpired settle between us. There was shared gratitude that Malachi was okay, sure, but we also realized we needed to be patient with one another. I needed Sterling to give me the space to ask questions and accept facts on my own terms. In turn, I had to make sure she knew I had an open mind—that I was willing to give her a chance to show me she wasn't crazy. Silently, we both accepted the terms set by the other.

I took in the library. It was perfect. Two walls were filled with floor-to-ceiling bookcases, which were equipped with a 5-rung rolling ladder to help reach the top shelves. To the left, etched into the wall, was a fireplace framed by a dark oak mantle. Big chunky chairs, that looked as if they'd swallow anyone up who sat in them, formed a semi-circle in front of the hearth. The back wall was mostly taken up by a big, wide window overlooking an expanse of sand and, behind that, the ocean. I knew instantly that I could spend all day here.

As if she could hear my sentiment, Sterling spoke up. "I love this room. It is one of my favorites in the house. You are welcome to use it as much as you want, along with anything else in the house. The others don't come in here as often. They aren't too inclined to the literary arts." A smile instinctively spread across her face as she talked about her friends.

"You can have your pick of any genre in here. I have no doubt you'd be able to find enough books to keep you more than occupied during your stay, and that's assuming you have a very niche preference."

"Oh, I'm not picky. When it comes to books at least," I added with a nonchalant shrug as my eyes rove over the titles nearest me.

Her smile shifted into one that made me feel as if it were for me and me alone. She walked over to stand beside me. Seeing her in my clothes, appreciating the library with me, made my heart squeeze. The deepest parts of me wanted nothing more than to make the most of the time we had together, regardless of how problematic the situation might b e.

Sterling was looking at me now. Our shoulders were inches apart, and I began to remember the electricity that followed her touch. I remembered how it had felt when she whispered in my ear the first night, and how her departure had felt as if it took a piece of me with her. Despite the dire situation, I had felt that missing piece slide back into place the second I opened my front door.

I could feel the warmth coming off her skin. Her eyes were deep pools that I wanted to drown in. I started to wonder what it would be like to reach out and touch her face—how it would feel to tangle my hands in her hair.

But I knew I shouldn't.

Aside from the wild stories, I had almost forgotten the other elephant in the room. Or rather, the bombshell femme fatale who had wanted to smite me when I had unceremoniously interrupted them. Eliza was waiting for Sterling right now. Probably in Sterling's bed if I was being honest with myself.

She was the reason why Sterling never called.

Sterling had shifted closer, standing in front of me now. She peered down at me, and I suddenly became aware that I was trapped between her and the wall at my back. It was only a small hint of movement, but I saw as she started to move her face towards mine. Just barely.

I turned my head to the corner over her right shoulder, stopping any further advancement. I stared straight ahead, seeing nothing in particular.

"Don't you have other"—I cleared the raspiness from my voice—"*business* to finish elsewhere?" A half-quizzical look passed over her face before she realized what I meant.

I dropped my gaze to the space between us and watched as Sterling took a big step back, increasing it sevenfold.

"Right. Eliza." She hesitated, somehow sounding sorry that she had a beautiful girl in her bed waiting to be ravished. I took a few steps into the library as she sidestepped towards the door.

"Well, I hope you enjoy the rest of your evening." Sterling cleared her throat. "We can talk more during breakfast tomorrow."

I nodded. "I'll see you then."

Sterling turned to walk out of the room while I started towards the chairs by the fire.

"Oh, and Kai?"

I turned back around to see her barely over the threshold, wearing that gorgeous smile I had seen on that first night on her face.

"Welcome to Soteria."

CHAPTER 9

"*I hope you enjoy the rest of your evening.*"

Sterling's words echoed in my head hours later. The haze in my mind had slowly lifted since I came to, and it somehow made things worse. Before, I had been solely focused on finding Sterling. Now, as I idly browsed the shelves, my senses came back into sharp focus. I was becoming more aware of how unfamiliar my surroundings were with every passing second, and it made me more restless than relaxed. It was hard to enjoy a place you had no knowledge of.

Well, that wasn't entirely true. I at least knew the name of where I was.

Soteria.

Any information I had started and stopped with the name. It held no meaning for me. Until it had fallen from her lips, I had never even heard it spoken. I didn't know anything about the house or its inhabitants. Aside from this room and my own, everything was alien to me.

No, I was far too uncomfortable to enjoy my evening.

I stayed in the library after Sterling left. I walked along the shelves and surveyed the titles on the far wall that I hadn't seen yet. Most were unrecognizable to me; some even seemed to be in a different language. I didn't bother to climb the ladder, preferring to stick to the shelves at eye level as I wandered around the perimeter of the room. Absentmindedly, I wondered who owned this massive collection, or the house for that matter.

I walked to the windows behind the desk. The beautiful gold sand sprawled behind the house. It eventually dropped off a sloped hill where a staircase had been built, making it easier to reach the beach and, past that, the cerulean blue of the sea. Waves came up along the shore, some crashing into rocks rather than finding sand. It was a steady thrum. The same one I had heard in my room earlier.

On the horizon, the sun was slipping down low. It painted the sky in reds and oranges, bathing the library in the last rays of heat for the day. I turned my back to the view and surveyed the desk. It was made from a heavy, dark wood, with a comfortable-looking black chair for the user to sit in. It was simple. No intricate designs to be seen. Drawers ran down both sides of the chair, but I found no interest in what was held within them. It was simple, yet elegant. Sleek.

Like the woman who had been sitting on it earlier.

Thoughts about Sterling seated there, the picture of ease, danced through my mind. Even in sweats, she still looked perfect. Then I remembered Eliza in the room. The image of her hands on Sterling, running them over her legs, made my stomach twist and effectively ruined my daydreaming.

I walked over to one of the plush chairs that faced the hearth and sagged into the thick cushion of the seat. It enveloped me like a soft hug, and I had sunk in so far that I wasn't sure I'd be able to get up.

She had never called because she was already with someone. Us meeting was nothing to her. Nothing more than a lone night out and, perhaps, too much alcohol.

A heavy sigh slipped from my chest at the thought, and I shook my head, berating myself. I had been drugged, brought to a stranger's home, and was in a place I was sure wasn't even on the map, and yet all I could think about was Sterling and Eliza. I had almost gotten past the night we had met. Almost. But then she reappeared, and I felt ease amidst the chaos. I remembered how beautiful she was and how her voice quelled the restlessness inside me that no amount of cleaning could tame.

If this feeling had come crashing down on me so quickly, perhaps I wasn't nearly as over her as I had led myself to believe. But none of that mattered now. There was nothing more to want. Sterling belonged to someone else. I felt a hollow ache in my chest at the admission but refused to let myself dwell. Staring into the empty fireplace, I forced my mind to clear of my emotions, tucking them into a box of their own. I needed to reassess my priorities.

I savored the final light of the day. Knowing I was not likely to find anything I wanted to read tonight, I fought my way out of the chair. As I started towards my room, I started to wonder if Sterling had thought to grab any of my clothes before she had whisked me away. I looked down at my naked feet as they passed from the rug onto the cool wood of the floor. In my anger, I hadn't realized they were bare.

I smacked into a wall so hard I fell backwards. I sat for a second, rubbing my head with a hand, when I noticed someone standing at my feet, the hallway sprawling behind them. *So not a wall.* With my pride hurting more than my head, I looked up at who stood before me. A familiar face, soft and apologetic, stared down at me. A dark hand was extended, and he helped me up when I accepted it.

The last time I had seen his face, it was full of pain. He had been bloody and beaten almost beyond recognition.

Malachi.

It was night and day from our first encounter. The planes of his face, the edges of his cheeks, and his jaw were more prominent thanks to the lack of swelling that had previously been there. He had rich brown eyes that were flecked with amber and gold. They were like nothing I had ever seen before. Standing next to him, I realized he was taller than I had thought last night. He had to be at least 6'5".

Malachi gave me a shy smile, dimples appearing on his perfect face. "My apologies. I should have been paying more attention," he said, his voice deep and smooth. I blinked at him, taking a moment to register what he was saying to me.

The image of his bleeding back came rushing into my mind. The agony that had been painted on his face was vivid as I tended to his savage wounds. The sorrow and worry that radiated from his friends had been tangible in the room.

But now, standing before me, he looked like the picture of health. There was no trace of the abuse he had suffered the night before. It was as if he had magically healed overnight.

You almost died in my house.

I brought myself back to the present, realizing Malachi was politely waiting for me to respond. He, no doubt, had also thought back to when we met. That is, if he even remembered seeing me. Perhaps I was just another stranger in this house. Though the way he had smiled at me suggested that he knew exactly who I was.

"Please don't apologize," I finally responded, "I was staring at the ground and ran into you. The fault is all mine."

"Allow me to share in the blame. I wasn't paying much attention myself."

I gave him a small smile and nodded. "If you insist. It saves me some embarrassment, at least."

Malachi chuckled lightly.

"Have a good night," I said, as I made to step around him. He allowed me the space to continue on my way, but before I had taken too many steps, his words chased after me.

"After nearly taking you out, I would hate to not formally introduce myself. I'm Malachi."

I turned towards him once again. "I'm Kiara," I replied.

"Oh, I know who you are. I have heard quite a bit about you. And, if the stories are true, I believe it is you who I have to thank for saving my life."

"It was nothing," I brushed off the weight of his words as I awkwardly tried to feign nonchalance. "Helping people is my job. It's something I'm used to."

"Nonetheless," he shrugged, letting the words hang between us briefly. "If you won't accept my thanks, would you do me the honor of a meal together?"

"Oh, I was just on my way to my room, actually."

"You're not hungry?"

I hadn't thought about it. How long had it been since I had eaten? I was about to decline the offer, letting him know I was in fact not hungry, when a rumble from my stomach filled the silence.

Malachi smiled, confirming he had heard the sound. "Come with me. I know where Sterling keeps the good food."

I followed him back in the direction I had come from. We passed the door to the library and came to the top of a staircase. To the left was another hallway that looked identical to the one on my right. He gestured for me to take the stairs first and followed a few steps behind.

When we reached the bottom, I allowed him to take the lead once again. The stairs ended in an open entryway. To the right was a living room. The windows allowed what little light remained to illuminate the furniture that filled the space. To the left, there was another hall that Malachi decided to walk down. We passed a couple of doors before coming across one that was open.

It led into a dining area that was attached to an immaculate kitchen. The stainless-steel appliances were flush with gray stone countertops atop black painted cabinets. Pots and pans hung from a rack on the ceiling above the island. On the back countertop, a spider burner was embedded into the stone that topped the stove. The refrigerator was to the left, while the countertop extended to the right. The sink was here, followed by more counter space where a coffee pot sat. Though the colors in the kitchen were dark, the open floor plan into the dining room and the wall of windows made it feel surprisingly light.

One of those windows looked as if it slid open and served as a door. There was a porch that extended away from the house. On it sat furniture around a fire pit. It looked like the perfect place to host a gathering with friends at the height of summer.

Malachi gestured to a seat at the island as he walked to the pantry door. "What are you in the mood for?" he asked as he disappeared behind the door.

I thought for a moment. It felt silly, but it was all I could think of.

"What kind of cereal is there?"

He stepped out once more, his face giving away no emotion as he stared at me. I was waiting for the teasing to start when a grin spread across his face.

"I have just the thing."

He disappeared once more, only to swiftly return with a box in hand. He placed it in front of me before going to the refrigerator for milk. I surveyed the packaging as he retrieved bowls and spoons before returning to his place opposite me. He slid the bowl and spoon over to me as I looked skeptically at the box. The box boasted about being high in fiber. It was a health-conscious cereal, something one would probably find in an elderly relative's cupboard.

I sank with mild disappointment. "Oh, on second thought, that's okay. I'm not a huge fan of—"

Malachi held up a hand to stop me. He reached for the box, popping it open and pouring its contents into my bowl. The cereal that appeared did not match the picture on the box. This was a cereal that seemed far more enjoyable. Where the box had advertised flavorless cardboard pieces, my bowl was filled with something sugary that promised to turn my milk chocolatey. The smell of peanut butter wafted into my nose as Malachi poured himself a bowl, too.

"Did I mention Sterling likes to try to hide the good food?"

"Well, in that case," I laughed as I grabbed the box and filled my bowl to the brim.

Malachi let out a rumbling laugh. "I knew I would like you."

I smiled back at him as I poured the milk, cereal spilling over as it rose past the edge of the bowl. I passed it to him and started to eat. It was so simple, but at that moment, it was the most delicious thing I had ever tasted. We sat in silence, and it was surprisingly comfortable.

"Does Sterling know you eat her food?" I asked.

"She suspects it. She knows that one of us has caught on to her latest trick. She will change it up once she catches on. We find out eventually, though, and the cycle continues." He shrugged unapologetically as he slurped from his bowl.

'One of us... We...'

"How many people live here?"

"Well, let's see. There is me and Sterling, of course. Then there are the twins and Roman. So five in total."

"Sounds like a full house."

"It is, but we don't mind it too much. The one who gets most annoyed is Eliza. But she isn't too hard to irritate." He beamed as if it were a great triumph.

"She lives here along with the five of you, then?"

"Eliza *is* one of the five. She's Callen's twin."

It made sense now. Why her eyes had seemed so familiar when we had met in the library. I had seen the softer version when her brother had been tending to Malachi in my living room.

"I heard you had the pleasure of making her acquaintance already," Malachi continued with a smirk.

"Who did you hear that from?"

"Eliza, as she stormed down the hall and slammed the door behind her. She was muttering about 'some Child of Adam waltzing in and interrupting her day.' I could only assume that it had been you. Well done, I must say. Getting her that mad is a feat that all of us have rarely managed to do. It's always great to see her ruffled." The teasing was evident. He talked about Eliza with the adoration of a brother who loved her dearly, despite her short fuse.

"'Child of Adam'? What is that? Sterling used the phrase earlier, too."

"It is a way to denote someone from the mortal world. Neither angel nor Nephilim, but simply human."

"Angels and Nephilim, huh? So, tell me…" I saw Malachi register the change in my tone. He sat up straighter, eyes wary. "Are you going to try and sell me the same story Sterling has been telling me?"

He sat there for a moment, weighing his words before responding. "I know what I know," he started slowly, "but I also know that, unless someone is open and willing to be told something, it will never feel like the truth to them, even if it is factual."

The way he spoke made it almost sound like a riddle. But it made sense. I knew I needed to be open-minded, and already, I was closing myself off. I looked down at my hands splayed on the cool stone of the countertop, unsure of what to say.

"Can I give you an unsolicited opinion?" Malachi asked sincerely.

I nodded.

"Sterling has never had ill intent in her life. She is not malicious or conniving. She holds those she cares about in the highest regard, and she only ever tries to do right by everyone she meets. The situation you are now faced with is, in part, her fault, yes. It could also be considered partially my fault as well. I was the reason she came back to you after a ll."

He paused, another apology written on his handsome face. I was going to tell him that it wasn't his fault, that the issues I had with Sterling were multifaceted at this point, but something made me feel as if he didn't need the explanation.

Malachi continued, "Sterling may make decisions that, in the moment, may be the best she could've chosen. The fallout happens later on. She had no intention of disrupting your life. And I can assure you that the choices she makes from here on out are only meant to try to right any wrongs. I love her like my sister. Hell, I could only dream that—"

He stopped abruptly, disappearing inside himself. It was brief, the haunted look that passed over him. His face was one of sorrow for only a second before he shook his head clear. "The point is, she never meant to hurt you. Sterling is trying to make it right in the best way she knows how. Please, don't fight her and make it even harder."

"It's just a lot to take in," I muttered quietly after a moment. "I mean, you meet a stranger at a club and have a great night with each other, only for her to bring her injured friend to you weeks later and then proceed to say that said friend is some divine being out of a religious text. To top it off, she drugs you, and you wake up to find her with some harlot wrapped around—"

I had gone too far. From what I had gleaned, Malachi also loved and cared for Eliza.

"I am so sorry, Malachi. That wasn't appropriate. And she's not... I mean, I don't know her but... I'm sure she is lovely, and her being with Sterling doesn't call for language like that. I'm sorry, I spoke out of frustration."

I was ashamed by my outburst and waited for Malachi to berate me further. Rather than becoming angry, though, he reached over the table and grabbed my hand. Giving me a knowing look, he said, "I know it cannot be easy. Any of it."

I squeezed his hand in gratitude. He was anything but judgmental. I was suddenly very grateful that I had quite literally run into him earlier o n.

"I'm glad you are healed," I said, not knowing what else to say.

"You and me both," he confessed. "Though now I have more issues to deal with. It makes me exhausted to think about it."

"What issues?"

"Nothing anyone else needs to worry about at the moment. Especially you. You have a lot to learn about this life before bringing the troubles of others into it." There was no condescension, only kindness and honesty in his voice.

Without warning, I was overtaken by a massive yawn. Malachi laughed and stood from where he had been leaning on the countertop. He stretched, and I stood too, reaching for my bowl to take to the sink.

He moved faster, swiping the dishes from my reach. "I will take care of these. You head up to bed. You have had a long day."

I laughed incredulously at him. "You're one to talk. I'm pretty sure there is still blood in my living room, staining my rug."

"And I will compensate you for that, starting by doing your dishes. Now go on."

"Thank you, Malachi."

"Please, call me Mal. It's what friends call me."

I grinned at him. "Kai." It was all I needed to say for him to understand.

"Goodnight, Kai."

"Thanks for the cereal." With that, I turned and headed towards my room.

As I passed the library, I realized that my room was likely the one at the end of the hall, the door still ajar from when I had stormed out. I was almost to my room when I heard a door open and close behind me. I turned to look on instinct, and saw Eliza standing there a few doors down.

Her eyes were daggers even in the dim light. The moonlight danced in her long hair, turning it silver, as she glowered at me. For some reason, I couldn't bring myself to break the stare in order to enter my room. She made a sound of disgust that she threw in my direction as she turned on her heels and stalked towards the stairs. I stepped into my room and shut the door, but not before catching the obscene gesture she had raised over her shoulder before walking out of sight.

I walked over to the bed, deciding that the breeze from the window was pleasant enough to leave it open. I stripped down to the boy shorts and sports bra I had on under my sweats and crawled under the covers.

I took the time to adjust the many pillows in such a way that I would always have one under my head, no matter how much tossing and turning I did. I looked around the room once more, appreciating the space now that I was no longer disoriented.

Mal had been right about one thing: a flustered Eliza was entertaining, albeit scary. It appeared that my mere presence in the house was enough to piss her off. It would come back to bite me in the ass, I was sure of it, but I couldn't help but giggle to myself at how ridiculous both of our encounters had been. First in the library, where she felt the need to smother Sterling in front of me, as if laying claim to some piece of land. And now the childlike behavior in the hallway. It was almost comical.

I tucked myself into the massive cloud of a mattress, relaxing almost instantly due to its sheer comfort.

I thought about the other things Mal had said. Tomorrow would be Sterling's first attempt to teach me about her world. I had promised to be open-minded in her pursuit to prove to me that this was real. I lay there wondering what the days ahead would hold in store, but I knew one thing for certain:

Tomorrow would be a new day, a clean slate. And I would need to let go of all my feelings for Sterling.

CHAPTER 10

It was all familiar. For the first time, I recognized my surroundings, and I was aware I was asleep. It didn't matter that I knew I was unconscious, though. It felt as if it were all happening in real time. The breeze ruffled my hair, and I smelled fresh grass all around me. Normally, my dreams were hazy around the edges, like an old photo exposed to time. This time, however, it was crystal clear.

I was in the clearing.

This time, Sterling was mere steps away. The weather was still perfect as she sauntered towards me, a lazy, lopsided grin on her face. She lifted her chin in greeting, her eyes dancing as they ran down my frame. She was happy to see me.

I felt my waking resolution waver within seconds.

She could be mine. Not in life. But here and now, in this slice of fiction, it could be real.

The fleeting thoughts unraveled quickly. I knew myself well enough to know that wanting something that wasn't meant for me would only end in devastation. Regardless of if it was while awake or asleep.

I doubled down on the promise to myself, sealing it in concrete. I smiled back as I tried to reframe my feelings to ones that were strictly platonic. When Sterling reached for my hand, I maneuvered away with a small wave. Confusion briefly touched her face before she recovered and accepted the small rejection gracefully.

She was staring at me the same way she had in the library earlier that afternoon, though we were not nearly as close to one another now. This time, it was as if *she* were the one entranced by *me*. We didn't speak. Time marched on, stretching this moment out longer than seemed possible, even for a dream.

Then I felt it.

The air began to soundlessly crackle against my skin. Every nerve ending I possessed was set ablaze. It wasn't painful, though. No, this was focus and precision. Untamed awareness. It was controlled adrenaline that was bottled up inside me, something only I could direct and bend to my will.

In the seconds that it took for the sensation to cover me, I looked over at Sterling and saw that she had not moved an inch. Whatever I was feeling, she was oblivious to it. My gaze was pulled from her to look over her shoulder at the empty space just a few feet beyond where we stood. The flow of energy coursing through me pulled my attention there. Something that could only be described as anticipation filled my chest as the air shifted around us.

The crackling intensity increased as scents of smoke and amber were woven in the wind. The new smell must have also registered with Sterling. Every inch of her went tense as she spun to look at the spot that called to me. The weather began to darken and change as it normally did. Clouds gathered in the sky and started to swirl ominously, foreshadowing the inevitable clash between Sterling and the shadowed silhouette.

The next few moments passed as they always did. The sky ruptured loudly, and Sterling leapt into action. She sprinted directly for the spot we had locked our eyes onto, as her sword materialized out of nowhere, perfectly seated within her hand.

"Get out of here, Kai!" The urgency was thick as ever, her skin three shades lighter than I thought possible. Sweat had started to bead on her forehead as I stood planted in place.

This was a noticeable difference. I was on edge, sure. But it felt different than the other times I had been in this situation. Thanks to the electric surge in my body, I felt powerful and sure of myself, despite still not knowing exactly what it was that we continued to face.

It was decided—I was not going to run.

My resolve kicked in, but before I could take a step towards Sterling, instead of the tree line, the violet light flashed towards the earth. But this time, it came down between Sterling and me.

I watched as sheer panic flooded Sterling's face seconds before the light separated us. "Kai don't—" Her voice was instantly hoarse from yelling, but she was cut off, words lost in space, as the figure made of darkness and cloud and smoke descended the path carved by the light. It was as if blinding starlight had mingled with the essence of pure darkness and created a wall that was both solid and soundproof.

The silhouetted figure, made from the darkest pieces of night, took shape from the ground up. Its eyes had the same violet-blue hues as before. And this time, they were fixed on me.

I rolled my shoulders back, standing taller, as I raised my chin. The shadow came closer until there was no more than three feet between us. The creature cocked its faceless head, and despite its lack of features, I could have sworn I felt condescension and mockery radiating from it.

"Kiara Novak," the voice crooned. Feminine and masculine notes intertwined as it spoke. No singular discernible voice could be made out as it continued, "It's a pleasure to meet you."

"I wish I could say the same, but you seem to constantly be ruining my dreams whenever I get close to something good." The steadiness that emitted from me was shocking, but I couldn't acknowledge it, lest it give way to something less in control.

"Oh, the angel halfling?" the voice sounded bored, "She is perfectly fine. You see, this was more of an A/B conversation, and she was having an issue C-ing her way out of it. I was happy to assist. You can have her when we are finished here."

"I don't want her."

"What you do or don't do with the golden child is of no consequence to me. I simply wanted to make a proper introduction. You see, I anticipate us needing one another in the future."

"I've watched you try to kill Sterling time and time again. If she is what you claim her to be, a Child of Angels, why would I trust you?"

"Kiara, my love, there are so many things you have yet to discover. So resistant to the real world around you. It's delicious really," the voice purred in a way that was both seductive and predatory, "how naive you are, and how unwilling to bend you can be."

"I like to stand by my convictions."

"It seems that's what you think, though it doesn't always prove to be true," the figure glanced slightly over its shoulder, towards where Sterling was standing behind the soundproof wall.

"I doubt, even if this were real, that I would ever need your help. You're vile."

A soft chuckle reverberated from the faceless form, its eyes shining brighter than before. Was it *amused?*

"In due time, I will relish bearing witness to your realization that not all evil is covered in the cloak of darkness. Right along with the moment when you admit that you do, in fact, need me."

"What makes you so sure I would ever need your help?"

"Because I know you have felt it. Even now, you still do."

The sentence hung in the air. I didn't need the creature to continue in order to know what it had meant, but it went on anyway.

"I will not be the first to teach you. I won't even put a name to what you felt in the air. No, that will be the responsibility of others. You may hone and master parts of it, sure, but one day you will crave what you felt tonight. That lick of power that's gracing your veins this very moment will be like a drug. It will call to you despite your feigned disinterest. You will learn to wield parts of it, but it will not satisfy your craving. Only then, when you have learned everything they are able and willing to teach you, will you seek me out. And I must say, my darling, I cannot wait for our time together."

The shadows moved slowly towards me with a feline-like grace. I refused to break eye contact as a swirling hand caressed my cheek, moving a lock of hair behind my ear. The touch was icy fire, the burn somehow electric.

"I won't interfere with your dreams further, though I do hope you can do better than the blonde back there." The shadow leaned to my left side, its mingled voice caressing the shell of my ear as it whispered, "I'll see you when the stars align, little dark one."

I sat up violently, surveying my surroundings. My chest was working violently as I tried to catch my breath. I was still in my oceanside room.

The gray skies outside my window began to streak with the blues and pinks of first light.

Everything was in place from the night before, save for the disheveled sheets that had fallen to the floor and the bedside lamp I clutched tightly in my hand. I couldn't remember reaching for it.

I focused on the consistent sound of waves running up to the shore, using it to steady my breathing. I gently set the lamp back in its place on the nightstand. As I collected myself, I could've sworn I felt the small hum of the electricity I had felt in my dream, though it was just a fraction. The more my heart rate slowed, the more the sensation dissipated. It made me start to question if it had even been there to begin with.

I lay back in bed and stared up at the ceiling as I tried to process everything that I had dreamt. There was consciousness, awareness, and it had the sharp lines of a memory rather than the smudged edges of a dream. It all felt strange.

In that moment, I felt annoyance and defiance, but there was no fear or sense of danger. I had felt an energy I'd never known. The shadow had said it was some sort of power, and with how potent it was, I was apt to believe it. There was something else that had been present too. A bigger feeling that I was only just realizing had come into play.

Curiosity.

I wanted to know more. Though I had been defiant, I couldn't help but admit that I wanted to seek out an interaction with this unknown being. There was a peculiar draw in my soul, and it made me restless.

I thought about what the smoke had whispered to me, so gently, *"'I'll see you when the stars align, little dark one.'"*

A big sigh escaped my lips, and I sank further into my mattress. The salt on the ocean breeze flowed through my window as I toyed with the idea that maybe, even in this new world, this still wasn't normal.

I wasn't sure if I should tell anyone about this. I hardly knew these people. Despite what seemed like good intentions, I was not so sure that I could trust them. After all, I still didn't fully believe Sterling. What if she was telling the truth? I didn't know enough about this world. If this dream really did mean something, could I trust her enough to tell her what I saw? Maybe I could talk to Malachi, but it would be hard to be aloof when I wasn't even sure what to ask. It only begged another question—could I trust Sterling's friends to keep secrets from her? I wasn't so sure.

Especially when the shadow and Sterling are constantly trying to kill one another.

I pondered my options for a moment longer, only finding more questions than solutions. With nothing else to do, I got up to start the day.

In the heat of my anger yesterday, I had not noticed much about my room aside from the windows and the sound of the sea. Against the far wall by the door was a light gray wardrobe. It matched the nightstand, as well as the bedframe and headboard. On the wall to the left of the bed, opposite the windows, was a closed door. I expected to open it and find another closet. To my surprise, when the door swung open, a private bathroom was revealed.

The room was almost as big as the bedroom. It was a full bathroom. It had a big clawfoot tub separate from the large rectangular walk-in shower. The vanity was large, though it only housed a single sink. Though there was a large rectangular mirror above the sink, there was also a full-length mirror that hung to the right of the door. The fixtures were a combination of black and silver, giving the whole room an elegant and contemporary look.

I had no toiletries with me, save for my toothbrush, which I found in a holder on the counter. At some point, I would need to ask where I could find someplace to buy the rest of my essentials, since I was meant to be here for at least a few weeks.

As I was brushing my teeth, it dawned on me that maybe, since she thought to bring my toothbrush, Sterling had thought ahead and packed clothes for me as well. I finished up in the bathroom and walked back into the bedroom, where I faced the wardrobe. I pulled the doors open to find a few familiar shirts hanging up, along with a heavy jacket and a couple of hoodies. The two lowest drawers were filled with folded pairs of pants. They varied from sweats to shorts to jeans. In the final drawer, my socks and underwear were separated by dividers that split the single space into thirds.

"I wonder who had the honor of doing this," I said to no one, and my cheeks instantly heated at the idea of Sterling delicately folding each lacey item that now rested on top of the pile.

I settled on a pair of light blue distressed jeans and a white t-shirt. I let my hair fall around my shoulders in its natural curl, volume added thanks to the ocean air. In the full-length mirror, I was pleasantly surprised to see that I looked more put together than I had felt these last few days.

I was walking over to the bench seat below my windows when I smelt the faintest scent of bacon wafting through the vents. Someone must have been making breakfast. My stomach reacted to the smell instantly, reminding me that I needed to eat. I stopped mid-step as I considered the possibilities of who I might find downstairs.

There was a chance I could walk downstairs to find either Sterling or Mal in the kitchen. That would be the best-case scenario. However,

I knew there was a chance that I would find one of the other two boys, Callen and Roman. Not having met Roman, and remembering Callen's icy personality, adding to the fact that I was coming downstairs hoping to eat food they may have made for themselves, was a recipe for an awkward encounter. With my luck, I would find Eliza at the helm of the stove, big knife in hand.

I stood contemplating my next move when I was interrupted by a knock at my door.

"Come in."

The door opened slowly, and Malachi popped his head around the corner, a warm smile painted on his face.

"I thought I would invite you down to breakfast before all of the other vultures caught wind and devoured everything in sight."

"You're my hero," I sighed with the relief of not having to gamble an awkward start to the new day.

Mal opened the door fully and leaned against the frame. He crossed his arms and raised a quizzical eyebrow at my enthusiasm over such a small gesture.

"I'm starving, but I was stuck debating my odds of survival." He waited for me to clarify what I had meant. "You know," I shrugged and changed my tone to one of seriousness, "Eliza, in the kitchen, with the knife."

Mal smirked, "You're lucky I'm an angel who has modern taste, otherwise that would have landed poorly."

"You being an angel has yet to be proven," I reminded him.

"Yes, well, angel or not, I make one hell of an omelet if I do say so myself."

"Then by all means, lead the way."

He turned and stepped over the threshold and into the hallway before throwing over his shoulder, "You were correct to worry about

Eliza. Even the bravest of us don't dare speak to her before 10:30 and two cups of coffee. A mere look from you, alone with her in the kitchen, would've changed the tone of the day for sure." He was joking, but somewhere in my soul, I knew Eliza was lethal enough that it could be at least a half-truth.

We made our way to the kitchen before anyone else had surfaced from their rooms. I helped set the table with directions from Mal on which cupboards held cups, plates, and flatware. Once the essentials had been set out, I took up my spot on the island chair from last night. Mal, despite my offers to help, had all but swatted away my hands.

"I can't help but feel that while it's in the name of hospitality, you not letting me help has more to do with a control issue." I popped a blackberry into my mouth as he turned towards me.

"I'm offended you would suggest that I am capable of such a thing." He winked before turning back to his creation. "You aren't known for your omelets by letting other people tamper with the process."

"Touche."

Footsteps echoed on the linoleum, and seconds later, Callen walked into the kitchen. His jet-black hair was in disarray, sticking out at all angles. His eyes met mine, and he gave me a stiff, awkward nod, which I returned with a half-smile. Whoever he had expected to see this morning, I was not on the list. His eyes continued to wander the empty space of the kitchen until they landed on Malachi who was humming under his breath as he moved about the stovetop. Callen immediately softened at the sight of his friend.

"I thought I smelled your cooking."

Mal turned to face him. "Only thing in the world that can wake up your sleeping ass."

Callen grinned, and he suddenly seemed so much younger. The laugh lines were obvious now, his eyes bright. Without the tension in his shoulders and the hard stare tracking my every move, I would have doubted he was capable of being so menacing. Whoever I had met that night, he was not the man standing before me now. This was the real Callen. Easy going. Relaxed. And the *complete* opposite of his sister.

Callen grabbed a plate from the table and brought it over to the stove. Mal plopped an omelet down and started to make the next, while Callen pulled out a chair. He set his plate back in its spot but didn't sit yet.

"I don't think I introduced myself before. After all, it was... Well, we were..." He looked quickly at Mal before shaking his head. "I'm Callen. I mean, I'm sure you know my name by now, but—" He shrugged, pink coloring his cheeks as he stammered through his introduction and further confirmed my assessment.

I gave him a small wave. "I'm Kai."

"Oh, we all know who *you* are," The voice was deep and male. Judging by my lack of recognition, I assumed it was the other member of the house I had yet to meet. I turned to look and found a tall, broad-shouldered man in the doorway. He had dark eyes and hair to match that touched his shoulders. Droplets of water from a recent shower still fell from the ends onto his fitted black t-shirt that hugged large, muscled arms. His skin was tan, and he had well-groomed facial hair. His eyes were alight with mischief as he sauntered into the room.

"We have had the pleasure of listening to Eliza bitch about you for the last..." He paused and smirked. "Oh, how long has it been?" He grabbed a plate and walked to stand beside Mal.

"Play nice, Roman," Mal warned gently, but there was a hint of seriousness in his tone.

"I'm only letting the girl know that she is a legend around here. No one has been able to piss Liza off the same way she has. It's truly impressive, albeit annoying, that that is all we have had to hear about for however long."

"Sit down and eat, you big buffoon. Kai, get a plate; the next one is yours."

I obeyed Mal's instructions, and as I passed Roman, he winked at me.

Taking my plate loaded with fruit, a fresh omelet, and perfectly crisp bacon, I sat at the table on the side opposite the boys. We were quiet for a minute as we ate, Malachi joining us after he finished making three more omelets. One was on his plate as he took the chair across from me.

"You know," Roman started to say between mouthfuls of food, "your sister is one scary piece of work." He was looking at Callen, who refused to take part in whatever game he was trying to start. "I feel real sorry for the poor bastard who ends up at the top of her list." He said this as he looked towards me. "You know, one time, she—" He stopped as more footsteps sounded down the hallway. "Speak of the devil herself. Good morning, Eliza dearest!"

The cheery tone of his words did not match the look on Eliza's face as she noticed my presence. "Since when do we let strays eat at the table?"

"Liza..." Callen's tone was gentle, but a warning nonetheless.

"Whatever," she scoffed and beelined it for the coffee pot. She made her plate and looked disdainfully at the seating arrangement, the only open seats being directly next to or somewhat near me. After a moment of contemplating her options, she turned her sharp gaze on Roman. It was admittedly impressive how long he was able to stare back at her, pleasant and unyielding. But he wasn't looking to win the war, and he chuckled before picking up his plate and sliding to the seat at the end of the table.

Eliza took up the spot next to her brother and began to eat silently, keeping her eyes on her food. The mood of the table shifted and was now one of a fragile quiet that was at risk of shattering when Roman inevitably burst into laughter. It was mere moments later that Sterling walked in.

"Good morning, everyone." She was bright and energetic, as if she had already been up for hours. I offered a small smile, the same one I had given to everyone else this morning.

"Omelet is by the stove for you," Mal informed her.

"It's okay, I think I might have some cereal this morning." I froze mid-bite as Mal and I made eye contact, guilt clearly written on our faces. Thankfully, no one paid attention to us as Sterling groaned from the pantry.

"Okay," Sterling popped her head out and surveyed all of us, attempting to tease out the guilty party, "who ate my cereal?" No one answered, but as Sterling turned her back to plate her omelet, Mal winked at me from across the table. It took all I had not to laugh.

Sterling sat at the head of the table, between Mal and I, and started in on her food. If she had felt the awkward energy in the room before, she didn't let it show.

"If you'll excuse me, I am going to get a start on my day. I'd hate to waste it stuck at the table shoveling food into my mouth like a bear before hibernation." Eliza lightly punched Roman's shoulder as he devoured another handful of blackberries. There was tenderness in the way she looked at him, the way she looked at all of them, before leaving the room, coffee in hand.

With her departure, the boys broke into conversation as they discussed their plans for the day. Malachi moved into the newly open seat between Callan and Roman. I couldn't help but smile as I watched the three of them. They looked like schoolboys scheming, creating a plan to wreak havoc in the school yard.

"I hope your room was comfortable last night," Sterling's voice startled me.

"Oh, yes. The room is great, thank you. And thank you for packing some of my stuff, too."

"Don't mention it. Feel free to rearrange anything you would like. I want you to be as comfortable as possible."

"I appreciate that."

She was silent for a moment before she said earnestly, "I'm sorry. I had limited what I took and had to pick what I thought was most essential. I hope the items I chose are sufficient enough."

I waved her off, "Don't think anything of it. I was surprised to find that I had anything here at all." I looked directly into her eyes for the first time. "It was really thoughtful of you, Sterling." She gave me one of those smiles, causing me to drop my eyes to my plate. I shrugged. "Of course, it's the least you could've done after kidnapping me and all." I looked sideways at her, grinning ever so slightly.

Sterling put her hands up as if in surrender. "You've got me there." She laughed lightly. "Is there anything more you need to do this morning?"

"I had to move some stuff around," I said sarcastically, "but I think my day is open now."

"Excellent. Well, if you are done with breakfast, we can start our day."

"Let me just clean up," I started to stand with my dishes.

Callen reached out his hand. "We've got the dishes. You guys get out of here."

"Are you sure?"

Callen gave me a lopsided grin as Malachi waved his hand in a shooing motion towards the door. I looked to Sterling, who only shrugged, not fighting the dismissal. She offered her curved arm out to me.

"Shall we?"

I nodded, looping my arm through hers as we walked out of the kitchen and onto the back porch.

CHAPTER 11

The porch faced towards the hills of sand and beyond those, the sea. While Fall had set in back home, the climate in Soteria was warm. The rays of the sun baked into the earth, promising to burn anyone who was too reckless with their time. Despite our proximity to the water, the breeze was mild, and it lowered the temperature just enough to make for the perfect day by the sea.

I released Sterling's arm as I stepped off the porch and towards the pads of stone that led to the beach. Wordlessly, I stripped off my shoes and socks and tossed them behind me as I wandered onto the sand. The heat on my bare feet was welcome at first, until it started to burn. I dug my toes in deeper until I found a cooler pocket. As I raised my head towards the sky, I closed my eyes and allowed myself to be swallowed up by the happiness that could only come from being by the ocean on a beautiful day. I didn't care that I could feel Sterling's eyes on me, and she didn't care to interrupt my moment.

I let the seconds pass, too content to care about anything that had happened or what was to come. For the first time in a long time, my soul was at peace.

I took a deep breath, letting the salt tickle my nose. "It's beautiful here."

"It really is."

I turned to find her leaning on her elbows against the chipped white railing that ran along the perimeter of the porch.

"I forgot how much peace comes from being near water." It had been at least half a decade since I had been near anything that resembled a beach. It had been just as long since I had felt anything like this.

"I'm glad that it helps you relax," Sterling observed with a smile. I walked back to where she was standing. Off to her left was a table and some chairs, which she gestured to. "Believe it or not, water makes a lot of people anxious. I'd hate for that to be the case."

"I could never hate the ocean. Some of my happiest memories were when I was running around the coast."

"Is that so?"

It was an easy response. One that left it up to me how much I wanted to divulge. If I chose not to share, it would have no doubt been fine. Yet I found myself quickly ready to share any part of my life with this woman. I shifted my gaze towards the horizon. "My aunt used to take me all the time. We would camp sometimes, but other times it was just a day trip. It could be a chilly, overcast day on a gray coastal shore, and it was still all laughter and smiles."

"That sounds amazing. Do you and your aunt still take trips like that?"

The ever-present grief I kept tucked away crashed down on my previous happiness. It must have been obvious because Sterling started to shake her head. "I'm sorry. That really isn't any of my business." Her cheerful demeanor dimmed as she mistook my change in mood for hesitancy. She waited for my response, and I could see her retreating into herself with every passing second.

"No, it's okay. I can appreciate you taking an interest in my life," I reassured, giving her a half smile that I hoped reached my eyes. Unable to hold her gaze as I spoke, I looked at my hands clasped on the table. "My aunt, Erica…" my voice was already shaking, "she passed away when I was seventeen. It was a car accident. She was gone before responders had arrived on scene. There was nothing for them to do."

The silence hung in the air for a moment before I felt the soft touch of Sterling's hand. I welcomed her comforting touch, letting go of my own hand in order to grasp hers. The gentle squeeze was warm and comforting as it assuaged some of the sadness in my chest.

We sat like this, looking out into the distance, content not to speak as the moment took its time to fade into nothingness.

"I like the ocean," Sterling confessed, "because I can't stand the silence. I feel as if there is constant noise in my head and, if there's nothing to distract me, I'll get lost in it all. Although there is a fine line between a distraction and overstimulation. I have found that the sound of the waves is perfect to drown out the mental mayhem. It's consistent, and I can breathe with the swell of the tides. It keeps the chaos at bay."

Her accent was heavy as she spoke, the vulnerability drawing out the tone of her homeland—wherever that was—and I was shocked by the seriousness and sincerity with which she spoke. But if anyone understood what she meant, it was me.

"Pure silence is utterly deafening." I returned the same gentle squeeze as I gave her a knowing glance.

Slowly, the ghosts dissipated from behind Sterling's eyes and was replaced with her sunny demeanor once more. "Indeed, it is. Well, I didn't talk up this whole day just to have you sit and listen to me drone on about the therapeutic purposes of a house by the sea. Put your shoes back on and let's venture around a bit."

I felt grains of sand embedded in my socks as I pulled them into place. "It never fails. No matter how cautious you are, sand will inevitably wind up everywhere."

"Beautiful things demand to remain memorable long after the moment has passed." The sparkle in her eyes was suggestive and mischievous.

"You sound as if you have experience with such things." We began walking around the porch, which I realized wrapped around to the front of the estate.

"Oh, I absolutely do. I would make it my mission to leave a lasting impression on everyone I'd ever met if I didn't already know that I was unforgettable," she winked at me over her shoulder.

I shook my head in pretend disbelief at what she had been trying to insinuate. "You know, when I had said that you wanted girls vying for a chance to be invited to play in the sandbox, I had no idea actual sand was involved."

"What can I say, Kai? I'm full of surprises."

I stopped mid-step as a genuine laugh escaped me. The sound set Sterling's eyes alight, and I couldn't help but smile. It was the first time I had laughed with her since that night at the club.

"But in all honesty, never once have I been able to avoid finding sand in all my personal belongings. And a lot of those items have never actually seen the sand."

"One of the many mysteries of nature, I suppose."

"If you ever discover the secret..."

"You will be the first to know," I promised, "So, you grew up here?"

"More or less. I spent a year or two out here before my mother and I moved. But in my early adolescence, I ended up living here once more, and I never left. It was a rough life," she teased.

"I can only imagine how hard it must have been. Do you have a big family? Even from what little I have seen, this house is huge."

"The occupants in the house varied throughout the years," she explained casually, "At one time, for about two years or so, we lived here, all three of us. It was the first time I had ever seen my parents cohabitate. You see, timing was not always in their favor. For one reason or another. As a child it, wasn't something I really questioned. I had my mother, and we were happy.

"Anyways, I was told my mother loved it here in Soteria, and that was why my father had had this house built for her. He is a...lavish man, you could say. The house may have been for my mother, but it was built in size and finery to lift his ego. We had more room than we knew what to do with, and since it was usually only my mother and I, she decided she would open it up to others. Friends, acquaintances, strangers, anyone who needed a place to stay during their travels were welcome. But, as I said, my mother and I didn't stay too long before moving back to our little cottage on some no-name island, where I spent the last few years as a young kid. Somehow, years later, I managed to end up owning this beautiful place. I guess you could say the rest is history."

I wanted to ask more about her parents and why they had left this amazing place. But if there was one thing I could assume about Sterling, it was that she was intentional in what she shared. The fact that she had barely mentioned her father suggested my prying wouldn't have been welcome.

Not missing a beat, she continued, "The house was moved into my name when I turned eighteen since neither of my parents had use for it any longer. They knew that I loved the place and, by some grace of the angels, it was given to me."

"That's so amazing. It must have been weird, though? I mean, surely if it was too big for you and your mom, it must have been monstrous for you alone.

"Of course it was. So, I naturally did what any young adult would do and filled it with my best friends. The gaggle of idiots in there has been the house's longest-lasting occupants, aside from yours truly," she said with unadulterated love.

We had rounded the corner to the front porch. An expanse of lush, emerald grass spread out before us, where a walkway led to an opening in a short white fence. From there, I wasn't entirely sure where it went. Sterling walked down the stone steps that came off the porch and strolled onto the lawn as she looked up at the house in reverence.

"This is home."

I stood gaping at the sight in front of me. The interior, or at least what I had seen of it, had been beautiful. However, there had been so much going on in the last twenty-four hours that the last thing on my mind had been the house.

It was gorgeous.

Before us stood a two-story house painted in a sandstone gray and trimmed in white. The top floor had three windows, the side windows identical to one another. What initially appeared as multiple smaller windows in the middle turned out to be a set of French doors that led out onto a small terrace. On the lower level, there were four pillars that ran across the front and helped support the cover of the porch. There were two more up against the house that held up the back two corners. Off to the left side, a white wooden swing swayed in the breeze while, on the right, a table and chairs similar to the ones in the back waited for occupants. The door sat between two wide glass panes and had glass paneling that allowed as much natural sunlight into the foyer as possible.

"It's perfect," I breathed out at last.

"You really think so?"

"Are you kidding me? It's absolutely beautiful, Sterling."

"That means a lot, Kai, truly."

We locked eyes and, for a moment, the world stopped. The warm way in which she spoke, and the enticing blue of her irises, had me in a chokehold. I let myself stare. I imagined what it would be like to brush the stray wisp of hair behind her ear. Based on the fluttering in my chest, I knew I wouldn't stop there, and I suddenly found myself wondering what her lips would taste like.

I cleared my throat, forcing myself back to reality. I'm sure it wasn't hard to convince anyone to move in. Tell me, how did you meet the...what did you call them? 'Gaggle of idiots'?" I laughed.

"That is a very broad question that consists of multiple stories." We started walking back towards the house, and Sterling gestured to the chairs when we reached the porch. "First, you have to understand the normal way in which we Nephilim grow up. Given this is supposed to be a day of learning, consider this your first lesson.

"Allow me to explain. The Nephilim raise their children differently in certain regards when it comes to both how and where we grow up, but the basics are fairly similar to what you would expect. We study reading and writing, science and math. Useful things that anyone would need in daily life. As we get older, some choose to study their hobbies in depth. They take up music, other languages, or art in all sorts of different media. It's very similar to public school, though we are in smaller groups.

"However, we have additional required studies as we age. We learn about strategy, critical thinking, and a multitude of histories. We learn about the Hosts of Heaven, the Archangels, and demons we eventually will learn to protect the world from. We must know their weaknesses, what strengths our ancestry blessed us with. The more we know, the better prepared we are to survive whatever situations we may find ourselves in.

"While knowledge is key, we also must train. We hone physical abilities at a young age in order to protect ourselves. Whether it is with weapons or hand-to-hand combat, we are exposed to it all. Are you with me so far?"

"It sounds like a big military school for small children, if I'm being honest."

"I swear it's not as scary as you're making it sound," she reassured me. "We use prop weapons until we are old enough, and skilled enough, to pick up the real thing."

"'Old enough,'" I repeated, my tone heavy with sarcasm, "I don't know that I would agree with that statement, but go on."

"Kai, a nine-year-old Nephilim child is *at least* ten times more adept with a blade than a grown adult from your world would ever be."

"What a terrifying thought."

She smiled at my fake horrified expression. "Some people have an aptitude for all weaponry or may even choose to specialize in a few. Others are content to become just sufficient enough in a small variety. We are all trained as warriors, but not everyone in our world ends up being a dedicated soldier."

"What do you mean exactly?"

"We are all physically capable of protecting and defending. However, we have people who choose different paths. People own shops and businesses. They teach and provide everyday services that you find in your world, though we have a handful of Nephilim delicacies as well. Some pursue a career in government. Then there are those of us who either choose, or are chosen, to pursue a life dedicated to serving in the shadows."

"I thought you said that Nephilim are meant to protect the human world? That you are all trained most of your lives only for a select few to choose that path seems counterintuitive to the whole purpose."

"I can see how that makes sense, not being raised in this world. Think of it this way. Some of us choose to be a part of a group that is able to be called to action when something goes wrong. We investigate situations that suggest demonic activity is involved. It isn't all war all the time, of course. For the most part, there are enough of us doing this job that we don't feel 'short-staffed' for lack of a better term. However, in times of distress, whether it be true war, natural disasters, or some other unfathomable situation, every teacher, business owner, and house parent alike is well-equipped to jump into action should desperation arise.

"But we are a people who are separate from Eden," she stopped when the name drew a look of confusion from me, "Eden is what we here like to call your world. Anyways, we wouldn't be able to survive if we were all nothing but soldiers. You need community and industry. Diversity in both skills and beliefs is necessary to create this, and it can help a civilization to thrive when it is all done correctly."

My attention had snagged on the shift in her verbiage. "I noticed you said 'some of us.' Is it safe to assume that means you are part of this soldier-trained group?"

"That is where the answer to your original question begins," Sterling said enthusiastically. She leaned forward with her elbows on her knees. "I was twelve and had already shown promise in combat techniques. In the preteen phase of life, we typically don't train co-ed. Eventually, they would mix us up, but at this time, I was strictly fighting other girls. Because I was so advanced—top of my class, actually"—she gave me a wry smile— "they wanted to expedite my training.

"I was placed with the boys, most of who had a year or two on me. One day, I was told that I would be getting a sparring partner, someone I would likely work with for the duration of my studies."

The memory swam so clearly behind Sterling's eyes, it almost felt as if I were watching it rather than hearing it.

"The first match was supposed to be a benchmark of sorts. The teachers for the boys wanted to gauge where I was before they continued with my training. The sparring ring was surrounded by boys, anywhere from ten to sixteen years old, and I knew none of them. Across the ring from where I stood was a lanky, pale, thin boy with a mop of black hair. He wouldn't even look up at me, just kept staring at his sneakers as the boys around us jeered and yelled. I had no doubts in my mind that I was going to wipe the floor with him."

"This is where you tell me you did exactly that because you're so gifted, huh?"

"Oh, not at all. I lost terribly," she laughed. "I thought 'there's no way this quiet boy could beat me. I'm the best,' and that was my first mistake. You see, Callen was the smallest of his age, but he was also the fastest. He learned early on that he could play meek, convincing his opponent that he was going to be an easy victory. Slippery as a snake and as cunning as a fox, that bastard humbled me quickly. I'd love to say that I made it ten minutes in the ring, but deep down, I know it was probably closer to five.

"I got the first punch in. Looking back now, I know he let me have it. It helped boost my ego and lower my guard. After that, he laid me out. I took three punches to the gut and one to the face in quick succession. Next thing I knew, he dropped low to sweep my feet out from under me, and I was on my ass.

"Most of the boys that age would have gone further, tried to knock me out or something. I was the only girl, and plenty of them wanted to show me that I was in over my head. But that wasn't Cal. No, he walked over to me, that sheepish smile on his face, and offered his hand to me. At that moment, I knew I had found someone who would have my back."

I could picture the smile she was talking about. It was the one I saw at the breakfast table this morning when he had stuttered through his introduction.

"I'm glad he put you in your place," I said playfully.

"It wasn't the last time either. I got better, of course, and I started to learn how to guess his next moves. I started to get cocky again. But then he grew a head taller and packed on 20 pounds of muscle."

"What I would give to see that humbled look on your face," fake longing filled my voice.

"Stick around long enough and you just might. He—well, actually, all the boys—keep me grounded *very* well."

"I may just have to then."

She grinned at me as a deep voice from behind made me jump.

"You don't have to be around too long. We humble Valkyre on the daily around here." Roman came up onto the porch, taking the steps three at a time. "Despite her best efforts, her hard-earned skills will always pale in comparison to my natural talents."

"Well, I suppose we can't all be freakishly large trees like you, Roman."

"If you're trying to hurt my feelings, it's not gonna work. In fact, you are only proving my point further." He winked at me playfully. "I am an original."

"The original ass maybe," Sterling retorted, "remind me why I let you live here and harass me every day?"

"Because your life would be immensely dull otherwise. Did she tell you how we met, Kai?"

"Actually, she had just finished telling me about her and Callen."

"You started your introductions with *him*? I am appalled, ma'am. You know I am your favorite, and our story is way more fun to tell."

"This entire chapter of my life started with Callen. I didn't know you until four years later, and when I first met you, I kind of hated you."

"I am hurt, Sterling. *Hurt.*"

"You're dramatic." She rolled her eyes. "If you would let me get back to it, though, I could tell her how we met."

"Well, by all means, carry on then."

"So how did you meet the others?" I asked, clearing my throat.

She thought for a moment on where to pick up. "Roman hasn't changed much in the years I have known him, but believe it or not, he was actually *more* of a loudmouth back then. He was always spouting off in our classes, but he could back up whatever trash talk left his mouth. So, of course, I already knew of him before we officially met. Roman is two years older than Callen and me—something he rarely lets us forget."

"It's important to respect your elders."

"One day," Sterling continued, ignoring Roman, "I was training when Roman and two other boys started to talk shit. Nothing serious, just stupid stuff sixteen-year-old boys would normally say.

"I eventually gave up trying to ignore them and told Roman to stop being a dumb prick, and to take his brainless friends elsewhere. Between my ego and his sarcasm, we were slated to spar within the hour. The deal was, if I beat him, he would put an end to the dumb remarks, and I would get to choose some form of public humiliation. If he won, I would owe him a single favor, no questions asked."

I looked curiously over at the well-muscled man next to me, a question on the tip of my tongue. "And yes," Sterling said, reading my thoughts, "he was a hulking neanderthal then, too."

"Not a very fair bet."

"It wasn't, but I was especially hot-headed in my teens, and I wasn't going to let any boy run his mouth, even if it meant getting my ass handed to me and losing a bet. People think I'm stubborn now? They should've met me then."

"She was unbearable. But it paid off at times. Even as an underdog, you were never one to back down from a fight," Roman mused with admiration. "We got in the ring and neither one of us held back. I had heard the rumors of this girl who thought she was hot shit, and I wasn't going to risk being subjected to her torture if the rumors were to prove true."

"Luckily, I had a certain grace and speed that his broad shoulders couldn't quite match. We both landed blows, and each of us was bruised and bleeding by the end of it all. I ended up in a pinch, though. Somehow, the brute was able to spin me around, back to his chest, arms around my neck, ready to choke me out. It would have been a fair win on his part, but I wasn't ready to lose. I let him lift me off the ground, and as he did, I kicked backwards hard and fast. And I aimed lo w."

She paused and started to nod with closed eyes as realization dawned for me. "You did *not*!"

"She did," Roman remembered so vividly he winced.

"I did. And he dropped like a sack of potatoes. I walked out of the ring without looking back at him. The boys all said it was a cheap shot. They thought it was fighting dirty, and it didn't count. Soon they were all saying there was no honor in what I had done, and that if I was going to fight like that, I didn't deserve to be there. They said that if I had to resort to dirty tricks to win because I was a girl then I wouldn't survive training with them. After hearing it enough, I started to believe it myself."

"But I would be damned if I let her doubt herself. Especially after being such a badass."

"A few days later, Roman found me in the dining hall. I was fully prepared for his anger. Instead, he held up a closed fist and waited until I bumped my knuckles against his. 'That was one hell of a way to win a fight,' he had said."

"It was," Roman shook his head in confirmation, "Honestly, most of those guys wouldn't have ever gone blow for blow with me just so they could tell me to shut the hell up, and I told her as much."

"You said 'you've got my respect, Valkyre,' and conceded that our bargain was still valid."

"You did earn it, and you still have it," he beamed proudly. "We were fast friends from then on, us and Mr. Green-Eyes."

"What did she make you do?"

"I picked the class with the most people, and the strictest teacher, and told him to streak through the classroom. I think there was something about having to do some sort of ridiculous dance, too. Callen's idea.

"That sounds mortifying."

"On the contrary," Roman wriggled his eyebrows.

"Really?"

"Maybe for anyone else, but not Roman. He actually ended up thanking me. See, by that point, we had started to integrate into co-ed lectures. He had a month's worth of punishments to face, extra workouts, the whole nine yards. But by the time he was able to have a life again, he had women lining up to go out with him."

"That's how Sterling earned the title of 'Best Wingman.' Once the ladies got a preview, they couldn't stay away."

"You really have no shame, do you?" Sterling shook her head in response. I turned to her. "What does it say about you that two of your closest friendships were built upon situations involving physical violence?"

"I suppose the professionals would suggest some form of masochism, but I like to think it just means we know how to have a good time."

"We have seen each other quite literally beaten and bruised. The closest friendships are forged in blood, you know. Now, if you'll excuse me, I believe Callen is waiting for me to kick his ass in the training room." He left us then, heading into the house to find his friend.

"So, what about Mal? How did you meet him?"

Absentmindedly, her hand came up to the right side of her shirt collar. I had never noticed the lighter skin that just barely peeked out from her shirt, running parallel to her collarbone. She adjusted the collar to cover the sliver of her scar. "I would hate to speak on behalf of angels. Even if it's only Malachi, it's bad luck. Let's just say I don't know that I will ever be able to repay him."

"I..." I had to swallow the lump that formed from imagining whatever danger Sterling had been in. "I'm glad Mal was there."

"Me too."

Sterling leaned back into her chair and closed her eyes for a moment. The breeze made the chains of the porch swing squeak quietly.

As much as I wanted to know, I couldn't bring myself to ask about Eliza.

I decided to go a different route. "So, does this count as my first lesson?"

"Let's consider it an abridged introduction. I would hate to drown you in information." She stood and stretched, and I followed suit. "How would you like an official tour of the house?"

"That would be excellent."

The interior was as beautiful as the exterior throughout the entire house. Most of the rooms I hadn't seen were storage rooms, bedrooms, and a very nice laundry room. She also pointed out the doors to the armory and the training room Roman had mentioned earlier, though we both felt it best to leave the boys alone when we heard a big crash followed by a lot of swearing. At the end of the tour, I had decided that the library was still my favorite room.

The last stop was in front of my room.

"If Malachi was truly an angel, wouldn't he have a power of some kind?" I turned to Sterling and leaned against my door frame.

"Well, typically yes. Angels can produce Heavenly Fire, something very key to the Nephilim. At minimum, it helps to forge weapons against our enemies. In its purest form, it is incredibly lethal."

"If you wanted to prove anything to me, you could just have him show me this magical ability, and that would probably do the trick."

"See, I thought about that, but Mal has fallen. He can't tap into that specific power unless the punishment is reconciled."

"I see. I suppose we will have to continue with your plan, then."

"You know I'm hurt you would even think that the thought hadn't crossed my mind," she said playfully as she drew herself to her full height. "I may be pretty, but I've also got a few brain cells."

"Based on the stories I have heard this afternoon, I don't know how much faith I have in those few brain cells. Too much head trauma," I teased. She shoved my shoulder gently, not having a retort readily available. We were standing close, but not like we had been in the library. This afternoon had been easy. We had talked about the house, and she told me stories of memories that had surfaced with every nick on the wall or dent in a door.

"Thank you for today," I said in earnest, "It helped me feel more comfortable here."

"Thank you for being willing to listen and ready to learn. Even if it was only about my friends and our lives here." Her steel blue eyes danced over my face, and her lips moved as if she were about to say something more. I held my breath in anticipation, still eager to know what was on her mind despite myself. Someone cleared their throat, drawing our attention to the hallway.

Eliza.

Whatever Sterling was about to say vanished in the second it took for her to take a step back. Eliza was standing in the middle of the hall with her arms crossed. The displeasure from seeing us together radiated off her in waves, covering the space in a thick blanket of her disapproval. Eliza turned on her heels and stormed away.

"I'll see you at dinner," Sterling assured me. She jogged to catch up with Eliza, and then they both disappeared around the corner as they went downstairs. I stood there, alone, trying to ignore the weight that settled heavily in my chest every time I watched them walk away together.

So much for strictly platonic feelings.

Deciding that there was no better place to avoid my self-pity than in the pages of a book, I pushed off the door frame with a sigh and headed towards the best room in the entire house.

CHAPTER 12

N o one was in the library, which, according to Sterling, was to be expected. I was perfectly content to browse the titles alone. I walked over to the window and opened it, allowing the sounds of the outside world to drift inward. The breeze somehow managed to bring the rays of the sun inside with it.

I walked over to the wall with the fireplace, running my fingers across the spines of books as I went. My eyes roved over the titles waiting for one to jump out at me. But nothing caught my attention. Not that I was trying all that hard to begin with.

That was the beauty of books. Even just being surrounded by them provided some sense of comfort, no matter where I was. When I was surrounded by books, I was never alone. I took solace in this as I continued to feel my way across the wall.

I made my way to the overstuffed chair that I had sat in yesterday evening. Just as I was about to flop down, I realized there was a black, leather-bound book on the cushion. I picked it up and realized quickly how dense the volume was. The title was not embossed on the front, and I had to use both hands to turn the tome in order to look at the spine.

'*Nephii: A Brief Nephilim History of Study and Tradition*'

I took up my place in the chair and began to flip through the pages. The vellum had the aged smell of an old text. Some pages had hand-drawn illustrations of various weapons and buildings, while others had depictions of creatures that could only be described as disturbing.

I stopped as one page caught my eye. The heading read '*Familial Law.*' I began to read.

"*The Hosts of Heaven have laws in place, such as the abolishment of creating new Nephilim lines through the union of angels and humans. Because of this law, and others previously passed down by the Archangels to the first of the Nephilim, we must also adapt the rules of Arcadia into law.*

In regard to the land of Eden, Nephilim shall maintain secrecy so as not to cause panic, incite chaos, or encourage the Children of Adam to become aware of and/or involved in activities linked to Heaven and Hell. Though a few mortals are seduced into the world of summoning and striking deals with demons, we do not care to promote it further through transparency.

"*Furthermore, we as a people must continue the bloodline of the Nephilim. The blood of angels is only ever diluted when mixed with that of a Child of Adam. It has been proven to be quite common that the offspring of Nephilim and humans lack much of the natural-born talent that would allow them to live a successful life among the Nephilim.*

"*For this reason, and the increased risk it poses to open our world to the Children of Adam, it is forbidden for any Nephilim to have any union, be it emotional or physical, with the inhabitants of Eden. Relations of any sort bring those mortal souls too close to the world of shadows in which the Nephilim live, and risk not only their safety, but the continuation of our people.*"

I looked up and into the unlit fireplace while I thought about what I had just read. In my mind, I felt the door I had previously closed on Sterling and I lock with a finality that was outside of my control. I sat with this information a little while longer when I realized what should have been painstakingly obvious to me from the start.

"I'm not supposed to be here."

"Unfortunately, no, you are not." Malachi's smooth voice startled me from the doorway. I stood abruptly, and the book clattered to the floor. Gracefully, he stepped into the room, picking up the thick volume from where it lay at my feet. He examined the page I had been reading, then looked back at me.

His face was gentle, honey brown eyes soft and understanding. "You have started to do your own research, it seems."

"I was just killing time. It happened to be in the chair when I went to sit down." I shrugged, suddenly feeling very tired.

"How was this afternoon with Sterling?"

"It was fine," I mumbled. "I got to hear about how she met the other two boys. She started to explain how Nephilim children studied and went to school, too."

"Correct me if I'm wrong, Kai, but it sounds like you doubt her less than you have in the past. Is that true?"

"Honestly, I don't know. It seems *too* elaborate for anyone to make up. Not to mention you're up and walking after suffering injuries that would have taken months to heal from." I walked over to the window and crossed my arms over my chest. "But then that means..." the words caught in my chest.

Mal walked up beside me, brushing his shoulder against mine. The warmth that came from him was comforting. "It means that the world as you know it has done nothing but deceive you. It means this," he shook the book between us, "is very real."

I ran my hands over my face and through my hair. Sighing, I asked, "She wasn't supposed to bring me here, was she?"

"No." One word, soft and simple. Final.

"Why did she then? Why risk punishment when she could've taken the memory from me and saved herself the trouble?"

"I cannot speak for her. But I have known her for several years now, and I know she always shows gratitude where she feels it is due."

"So, you're saying Sterling brought me here because she was grateful?"

"Possibly, I know I am, and I would have been disappointed to not have met my savior," he paused, "I also know that after Sterling met you, there was something different about her."

I turned to face Mal then, searching his face for any sign that he was holding back. If he was, it didn't show.

He went on, "She could have taken your memories, sure, but Sterling would still have to hold onto the memory of you. I think she was hoping that once she got you here, the solution would appear easily. Unfortunately, that has yet to be the case."

"Well, according to the law, it's not allowed."

"It isn't. And Sterling is a strict rule follower. Sure, she made reckless decisions when she was younger, but when it comes to the law, she respects it greatly. I think that's what makes this even harder for her."

"She was reckless when she was younger?" I could hardly picture it.

"Oh, yes. Those three were *terrible* at doing as they were told and rarely followed protocols. It's amazing that they survived their adolescence. Though I have to admit I am grateful. It is because of their foolishness during their youth that we met."

"How *did* you meet, exactly?"

"Did Sterling not share the story?"

"She had said it would be best to let you tell it. Something about it being bad luck to speak for angels."

"She is so superstitious," he said lovingly. "Well, where to begin? Sterling was probably eighteen at the time. There had been rumors of a particularly nasty demon nest floating around. Our lovely trio had been tasked with going in to do some reconnaissance. They were specifically instructed to not engage the horde. Naturally, three adrenaline-fueled teenage warriors only saw a challenge."

"They tried to fight the..." I couldn't bring myself to say the word. Saying it felt like I was admitting to the truth of it all.

"The demons. That is correct. They thought it was something they could handle. Given the fact that they are three of the most talented warriors their generation has seen, it was reasonable. It wasn't their fault that the dispatch had not included the fact the nest was home to eight fully grown *Daemoni*. Even the most skilled Nephilim can only handle one at a time on their own."

"They were outnumbered then."

"Severely. It did not help that, typically, these demons usually live in groups of four or five. Sterling and the boys just assumed leadership was being overly cautious. Like any other group of teenagers, they went into the house and disturbed the beasts. It was too late to call upon the Nephilim leadership for help by the time they realized they were in over their heads. Sterling called out to the Angelic Host. She begged for aid, even if it meant her friends' lives in exchange for hers. But no one came."

"Why not?"

"Angels are not forgiving creatures. The Host knew that the boys and Sterling were out of line. And there is...history the angels had to consider. Politics is nasty business even in Arcadia."

"Politics or not," I murmured incredulously, "They were just kids. They needed help."

"Unfortunately, that's a hard sell for immortal beings who believe in severe consequences. To them, mortal life is fragile, weak, even in regard to the Nephilim. Three mortal souls are a small price in their eyes."

"That's terrible."

"It is. But you saw what they are capable of in regards to their own," he said sadly, pointing to himself. "Imagine the heartlessness for teenage soldiers who do not follow commands."

A small shudder wracked my body.

"I happened to hear the call, though. I could not bear to sit by idly and watch such innocent souls be condemned. So, I stepped in. Just in time, too. A *Daemoni* was only moments away from tearing into Sterling's chest. I was able to pull it off of her and dispatch it properly, but not before a single talon tore into her."

"I saw part of her scar today."

He nodded solemnly. "The rest was history. Sterling was so grateful that she said I could stay here whenever I liked. Eventually, it felt more like home than Arcadia ever did. One day came when I decided to never go back."

I shook my head in numb acknowledgment. I had only been partially listening as I tried to imagine a world where Sterling didn't exist. It was impossible.

"I still sometimes lie awake at night thinking about what would have happened if I had not reached them when I did," Mal admitted, reading my mind, "It makes me nauseous every time."

It made my stomach curdle.

My legs were shaky as I pulled out the desk chair and took a seat. Mal followed suit, sitting on the edge of the desk to face me. "You care for her, don't you?"

"Does it matter? Nothing can be done about it," I said, resigned.

Something like empathy colored Malachi's features as he reached for my hand. "For the record, though I know it doesn't change the situation, I'm glad Sterling brought you here so that I was able to meet you. We will figure everything out as it comes. I have a feeling we have not yet learned all that we need to know in order to fully see the situation at hand."

I gave his hand a squeeze in thanks. Then, ready to move the focus from me, and emboldened by his directness, I asked, "What about you, Malachi? Any great loves to speak of?"

"I have lived a long time, Kai, and I have learned to love people from afar because of that." My confused look prompted him to go on. "My people are not the warmest, and finding love does not happen for everyone. Especially when you are an outcast like me. My sister understood me best, but issues arose that caused a rift in our relationship, and she left. After that, I was truly alone.

"There was someone once, after my sister had left. I thought I had never been happier. We were inseparable. I thought I was in love, but it was short-lived."

"What happened?"

"Angels are no longer allowed to be with humans, as you know. So, they brought my lover and I before the courts. We were tried before the council and were unable to deny that we had broken the law. Of course, we were found guilty and punished. My mortal lover was sent away, all memories of us erased. I was kept under strict supervision, something akin to house arrest, and suffered my own punishments.

"I gave up on any source of romantic love after that. Instead, I would watch how the relationships of others would unfold. I would live vicariously through the love given to others by strangers."

"That's heartbreaking."

"For a time, it was hard. That is, until I moved into this house, and I was able to feel like part of a family. I still long for that love of my life, of course, but I feel closer to it now than I have in many, many years. Here, I have learned that romantic love is not the only love that can make a heart swell with happiness."

"Maybe you will find someone like her one day, someone you can have that life with."

"I've only ever been reminded of him by one other person, but that is a bridge that I could never cross."

Him.

"Oh my gosh, Mal. I am so sorry. I didn't mean to assume anything."

"I know you meant no offense in any sort of way, and none was taken." His smile was genuine.

Outside the window, overlooking the sea, the sky was turning to a shade of navy. I was only just beginning to realize how much time had passed as I saw the violet and pink streaks chase each other through the sky. The chill seeped into the room, causing me to shiver and cueing Malachi to close the window.

I gave him a grateful nod as I reached for the book that he had sat next to him on the desk. "Do you think it's worth reading this whole thing?"

"I would say so. Knowledge is power after all, is it not?"

"Some would say ignorance is bliss."

"You could always flip a coin and see what happens. Make it a daily routine. To read or not to read."

"That could mean too much excitement for the day," I said sarcastically.

Somewhere in the house, there was a large crash. It sounded vaguely like glass shattering. Within seconds, Roman and Callen rounded the corner of the door and entered the library.

"Mal, my friend, we gotta get the hell out of dodge," Roman intoned without hesitation.

"What do you mean? And what is happening down there? I thought you were trying to balance spinning plates on sticks again."

"That's why we need to leave," Callen murmured. He locked eyes with Malachi, and for some reason, I felt the need to look away.

"Eliza is probably going to burn the house down with Sterling in it. I don't feel like being around when that happens," Roman continued. "I would rather be drinking than roasting like a marshmallow."

"No one thought to try to break up the fight before my kitchenware became collateral?" Mal asked incredulously.

"To call it a fight would imply that both parties are playing offense. Sterling is just kind of letting things happen, occasionally protecting vital organs. I wanted to watch initially, but Cal insisted that we stay away from it." He started to fake a pout, but it didn't last long as he said, "So we decided to collect you and head into town for a few rounds. Get your ass up and let's go."

They hadn't seen me. The angle that Mal had been sitting at seemed to obscure me from sight. He shifted so that I came into view. Callen immediately blushed, giving me a nod of acknowledgment with a shy smile. Roman grinned from ear to ear. "Sorry, I didn't see you had company, Mal. How's the human doing?"

"Oh, I'm just living the dream."

If he heard the sarcasm in my voice, he didn't acknowledge it. "Excellent," he replied cheerfully.

"Roman, I'm in the middle of talking to Kai right now. I am not just going to leave her all alone."

"Perfect, you can bring her too!" His mood was absolutely jovial. "She would probably be safer out of this place with Liza in the mood she's in anyway."

Another shattering noise resounded through the house, as if to emphasize his words.

Mal dropped his head into his hands. Callen looked as though he was trying to work through a breathing exercise. Roman looked like a young kid in a candy store. "I believe that's our cue to leave, gentlemen." He turned to step through the doorway, which, I now noticed, he barely fit through thanks to his wide shoulders and towering height. Cal joined him in the hall, and they both looked expectantly to where Malachi and I still sat.

"You do not have to come, of course, but I do agree with Roman. This house is not going to be quiet or comfortable for the next few hours." He laughed, mostly to himself. "And not for nothing, Kai, but I feel like you have earned yourself a drink."

A mischievous grin I wouldn't expect from Mal spread across his face as Roman cheered, "Yeah, Kai, come play with the big boys!"

Callen smiled and nodded slightly, signaling that he, too, was okay with my addition to the group.

"*—jeopardize it for what?!? The Stray?*" Another crash. "*GO TO HELL!*"

"What is the safest and quickest way out of here?"

The three boys started to laugh almost uncontrollably. Without another word, Roman inclined his head for us to follow him down the stairs. He went first, checking to make sure that the coast was clear.

Once he was certain no one was around, he waved us frantically towards the door. We all slipped out, the door closing soundlessly behind us.

I was startled when Cal and Roman broke into a run down the steps and towards the opening in the fence. Mal looked back at me with a casual shrug before he took off after his friends.

"When in Soteria," I said to no one before chasing off after the boys. They were all much taller than me, and I had to sprint to make up the bare minimum ground. They had run so effortlessly. Meanwhile, I was heaving, trying to catch my breath before I had even made it a yard from the fence line.

My sprint slowed into a run, before it became a jog. Thankfully, the three men had stopped on the path. It was obscured from sight of the house thanks to tall shrubs. Jogging the last few steps, I finally rejoined them. I stopped, bent over, and dropped my hands to my knees in an attempt to not let them see just how out of shape I was.

"Sorry for the jog, Ace. We aren't used to people with such low stamina," Roman poked at my side. Clearly, I hadn't fooled them at all.

"We needed to get to a covered spot just on the off chance someone decided to look out the window," Mal amended, shooting Roman a look of disapproval. He held his hands up in surrender, though the smile didn't fade.

Callen jumped in. "We will walk the rest of the way. I see no reason to ruin a perfectly good drinking night with exercise."

"I can get behind that 100%," I said as I stood up. We began walking in silence. The air was cool, and the sun had almost finished setting.

Next thing I knew, we had come to what looked like a small town. To the right, the second building we came across had the door open to the street. Chatter and music poured out of the pub, inviting all who passed to come in and spend their money.

"I hope you can drink better than you can run, Ace."

CHAPTER 13

T he pub was named *The Raven & Rose*. The inside was raucous. People were singing along with the live band, many already intoxicated despite the early hour of the evening. The light was soft and yellow in the fixtures lined throughout the establishment. The brick-and-mortar walls were worn, yet somehow classic. It was tame in some ways compared to any club I had been to, but wild in other respects.

The music was not electric and pulsating, so loud that you couldn't hear your own thoughts. However, the groups of people, young and old, singing along with the band was a dull roar at minimum. The drunken laughter weaved in and out of the voices, trying to keep time with words I didn't understand. And yet, I felt antsy to join in the clapping and dancing that took place before me. The atmosphere was intoxicating all on its own.

Roman made for the bar without hesitating. "What is your drink of choice?" I thought this was the most serious I had ever seen him, and I felt as if there was a right answer.

I thought for a moment before responding simply, "Dealer's choice."

His eyes danced as he nodded and turned back to the bartender. "You just made your first mistake," Callen smirked as he and Mal came up on either side of me.

"I came to play with the boys, so that's exactly what I'm gonna do."

"Angels help us." Mal looked to the sky, shaking his head, though he was smiling broadly. Roman appeared at the table we found, holding a tray with four shot glasses filled with clear liquid. Each shot was paired with a glass that was filled with golden amber sloshing over the sides.

"I think it's a bad idea to mix this early on," I eyed him.

"This is what happens when you let Roman order first," Cal explained, "He is never one for good ideas. His only goal is to ensure that everyone ends their night by throwing up everything but their memories."

"Although I *do* encourage the purging of memories on special occasions." Roman raised his shot glass before throwing it back, not bothering to wait for the rest of us. "Come now, ladies, let's not let perfectly good liquor sit in squalor."

The three of us picked up the remaining shots while he toasted once more with his amber drink. Wordlessly, we all raised our shots and then tipped them back. It was a sweet taste, not like anything I had ever had before. It wasn't sickly sweet like a liqueur, though I felt the heat instantly in my chest, like I might have with tequila. The taste that made most people gag was absent. It was amazing.

I was acutely aware that all three of them stared at me as I downed my shot. "That was delicious. What is it? It's unlike anything I've ever had before."

Roman stifled a laugh as Callen looked wide-eyed at me. "It's called *caelacrimae*," Malachi said, shooting them a stern look. "It's a specialty for the Nephilim and angels that involves a special fermenting process. Though I don't know much about that process."

I sipped from my bigger glass. "So, the Nephilim drink whiskey sours, too?"

"Of course!" Roman exclaimed. "If it's not broken, don't fix it." He drained his glass. "I'm getting another round, and those better be gone when I come back."

I looked around the pub as more people filed in, filling what little empty space had been available. My eyes caught on a single spot on a far wall. Etched into the wall was a backwards 'N.' The tail on the left, which would continue to be drawn upward, was slightly smaller and at a steeper angle than the rest. From the top of that tail, another line was drawn downward, following the steep angle before leveling out into a flat line that crossed the rest of the backwards 'N.' The flat line ended in a single solid circle.

"I've seen that before," I pointed to the wall as I took a big drink from my glass. My words already felt heavy as they left my lips. "Sterling has that tattooed behind her ear."

The two boys tensed ever so slightly, though my head was starting to feel too light to pay it any mind. "What does it mean?"

"It's the sign for the Archangel Gabriel." Callen shrugged, sipping from his drink. "The older Heavenly Hosts helped to create the Nephilim lines, but it all started with the Archangels. They were the ones to see the need for our service. They wrote down Heaven's law, and they continue to oversee the growing situation between Heaven and Hell." He stopped talking, glancing at Malachi. I couldn't prove it, but I swore I saw Cal wince slightly.

"Some histories have written that, while all Nephilim come from angels, the most emboldened warriors come from a line involving the blood of the Archangels," Mal picked up the explanation as Callen drank. "That's not to say that the signs are strictly reserved for those who bear the blood. It's like humans and their Saints. Some pay respect and ask for guidance from different Archangels. Gabriel is but one among several. There is Ramiel, Uriel, Raphael, Michael—"

"I think my aunt prayed to Michael," I interrupted, mindlessly playing with the pendant that hung from my neck, "I knew she was spiritual, but we never set foot in a church that I can remember."

"A lot of the Children of Adam pray to Michael and Gabriel," Malachi confirmed as Roman came back to the table.

He handed out drinks to the others before placing two more shots of *caelacrimae* in front of me, along with another whiskey sour.

"Drink up! Consider the extra shot a gift." He shot me a wink as he put his two shots and a drink onto the table.

"A gift for what?"

"Surviving in our house of madness, of course."

"I'll drink to that," Mal agreed, raising his shot.

"Here, here," Cal followed suit, and I did the same, tapping my glass to theirs. As soon as the liquor went down, Roman toasted me with his second shot, "And here's to bad decisions!"

I threw it back once again, then drank deeply from my fresh drink. I'd be lying if I said the cheers and claps that came from the three boys didn't make me smile. Setting down my glass, I turned to Mal.

"If you're an angel, aren't you supposed to be pure? Doesn't that include not drinking?"

"Mal? Not drink?" Roman laughed deep in his chest, causing my head to whip around to him.

"Malachi Swordson is one of the worst of us," Callen added, "He has been known to drink Roman under the table a time or two."

I glanced back at Mal as he sipped his drink. "Is that true?"

He raised an eyebrow playfully as he shrugged. "I guess you'll just have to find out."

I shrugged back, "So be it," and I finished my drink once more. I stood to stretch my legs only to stumble into Callen with a surprised, "Whoa!" He caught me without missing a beat. Steadying me, he waited to let go until he was sure I had regained my balance. He gave me a polite smile while the other two tried to conceal their laughter. If I was supposed to be holding my alcohol like them, I was doing a terrible job of it now.

"My tab is open. Go get yourself another drink, but tell the bartender you're cut off from *caelacrimae*."

"I thought we were making poor decisions tonight?" I teased, dropping my voice to its deepest octave in an attempt to sound like Roman.

"Absolutely! But I can't have you dying of alcohol poisoning, that would be zero fun explaining to Sterling."

"Hold that thought." I meandered to the bar, swaying slightly as I picked my way through the crowd. True to my orders, I only asked for another whiskey sour. While I waited, leaning back against the bar, I watched as people sang and danced. I found myself drifting in my thoughts as I wondered if Sterling had ever danced here before. The image of her spinning around with the boys, as they drank and laughed, filled my mind. It made me wish she were here tonight.

Given my few interactions with her, I could not fathom Eliza here with the boys. She seemed so serious and angry. This place was happy and carefree. I took the time to consider that perhaps she wasn't always in a vile mood. Before I came along, had she been pleasant? Maybe even fun?

The bartender pulled me from my thoughts as he handed me my drink. I made my way back to the table with minimal sloshing, just in time to find Roman with his arm around Callen, singing loudly and obnoxiously with the band. Callen blushed deeply as more eyes turned to them. Mal's eyes sparkled as he watched his friends. No. As he watched *Cal*.

The song finished, and Roman sat once again. The relief was palpable as it rolled off the black-haired boy to my right, attention finally falling away from our group, though Roman had yet to stop screeching. "Always so serious, little Cal," Roman tutted at his friend happily.

"I'm not serious," he protested. "I'm...I, uh..." He searched for the words frantically, but apparently, they evaded him. The glaze in his eyes told me that his drink wasn't helping him.

"He's quiet and laid-back," Mal offered when words failed Callen.

"Yes, that's it. I'm laid-back. Thank you, Malachi," he beamed across the table as they tapped their glasses together. After a sip, "My sister is the serious one." Roman nodded, not disagreeing with this statement.

My drinks got the better of me, and I asked, "Do they always fight like that?"

Surprisingly, Callen answered first. "They never used to. Only when they started sleeping together did the bickering start. Even then, it's been worse the last week or so."

"Bickering after they started..." I paused, not able to bring myself to repeat what Cal had just said, "started going out. That must still take a toll on the house after all this time?"

"'All this time'?" Roman repeated.

"Well, yeah, they have been together for a while, haven't they?"

"Oh, no," Callen responded. "At least, I wouldn't call it a while. I would say four weeks at most."

Four weeks? That was around—

"Hey! Didn't Sterling meet you at *Arcane* around that time?" Roman asked, getting excited as he put the pieces together.

"If it's so new, then why do they fight? Especially if they didn't before?"

"My honest opinion is that Sterling doesn't actually want her," Roman said into his glass of ice. The table shook as he yelped in pain. He shot a dirty look at Mal, who had kicked him under the table.

"Wingless bastard," he mumbled, rubbing his shin. "I'm being serious, though. Liza can be a royal bitch."

"*ROMAN!*" Mal yelled at him. He was halfway out of his seat and looked as if he was ready to punch his friend.

The man put his hands up innocently. "I say it with love. I mean it in the most endearing way possible, just like when you guys call me names. If some stranger walking down the street calls me a prick, I'm gonna wail on him. But with you guys, we all know it's true. And I'm just saying that, as of recently, she has been on a war path, and it can get ugly when she is like this." He turned to Callen, who was sipping his drink quietly, his face pale. "I know she is your twin, but that also means you know more than anyone how right I am. We can all love her and be ready to defend her while also owning the truth. The two can mutually coexist."

"You're right," Cal exhaled slowly. "She is not a nice person 70% of the time. But within that 30%, she is the most loyal person you'll ever meet."

Malachi sat back in his chair, crossing his arms tightly, as Roman went on, "I don't think Sterling likes her; I think it's just a distraction." They all looked at me briefly before finding their drinks, a spot on the table, or literally any other spot to look at. But I am too tipsy and too consumed by the small flicker that comes to life in my chest.

Suddenly, I can't tell if the heat is from the booze or a new hope slowly devouring me.

"In all honesty," Roman continued, "I don't think Eliza wants Sterling much either. Think about it for a minute. The two of them have had *years* to pursue one another. Aside from a brief flirtatious comment every few months, neither one of them has ever made a move." He tipped his head back to get every last drop out of his glass.

"No, if you ask me, Sterling needed a distraction, and Liza wanted a game. And she is *very* competitive." This time, Roman looked directly into my eyes, and I had to be the first to look away. My cheeks felt warm, and my head was starting to spin.

"Another round then!" Malachi surprised us all as he stood. "When I come back, there'd better be more singing and idiocy. Don't stop until Callen is as red as a strawberry." He winked at me, then stepped into the crowd. I was grateful for the sudden change and, shortly after he left, the band started up a song.

It was one Roman seemed to know better than the last, and by the time Mal had come back, the man had climbed onto a pool table where he was attempting to serenade two women. The word 'serenade' could have been used *very* lightly.

"Shameless," Mal said as he watched his friend across the room. Eventually, Roman and the women joined us. The next few hours passed with more drinks and jokes. The boys shared stories, mostly ones in an attempt to embarrass Roman as he entertained the girls.

The sun had set hours ago, and I knew that it was time for me to cut myself off. Callen and Mal seemed to share my sentiments. As we stood to leave, Roman followed us to the door, only to tell us not to wait up. He turned back and sauntered over to the table, placing an arm around each of the women as he sat down. He flashed an award-winning smile, signaling us to leave.

"Whoring bastard," Callen laughed when we stepped out of the pub. I laughed along with him as the three of us began the walk back.

My head was fuzzy in all the best ways as we stumbled our way back. Laughter filled the air while Callen and I tried to remember the words to one of the songs the band had played multiple times by request. Never mind the fact that those requests had been from all of us.

The walk felt shorter on the way back, the chill in the air barely registering against the bare skin of my arms. We quickly came up to the steps that led to the front door, and Mal had to remind us to be quiet as we entered the silent house.

"Anyone care for a nightcap?" Mal asked. Callen agreed that he could use another drink. Though the invitation was open to both of us, I couldn't shake the feeling that they would prefer to be alone. Not that they would ever tell me that, of course. They were too nice and would have gladly accepted my company as well.

"I think I am going to pass this time, but you two enjoy yourselves." I began to walk up the stairs, only to turn around again. "Thank you for tonight. It was the most I have laughed in a long time."

They both smiled at me before they said their goodnights and headed towards the kitchen, as I headed up to my room.

I was perfectly happy to retire to my room, but I wouldn't be able to fall asleep. Though I knew I wouldn't be able to retain anything I read in my current state, I decided to stop in the library to grab the book Mal had left on the desk. I walked down the hall, still humming the song Callen and I had been trying to sing on the way back. The song was broken up, peppered with spots of laughter as I bumped into the wall here and there.

The lights were on in the room, dimmed to a soft glow. I noticed the fire, more ember than flame, in the hearth, before I saw Sterling in the chair across from the mantle. She turned at the sound of my footsteps as I wandered into the room.

"Well, hello there," I said, bringing two fingers to my forehead before flicking them forward in a drunken salute.

"You seem to be in great spirits," she replied dryly as she turned back to look at the fire.

"I had the best night I have had in a long time thanks to your friends."

"Is that so? Where the hell did you all get off to?" I walked a little farther into the room, tripping over my own feet. I laughed as I unceremoniously lowered myself to the floor. Sterling stood to look down at where I sat, still giggling slightly. "Are you *drunk*?" she asked incredulously.

"You're one to talk," I laugh, pointing to the half-empty glass in her hand.

"Unbelievable," she scoffed, and circled back around to her seat in the center-most chair, taking a long pull from her glass.

I wasn't sure exactly what it was that did it, but something snapped inside me. Where there was once humor now lived annoyance. She was clearly upset, but she did not need to take away the joy of my evening.

I stood quickly and came around to stand between her and the fireplace. "We went to the pub," I said defiantly. I took in the sight of her. She was in a black button-up, one where the buttons were tucked under another layer of fabric to look seamless. She had it undone one button too low to be casual. The light gray of her pants and the midnight black of her shirt made her skin scream with its golden tan.

Her normally perfect wave of blonde hair was in a slight disarray, probably unnoticeable to most. She pinched the bridge of her nose with closed eyes while her other arm draped over the arm of the chair. Long, slender fingers, decorated in silver rings, gripped her glass by the rim. Her ankle was crossed over her knee. This was a new version of Sterling, one I wasn't entirely sure I could navigate well, given my current state.

"What did you drink at the pub, Kai?" She didn't look up.

"What does it matter? I had a few drinks just like everyone else."

"What. Did. You. Drink?" The clipped tone surprised me. It only fueled my annoyance more, edging it towards anger.

"I had several whiskey sours if you absolutely need to know. And a couple shots of *caelacrimae* as well.

"And whose bright idea was it to drink the *caelacrimae*?"

"Roman bought the first few rounds, but we all drank together." I didn't understand what the big deal was.

Sterling stood abruptly, throwing her arms up in the air. "Fucking idiots. All of you!" She walked over to the front half of the desk, placing her palms flat on its surface. Her glass sat next to her right hand.

"I'm sorry?" I asked, exasperated by the anger she was directing towards me.

"You are smart enough, and everyone has big enough mouths, that I'm sure you have figured out by now you aren't supposed to be here, Kai." She turned back to face me, her chest moving faster with her agitation. "If it got around that you were *here*, it would make my life immensely difficult, probably causing a lot of issues for the rest of them."

It felt as if she had finally realized the depth of her mistake. She knew she shouldn't have brought me here, and she was about to say as much. If I thought about it enough, if I anticipated the words she might speak, it would be enough to make me cry. But that was something that I refused to do here.

I stormed over to the opposite end, grabbing the book I had come for. I spun on her once again. "Well, I'm sorry I didn't want to stay in this house while you and Eliza fought all fucking night. Unless that's why you're really mad? Because I wasn't here to witness the show?"

"And what the hell is *that* supposed to mean?"

"Oh, Sterling," I said, my tone sickly-sweet. I took a few steps towards her, closing the space so that we were practically face to face. Reaching around her, I picked up the glass on the table. I drained what was left of the straight whiskey, without breaking eye contact, and placed it back on the table. Her eyes were storm clouds of gray. "It means if you want to fuck someone who makes you miserable, that's your choice. But don't make the rest of us suffer with you. Don't make *me* suffer with you."

"You are talking nonsense."

I moved to her left side to whisper into her ear, "Pray to Gabriel, maybe he will explain it to you." And then, because I had the burn of whiskey in my chest, I brushed my lips feather-soft over her tattoo before pulling away. They sang with electricity as I took a step back.

She reached up to where my lips had been. "How do you know what this is?"

"Same way I learned that you decided to sleep with Eliza the night we met at *Arcane*," I let the venom seep into my words, "your friends told me."

Sterling sighed in exhaustion, but I wasn't ready to stop. If she had wanted a fight, she was going to get one.

"They told me that you follow rules to a fault. Is that why you are suddenly so angry with me tonight? I'm a walking regret, aren't I? Did you finally look at me and realize I was the biggest mistake of your life? You broke the law. You're trapped in a *miserable* relationship for reasons that apparently only make sense to you. Honestly, do you blame me for your relationship with Eliza?"

"Lower your voice, Kai." Her warning was cold.

"No, you brought this on yourself. Rather than do something selfish, rather than admit to anything that is against the rules, you turn yourself into a martyr. For God's sake, you don't even want her, Sterling!"

"Oh, and you think you know what I want?" Sterling's face changed. A flicker of some emotion I couldn't place passed fleetingly and was replaced with something akin to cruelty. "Just what do you think I am trying to avoid admitting to? That I am *attracted* to you? What gives you even the *smallest* idea that you are even *close* to what I want?"

It was a slap in the face that sobered me up quickly and dropped my voice to a whisper, "Go to hell."

The room went black. The embers of the fire mingled with the light of the moon, giving us a ghostly sliver in the darkness.

"That's just great," she yelled out, "The power going out is exactly what we all needed."

"Goodnight, Sterling."

I turned to leave, but she seized my wrist in her hand. Her grip was tight as I tried to instinctively pull away. Rather than let go, she pulled me back to face her, closer than before.

"What the hell are you doing?" I was shocked as my mind tried to process what was happening.

"Something selfish." Within seconds, her other hand was at the nape of my neck, pulling me to her. A gasp escaped from my chest as our lips crashed together. I stood still for a moment, frozen with shock.

And then I kissed her back.

I stepped into her body. The hand that she wasn't holding traveled to her waist, pulling her closer to me. The pressure of her body was intoxicating.

Her lips were soft, though their response was not. She kissed me hard. The tip of her tongue outlined my mouth, and I gave her what she wanted. I could taste the whiskey on her breath as she explored my mouth. She set the rhythm, kissing me deeper as her fingers tangled into my hair. I felt a tug then. Using her grip on my hair, she tilted my head back, lifting my chin up towards her. The height difference worked to her advantage as she lost herself in the kiss.

My hand slid from her waist and up along the side of her body before I wrapped it over her shoulder, hoping to somehow get closer. Our breathing became rapid, and I couldn't tell my breath from hers with her chest moving so closely against mine. The thought only made it harder to breathe, and a small moan escaped my lips.

Sterling groaned in satisfaction. She spun us so quickly that I didn't realize what had happened until she had backed me into the desk. Without breaking the kiss, she let go of my wrist only to take the book out of my hand and toss it somewhere away from us. With both hands free, I locked them together behind her neck. I stood up on my toes, trying to eliminate any possible space.

She took advantage of my lack of balance, placing her hands on the back of my thighs, lifting me up onto the desk. The surprise had me breaking away from the kiss, only to have her replace her lips on my neck. Her hands moved up my thighs to my lower back and pulled me to the edge. I widened my legs, allowing her to fill the space between them. Heat filled my core as she kissed from my neck to the right side of my collarbone. She trailed her tongue over the middle, kissing the left side, and working her way up once more. Pausing at the hollow of my neck, she placed a gentle kiss, and then she sucked hard.

It was unbearable, and I knew there would be evidence of what we had done here if it wasn't stopped quickly, but I didn't have the willpower to disrupt her. It was over in a single, rapid breath. I began to protest, but she kissed along my jawline before biting my bottom lip and gently pulling away. I moved my hands to her face, needing more of her. But her left hand slid to my throat.

Sterling squeezed gently as she pushed me backwards. My back made contact with the desk as her right hand rotated from my lower back to grip my hip. She was leaning over the top of me, kissing below the base of my ear. "You aren't close to what I want," she breathed out raggedly, "You are exactly, absolutely *everything* I want." She nipped my earlobe, and I shuddered beneath her as she moved her head lower.

My shirt had ridden up, and now her nose trailed gently over my exposed lower abdomen. With her hand still at my throat, she moved her head to the hollow created by my stomach and the hip she held on to. There, she began to leave agonizingly slow kisses. My hands twisted in her hair, pulling harder than I intended.

It elicited a small laugh from Sterling, but she understood what I was trying to say. Gripping my hip to the point that her fingers were digging in, she kissed my stomach hard. She pulled me to her while I pushed. Sucking, biting, running her tongue over the spot. And then she would repeat it all.

There would be proof of her actions there tomorrow. And I don't think either one of us cared.

I glanced down only to find her eyes were already on me, watching as I lost myself in the feel of her touch. "God," I sighed, dropping my head back to the desk as Sterling continued to kiss across my stomach.

She slid her mouth up my torso over my shirt. Her hand followed. It stayed on my side, sliding under my shirt. My skin was on fire everywhere she touched. As I wrapped my legs around her waist, I could feel the aching discomfort between my legs that begged for more.

Her hand went to my chest, over my sports bra, and I arched into her touch. I didn't want her to be gentle. I wanted her to grab me now like she had grabbed my wrist.

I buried my face in the crook of her shoulder. The smell of sandalwood and vanilla filled my nose and made my eyes flutter shut. I kissed her neck, tasting the salt on her skin. A sound of contentment slipped from her, and I could feel it reverberate under my lips as I continued to work my way up her jaw. She arched her back, hips moving forward as she allowed more of her lower body to press into mine.

Sterling held her position there for just a moment longer, as if she could feel the heat spreading from my center and out through my body. It was almost impossible to control the urge to move underneath her. Anything to create extra friction between us.

Letting go of my throat, she reached behind her neck where my hands gripped tightly. She grabbed my wrists in her slender, strong hand and pinned them above my head as she kissed me once, slow and deep. In that one kiss, I could feel every moment of desire that had passed since we had met. I met hers with a desire of my own.

"Sterling," her name was a whisper into her mouth. It was dripping with suggestion, begging her for everything she already knew I wanted.

She groaned against my mouth as she massaged my breast with the hand under my shirt. I could no longer resist the urge. I rolled my body underneath her in time with her movements, wishing that my bra wasn't preventing me from feeling her direct touch.

Sterling slid her hand to her left, slow and teasing. Before she could grasp my other breast, I felt something tug on my neck. The kiss broke, and she looked down to see what had caught on her hand. She released my wrists as she pulled back in order to see the silver chain she pulled out from the top of my shirt. It was the necklace that I had been messing with while at the pub. On the pendant, a graphic depicted Saint Michael.

Sterling froze.

"It was a gift from my aunt," I told her as she stood from her place on top of me. The lights flared to life, illuminating the disarrayed state we were both in. I sat up on my elbows, confused by the sudden tension in Sterling's shoulder.

She wouldn't look at me, preferring the ground over my eyes. "I'm so sorry, Kai," she ran a nervous hand through her hair, trying to smooth it out. "I took it too far. I just...I'm drunk and I wasn't thinking. And it just—it can't happen. Not now. Not ever again. It was a mistake."

Silence hung between us. My only acknowledgement was to nod. I knew what she meant, but it didn't ease the sting of her words.

"I told you it was something selfish." She laughed without humor.

"In all fairness, I told you to do something selfish," I said, trying to lighten the suddenly heavy mood.

Sterling looked up, locking eyes with me. "I'm sorry," she repeated. "Goodnight, Kiara." With my full name hanging between us, she turned and walked out of the library, not waiting for a response. But I wasn't focused on her departure. I was focused on her eyes.

When she had finally looked up at me, her eyes had been different. The cerulean blue that I had grown so accustomed to was no longer there. They had morphed into a light hazel color. It was so light, as if it were on the verge of transitioning into gold. They looked as if they were about to burst into flames.

Just like in my dream.

CHAPTER 14

What the hell just happened?

I remained on the desk. My mind was swimming, though it was adrenaline rather than alcohol that made me dizzy now. The taste of whiskey still danced on my lips, Sterling's touch a ghost on my body, as I pulled my shirt back into place. A splash of color had already started to blossom on my hip where her lips had been.

My head fell into my hands, and I tried to take a deep breath in a poor attempt to stop the thundering in my chest. It took several minutes for my heart to ease into something slower, eliminating the roaring in my ears. Emotionally, I was being pulled in multiple directions, questions and longing at war with one another in my soul.

Had she really meant what she said? Does Sterling truly want me?

It didn't matter, did it? The law was set in stone. Besides, she said it herself, she's drunk, and it was a mistake.

Despite the hasty dismissal, I still craved her. Not only did I want more of her touch, but *I* wanted to touch *her*. Whatever control had slipped in her mind had been replaced by the desire to control the situation between us. And all she seemed to have cared about was having her fill of my body. Sterling had been entirely focused on *me*. The thought made me insatiable.

I replayed the moment she walked away over and over again in my mind. Her hair had been a mess from my hands running through it. The look on her face as she apologized for stepping out of line mingled with something akin to pain. It was as if the realization of what our actions meant was difficult for her to swallow, but walking away from whatever private moment we had shared was downright painful.

And then there were her eyes.

I hadn't noticed until then that they had altered their color. But as I thought back through everything, I realized that the glow from the embers and moonlight may not have been solely to blame for the way her eyes had shone as she had looked up at me on the desk. They may have been ablaze before we stopped.

Shaking my head, I slid off the desk. I needed to sleep and clear my head.

Maybe Malachi would know what that had been about. Surely if anyone in the house could be trusted with something like this, it would be him. I tried to quiet my thoughts as I walked towards my room, turning off the lights to the library as I went.

I had barely taken two steps into the unlit hallway when someone behind me cleared their throat.

"Son of a bitch," I exclaimed as my hand reached for my chest. I spun around to find the silhouette of someone who could only be Roman.

"My mother is a piece of work, don't get me wrong. However, I don't think 'bitch' is the word I would use."

"You scared me! What are you doing here? Weren't you supposed to go home with one of those girls? Or did they think better of their drunken decisions?" I teased.

"There were roommate issues that came up, but I am nothing if not a gentleman. I offered up my room to them instead." My eyes had begun to adjust in the darkness, and it was just enough that I could see him clearly. Roman was holding a bottle of what I did not know and was wearing nothing but black sweatpants that sat low on his slim waist. He was well muscled, every line defined in his abdomen, chest, shoulders, and arms. His long hair had been tied on top of his head, and he wore a devilish grin as he waited for me to put the pieces together.

"It's rude to keep a lady waiting, Roman, let alone two." He only smiled broader, happy that I played along rather than chastise him.

"They needed a break," he said coolly. "I went to get something to drink," He gestured to the bottle in his hand, "and I was heading up the stairs when I heard Sterling yelling. I figured she and Liza might still be going at it. I got curious." He shrugged.

Oh no.

"So, you *spied* on us?" I asked incredulously.

Roman laughed. "Relax. I didn't see"—he paused, looking at me teasingly— "whatever may have happened. By the time I got to the top of the stairs, the lights were already out. I was ready to come in and save Sterling from the wrath that is Eliza, realizing voices were no longer raised. I almost walked in until I heard *your* voice. Just one name, actually." Roman gave me an implied look.

I couldn't help myself—I hit him in the arm. He cackled. "You really have to work on that punch. That wouldn't hurt a fly."

"I can't believe you just stood here!"

"Kai," he said, all humor erased from his tone, "I promise you it wasn't like that. I heard your voices, and it stopped me in my tracks. By the time I processed *what* was going on, Sterling was already walking out of there. I would've gotten caught by her if I tried to make it back to my room."

"And yet you didn't hide from me? Why?"

"Because I stand by what I said tonight. You remember the story from today? About how Sterling and I met?"

"Yes, Roman, I remember, but I hardly see how it's relevant right now."

"I am friends with Sterling because she has never been afraid to be straight up with others. She is honest to a fault and would be willing to take a beating before she stood by and let some idiot disturb her peace or that of another."

"That's great, but I'm still failing to see why you didn't bother to hide from me."

"Again, I stand by what I said at *The Raven & Rose*. Sterling and Eliza are nothing more than a game of distraction. And in the last month, my friend, who is more like a sister, has been nothing but dishonest with all of us, including herself. And it is tearing me apart to watch her struggle against herself." Roman spoke quietly, his eyes dimming. "She is most herself when you're involved, though. When Sterling mentions you, sees you, or hears your voice, it's different. This morning at breakfast, she was the girl I met over a decade ago. For the first time in a while, she wasn't lying to herself."

"Roman..." I didn't know what to say. "People are always better versions of themselves when a crush is around. It's just a side effect from having someone new in the house."

"No, Kai," he objected, "I have seen Sterling with girls in years past. Ones she genuinely liked and would spend a lot of time with. But there is something different about how you two interact. I can't explain it exactly. You're good for her."

"It can't happen. You guys all know that. I know that. There are rules and punishments. Not to mention, Sterling is all but married to the law from what you have all told me. You heard her apologize before she left. She thought it was a mistake even before it had a chance to s tart."

"There is a lot you don't know about all of us. About Sterling. It's not a bad thing, you just haven't been here long enough. But I can promise you one thing. Sterling won't see this as a mistake. Not in the way you are worried she will. There are things that just have to play themselves out first."

"Are there any 'things' you *can* tell me about?"

"Well, first, we have to work on that weak ass punch. You won't survive here if you can't throw down." He grinned at me, playfully hitting my shoulder with his drink.

"Noted," I gave him a small smile. "Say, don't you have guests waiting on you?"

"They already got to experience my company once; they know the wait is worth it."

"Arrogant prick." Roman laughed as he stepped past me, heading towards his door.

He was walking backward. "Arrogant prick or confident charmer?"

"I said what I said," I teased back. I walked past him, slowly heading for my room.

"Kai, she's as stubborn as she is gorgeous, and her heart is in the right place. Don't give up on her."

I gave him a little nod. Satisfied, he went to open his door. I stopped him.

"Have you ever noticed that... I mean, have you ever seen..." I felt crazy, trying to ask this question. Roman stood waiting patiently, hand resting on the door handle.

"Her eyes," was all I could manage at first. "Have you ever seen them change?"

He glanced down to where his hand was. It looked as if he was debating how he wanted to answer. Or if he wanted to answer at all. His dark eyes found mine, a lopsided grin on his face. "In due time, Kai. Goodnight." And then he disappeared into his room.

What the hell does that *mean?*

Exhausted both physically and emotionally, I shook my head and went to my room. I felt as if Roman had only confused me more with what he had been saying. Everything had been so cryptic, and while I could appreciate the fact that the boys never wanted to speak on behalf of others, it was making my first two days here complicated.

I walked into my room and immediately flopped onto the bed. I kicked off my shoes and jeans, not caring to find pajamas in one of the drawers that held my clothes. I rolled my way under the covers, tucking myself in as snuggly as possible.

The day raced through my mind as I reflected on the events that had transpired. Breakfast. My talk with Sterling as we explored the house. Spending time with Mal, followed by drinking with the boys, as I got to know them better. The power going out and the kiss that I had been craving for so long. *'You are exactly, absolutely* everything *I want.'*

I replayed that last part over and over again, leaving out how Sterling had looked before she had walked away from me. It had been selfish of both of us. In allowing ourselves those brief minutes together, Sterling was likely somewhere angry with herself. As for me, I knew I would long for more. I'd drive myself crazy wishing for something I couldn't have. But the damage was done, and in that moment, it had been more than worth it. For tonight, I'd allow myself to drown in the memory of our connection, however short it may have been.

The images behind my eyes rocked me to sleep. As I began to lose consciousness, the last thing I remembered was that I had left the damn book in the library again.

The sun flooded my room through windows that had been irresponsibly left open. The heat of the day was already apparent as it baked me where I lay in bed. The attempt to open my eyes failed miserably. The moment I tried, I was hit with a pain in my head like no other. It was immediate and almost as blinding as the light itself.

Despite my body's protest at the movement, I forced myself to get up and walk to the bathroom. The light remained off as I all but crawled to the toilet. The tile felt cold under my bare legs, which helped center me as the world tilted sideways in my mind. Not centering enough.

It wasn't long at all before my head was dangling over the toilet's edge. The legal poison I had ingested was being rejected, along with what little food I had had since being here. My body purged itself, and it felt as if it was never going to end. That is, until it finally did.

Ten minutes later, I was leaning against the wall, still on the floor. A thin layer of cold sweat covered my forehead and neck. My abs hurt from the work they had put into betraying me. I had nothing left to give. However, as the bouts had grown less and less, the spinning had also decreased slightly. It was finally bearable, though my brain still pounded violently in my skull.

I recalled Callen saying something last night. *'His only goal is to ensure that everyone ends up throwing up everything but their memories.'* Clearly, Roman had succeeded. I was torn between wanting to hit him and not wanting to hear some sarcastic comment about 'not being able to hang with the boys.' I settled on the latter and decided it was in my best interest to rinse off in the shower.

Once I felt more like myself, I stepped back into my room. The air wafting through the window was hot, persuading me to choose a pair of athletic shorts and an oversized, light t-shirt. With my hair up in a bun, I knew it wasn't going to get much better than this.

I hobbled out of my room, automatically heading to the kitchen, where I hoped Mal would be. Sure enough, he was seated at the island. A cup of coffee was in one hand while he scrolled through his phone with the other. "Good morning." He hadn't turned around, nor had my steps been loud, and yet he was already greeting me before I even entered the room.

I made a sound in the back of my throat that was somewhere between a groan and a growl. I poured myself into the chair beside him. My arms folded onto the table in front of me, and I buried my head in the darkness.

"How was *your* night?" Mal asked casually.

My breathing paused for a moment, everything tensing. I was deciding how I would repay Roman for running his big mouth, but came up short. I was so focused on surviving the pounding in my head this morning that it had drowned out every thought, including what had happened between Sterling and I, until now.

I decided to proceed with measured caution. "You could say it was...eventful. How about yourself?"

"A nightcap with Callen is always a nice end to a night out. It's like the bow on a present that wraps everything together harmoniously. Luckily for me, he was also prepared with water, which ultimately saved me from a terrible morning." I could feel his silent laughter next to me as, I assumed, he assessed the poor shape I was in. "It seems you weren't as fortunate, my friend."

I lifted my head to take a look at the immaculate man next to me. He was fresh and ready for anything the day could throw at him. He smiled and pointed to the counter. "The coffee is over there; it's fresh."

"And he continues to save my life," I said with gratitude as I walked over to the cabinet of mugs. Grabbing one down from the shelf, I poured a full cup, still steaming. I took up my seat next to Malachi once more, who generously let me sip on my coffee before we continued conversing. Slowly, the intensity of my headache began to decrease.

"Is anyone else awake?" I asked.

"I heard someone on the upper level very early this morning. Up in the training room. You have been up there before, haven't you?"

"Sterling was about to take me up there, but thought better of it when Roman was yelling profanities at Callen."

Right, well, we have filled it to function as a training room, though it is basically a large attic space. Callen is not one to train after a night out, and Liza rarely goes up there willingly, so I can only assume it was Sterling."

"Does Roman not train after a night out either?"

"I hadn't thought he had come home yet?"

So, he didn't know that Roman had brought the girls here. That meant Mal hadn't heard about what he had seen after all. "Oh, he came back last night. With company."

"Of course he did." Mal shook his head. "Were you fortunate enough to meet them as they came into the house?"

"No, I ran into Roman in the hall outside the library. He actually scared the shit out of me."

"He was wandering the halls while he had a woman in his bed?"

"*Women,*" I corrected.

"What in the world was he doing in the hallway then?"

This was it. "He ended up kind of trapped out there when he was coming back from the kitchen. You see," I turned my body to face him directly, "he heard Sterling and me. I went looking for a book when we came home and had found Sterling in the library. One thing led to another, and next thing I knew, we were arguing. Until we weren't..." I trailed off, hoping to imply the right things. Then I hurried to continue, "Roman had heard Sterling's voice and thought it was Eliza on the other end of the conversation. He was up the stairs by the time the fighting had stopped, and he was shocked to hear my voice instead of Eliza. He couldn't make it to his room before Sterling left the library, but he felt the need to scare me half to death when I stepped out." I waited apprehensively to see how Mal was going to react. For a second, I panicked, suddenly worried that Mal would be angry at Sterling, at *me,* for sneaking around behind Eliza's back. Despite their sentiments last night, she was still one of them after all.

"Shameless bastard," was all he said. His tone was light and un-bothered. I looked for a change in his posture, but there was nothing to suggest ill feelings.

"'Shameless bastard'?" Roman boomed from the doorway. "Are we already talking about me this morning?" He looked the same as when we had talked in the hall last night, wearing the black sweats and nothing else, although his hair was down now. "I am truly flattered."

"Will your guests be joining us for breakfast this morning? Or did they have the good sense to leave before dawn when they would have to look at your face in the daylight?"

Roman grinned brightly. "I just saw them out, so unfortunately, it'll just be me for breakfast. And make it something greasy, will you, Mal? I'm on the verge of a hangover."

"Serves you right," I mumbled into my coffee. Malachi stood and walked over to the stove, where he began removing things from the cupboards.

"And how are *you* feeling this morning?" Roman gave me a knowing wink behind Mal's back.

"I feel better than you look," though, as I said it, I had to admit he didn't look hungover at all.

"Then you must feel like a million bucks. I mean, I know I always feel great after, well, you know."

I ignored him, drinking my coffee deeply. Mal turned enough to give him the side eye. The smell of bacon started to waft through the air, reminding me I had nothing in my stomach.

"Sorry, Malachi—inside joke between old friends here." He shrugged innocently. "You had to be there."

"I already told him, Roman."

"I missed story time?" Roman asked disappointedly. He took the chair Mal had been sitting in and spun it towards me. "I want the details."

"What is this, a frat house? I'm not telling you anything. Besides, I didn't tell Mal specifics either," I said, exasperated.

"Come on, Kai, indulge me," he whined.

"You're a pig, Roman," Mal called from the stove.

"I don't mean it in a creepy way. I mean it as a friend."

I drained my coffee cup and stood to get more. "No."

"Fine," Roman pouted. "But if you were a man, you would have totally told us, just saying."

"I doubt that she would have," Mal finished off the conversation. "I have a feeling Callen is going to be sleeping most of the day and that Eliza will be avoiding everyone due to the potential aftermath of last night."

"Lucky for us," Roman mumbled under his breath.

"That being said, it'll probably just be us for breakfast, so I'm going to keep it simple." He made a mountain of eggs and hashbrowns to go with the bacon. We took turns making toast and plating our food. At first, I thought that Mal had overcooked, but when I saw just how much Roman

was able to shovel down, I began to fear he hadn't made enough.

We ate in contented silence. Mal finished first and excused himself. "If I sit here too long, the day will be lost." As he walked out of the room, Roman went back for his fourth helping of eggs and toast. He had already polished off the bacon.

"I think Mal's cooking saved me from a terrible hangover," he said after clearing his plate once again. He put his dishes in the sink and grabbed a bottle of water from the refrigerator. "Now, if you'll excuse me, I will be sleeping in a hammock for the duration of the morning.

"Don't get too sunburnt."

"But that isn't nearly as fun."

I waved him away as I walked over to put my plate in the sink.

"Kai," Roman said.

"Yes?"

"If I crossed a line earlier, I'm sorry. I've been told I can take things too far, and if that was the case, I want to apologize. I figured you would have told him, or that you were at least going to."

"How did you know that I would tell him?"

"Because we all tell Malachi everything. He could probably ruin this whole house if he were a more vengeful sort of angel."

His voice was soft, the apology genuine. And he was right, I was planning on talking to Mal about everything. In all honesty, I wasn't even mad about what had happened this morning. Roman had been teasing me as if I had lived here for years.

It felt like I was one of them.

"No harm, no foul," I smiled at him.

Relief flooded his face as he nodded before walking onto the back porch and out to the beach. I stayed in the kitchen. I cleaned up what little had been left out to the best of my abilities. When there was nothing more to be put away, I decided an afternoon sleeping in my bed wouldn't be the worst thing in the world.

I climbed up the stairs, and when I landed on the platform, I heard voices in the distance. Muffled words flowed from somewhere to my right, down the hallway that housed the armory and training room. I couldn't help myself. Driven by curiosity, I followed the voices. As I got closer, the realization dawned on me that I could no longer give Roman grief for spying on me.

A door sat open on the right at the very end of the hallway. When I peered inside, I found a narrow staircase leading up to what I could only assume was the training room.

"You're being a pessimist," came Mal's voice. I stepped behind the door to ensure I would not be caught eavesdropping.

"Yes, Malachi, please tell me how negative I'm acting. It really helps me solve the situation." *Sterling*. She sounded exhausted and tense.

"If you would actually listen to what I am telling you, you would see that maybe there *is* a solution. Maybe things aren't as...dramatic as they seem."

"It only seems *dramatic* because it's not your head on the line." She grunted, and the sound was followed by a loud thud that startled me.

Mal's tone changed. Though it was still gentle, there was an underlying bite as he spoke, "Do not act as if I do not know the burden of being under scrutiny because of my differences or because of my family, Sterling. I have played the game far longer than you have been breathing."

She sighed heavily. "I'm sorry. I don't mean to take it out on you. Or her. Or anyone for that matter," she said, resigned. "Do you know what happened last night?"

"I know that whatever happened was enough to drive you up here at four in the morning, and to make her blush when she glazed over it at breakfast."

"She was going to walk away. I had said..." Her voice broke slightly. She cleared her throat. "I said something cruel. Kai got under my skin, and I lashed out. I couldn't let her leave. Not like that. I didn't have a plan for what would happen once I stopped her. And I just lost control." Her voice got quieter. "I kissed her, and then I couldn't stop. I was consumed by alcohol and my emotions. It was only when I was looking at her necklace of Michael that I remembered my place and t he rules."

"You are allowed to have feelings, my friend. You try so hard to follow the laws of Heaven that you forget you also have pieces of humanity to account for."

"It doesn't matter, Mal. There is nothing there. There can't be. Even if there was a sliver of anything, it's over. I told her that before I walked away. She knew *before* I messed up that we couldn't be together anyways."

"If there was nothing, then why have you been moping up here all hours of the morning?"

"Because *'I'm allowed to have feelings,'* remember?" Sterling threw the line back at Mal. Before he could reply, she apologized quickly. "I'm sorry. Again. Everything has become so convoluted since we met. And for what? A moment of lust?"

"I would hardly call what emotions you're lying to yourself about just lust," Mal muttered.

There was a pause where I imagined the icy glare Sterling shot Mal. "And now," she went on, ignoring him, "I have to figure out how to take her back home."

What?!

"Sterling, that isn't fair to either of you."

"Well, I can either do that and maintain some form of secrecy about what I have done, or we can play it out until someone discovers our secret, and I have to answer for my actions. Which will likely also drag you all into the mess."

"Sterling, you have another option."

"And what is that exactly?"

"Let her attempt Metanoia." Mal's voice was evenly measured. He sounded as if he were speaking to a nervous animal.

"Absolutely not." Her voice was steel snapping closed. "Are you out of your mind, Malachi?"

"I think I could plead a very good case as to why she would be capable, given she is allowed enough time to prepare, that is."

"It could kill her, Mal. Humans were not made to withstand such a trial."

"You said so yourself," he continued with his slow, calm tone, "when you brought her here and the elixir was wearing off, she was paralyzed. It didn't *only* make her sleep. She also was able to drink *caelacrimae* like any of us would. We watched her carefully. The reaction to an acrid, bitter taste that you would usually expect was nowhere to be seen."

"So because she has been able to indulge in our drinks, you are ready to send her to her death? Purely on a hunch?"

"I would say it is more of a theory than a hunch," Mal defended. "I feel like she will continue to reveal herself if allowed the opportunity to do so. And that is something she can only do here."

Another thud came from above. And then another. "What if you're wrong?" Sterling's voice was barely audible.

"Then I will do everything I can to correct my mistakes. But I have faith in my theory. I have faith in *her*, Sterling."

"But what makes you so sure? Is there more you aren't telling me?"

There was silence for a moment. "I'm not sure yet."

"Mal?"

"Sterling, I need you to trust me on this. Train with her. Teach her what you can and let it play out. And if I'm right," He paused and I imagined the soft understanding smile Mal gave his friend then, "you could possibly have everything you've ever wanted."

"How do you know what I want?"

"Because you are a dear friend, and I know you all too well."

"I hate this idea."

"I would never put her in danger intentionally. Aside from owing her my life, I actually enjoy her company."

"If you see her first, you can bring it up to her. Offer the opportunity, but don't force it on her. Kai will make her own choice. If I am not downstairs before you talk to her, send her my way."

"I promise it will be okay, Sterling."

"Don't make promises you can't keep, Mal. It'll ruin your credit score."

I leaned my head against the wall and closed my eyes as I heard a soft laugh leave Mal. There was a thud once more. Then a second, and a third. The frequency picked up as the sound deepened. I opened my eyes, ready to sneak away to my room. When I went to leave my hiding spot behind the door, I came face-to-face with Mal. He placed a hand over my mouth before a startled sound could escape me. With his other hand, he held up a finger to his lips, gesturing for me to be quiet, before pointing down the hall in the direction of my room.

I nodded as he took his hand from my face. Gently, he eased the door away from me so as not to risk any accidental noise. Clearly, Malachi was biting at the bit to be the first to talk to me. It was just as well, I hoped he had a good explanation for me. One that wasn't cryptic.

Whatever the sound upstairs had been, it had stopped. It was now replaced with the faint sound of Sterling breathing fast. A new urgency settled over Mal as he gestured rapidly for me to follow him. Together we walked quickly and silently until we were safely in my bedroom.

"Well done, Roman 2.0," he said sarcastically.

"What was all of that about?"

"Do you want the short and simple version?"

"That is all I have *ever* wanted this whole damn time, Malachi." I sat on my bed with a deep sigh. "Tell me."

"I have a strong feeling that you are Nephilim, Kai."

CHAPTER 15

I stared at him blankly. He waited, allowing me time to wrap my head around this new revelation, though as the silence stretched on, I still had no response for him.

"Mal, that doesn't make any sense."

"I think it makes perfect sense. You heard my conversation with Sterling, did you not?"

"I did, which is basically the equivalent of hearing someone speak in tongues," I started to speak faster, air suddenly not filling my lungs fast enough, "except for the whole 'send her to her death' thing. That was crystal clear. I have no idea what's going on here."

"I understand that you're overwhelmed and that—"

"That is an understatement. I think everyone in this house forgets that I have been here, consciously, for two days now. Before then, I was a normal person. I worked. I had friends, a life. Then I met a woman at a club and watched her, weeks later, pace my room as she told me that angels and demons warred in secret and that she, along with a whole civilization, was tasked to protect us mortals. And now you're telling me that *I* am also one of these people? I didn't know this world existed until you were *bleeding out* on my floor, Malachi!" My voice went up two octaves. Something akin to a sob erupted from me while I tried to catch my breath. As the words came pouring out, I started to realize that I hadn't worked through the last three days.

When traumatic events happened at work, we did our best to debrief as a team. We talked with one another, sometimes cried together, whatever it took to alleviate the grief and stress by even a fraction. I had allowed myself no such reprieve since I saved Mal. *How could I? It's not as if I have had much downtime.*

Mal came over and sat beside me, placing a gentle hand on my shoulder. "Kai, I cannot sit here and pretend that you have not had to contend with a lot of things in a very short time. To say that it is not affecting you would be to lie. And it should be eliciting a big response. If we are right about this, it will change your life. Immensely." He paused, assessing me to ensure that I wasn't on the verge of hyperventilating. I gave him a nod, in part to show that I was okay, but also to urge him to continue.

"I apologize that we have all been so secretive. You live with the same group of people for a time, and you learn all there is to know. Dreams and desires, shames and heartbreaks, we eventually share everything with one another. Suddenly, when someone new comes in, well, it's hard to not feel like you may reveal someone else's secret at any given moment.

"The past being protected at your expense is not fair to you, though. I will do my best to be as transparent as I can from now on. If I am unsure about whether I feel it is my place to share, I will direct you to whoever it pertains to. I will talk with them as well. Hopefully, we can all make this as easy for you as possible going forward."

I took a breath in and released it slowly. "I'm sorry. I..." I was frustrated with myself now. "I don't know what that was, but I apologize. I know I can handle stress better than I have been recently."

"Kai, you have done nothing wrong. In case you haven't noticed, we have not all been our best either. And we live in a constant state of stress," he huffed half a laugh, "You would think that for a group of seasoned warriors and an angel, a new house guest would not have caused such a disruption in manners." I laughed, though it was half-hearted. Mal's kind eyes watched me carefully. "We can wait until you are ready."

"I'm ready." He started to protest, but I stopped him, "I promise, Mal, really. Just be ready to take your time, okay? Now, start from the top."

He nodded before deciding the best place to begin. "You fell asleep prior to arriving here, right? Do you recall the paralysis you felt as you were waking up?"

"How could I forget? I—" A lump formed in my throat as I relived those moments of panic. "I have never been more scared in my life."

"I can only imagine. Strangers show up at your door, and the next thing you know, you're waking up somewhere foreign, with almost none of your senses. Any reasonable person would be terrified. Sterling said you mentioned it when you confronted her. Tell me, how did she respond?"

"She was stunned. Genuinely. Even in my anger, I could see she had been caught off guard. She felt awful about the effects it had on me."

"Well, what she had slipped in your drink that night was a special drought. The intended purpose was to send you into a deep sleep, allowing Sterling to bring you here without you knowing the way."

"In case I changed my mind and tried to leave."

"Precisely. Though I can't say you would have been able to find your way back to Eden, clever as you are," he smiled softly, "Anyway, for the Nephilim—and, to some extent, angels—that specific drought doubles as a paralytic. One that can be dangerous when not measured correctly.

"The Nephilim's physiology, thanks to their ancestry, has allowed for several differences from the Children of Adam. Some are advantageous, while others have been manipulated in order to exploit weaknesses that are not found in mere mortals.

"While you were not given a lethal dose, thankfully, Sterling also did not believe she needed to be as precise in her concentration. This, I believe, inevitably led to the pain you experienced when first waking up here."

"That isn't too far-fetched, I suppose...but it's not concrete proof, either. What else backs up your theory?"

"When we went out to the pub last night, Roman ordered several rounds of *caelacrimae*. You had quite a few of those shots, right?"

I gave him a quick nod.

"Tell me, how did it taste?"

"It was probably the best drink I have ever had in my life."

"That is because it is a product of angels, Kai. In its literal translation, it is named '*Tears of Heaven.*' Humans who stumble upon the liquor often find themselves immediately spitting it out and running for the nearest purgeable liquid. It leaves a terrible taste that typically lingers for quite a while."

"Why would your people make something taste so awful intentionally? Have they never heard humans describe things as 'heavenly'?"

Mal chuckled. "It is to deter them from seeking out angels and anything else celestial. They do it to keep the worlds separate. To keep the Children of Adam safe."

"I see." Another sigh escaped me. "Mal, these are facts of your world, and I have no doubt you're right about *how* these things are supposed to work. If we were talking about anyone else, I would support your theory."

"But not in this case?"

"It just sounds crazy. I mean, it's *me* you're talking about. I grew up with my aunt. It was a beautiful, perfect, normal life. Sure, I know very little about my parents, other than Erica missed them from time to time. But I can assure you they were not children of divine beings."

"Stranger things have happened. And while I feel that those two situations alone provide a concrete base for my theory, I do agree with Sterling. Something is different about you. But where she sees it as a personal weakness, her pinning over you, I feel there is more to it."

"I'm not following you."

"We have all done a terrible job of explaining things to you, as you pointed out earlier. It's just that you have seamlessly blended into this house and the circle of those who reside in it. It makes it hard to remember that you haven't been here more than a couple of days. I mean, for crying out loud, you and *Callen* were singing drinking songs on the way in last night. He is the sweetest person to walk this Earth, but he is also very reserved with new people. This is not the case with you, however."

"Perhaps it's my infallible charm," I teased.

He gave me a small laugh. "You are indeed very charming. But it is more than that. Something more central to you than good manners and a pretty smile. I am a huge proponent of you testing to prove that you are, in fact, Nephilim."

I waited a beat, curious to see if he might add more. Nothing. Malachi simply held my gaze, unblinking. Finally, I asked, "What is this test?"

"It is called Metanoia. It is a task to test your abilities. Most Nephilim tend to prove this while in their later teen years by facing demons on mandatory patrols while in school. It has rarely been seen that an older outsider wants to prove they are truly a Child of Angels, but it happens nonetheless. This test has been put into place for those specific cases."

"What cases would require an exception like that? Can Nephilim fail out of school?"

"No. Even if someone is not fit to be a warrior, they would simply be trained in some other discipline. Regardless of physical capabilities, a child born and raised in a Nephilim household will always be considered as such.

"The rare instances where it has been seen that someone requests to face this trial are usually when a Nephilim child seeks this place out. Typically, this is someone who was raised in Eden, around the Children of Adam, but has Nephilim parents who chose to leave this life behind. In order for them to seek out an approval to test, they must first know that Soteria exists. They have to know how to find it in order to approach the council with their formal request. That—being able to find Soteria, I mean—is almost proof alone that they are Nephilim. Their parents will have told them what to expect, should they choose this path. They come prepared, aware of what must be done, and should pass with relative ease."

"So, you have seen this test before?"

"Once—long, long ago. Angels can be present for it, but at least one Archangel must observe the test. Though the Nephilim are their own people, they are the messengers of Arcadia. The Archangels will have the final say."

"Did they pass? Whoever it was that you observed during their trial, I mean?"

Mal's shoulders sagged slightly as he diverted his eyes from mine. His thoughts were far off as he spoke. "Her name was Evangeline.

She performed well, better than some Children of Angels would have, despite being brought up learning at a young age. She was both lethal and lovely as she battled her chosen demons. Sharp as a blade when strategizing."

Despite the words of praise, his tone was brimming with sadness. "What happened?"

"Both the Archangels Michael and Gabriel were presiding over judgment that day. They stepped away to discuss their thoughts privately. For whatever reason, they came back with a decision to deny Evangeline the right of being deemed a true Nephilim." He continued to stare at the floor, unblinking.

"Why would they do that?"

"There were rumors, of course." He shrugged, turning back to me. "But nothing ever came to the surface with evidence. It was nearly two hundred years ago. I was younger than I am now, and oblivious to the politics of Heaven. I am afraid I didn't have the appropriate connections to dredge up the true nature of their decision. After a time, it no longer mattered. The chatter subsided swiftly among the Nephilim, and the angels didn't care much about any of it to begin w ith."

"How old are you?" I couldn't stop the question from tumbling out.

Malachi laughed softly. "I am eight hundred years old. That is still young in the eyes of some of my people, though unfathomable to those I now spend most of my time with."

"You look good for your age," I attempted the joke, though I was sure he had heard it before.

Nonetheless, he gave me a winning smile. "I appreciate that, Kai. You wouldn't believe the number of grandfather jokes I have endured from Roman alone. He has an uncanny ability to make the last few years feel longer than my entire existence. I will give it to him, though, every few months, he does think of something new that makes me laugh."

I could imagine the boyish grin that would consume Roman's face in triumph from getting Malachi, or anyone really, to laugh at a joke at their own expense. He expressed his love for his friends through his humor, and the better it was received, the happier it made him.

"Going back to the situation at hand, do you understand everything so far?"

"I believe so. What would it mean if I passed?"

"Well, that would be up to you. Should you choose to, you could stay here and continue to train. Carve out a life for yourself with the Nephilim, however that may look. I'm sure Sterling would let you stay as long as you wanted. You could also choose to go home. But even when choosing that, you would have access to come and go from Soteria and other Nephii provinces as you pleased. No memory would be taken from you. And no punishment would be passed down to the h ouse."

He added the last sentence hesitantly, already anticipating my next question. Still, he waited for me to ask.

"What happens to you all? If I fail? Or if they discover what has happened?"

"I cannot fully say. Sterling will presumably try to take all the blame. Of course, the council would never allow that, though she would receive the worst of it. I am clearly not the favorite among angels right now, either"—he glanced just behind his shoulder— "which grants us no favors."

"I want to know the specifics, Mal."

He sighed heavily. "Any number of things. They could separate all of us to start, taking the house away from Sterling. Demoting Callen and Roman would be a huge dishonor, especially for Roman, who lives for the fight. Eliza may get sent home to her parents in Etnos. That would be the least terrible thing, though still punishment enough for her to be miserable for the rest of her life."

"You really believe her being sent back home would ruin her life?"

"You don't understand what it was like for her there, Kai. They are still very conservative in Etnos, as are the twins' parents. They thought that the education of girls prior to their teenage years in Soteria was not appropriate for Eliza. While Callen was sent to train out here, her parents felt Eliza would fare better living as their mother had. They all but trapped her on that island as they tried to force her into their idea of a 'proper' woman. In their eyes, she should be a boutique owner, married and raising the next great generation of warriors. But she herself is a born fighter, and was able to claw her way into Soteria when she was seventeen, all but running away from a predestined future."

"I had no idea," I whispered.

Malachi waved a hand, "Nor did I expect you to. But in order to understand the gravity of what going back to Etnos would mean for Liza, you needed to know that. She would be sent back, and they would likely isolate her into a 'profitable' union."

"Profitable?"

"It's considered such when naturally talented females inclined to battle are married to high-ranking warriors. They then take on the duties of housewife and mother. Both of which are roles that seem utterly abhorrent to Liza."

"That's terrible." Though I felt no warmth for her, I would not wish a life of someone else's design on anyone.

"The punishments of the others are not the worst of it. Sterling would be pulled from her position, publicly shamed, and likely beaten. She would be made an example for both Nephilim and angels.

They would take everything from her and lock her in some dark space until she forgot everything she had ever known."

"All for bringing me here?"

"For that, for having anything resembling feelings for you, for hiding it for so long. The list would only grow from there. Every little indiscretion would be scrutinized. They could go back years and years and make her pay for every single mistake."

"But you all have said she follows rules almost to a fault. Wouldn't that grant her some leeway?"

"Sterling has an...interesting past. One that did not allow for many mistakes to begin with. Besides, she is a soldier. And what good is a soldier who gets a taste for breaking rules without being reprimanded? They fear losing control. Especially of her."

"And what about you?"

"I suppose I'd go back to my people. Any chance of redeeming myself and getting my wings back would be gone. If they haven't already burned them, they would be ashes by the time I returned. I would live in servitude to whoever wanted to purchase my time from our governing body. In whatever way they preferred."

We sat quietly for what felt like ages as I digested what my new friend was telling me. I couldn't imagine them all not being together, let alone everything else. Sterling, beaten and bloody in front of a crowd. *All because of me.*

"That is a lot of pressure," I murmured, mostly to myself. My eyes were staring at the floor unseeing as the weight settled on my chest.

"What if you're wrong and I'm—" my throat had dried and I tried to clear it, "What if I try and it's not enough?"

Mal grasped my hands in both of his, his brown eyes soft and calming as he said, "Then you will have tried to win a battle that fate decided long ago wasn't meant to be won. Sometimes fate has its own plans, despite the choices we make. However, choosing to face a challenge, regardless of a possible predestined outcome, choosing to fight rather than accept it, is a far more courageous feat than most would ever dare to undertake. Especially when doing it in the name of those they care for."

Mal somehow knew me well enough to know that I had already said yes before he had even told me what I was agreeing to. I knew it could possibly help him, help the others. I would do whatever I could to stop something from happening to them, even if I lacked the faith that Malachi seemed to have in me at present.

I gave a shaky breath and nodded, squeezing his hands tightly. "You will have time to prepare," he assured me, "as much time as we can get you. And you will be learning from some of the best Nephilim in several generations. But don't tell them I said that," he added lightly with a wink.

I dug deep for a smile. It was less for the joke and more for my appreciation that he was trying. "When do we start?"

"Sterling is likely still up in the training room. Talk to her first so that she knows what you have decided to do. We will coordinate and make a plan from there."

I squeezed his hands again, letting the ease in his demeanor wash over me as much as possible. We both stood then, dropping our arms to our sides. Mal gestured for me to lead the way out of the room and, as I grabbed the door handle, I turned back to him once more. "Why do Sterling's eyes change color?"

"That is one question I know I cannot answer. For that, you have to talk to Sterling." I groaned, and he laughed at me. "In due time, Kai. In due time."

"That seems to be the popular phrase around here," I said, disgruntled. I opened my door and we both ventured into the hallway.

We walked together until we came to the stairs. From there, Malachi went down the steps while I continued straight towards the attic door. The stairwell was small, and as I made my way up, I was aware of the thudding sound from earlier this morning. When I reached the final step, I could finally make sense of what it was.

The attic was a single floor that spanned the whole length of the house. There were various spots dedicated to specific equipment that Sterling had briefly mentioned the other day. The wall with various swords and other handheld weapons was neat, organized by both size and material. Off to the side of it was a circle that had been painted on the floor, and had a bowl of chalk set on either side. In other places, ropes hung from the roof, dummies lined the walls, and mats of various sizes were stacked neatly. On the far back wall, there were silhouettes of human forms painted, along with other shapes I couldn't identify. The sound drew my attention to this wall, and I saw several small knives embedded there. Each one sinking into what would be a lethal point on the painted target.

In the middle of the room, several paces away, stood Sterling.

I stopped in my tracks, noticing her discarded shirt seconds before I gaped at her back.

The tattoo was beautiful. A pair of intricately drawn wings spanned its entirety. It started at her shoulders, covering them completely. As it snaked beneath her sports bra, I could tell it fanned out slightly there, only to begin to thin out once more. Each wingtip touched, meeting to come to a point midline between two dimples in her back, leaving a skinny oval of tan skin untouched.

Her shoulders rose and fell as she breathed hard, no doubt having been throwing these knives for several hours by now. She had just thrown another knife, and I watched the muscles in her back start to relax one by one as she returned to a more neutral position.

"I like your tattoo."

Sterling startled, spinning quickly with an elegant grace. She had a sheen of sweat over her entire body as beads ran down her temples, down her chest, and over her stomach. The way the light hit her golden skin, she seemed to glow. It was hard not to stare as her breathing quickened in surprise, moving her chest rapidly. The contours of her flat stomach deepened momentarily, helping maintain her balance from being upended by the swift movements.

"I'm sorry," I said, trying not to sound breathless myself, "I didn't mean to startle you." Her eyes were an electric shade of blue, lit by the endorphins of physical activity. Blonde hair was piled on her head, but strays had started to fall around her face in perfect disarray.

I wanted more than anything to move them away from her face.

"It's fine," her accent was thick as she caught her breath, "I'm not used to people sneaking up on me. It has been some time since it happened, if I am being honest." Sterling began to relax once again, her breathing coming back to a regular rhythm. She walked over to the wall, where she began pulling the knives away. Some were lodged deeply into the wood, and I observed keenly how removing them accentuated her defined arms more as they put in extra effort to work the small blades free. Her hand tightened around the hilt of a particularl y difficult one.

Like how it had tightened around my neck.

Before I could stop myself, I was thrown back into the memory of last night. Those arms, her hands, holding my body in place. How they had moved me in whatever ways she had wanted. The grip of her hand on my throat as I tasted the whisky on her tongue—

"Kai?"

"Yes?"

"Did you hear me?"

Shit, what did she say?

Sterling saved me the embarrassment of saying that I had, in fact, not heard her at all. An arrogant smirk crossed over her features briefly as if she had heard my thoughts but vanished just as quickly as it had appeared. "Is there something you need?" Her tone was indifferent, as if I were a needy child cutting into valuable time that was not to be wasted.

Tired of waiting for a response, she returned her attention to the target on the wall. It was then that I remembered this was the first time we had seen each other since she had left me alone last night.

"Mal sent me to find you."

"Did he now?" She worked the last knife free and went back to her spot in the middle of the floor.

"How are you?"

She scoffed. "Surely Malachi didn't send you to see how I'm *doing*." Sterling dropped the knives beside her feet, save for one.

"No, he didn't; I wanted to know. Things were... Things left off on an abrupt note. You seemed flustered. I know I was."

I could've sworn I caught a glimpse of hopeful surprise as she stared at her weapons on the floor, intent on separating them equidistant from one another. Maybe I had imagined it.

Quieter still, eyes to the ground, "I just wanted to make sure you were okay." I chanced a glance up at her.

Sterling combed back her hair with a free hand and sighed. "I'm as okay as I can be, Kai." Her tone was resigned and tired. "Are you okay?"

"As okay as I can be." She gave me a small nod before turning to take aim at the wall again. Pleasantries out of the way, she asked, "What did Mal send you for?" Then she let her knife fly. It sank into the left shoulder of the target with a hollow thud.

"We talked," I started as Sterling reached for a new blade and prepared her aim, "and I decided I want to train so that I can attempt the test of Metanoia."

The words came out as Sterling made to throw, entirely distracting her when she released the knife. "What?" she squawked out as it missed the target completely, striking an unpainted piece of the wall off to the right. "You're serious?"

"Yes," I squared my shoulders, prepared to stand my ground. I stepped closer to her as she reached for another knife. "Mal said the two of you had talked and that, as long as it was my choice, you would train me. This would help, wouldn't it? It could save you and the others?"

Sterling fidgeted with the knife, patting the flat side in her palm repeatedly. "It's a small *theory* that Malachi has decided makes sense to him. So, of course it must be fact. Honestly, Kai, I know he is convincing, but where is your sense of self-preservation?"

I ignored the dig as I got closer still, just an arm's length away now. She started to pace in small steps. "Don't you trust him?"

"I do, but I don't like to gamble, let alone with the lives of others. *Especially* not yours." The disinterested mask slipped to reveal the raw emotion behind the words.

I had to repress the chill of excitement that ran down my spine.

"Well, I trust him. And I've always had decent luck."

"Fool's luck is more appropriate," Sterling corrected. She was standing behind me now, having circled her way around the space I occupied.

"Luck is luck," I said, spinning around to face her, "and I'll honestly take whatever I can get."

She stepped directly towards me. "You know I can't guarantee your safety?"

"I know."

Another step. She was standing directly in front of me, almost toe to toe. The scent of sandalwood and vanilla that came from her was intoxicating. It took all of my willpower to not breathe it in deeper. I wanted to taste her skin. I wanted to reach out and grab her hips, use them to close the distance.

But I didn't.

I met her gaze, having to look up slightly into eyes that had started to darken with every word we spoke. Sterling wanted to change my mind and hated that she had no control here. Her jaw tightened imperceptibly. She started to blink less frequently as her eyes narrowed slightly. Despite her best efforts, it was always her eyes that gave away her true emotions. Right now, they showed clouded fear.

"You know you could die, right? Something awful could happen, and no matter what I tried to do, they would not let me interfere."

"I understand."

Sterling looked to the rafters, shaking her head incredulously as she turned her back to me. "She understands," she groaned at the ceiling, throwing her hands up. "Of course she *thinks* she does." Within a tenth of a second, the air shifted, right before Sterling turned back to me abruptly. Her right arm was already in motion as she brought it forward, releasing the knife she had been toying with. Our eyes connected as it went flying with sure precision.

It moved fast, but its path was evident as I watched it come towards me. Not towards me. Just *beside* me. It wouldn't touch me if I stayed in my spot. I remained rooted in place. I felt the air stir by the right side of my head as it passed by, lodging into the center of the target.

I did not flinch but kept my eyes locked with hers.

Whatever resolve was set behind my gaze must have broken down the last of Sterling's resistance. Looking to the ground, she let out a tired sigh, but when her eyes landed on me once again, she gave me a single nod.

"Let's begin."

PART II

"In the middle of the journey of our life I found myself within a dark wood where the straight way was lost."

Dante Alighieri

CHAPTER 16

That evening, Sterling went over the process of Metanoia and what would be expected of me if I chose to see this through. The lingering hope that I would reconsider my decision danced lightly over her expression for the duration of our conversation. That is where her protests started and ended, though. Despite her fear of the outcome, she knew I had made up my mind and that I would not waver.

Her explanation was not so different from Malachi's. She repeated the basics of the trial, along with how it was judged by both Nephilim leaders and at least one Archangel. The possibility that I might not pass, and what it could mean, wasn't brought up by either of us.

She didn't need to voice what her greatest fear was any more than I needed to be reminded of what hung in the balance. It had been said once, and subconsciously, we both agreed that that was plenty.

We were sitting on the floor of the training room. The last light of day poured the blues and violets of dusk through the window as our conversation came to a close. Sterling was sitting with her arms wrapped around her knees, another knife in hand. She twirled it absent-mindedly as she glanced towards the window.

"Better get some rest," she looked back at me, "you are in for an extremely long day tomorrow."

I got to my feet as Sterling moved to do the same. While I started for the stairs, she went the opposite way. She flicked on a light before returning to her pile of knives. It was seconds before the one she had been holding was embedded into the wall, vibrating in the dead center of the target.

"You aren't going to call it a night?"

"It's not me who has twenty years of training to catch up on," she kept her back to me as she adjusted her stance, new blade in hand. "Twenty years, at the bare minimum that is." This sounded less teasing than more of a hard fact.

Though she was less than thrilled by my decision, we had come to an amicable place throughout the evening. Or so I had thought. However, the cold indifference was present once again. We still hadn't talked about the other night in great detail, but I had figured she would rather just let it go. If it had meant we were able to put the awkwardness behind us, I would have been more than happy to leave it alone. But here we were, separated by sheets of ice put up by Sterling.

"What the hell?"

This made her pause as she wound up for another throw. Dropping her arm, she turned back to me, raising an eyebrow in response as if to say, *'Yes?'*.

"Why are you acting like this?"

"Like what?"

"Every time I think we have made progress, you change your mind. We get into a fight, and you are sweet and apologetic. I hang out with your friends, people who *you* wanted me to feel comfortable with, only to come back and have you angry with all of us. Then you kiss me and throw me onto a desk, before walking out abruptly and telling me that it was a mistake. Even now, just when I think we have come to a place where we can be normal, you start to act like an asshole again." I was doing my best to keep any emotion out of my voice, but in doing so, I started talking faster. "You are hot and cold, and I can't keep up with you. Do you care about me? Do you hate me?"

Sterling crossed her arms, and her jaw tightened. "I'm sorry that you feel I have been unfair to you. I made a mistake when I brought Malachi to your doorstep, and I have made mistakes since then." She was clearly referencing the kiss. "I take the responsibility for the situation I put both you and my friends in, and I want to remedy that. I'll see to your training, but there needs to be a line drawn. Whatever drunken choices I made, whatever whims I gave into, those are choices that will die in the past. I don't want to be uncivil, and given time, I hope we can find common ground."

Everything she was saying was formal, impersonal. Not at all like what she had said to Mal earlier. Though it stung, I nodded once and turned for the stairs.

"Kai," Sterling said, causing me to turn around mid-step. "I still mean what I said. It was a mistake. And I am so sorry. It was all words and actions induced by alcohol and stress. That doesn't excuse it, but the sooner we both acknowledge it for what it was, the better off we will both be. Besides, I have Eliza to think of."

If the small possibility that maybe this all meant I *could* be with Sterling in the end had started to pry open that locked door, Sterling's words soldered it shut. Roman had been wrong; Sterling regretted what had passed between us. Whatever everyone else believed to be true, Sterling did not feel the way they had assumed. Her actions, the moments where I had hoped she could have felt something for me, were all motivated by the guilt of putting me in this situation.

"Yeah," I muttered quietly, "you made that *very* clear last night." I turned and descended the stairs. The hollow sound of knives hitting the wall sounded one by one as I walked to my room, hoping that sleep would claim me quick.

It was anything but easy.

The following morning, I awoke to a loud, demanding knock at my door. My vision was blurry from sleep, and I rubbed them clear as I opened it. I came face-to-face with Roman, looking bright-eyed and ready for the day ahead.

"Rise and shine, Child of Adam! We have work to do." I looked out my window and saw that dawn had not yet broken.

"What time is it?" My voice came out cracked and dry.

"Time to get to work on those little chicken legs," he said with a glance and a laugh.

"Give me ten minutes," he started to say something about me not going back to sleep as I shut the door on him. Roman didn't open it. Instead, he began tapping on my door in such a way that would ensure I would come back out, if only just to punch him for being obnoxious.

I brushed my teeth and quickly threw my hair up. After dressing in a pair of leggings and a t-shirt, along with a pair of black and white running shoes, I was ready to face him once again. I opened the door, abruptly stopping the tapping.

Roman gave me a once-over and shrugged. "I suppose you won't need to train if you face your trial looking like that. The demons will be terrified by the sight of you alone."

"Sorry, I didn't realize training was a beauty pageant. Should I change into something you deem more likable?" There was a bite to my tone.

"Whoa, easy there, killer," he held his hands up in surrender, "All I meant was you look exhausted. But if looks could kill, you might just be a lethal weapon after all."

I rubbed my eyes again, "I'm sorry, I barely slept at all last night."

"You were that excited to train with me? Wow, I am truly flattered."

"No...Actually, I didn't even know I would be meeting with you today. I actually expected you to be shorter, blonde, and a tad more feminine if I'm being honest."

"No one told you? We decided to divide up your training based on what we are best at individually."

"And of course I get to deal with you first thing in the morning."

"Hey now," Roman said in mock offense, "I am a delight. And besides"—he ran his eyes over me again— "you need to work with me before you can work with almost anyone else. Your body won't hold up while training with the others without getting hurt." This, he said without a hint of humor. He stepped aside, gesturing with his hand to the hallway. "Shall we?"

I stepped out of my room, and Roman closed the door behind me as we walked towards the stairway to the training room. "Why did you guys need to break up my training?" I asked him.

"Well, of course I am the most skilled out of all of us when it comes to combat, but you have all day free to train, and I do not, so we had to split up the sections." He shrugged, but his grin was full of humor.

"That and Mal suggested you might benefit more from learning from our combined strengths."

"And what is *your* specific talent, exactly?"

"My favorite, of course: weapon handling. But to start off, I'll also serve as a conditioning coach of sorts. We need to work on strength and endurance before you can progress to anything else too advanced. Because of that, your first week or two will be strictly with Mal and I."

"I'm not in terrible shape," I mumbled sheepishly.

"Not for a Child of Adam, but you even said so yourself that trying to keep up with us the other night was hard." He flinched when I raised my hand to my neck, as if he were expecting me to hit him for the reminder. "Besides, even if you were an Olympic athlete by mortal standards, that's nothing compared to what is expected of a Nephilim to be in fighting shape."

We reached the stairs and entered the training room. It was empty, save for us. "And what will I learn from everyone else?"

"Callen is fast and calculating. He will be teaching you agility, strategy, and the importance of being able to combine the two in order to defeat an opponent. The time with him will be filled with sparring using both hands and weapons. In that time, you will learn how to strategically observe your opponent's use of the two.

"Malachi will mostly teach you history and demonology and, later on, will serve as a reviewer of sorts to bring together all you have learned. He will be a blind opponent in the sense that he has no idea exactly how you have been trained. You will fight as any two opponents would. He will be as calculating with you as he would any of us, if not more so.

"I'll be showing you proper weapon use and hand-to-hand combat," he added cheerfully.

"And Sterling?" I asked hesitantly.

"She will have her part in this later. But for now…she felt it was best if we took on the bulk of your education." His tone was neutral, but he couldn't look me in the eyes as his words registered.

Disappointment crashed into me, though I shouldn't have been surprised. But, despite the pain in my chest, I released a small breath I hadn't realized I had been holding. He hadn't mentioned Eliza, and that was a silver lining I could hold onto. As if he could read my mind, Roman added, "We all felt it would be best if Eliza wasn't left alone to train you. Of course, she may serve as a great final sparring partner before your test. She would give even the strongest demons a run for their money, given the fire in her eyes when she sees you."

I rolled my eyes but nodded. I was grateful that I would not have to spend time alone with her, much less learn in front of her. I was most awkward when I was learning, and it made me uncomfortable even in the best of situations. I could not fathom having Eliza as a teacher.

"Although you may be begging to train with Eliza after I'm through with you," Roman laughed.

I squared my shoulders, trying to look taller. "Do your worst," I challenged.

A feral smile crept across his face. "You are going to regret that."

Roman was right. After a grueling six hours of conditioning, I could hardly move. I had been slow, too. He gave me a list of workouts with low reps and many sets, and only when I was finished would we move on to the next thing. The deal was that the length of time required for our early lessons would depend on me and my ability to complete the list he came prepared with every day. I was starting to think that it was never going to end as I struggled through pushups. My arms felt like noodles, and I had long since resorted to using my knees in order to keep moving. Even then, my effort at this point was sad at best.

I was struggling to push myself up, and as I shakily reached the top, Roman finally spoke. "Stop." It was all I needed before I allowed myself to collapse flat on my stomach. I was breathing hard, and my arms were already starting to cramp. I could feel the bruises forming on my knees.

I wanted to roll on my back but decided against it. The several core exercises I had previously done made the movement all but impossible. "I hate you."

Roman laughed his deep rumbling laugh. "You'll be thanking me when you are surrounded by demons. Or in the ring with Cal. That one is a quick little bastard, I tell ya."

"I can't move anything. I can't even roll over."

"Breathe through it. Take a breath in and breathe out as you move."

"I'd rather stay here forever, thanks."

"Being able to fight through the pain is important too, you know. It can mean the difference between life and death. Do you know how I do it?"

"You have two brain cells and a high pain tolerance?"

Roman smirked before he gently poked me in the ribs with his foot. I hissed in pain and attempted to scoot out of his reach. I didn't make it very far.

"You're so clever," he said teasingly. "No, it's nothing like that. It has nothing to do with our physical capabilities. One of the greatest weapons we have to survive pain is our minds. Does it take it away? No, but it helps us bear it, helps us try to understand it to a point where we can co-exist with it. The mind can protect us in more ways than some armor can, and it is astounding. I'm not saying I would go running into battle without any physical protection, but you of all people should know what I mean."

"And why is that?"

"Pain is both physical and mental, Kai. You lost the only person you've ever had in your life at a young age. Your career centered around helping those who were suffering, trying to survive their worst days. You have seen things, lived through moments, that many do not experience even in their worst nightmares. That leaves scars on a person's soul. Yet you endured. How?"

"I...I don't know," I thought back to my most recent loss—the night that James died. "I guess I just picture this box in my head. When my feelings or the emotional strain of a situation are too much, I shove it in there. It's easier to digest when I can try and control the release bit by bit rather than all at once."

"Exactly, but it doesn't mean it's no longer there. You're still working hard, still struggling to exist with it, but you are not letting it control you. It finds everyone, some unfortunately more than others. Some days it is stronger, and that's okay. It doesn't mean you've failed. You keep fighting, and that matters. The more you learn how to manage it, the stronger you will become."

I stared at him for a moment. "Roman, that was surprisingly deep."

"I'm not just a pretty face; I can have a profound thought now and again. But stating the truth isn't going to get you out of this. C'mon, Kai, this is the easiest it's ever going to be. Best to start now."

I groaned, knowing I wasn't getting out of this. I took a deep breath and squeezed my eyes shut as I willed myself to move. Everything was on fire. Muscles that I didn't know I had ached deeply, and my body begged me to stop. Doing as Roman had told me, I slowly exhaled through the movement. Next thing I knew, I was on my back, the aching receding.

"Good. Now, get up."

"What?"

"You heard me. You are going to be hurting endlessly for the next few days, and I need to see that you can still manage." I rolled my eyes at his look of fake concern. Sitting up alone was agony, let alone fully standing up. *This is going to take some time.*

Roman all but laughed at my struggle. "You are supposed to meet with Mal in the library around 3. But honestly," he hesitated as a small whimper escaped me, "Seeing as how you seemed to be set on moving at a snail's pace, you may not make it down the stairs until then. I'll let him know you will see him closer to 5."

He began walking to the stairwell. "Wait," I managed to squeeze out as I sat all the way up. "You're just going to leave me here to struggle?"

He pretended to consider it for half a second before responding, "Oh, absolutely. It'll take you a while just to stand, and that's not even considering the stairs you have to climb down, and I'm afraid I'm too hungry to hang around."

"What if I fall?" I knew I was being dramatic, but I wasn't going to let him leave me to suffer that easily.

"Then I will be sad to have missed seeing it. I wish you the best of luck. Ciao, Kai!" With that, he turned and lightly jogged down the stairs.

"Rat bastard," I called after him, which received a genuine laugh in the distance. I focused on breathing through each motion as I made it to my feet. Every movement required time, and I had to take breaks after each shift in position. Within ten minutes, I was standing, or more accurately swaying, on my feet.

Truth be told, the focused breathing had helped to some small extent. But with how much pain I was in, I would take whatever small reprieve I could get. Placing one heavy foot in front of the other, I made my way to the top of the stairs. "Let's get this over with."

It took me another 20 minutes to limp my way down the stairs. Another 10 minutes before I crossed the threshold of my room, and all but collapsed into my bed. Every part of my body felt as if it had been filled with lead, and I still had the strength of a cooked noodle.

I know Roman was being sarcastic when he said it would take me hours to get back downstairs, but I was grateful for the extended break, nonetheless. It was just after noon by the time I had made it back to my room. I had plenty of time before I needed to meet Mal.

There were a lot of ways I could fill the time. I was hungry. I knew I should shower. I could vaguely recall Roman saying something about the importance of stretching, and how it was best to do that after my muscles were warm. All these thoughts flowed through my head, but ultimately, I acted on none of them. The last thought I had was how badly it was going to hurt getting out of bed once I woke up.

I was awake in time to take a shower and change gradually. Everything was extremely stiff, but the hot water helped to ease some of the pain. I was almost walking normally by the time I hobbled into the library. Mal was perched in a chair, an open book in hand. He looked up and gave me a warm smile as I walked towards him.

"I can see Roman really made you work for it today."

Clearly, I wasn't moving as well as I thought. "I think he is trying to kill me."

Malachi chuckled. "On the contrary, I think he is trying to make sure you stay alive. For all his jokes about torturing his students, he always means well. Though I don't doubt he gets a kick out of watching us struggle at his hand."

"Honestly, he isn't a bad teacher," I admitted genuinely. For all his sarcastic remarks and jokes, he was patient and encouraging while we worked. He never made fun of me for being slow or weak. His criticism was constructive and gentle. Overall, he was one of the best teachers I had ever had.

"Care to sit down?" Mal gestured towards my favorite overstuffed chair.

"I would love nothing more." I flopped into my seat, wincing at the impact. Mal looked amused. "So, I hear you are to be my tutor and eventually make sure the others do their job well enough?"

"That just about sums it up, yes."

"Can I ask you something?"

"Always."

"I'm not complaining about how you all broke up the sections, but why are you *only* teaching me the histories?"

Mal closed his book and leaned forward a little. "We all thought I was best suited for the histories because I have been in this world the longest. Some of what I will teach you, I was present for. I will also serve as the so-called 'reviewer' because I am the only one to have ever seen someone test. We all figured that I would be the closest thing to measure you up to the task that may await you. And besides," he continued, his tone softer now, "although I am mostly healed, I am not fully recovered, and I fear any combat training from me would do you a disservice. Not to mention, angels and Nephilim train differently."

I nodded, "So what have we got planned for today's lesson?"

"Tonight, we will go back to the start of the Nephilim."

"Were you around for that?"

"Oh no, that was nearly a couple thousand years ago. Do you know the general story?"

"I think so. It was realized that children of angels and humans were different than those of mere mortals, but they weren't quite like their angel forebearers, either. In the end, they decided that the Nephilim would be able to keep the demons at bay, but allow the angels to return to Arcadia."

"Very good. You are correct. At its roots, that is exactly what happened. However, in the beginning, angels were laying with humans simply because they could. There was no specific reason for it other than mutual attraction. Even Archangels were siring children with residents of Eden. Their offspring were the strongest of the Nephilim, of course, seeing as how a stronger line of divinity flowed through their veins. It was a few centuries later when the laws came into effect, prohibiting angels and Archangels from bedding humans. Nephilim were once not as restricted as they are now, though. They could be with whomever they desired, save for the Hosts of Heaven. But it wasn't long after that laws were put in place for the Children of Angels, too. Humans were dying needless deaths due to their exposure in our world. Strong Nephilim lines were starting to become weakened by mortal parentage.

"Though the laws made sense, the Nephilim race needed strong lines to balance out what had been lost. Once this became obvious, the angels were allowed a small window of time where they could seek out humans to procreate with, provided they were honest with whomever they chose. The Child of Adam needed to openly accept their role in this. They would be given special privileges in exchange for their children being raised by the Nephilim.

"Some angels and Archangels slept with Nephilim, eager to see if the bloodlines would be stronger with these pairings than those with mere mortals. It is still speculated about today, though no longer in practice. Now, Nephilim are simply meant to seek love within their own people. Given the hazards of the lifestyle, and the sheer insanity attached to the truth of it all, it is a small sacrifice if even one at all."

I listened to Malachi talk about the dawn of the Nephilim people. How their governing body was elected, how the education systems were designed, and how historical events led to certain laws being implemented. Before he dismissed me for the night, he handed me the *Brief History* book I had left earlier. "This may be a nice abridgement of some of the topics we will be discussing."

"Thank you. I meant to grab this the other night. I...got distracted and forgot."

Mal gave me a small nod, understanding exactly what the distraction had been. "Don't bother reading it tonight, though. For now, take care of yourself. A hot bath with some of those Epsom salts will work wonders. Have you eaten?"

I shook my head no, my stomach growling loudly in the silence.

"I'll make sure food is sent to your room. Get some sleep. *Good* sleep. Tomorrow will be worse than today was." We both stood, Malachi moving effortlessly compared to me. I gave him a hug and thanked him for both the lesson and his kindness, and then I made for my room to rest my aching muscles.

As promised, a dinner tray full of pasta, chicken, salad, and bread was waiting on my nightstand. I had not realized how hungry I was until the smells wafted through my room. No time was wasted as I scarfed the food down while silently thanking Mal. The fresh pasta filled me with warmth and comforted me more than anything had in a long time. With a full stomach, sprawled out in my soft bed, I fell asleep despite the light that still seeped through my window.

The next week and a half of my training consistently progressed in the same way as my first. I would spend the mornings working out with Roman and the evenings studying with Mal. Malachi had been right when he said the second day would be worse. I had awoken to tight muscles that ached with each and every breath I took. When I came face-to-face with Roman, he merely laughed at me. "You didn't stretch, did you?" Without another word on the subject, he conditioned me mercilessly. I tried stretching that night at his suggestion. Though I would never tell him, it did help some. However, the burning with every move I made continued, demanding to be acknowledged.

Another constant? I was exhausted. I took most meals in my room, sleep quickly finding me afterwards. Typically, everyone in the house was still asleep when I slipped into the kitchen for a quick snack before the start of my day. Some evenings, I ate while studying with Mal. Because of this, I rarely saw the other residents of the house. Some part of me was okay with this fact. I was too tired to offer good company to anyone, and any free time I had, I wanted to fill with sleep. And yet, I would catch myself longing for some interaction that wasn't combat training or a demonology lesson. It wasn't only time with Sterling that I longed for, either. I missed how it had been the first few days after I had arrived. All of us having breakfast together, midnight snacks with Mal. The normalcy of it all tugged at my soul, and one night, despite being entirely spent, I found myself wandering down the stairs towards the activity in the dining room.

I walked down the hallway but stopped just before entering the kitchen. The sound of delighted conversation filled the space as voices, both male and female, spoke over one another only to be smothered by laughter. For a reason I couldn't pinpoint, I silently positioned myself so I could just barely make out the table. They were all seated there—including Eliza. She was seated on the right side of Sterling, sitting in the seat I had occupied during my first few days in Soteria. She smiled a dazzling, perfect smile at whatever Callen had said. Collectively, the table erupted into laughter, save for Roman, who threw a roll in the direction of Sterling. Not a moment passed before he was smiling with them, though.

My heart squeezed when I realized that this is who they were to one another. This is how the house always felt. At least it *was* until I drunkenly stumbled into Sterling's life. Now I was the cause of an obvious rift between Eliza and the rest of them. Between Sterling and her sense of right and wrong. I let myself be blanketed by my pity only until I reached my doorway, ensuring that I discarded it before crossing the threshold. Eliza's joy was a rare sight, burned into my eyes as if I had looked directly into an eclipse. The best thing I could do for them was give back what I had put in jeopardy—their lives.

I didn't seek out extra company after that night.

To their credit, Malachi and Roman had been doing a great job in their respective lessons. And we did talk during that time. But the roles of student and teacher were ones that we all fell into quickly. In those moments, our friendship was a secondary thought. Our common goal—my not dying—served as a constant reminder of how valuable this time was.

About halfway through the second week, Roman allowed me to pick up a sword. When he let go, allowing me to bear the full weight of the weapon, I fought to keep it up. Arms shaking, the tip of the blade fell to the ground with a loud clatter.

"Honestly, you held it longer than I expected," Roman mused as I set the hilt on the ground.

"I'm screwed, aren't I?"

"Not necessarily. Plenty of Nephilim choose not to use swords. But the keyword there is '*choose.*' If they had no other option in a given situation, any Nephilim would still be able to use one at a proficient level."

I looked down at the sword, doubt filling my mind. My face must've betrayed what little self-confidence I felt because Roman came over to me and gently placed a hand on my shoulder.

"We will get there, Kai. Besides, this is a fully weighted sword that would be wielded best by someone like me."

"A pain in the ass?" I asked quietly, trying to lighten the heavy mood filling the room.

"Exactly," Roman beamed, "So, we will start with something smaller. And if, when everything is said and done, you can wield that blade there, then you get to call yourself more of a man than Callen, and he will owe you a drink."

"You know I've been told it isn't right to make bets on behalf of others."

"On the bright side, if you fall short, in his ignorance, he won't know to come collecting."

That afternoon ran longer than usual as we explored different weapons. Knives, swords of various sizes, bows, and a slew of other miscellaneous tools Nephilim used in battle. Our lesson was coming to a close as I was trying out a set of throwing knives similar to the ones Sterling had been using when we had last spoken. Of the three I had thrown, none had sunk into the target.

"At the very least, you might manage to bruise your enemy, if not only piss them off more."

I rolled my eyes at Roman, frustrated with my lack of success. "Aren't you supposed to be encouraging me? Telling me 'you've got this' or something inspiring?"

"Yes. I'm encouraging you to figure it out, or you'll be a demon snack. Very inspiring if you ask me. Now come on. You need something to eat, and you're going to be late meeting Mal."

"I'm not done with this lesson yet."

"It's only day one, don't be so hard on yourself. You have tomorrow and days after to practice."

"Roman, I'm not done," I said curtly.

He sighed and shook his head. Free strands of his dark curly hair had escaped from the majority that had been pulled back. The hair now fell into dark eyes that stared back at me. I couldn't be sure, but I was almost certain that behind the feigned annoyance of being defied, there was *pride*.

Roman walked over to the spot on the floor where my knives had fallen. He picked one up and walked towards me, spinning it expertly in his hand.

"You get one more chance. Then I will carry you out of here myself." He tapped the flat side of the blade in my palm twice. "Make it count, Daughter of Adam."

Something stirred in me as I took the blade. I felt the frustration that had been building over the last week start to seep into my psyche. I missed the regularity of my old life, missed not living in confusion. I felt so far from what Malachi thought I was—what the others hoped I could be, for their sake. And being reminded that I was a Daughter of Adam, doomed to fall short of divine expectation, only fueled my emotions.

I felt more awake, more alert. My muscles were tense and ready to spring at any moment. The resolve settled over me—one that would not allow me to accept an inevitable failure so easily—as I took the knife from Roman, nodding once. I rolled my shoulders back, standing taller with something akin to confidence pooling in me. I weighed the small blade in my hand, looking for the balanced point. Taking a deep breath, I pulled my arm back. Almost without my conscious permission, I let it fly.

I don't know how but, in my bones, I knew its exact path. And I knew that it would find purchase this time.

It wasn't long before what I felt was confirmed as a hollow sound filled the silence. Stuck in the center of the painted human target was my knife. I looked over my shoulder at Roman. There was no question of whether he was proud now. He radiated delight. "Where the hell did that come from?"

"If I could tell you, I would. But when I threw it, I knew it was going to stick. It just... It felt *right*."

"Hold on to that feeling, from start to finish. We are going to hone the hell out of it!"

I nodded, smiling back at him, and then started for the stairs. "Now I'm ready to be done."

Roman chuckled. "Of course you are."

It wasn't long after that that I started working with Callen. I had missed the shy boy with the small, sweet smile. That is, until he knocked me on my ass, while Roman stood laughing in the background. I was still getting used to the basics of swordplay, so Roman and I had agreed that simulating the use of one in combat by using a wooden dowel would be in everyone's best interest.

We hadn't been in the ring for more than three minutes, and Callen had already taken me down. His dowel was poised just above the center of my chest, and my mind reeled at how this had happened. I hadn't even seen him move towards me. Next thing I knew, I was on the ground, feet swept out from under me.

"That means you're dead, Kai," Roman jeered from the sidelines. Callen gave me a small smile in apology and offered me his hand. "We all told you he's a quick bastard."

"You really came out of nowhere, Cal," I said to the dark-haired boy in front of me.

He shrugged. "You were so focused on how you were going to wield the dowel. Your attention being set on your arm movements meant you weren't paying much attention to me, much less your own feet. Lesson one, you have to be aware of *exactly* where you are in space just as much as where your opponent is. You need to know how your adversary perceives you. It gives you an edge. One that allows you to disguise your next move."

"It's so much to think about at once."

"That's what I'm here for," Cal said lightly. "Where most of us just do it naturally," he looked to Roman, "only some of us have the ability to *teach* it."

"Guilty," Roman said, holding up his hand, looking anything but.

"And where some are built like the mountains, the rest of us have to be a little more calculated in battle. We can't just go charging into throngs of demons, taking out half because we simply ran into them."

"Okay, that happened once," Roman exclaimed, "Don't hate me because I'm big and strong and you were built gangly, Callen."

Cal gave his friend the finger before smiling back at me. "Let's start from the beginning."

He walked me through his mental process of assessing his opponents. "The battle begins long before you step in the ring. I started watching how you walked, how you handled your weapon. Body language can betray almost anybody, whether we want it to or not. You use it to your advantage."

Something stirred in my mind. A story Sterling had told me about the boy in front of me surfaced. How he had knocked her down in a similar way. "Do people forget their feet often?" I asked.

"It tends to be an easy spot for me to attack after long enough."

"You played Sterling, didn't you? You knew she thought she had it in the bag the first time you fought."

His emerald eyes sparkled with the memory. "I did. Back then, I never sparred for fun the way the boys my age did. It was a rare thing when people saw me fight, and I liked it that way. She was strong and had something to prove, but her losing that fight between us saved her from having a bigger target painted on her back, I think." He considered something for a moment. "Now, when we all spar, it's a lot harder because we know one another's tricks."

Roman stood in the corner, smiling and nodding along.

"You were at a disadvantage because I know what Roman has and hasn't taught you. I know you aren't comfortable with weapons yet. This is all because I live in the same house as you. But let's say I didn't know any of this.

"I would have been able to read it from the way your arm that held the dowel kept adjusting, unsure of where it should be versus what was comfortable. You kept looking at it, too. It stole your concentration from what was in front of you. Your hips gave away every move you were about to make, angling towards wherever you wanted to go. Your eyes would follow when they weren't trained on your dowel. You looked exactly where you wanted to strike, allowing me to guard myself long before you swung. And because we never faced one another before, you didn't know how quick I truly am," Callen explained.

Eventually, Roman left, and Cal and I continued to talk about strategy. He told me stories of sparring, battles with demons, and anything he thought might be helpful. I asked as many questions as I could think of, anxious to drink in any advantage that was offered to me.

"Don't worry," Cal said as we were cleaning up the training room before we left, "we all had to find out the best ways to expand our talents. You'll figure it out soon enough."

"All of you have been doing this since you could walk," I reminded him.

He nodded. "You're not wrong, but we have all had the odds stacked against us at one point or another. Sterling was a girl among boys and, worse, eventually a woman among men. Many didn't want her to succeed purely because of their pride. They never gave her an inch, and she had to work twice as hard just to show them that she belonged there. And even harder to make them sit down and shut up.

"Roman excelled in the physical areas of our education, sure, but he was blocked academically by every teacher and tutor he came across. He is smarter than people ever gave him credit for. Where I may be able to strategize against someone I'm fighting, he could lead armies on multiple fronts. But our teachers refused to let him ever test as a strategist because they had already made up their mind that he was only ever meant to be a soldier, not a leader. He turned his physical advantage into something that eventually made them listen to him.

"For me...Well, I was very small for my age. Truth be told, I was sick. Some childhood illnesses that stole any nourishment from me before my body had a chance to absorb it. It made me weak and fragile. I was bullied by boys in our year, as I'm sure you've been told. To the dismay of my father, I was not the strong warrior he had prayed for. Despite my illness, he demanded that I still work and train as any boy would. It was exhausting mentally and physically. Having a parent that was determined to make you into the version of yourself that they had always envisioned is hard enough, but when it's nearly at the cost of your life..." He shook his head, lost in a moment. "It's hard to understand why you would want that relationship to still work out.

"Anyways, the pain of training was nothing compared to what I went through while sick. When it was at its worst, my bones felt hollow and ached deeply. It was as if I could feel my muscles ripping apart and knitting themselves back together again, merciless and slowly, as my joints would start to swell. Nothing at first made it better, and I would spend days curled up waiting for it to end. But I came out on the other side of it all, still painfully at a physical disadvantage, though."

"How did you get better?"

"I never really did. I manage my symptoms well enough now, though some days are worse than others. I have medicinal remedies to keep the reactions at bay, mostly, and I have learned what diet suits me best. But ultimately, I give my father credit. He sent me here to train with the elite, and I quickly learned that I was more observant than my counterparts. I learned what I needed to do to survive. And what I needed to do to never get sent back home."

"Your mom never stopped him from pushing your training?"

"They are very traditional where I am from. My mother was raised to believe her place was under my father's rule and that she should not defy him. She is a tender woman, and I know deep down it hurt her to see me in pain."

"You said you still want that relationship to work out? Why?"

"It's a hard feeling to explain. I was angry for a long time, but eventually I knew my anger alone wouldn't propel me through the world. Not without eating away at my soul. Once I allowed my anger to start to dissolve, I was able to see the other side of it. My parents were born and raised in their traditions. It's all they know. In some backwards way, my father doing what he did was out of the deepest love. A man who cannot protect his family is better off dead in the eyes of the people in Etnos. He is cast out by everyone and left to his own means, which on the island is equivalent to nothing.

"In a way, he made me as strong as he did so that he could send me here. I may not have been the strongest, and I may still have failed in his eyes. But I wouldn't have been turned away from society here. I still would have had a chance at a life. My parents are imperfect, but they did the best they could within the ways they were taught to view the world. For that, I do not fault them. We had a happy childhood outside of these things, and though they are not minor issues, I still love them, and I cling to those good times. That being said, I am still allowed to set boundaries regarding what I am willing and unwilling to share with them. For the sake of my mental health as well as our relationship."

"And Eliza?" I asked cautiously.

"Her situation with my parents is not something I can pretend to understand. Other than the fact that we both couldn't fill the roles our traditions required, there is nothing similar. I can no more pretend to imagine being a woman in her shoes any more than she can say she understands how much that illness took from my soul. Even as twins. Our experiences shape how we walk this earth, and her relationship with our parents is not mine to influence. I can only hope that one day we can all be in a room together, one more time, even if it's to shout and argue. I'd prefer that over only three of us together, mourning in silence."

I let his words sink in. "They are lucky to have a son as understanding as you."

"We all deserve grace and compassion, and we need it most when we are at our worst, don't you think?"

I nodded, and he smiled briefly. "I've got the rest of this up here," he said, gesturing to the dowels and books about psychological warfare we had spread out on the floor. I thanked him and made my way to the library, where Mal was waiting for me.

CHAPTER 17

It had been six weeks since my first day of training. I had settled into my routine easily and had even found time to read for fun during the day. But just when my workouts started to get easier, Roman would increase the repetitions or the weight of the sword. I lasted longer in the ring with Callen, though I knew he was holding back for my benefit. Mal and I continued to study history and notable wars, as well as demonology.

He quizzed me weekly on what strengths and weaknesses belonged to certain Creatures of the Night. Some of these study sessions ended up involving not only Mal and I, but Roman, Callen, and a bottle of wine. We would eventually fall into a drunken game where we debated what demon would win, given it had attained a superpower of some sort. This usually ended in my suggestion winning by vote of both Malachi and Callen, leaving Roman to pout only until a new round had started.

We still worked tirelessly, but I didn't feel isolated anymore—things had almost returned to normal, at least between me and the boys. We drank and teased one another. The seriousness of our lessons disappeared with the setting sun each day, allowing us a few hours to simply enjoy one another's company.

I didn't see Sterling.

I was reassured by Malachi that she hadn't abandoned me. One night, after Cal and Roman had retired, it was just the two of us in the library. His expression all but begged me not to lose faith in his friend.

"She's given up on me."

"That is far from true."

"Then what is it?"

"She...she wants to make sure you are as ready as possible. I think that a part of her worries your studies with her would be filled with distractions that would keep you from reaching your full potential."

"Oh, why? Because she's so good looking, I can't contain myself?" I was acting like a petulant child.

"More because her fear for your life, her not being impartial to you, would distract *her* from teaching you. For all the fun we still have together, there is a huge consequence attached to these outcomes, Kai."

And he was right. The heaviness of the situation was not lost on me. No matter how tired I was, I carried it with me. It crawled into bed with me every night, weighing on my chest as I slept. That night, it was too much to bear. Sleep couldn't find me, and I finally gave up. I threw the covers back and made my way out onto the back patio.

The chill in the air was a welcome respite from the never-ending heat of the day. I made my way to the banister and looked out towards the water. The horizon was no longer visible as the night sky blended into the swell of the inky black sea below. Had it not been for the roar in the distance, the scene would have been nothing but a starless void with no hint as to what may lie on the other side. An involuntary shiver snaked down my spine, and I pulled my sweater tighter around my shoulders. I was grateful for the waves; they were my anchor of familiarity in a world still so foreign.

But was my old life something I wanted back now? I racked my brain trying to imagine what life would be like had I never met Sterling. If I had stayed home the night of that boy's death, instead of trying to drown my sorrows in booze and strangers, I wouldn't be finding myself subject to a deadly trial. Maybe I would be at the hospital laughing with my coworkers as we struggled to make it through our last shift. I could be getting ready to meet friends for the opening of a new restaurant. Hell, what if I had met someone, and we were heading on our fifth date?

The swirling thoughts dissipated as quickly as they formed. The consistencies of my past life, which usually brought me joy, now seemed to have the color seeped out of them. I recognized the intricacies of my work relationships. There was something baffling, I realized, about sharing traumatic experiences——being able to blindly trust someone in a stressful moment——but not knowing something as basic as when their birthday was. In truth, I didn't *know* them. There was a sad truth in knowing deep down I wouldn't be meeting friends. I would be home, alone. My close friends had relationships, kids, careers that didn't afford as much free time. Besides, I couldn't remember the last time a new restaurant opened up in my part of town. But what was even harder to admit? I knew I wouldn't be on a date.

For all the stress and emotional whiplash of the last few weeks, all of the pain and confusion, I knew I would make the same choice again. Regardless of the hardships, I loved the new friends I had made. I felt strong in this new life, and the unknown of my future was infinitely more enticing than the mundane comforts I had left behind. But above all else, I knew I would never choose a world in which I hadn't met Sterling. Her emotions had been erratic at best, but that didn't matter. From the moment she spoke to me, my life's trajectory shifted, and by some miracle, it felt as if I was finally orbiting around the right spot. I felt her aura as it moved through the house. Those weeks after we had met, I was aching and hollow in a way that felt what I could only assume was something akin to being incomplete. And after we had kissed? My world was on fire. No, I would gladly walk the path yet to be revealed rather than go back to how things had been.

"What the hell are you doing?" I asked myself. I startled when someone scoffed behind me.

"What you're doing is ruining my me time," Eliza shot back. I couldn't see her face, but the sneer laced her words.

"You scared me."

"If you startle this easy in the dark, you are in way over your head with the whole 'I wanna be Nephilim too' bit."

"I didn't mean to disrupt your night. I thought everyone was asleep."

"Well, you thought wrong. Consider my night tarnished," she murmured. It was only after a faint glow illuminated her features that I realized she was speaking around a cigarette as she lit it. The smell of smoke joined the salty sea air as Eliza snapped her lighter shut with a click.

"By all means, don't let me continue to be an inconvenience," I shot back, "the porch is big enough that I don't have to intrude on your alone time." I started to walk around the backside of the house so as not to cross in front of her.

"Okay, fine," Elizia groaned, "if you can stand there quietly, you can stay."

I hesitated, momentarily torn between my desire to be close to the ocean and my instinctual avoidance of Eliza. Damn desire, rarely did instincts win where it was concerned. I went back to my spot on the banister. "Thank you," I nodded in her general direction, "I just couldn't fall asleep and——"

"That's the opposite of being quiet."

"Right."

The tense silence hung in the air. It was more uncomfortable than if she had been hurling insults my way the entire time. I was beginning to question my decision to stay when Eliza started shifting in her chair. Clearly, I wasn't the only one who hated this particular silence. Still, it surprised me when she broke it first.

"You like the ocean?"

"Yea——yes," I stammered as surprise filled my tone. *Is she actually trying to have a conversation with me?*

"Sterling had mentioned that you did. Something about waves and silence being loud. Which makes zero sense to any sane person."

"She told you that?" My heart immediately started to beat in my chest, and I questioned if I should be excited that she had remembered this about me and had bothered to mention it, or if I should feel self-conscious because they had been talking about me.

"Don't get all schoolgirl on me, Stray. It had been a minor note about you, an afterthought, before we moved on to...other topics. Needless to say, she didn't have many thoughts after that." Eliza blew out a line of smoke coolly. My eyes had adjusted by now, and I could see her suggestive smile. I couldn't stop the sound of disgust that emitted from the back of my throat.

"Is that really necessary?"

"What?"

"Your entire attitude towards me."

"You must be feeling sensitive. I have no idea what you're talking about."

"For God's sake! The innuendos, the digs, the fucking nickname! Why are you so determined to make my life a living hell?"

"Oh, please. You're being dramatic."

"It's glaringly obvious that you hate me. You make it clear the second I walk into a room. But what doesn't make sense is why you hate me so much. Is it about Sterling? For crying out loud, Eliza, she's with you. In whatever twisted game this is to you, you won. Is that not enough? Do I need to be more miserable than I already am in order for you to be satisfied?"

"I don't *have* Sterling. And for the record, she doesn't have me, either. Not that I owe you any type of explanation, but we are not in love. She is as free to walk away from me as I am to leave her. No strings. But she hasn't yet, though even when she's there, she seems far away. In all honesty, I would respect her more if she walked, but she is so fucking determined to prove something to everyone. We all know the only one she has convinced is herself."

"What do you mean?"

"That night that you and the boys got belligerently drunk? I know about what happened after. Your little rendezvous in the library."

"Eliza, I..." My palms were sweating, "It was just a kiss. It didn't go any——"

She dismissed me with a wave of her hand. "I couldn't care less if the two of you fucked until dawn. Like I said, no strings." She took a drag from her cigarette. "Even if I do hate losing. No hard feelings."

"Then I'm confused. If you truly don't care, why do you lash out at me every time a quip comes to mind?"

"It's partly because they just come to me, and it'd be such a waste of my talents. But you were somewhat right about one thing."

"Which is?" I prompted when she didn't go on.

"I don't hate you, but I do hate your presence in this house."

"How is that any better?"

"I'm sure that, as a person, you are decent in your own boring, Edenite way. In another life, I may not have ever given your existence a second thought. But you're here now, and that causes me strife. You're not dumb. You know what the consequences are for everyone in this house if we get caught with you here. Everyone that I have ever loved and cared for stands to lose everything because they cannot pull their rose-colored glasses off long enough to see the liability you truly are. Especially Sterling."

"She understands the––"

"Do you know why Sterling and I started sleeping together? She stormed into my room like a bat out of hell the night you met at *Arcane*. I asked if she was okay, but I couldn't even get the question out before she kissed me."

My stomach rolled, and I turned to face the beach, partly so Eliza couldn't see me wince and partly so if I threw up it wouldn't cover the porch.

"Relax," she muttered not unkindly. "I'm not going to tell you the gruesome details of our tristes. Anyways, I pulled away in shock. We had always had a friendly flirtation, but neither one of us had ever remotely thought about crossing that line. Clearly, it was written on my face because she started apologizing like a maniac. Once I got her to stop saying 'sorry' on repeat, I told her I needed an explanation.

"'I met someone,' was all she'd said at first, and I made some smart-ass remark about how I was flattered she decided to kiss me instead. She was dead serious as she looked at me, 'It's different, Liza. There is...more to her.' I told her I was happy for her, but still, it wasn't adding up why she was so frantic.

"'It can't happen. For so many reasons––like the fact that she is a Daughter of Adam––I can't seek her out again. I need your help, Eliza.'

"From there, she laid out her plan; I was supposed to help her forget about you. I think in her mind, the sex was less about being the mechanism that helped her forget, though. If you ask me, I think she was relying on her deep sense of honor, pretending that it was something more between us so that she would never let herself think about you. You know her. She would never hurt someone she loved. And we did love each other. We *do*. But it's a love forged in childhood memories and friendship, and it apparently didn't stop her from trying to have her way with you."

"Again, Eliza, nothing happened."

"If your pendant depicting one of the strongest Archangels hadn't reminded Sterling of her indiscretions, would either of you have stopped it?"

I shook my head.

Eliza scoffed, "At least you're honest. When we were fighting that night, it wasn't about my jealousy. It was about the fact that she had become extremely lax with you. She was flirty and inviting, and I knew that the battle to see reason was already lost. Since you woke up and found us in the library––which is where I intervened before she could be found sitting at your bedside––she hadn't touched me. I tried to play the girlfriend role and make a move. Sterling reacted to my touch as if it were a red-hot brand. I was reminding her about why we had started sharing a bed in the first place, but my pride was hurt from being rejected, regardless of who or why. I started yelling at her.

"I told her that she was an idiot. I had disrupted the house with this fake relationship that no one really believed, and it had been slowly eating away at our friendship. Despite all of that, I had kept it up because I cared about her. And instead of holding up her end, she had brought you into our home. I reminded Sterling that she was the one we all looked to and that I had lost my faith in her. I told her that I had never known someone to be as weak and as selfish as she was."

I thought back to that night as Sterling had caught me by the wrist.

"What the hell are you doing?"

"'Something selfish.'"

And then we had kissed.

"You guys had been fighting before I got here, though," was all I could say as I remembered the boys telling me the bickering had started weeks before.

"We were," she agreed. The fair silver glint of her hair piled on top of her head bobbed as she nodded. "She managed to stay strong in the beginning. I washed your number from her hand. She didn't mention anything about that night, and I thought maybe she would be able to get past it. Of course it wasn't that simple. Sterling started lingering in front of the doors of *The Arcane Club* when we would go out. One time, she almost went in looking for you, and I had to pull her away. That was the night we argued for the first time. She started talking about you in her sleep, too. For a reason I will never understand, Kai, you are a siren song, and she is the sailor who has been on a ship for far too long. She's infatuated."

"Was," I corrected, "She barely looks in my direction these days."

"She threw her moral compass, along with her fear of consequence, out of the fucking window. She compromised her integrity, her honor, all because of a single moment with you. The fundamentals of who she is, completely discarded. Can you blame her? Besides, it's probably for the best if she never bats an eye at you."

"What if Mal is right and I *do* belong here? Would it really be so terrible?"

"Even if he is, even if your whole suicide mission to face Metanoia is successful, you are a stranger, and I don't trust you. Especially not where my family is concerned. Sterling cannot live her life feeling as if she has thrown away everything she has ever worked for because she was obsessed with a girl, and if I have to save her from herself, then so be it. I would, I *will*, choose them over anything or anyone, including their own delusional happiness. And you will find that they feel the same. We have survived too much together to let someone come in here and make us question our loyalties to each other. I mean no disrespect when I say this; You're an outsider who will always be on the outside looking in. And if I could have you out of here by first light, it would be in the best interest of this entire house."

"Don't tell Roman he was right," was all I could think to say as the night's revelation sank in. "He would be unbearable."

"That he would be," Eliza conceded as she tilted her head back and blew out a long line of smoke.

We remained in our respective places as a new type of silence fell over the two of us, and a clearer picture of Eliza slid into place. She was right. I was an outsider, and it was crazy of me to think that, when it really came down to it, I could ever truly be one of them.

Morning arrived quicker than I wanted. I ascended the stairs to the training room, attempting to anticipate what Roman had in store for the day. But it was not Roman I found waiting for me.

Sterling stood in the middle of the room, looking out the window into the front yard. Her golden hair was pulled into a long braid running down the length of her back. She wore black pants and a black fitted jacket.

"I thought I was meeting Roman today."

She must have heard me coming up the stairs because she showed no signs of being surprised. "Roman had other business to attend to today. He and the others have also reassured me that you're ready to include my training sessions in your schedule." She turned to face me.

A small part of me felt proud at the praise from my friends. *They think I'm doing good.* "So where do we start?"

"Step into the ring," was all she said as she unzipped and removed her jacket. She was in a black tank top that hugged the outline of her body. As she turned to hang up her jacket, I saw the upper curves of the wings inked on her back. They were visible on either side of where her top met to run up her spine.

"What?" I asked, confused. "This is our first lesson, though. You haven't *taught* me anything."

Sterling walked to the ring that was drawn on the floor between us. "They said you were ready, and I want to see what that means."

Incredulously, I shook my head and stepped to meet her in the ring. We circled one another for a time before Sterling lunged. She was fast, and I was not ready to counter. Her fist caught my shoulder as I turned, unable to block properly. She landed a knee into my unprotected abdomen and knocked the wind out of me before stepping away.

I steadied myself, resuming my guard. This time, I moved toward her, looking to land a jab to her side. But I miscalculated, swinging into thin air as Sterling kicked at my kneecap. As my leg buckled, her fist found purchase in my ribs, and I fell to the floor.

She stood looking down at me, barely working to breathe despite how fast she had moved.

"I think they oversold your preparedness. I'll let them know to touch base with me in another couple of weeks." She turned away from me, walking to retrieve her jacket as I scrambled to my feet.

"You're leaving?" I asked, shocked.

"You aren't ready," was all she said as she walked across the ring to the stairwell.

"Do you want me to fail?" She hesitated, her hand hovering over the banister. "Because right now it feels like you want me to."

"How could you even think that would *possibly* be the case?" she asked quietly, her back still to me.

"The last time we spoke, you said you would train me. Then, come to find out, every day I'm working with the boys, not you. I haven't seen or spoken to you in *weeks*, and then you come up here, land two blows, and decide that I'm not worth your time? After you haven't taught me anything?"

Sterling turned to face me, eyes gray and grave. "Don't be ridiculous, Kai."

"You don't get to just walk away. I don't care about whatever reason you may have. This is *my life*, and everyone seems to be on board with helping me, except you. You brought me here, and now you have to play your part, regrets or no. I can set aside my feelings, so why can't you?"

"You have no idea what—"

"Damn it, Sterling! I am tired of being tiptoed around. I am tired of being told I don't know this or that. For once, give me what I deserve: a fighting chance at surviving this." She stood in place, staring at me.

"You once told me you were as good as your word. It's what brought me here to begin with. So, stand by it now and train me for fucks sake!"

She dropped her jacket to the floor, closing the space between us in three long strides. "Is this what you really want? A *real* fight?"

"Yes," my tone was clipped. I set my shoulders and raised my chin slightly. In that moment, I hated that I had to look up at her in order to meet her gaze. "Don't hold back. If you're going to hit me, do it like you would with anyone else. I don't want special treatment."

Her demeanor was cold. "Fine. Have it your way." She walked to her side of the ring. We circled one another for a fraction of the time now. In those moments, I reminded myself to think about my lessons with Callen. *What can I use to my advantage?*

Sterling's fist came towards my face. I barely had enough time to move my head. Her fist found air; the momentum from her follow-through caused her to twist more than she had planned. Rather than finish the spin, she stopped. I took the opportunity, releasing two quick jabs to the right side of her rib cage. A sound came from her, but it was more from surprise than pain.

She recovered quickly. As I advanced towards her, back still partially to me, she dropped low when I swung for her head. Swiftly and still crouched, Sterling spun to face me and stood fast, breaking my guard with a swift motion. She grabbed my shoulders and pulled me towards her as her knee came up to connect with my stomach. Air sailed out of my lungs as I doubled over, but before I could catch my breath, the left side of my cheek was met with Sterling's right hook.

Stars began to form at the corners of my vision as I stumbled backward towards the edge of the ring. My ears were ringing, the left side of my face throbbing with heat, already starting to swell. I reached up gingerly to touch my cheek as I tried to force my lungs to catch some reserve of air. It was then that I felt it. The air crackled around me. It wasn't nearly as strong as it had been before, but it was present, nonetheless. I rolled my shoulders and took up my stance once again as I stepped closer to the center of the ring.

I didn't think that I could beat Sterling, but I was determined to give her one hell of a fight. I thought through what I had learned once again. Sterling was too seasoned to make little mistakes, like looking where she would move next or favoring one side to strike.

But she doesn't know that I know these are mistakes.

Everything moved at about half the speed it normally would. I glanced down, as if I was going to aim a low kick to her knee, moving my body to look as if I had planned to do just that. As Sterling reached to block, and hoping to catch my ankle in the process, I switched up my stance and brought my left fist down on the right side of her face. Taken by surprise, she left her core open. There, I delivered three quick jabs to her stomach. Sterling turned her face towards me and immediately saw the second left hook aimed for her face. She blocked it, aiming to sweep my legs out from under me. She was successful at knocking me backwards, but not before I grabbed her shoulders, bringing her to the ground with me.

I felt the sensation of falling for what felt like an impossibly long time before my back met the floorboards. I held on to what breath I could, but even that was lost as Sterling came crashing down on top of me, driving an elbow into my right side as she did. I wrapped my arms around the back of her neck, my left arm looping under Sterling's right. If I kept my elbow perpendicular to my body, she wouldn't be able to move her arm past my shoulder. I had effectively trapped her upper left arm to her side, but she was still hitting my ribs. One particular punch landed harder than the rest, and my tension on her neck loosened just enough that she was able to gain more motion in her right arm.

Another punch to the left side of my face almost had me yelling out in pain, but I remembered what Roman had said about breathing through it. Instead, I tightened my grip again, shoving down my desire to give in to the pain. I planted one foot against the floor while dropping the other and used all my strength to roll us to the right. I loosened my grip just enough to drop two quick elbows to Sterling's face. Blood sprang from her nose, providing enough of a distraction for me to pin both her wrists under my left hand.

Straddling her hips and using part of my weight to pin her arms, I looked down at her. The blood from her nose was starting to run down her cheeks. Her chest was rising and falling fast as she worked to catch her breath. She raised her chin up towards my raised right fist, "Are you going to take another swing?"

I dropped my arm, my left hand releasing her wrists. "No," I said as I wiped sweat from my brow. To my surprise, my hand came away red. *So not sweat, but blood.*

"Big mistake."

Within seconds, I had been flipped over, headfirst, and landed on my back. Sterling was over me now. Her ankles and feet wrapped around mine, locking one leg on each side of her hips. I scrambled to do anything to counter, but she caught a wrist in each hand with a vice-like grip. She wiped her nose on the back of her forearm before lowering herself onto her elbows, which were placed on either side of my head.

"Never stop until someone yields or is dead. Otherwise, the fight isn't done." We were so close I could almost taste the salt on her skin. I felt every inch of her body pressed up against mine as we both breathed quickly. The weight of her was unbearable, the proximity like a drug. Her eyes were alight with something that set me on fire. I felt a deep ache growing in my core that had nothing to do with the match, and I knew I would let it consume me.

Suddenly, my conversation with Eliza was replaying in my mind.

"'She threw her moral compass, along with her fear of consequence, out of the fucking window. She compromised her integrity, her honor, all because of a single moment with you. The fundamentals of who she is, completely discarded.'"

Whether it was hate or love, I'd be damned if I let it ruin her further.

"I yield."

Confusion spread across her face as I said this, but she didn't move. "I yield," I repeated. "I'm done, Sterling. Now please, let me go." Realization dawned on her finally, clearing the dreamlike haze, and she quickly scrambled up. Taking her outstretched hand, she hauled me to my feet before taking a step back. Her nose was still bleeding.

"I'm sorry about that," was all I could say as I gestured towards her face.

"This is nothing," she waved me off. Her ice blue eyes ran up and down my body, assessing for any visible injuries. "I'm sorry about your eye."

I shrugged. "I'm the one who said don't hold back."

We were both quiet for a moment. After six weeks, it was a lot easier to fight one another than to speak. Sterling looked at me from the corner of her eye. A small smile played on her lips. "That was one hell of a fight, Kai. I'll give you that."

I smiled in return. "My teachers have been good. Guess I have them to thank." Sterling nodded her agreement as the door opened to reveal Malachi.

"I thought I'd find you here," he said to Sterling, "we've been dispatched to an industrial area in the States. Apparently, a small pack of *Epiales* has set up camp in a factory, and it doesn't appear they want to leave anytime soon."

I watched as Sterling's mindset instantly switched, transforming her into the seasoned leader she was. "How many are there?"

"Five, I believe."

"Casualties?"

"The custodian on tonight's shift, unfortunately. But no one outside of that. No other Edenites are aware of their presence at this time."

Sterling nodded. "Have everyone geared up and ready to leave in ten minutes. Will you be joining us?"

"I think I just might," Mal replied. I could tell by the way he shuffled his weight from foot to foot that he was anxious to get in on the action. I didn't know if he had been out since he had lost his wings. "What of Kai?"

Sterling barely glanced at me, but before I could protest, she said, "Find something that fits her. She can come along for the experience. I don't think that she should need it, but it's best to make sure she is armed in some capacity, too."

I looked back and forth between the two, utterly bewildered. *She's letting me come?* Malachi barely held back a smile at my reaction as I quickly thanked Sterling before following him down the stairs and into the hallway. Concealed in the excitement was a single fact. I was about to face my first demon.

And I was terrified.

CHAPTER 18

I followed Mal to a hallway closet, where he began to flip through clothes. "I'm sure we will be able to find something suitable for tonight." He came back into the hallway holding up two hangers. On one was a pair of black cargo pants, while the other had a dark gray jacket. "Do you know if you have a black thermal in your wardrobe?"

"I think so. If not, I have a black long sleeve at the very least."

Malachi nodded. "Sleeves are important. But the thicker the material, the better. I will leave these to you," he handed me the clothes. "I'll meet you outside your door shortly, and we will fit you with some weapons."

We parted ways, going to our respective rooms. Once inside, I caught a glimpse of myself in the mirror. The gash over my eye was still bleeding. A small trickle had started to roll down my face. I cleaned it quickly and made a note to ask Mal for a bandage before we left.

I looked through my wardrobe and was surprised to find that I did have a thick, thermal, black, long-sleeved shirt. I dressed quickly. The pants were big on me, and as an afterthought, I decided to use the black belt that had been mixed in with my things. I tucked my shirt in and grabbed the jacket off its hanger. I pulled it on, impressed at how light it felt. The material was something akin to leather, but it was half the weight. I flexed my arms, hugging them to my torso. It moved easily with me. It fit perfectly.

I pulled back my hair and slipped on my black running shoes. As I approached the door, I heard a knock from the other side. Pulling it open, I found Mal. He was dressed in black and dark green. In his hand, he was holding a pair of black boots. "These will likely have better grip and mask the sound of you walking better than those would," he gestured down to my feet.

I started to trade my shoes for boots, and Mal leaned against my door frame. "They are a little big, but better than loud and slippery."

"Thanks for finding all of this for me."

"No thanks necessary. We will make it a point to get you items of your own. Ones that fit properly." He smiled at me as I finished lacing the last of the boots, and gave me a once-over, seemingly satisfied with what he saw. "Are you ready?"

"As ready as I can be, I think."

"Then follow me."

We walked down the hall towards the training room stairs. Mal took a left, entering through the doorway of the armory. He flipped on a light, and we were met with walls of weapons. Swords of all sizes sat displayed along the back wall. Spears and shields were hung on racks throughout the room. Every kind of weapon you could think of seemed to be present.

"We tend not to use these much. Everyone has their own small personal collection they store in here as well. But it is always good to be stocked in a pinch. Now, let's see what works for you."

In the end, I settled for a set of six throwing knives. The pants had three slots on each side, perfectly made to hold these smaller blades. Mal suggested I also take a short sword.

"Though I doubt you'll need any of this, it is better to be somewhat prepared." He fitted a sheath with a strap to my back, allowing the sword to run parallel with my spine. "How do you feel?"

I shifted my weight back and forth. "Pretty good. It's all a lot lighter than what I had expected."

"Yes, well, we have to be able to move fast yet remain safe. There are special Nephilim tailors who create fabrics specifically meant for fighting gear. Plus, it helps that this sword is ten times smaller than the one Roman kept throwing into your hands."

"Not terrible in style either." We walked back into the hallway, aiming for the stairs to the main entryway.

Mal smiled at me, "The Nephilim, warriors especially, inherited some sense of pridefulness from their angelic blood. They do not like to do anything without some level of flashiness."

"You're telling me that the theatrics Roman indulges in daily are *hereditary*?" I ask with mock horror.

He laughed. "Unfortunately for his future children, I am afraid it may be so." The humor settled in the air as we reached the top of the stairs. We paused there, and Mal turned to me.

"Are you ready?" he asked me once again. His tone was more somber than when we had been in the doorway of my room. The relaxed way he leaned against the frame was now replaced with a light yet tense energy that emanated from him. The weight of what I was about to encounter was sinking in.

"I realize I don't know what I'm doing," I said hesitantly, "but I trust you guys."

"Good. That is an important part of these things. Trust those of us going into the fray with you. Listen to what any one of us tells you. These demons are cunning and quick. Slippery like a serpent with serrated talons that are sharp as a tack. Their teeth are like razor blades, and they are extremely driven by any given chance to rip out your throat. Though they will settle for whatever internal organ they can g et."

I felt the color drain from my face slightly. We had been discussing demons in our lessons, but this was the first time my education was related to something I would be face-to-face with in a short time.

"As awful as it sounds," Malachi continued in a gentle voice, "it lends us an advantage. Because they are so, let's say, 'food-driven,' they hyper-fixate on that single goal. It makes them predictable."

I take what little comfort I can from this as I turn to head down the stairs.

"One second." I turn to look back at him. He lightly slides two fingertips over the gash above my eye. I felt a slight tingling sensation, and then, as quickly as it started, I felt nothing once more. Reaching up to touch it, I was surprised when my fingers met healed skin rather than the open wound that had just been there.

"How did you do that?"

"I may not be able to summon the Fires of Heaven without my wings, but I still have a few tricks up my sleeve." He gave me a wink before gesturing towards the stairs. "The others will be waiting for us."

He was right. As I cleared the last step, four pairs of eyes looked at me from the room off to my right. Sterling was dressed similarly to what she had been wearing this morning, but she had traded her thin athletic jacket for one of the black Nephilim battle jackets. The other three were dressed in various shades of blacks and grays, though Eliza was more adorned in a silver of some sort amidst the black material. It matched the color of her hair. The pants that both Sterling and Eliza wore hugged their legs more than the ones that the boys wore. Where the latter was wide-mouthed, almost equivalent to a boot cut, the girls wore something more closely resembling joggers. Looking down at my own gear, I now realized just how big my pants were on me. There had been a buzz in the air. It was one of adrenaline and excitement between friends. But, like always, the mood instantly shifted when Eliza saw me

.

"You can't be serious."

"I'm sorry?"

"You don't really think you're coming with us, do you? I mean, you don't know *anything* about what we do."

"Liza," Callen whispered, trying to stop his twin.

"You have been practicing or whatever it is you call it in the training room for a few weeks. We have trained together for *years*. You are just going to slow us down, Stray."

"Liza, stop." Callen's tone was sterner now, but she didn't acknowledge him.

"Nothing more than a liability," she sauntered to stand in front of me. Her top was revealing, especially for something that was meant to protect her in a fight. The V-neck of her shirt dropped lower than most. I noticed that her boots were adorned with heels and couldn't begin to fathom how she walked in them. Much less fought demons. "But hey," she said sweetly, "maybe the demons tonight will take care of you. It would save this house time in training you purely on a *hunch* that you could ever be one of us."

"Enough." It was one word, but it was filled with a command saturated with disapproval. The room felt as if it dropped several degrees. I looked to where Sterling stood, fists balled at her sides, her jaw clenched. She was as solid as stone, and her eyes were just as hard. "I gave the order for Kai to come. I expect *all* of you to protect her in the same ways you would one another, if not more fiercely. She has come far and has farther still to go. Any failure to treat her as you would other Children of Angels, specifically as one who lives in this house, will be considered as defiance of a direct order, and you will answer to me." I had never heard this level of strictness in her voice. Sterling looked around the room, gaze stopping on Eliza. "Do I make myself clear?"

Eliza nodded and walked out of the front door without another word. "Callen," Sterling started.

"I'm on it." He followed his sister, jogging down the steps after her. Roman followed behind soon after. Then, it was Sterling, Mal, and I who were left standing there.

"So, how do we get where we are going?" I asked gingerly.

Despite Soteria being far removed from any traces of Eden, the trip was quick. Malachi explained that, under normal circumstances, he would open a portal that would bring us directly to our location. However, since his fall, he could no longer channel enough angelic power to summon one.

"So, what do we do now?"

"We travel the old-fashioned way," Callen provided.

As he said this, Sterling pulled something out of her pocket. It was a glass orb, known as an Agni. These were angel-made, and when forged, a small amount of Heavenly Fire was deposited within. Nephilim could not create Heavenly Fire from nothing like the angels, but they could be taught to call for it through imbued objects, so long as it had been encased and blessed by the sign of an Archangel. Most Nephilim carried one as a source of light.

The sigil of Gabriel that had been etched into the clear glass of Sterling's Agni started to glow. I watched in awe as she cupped it tightly in both hands, eyes closed in concentration. There was a bright flash. As my eyes adjusted, I registered the swirling green light in front of us where the front door had been. Without hesitating, Eliza stepped through, followed by the boys.

"What is that?"

"It's still a portal," Sterling reassured. I could see the hint of amusement that danced in her eyes as she watched my curiosity take shape. "Malachi's portal would be a direct shot. But the Nephilim have to get around undetected somehow. So, Arcadia granted us the ability to use some of their power. But it comes with stipulations. You have to be adept at reaching for Heavenly Fire and controlling objects that have been imbued. The portals are also tied to fixed points—specifically houses of worship."

"Does the type of religion matter?"

"Not at all. Worship is worship as far as Arcadia is concerned. It will take us to the nearest point of our desired destination."

"I see. Does it...?"

"Feel like you're falling through a void?" she grinned wryly. "Oh yeah. The first time will make you a little queasy. But I promise it will pass quickly. Do you trust me?"

"Of course."

"Then after you, Ms. Novak."

I stepped into the light and immediately felt weightless amidst the fall. I found my stomach in my throat, ready to relieve me of my dinner. In an instant, my feet hit solid ground. I stumbled with the impact and was grateful for Callen who was able to catch me before I fell on my face. My cheeks heated as I thanked him and I heard Eliza scoff before Sterling stepped through.

I looked around, taking in the massive cathedral that stood before us. Stained glass windows projected an array of colors onto the steps, covering us in the warmed hues of the mosaic.

"I thought we would end up inside?"

"It's a lot harder to get in and out undetected if they have closed for the night. The stairs are still considered hallowed ground," Callen explained with a shrug. He started down the steps of the Cathedral and we all followed as dusk started to fade.

We walked in silence for a short time, arriving at the warehouse as darkness began to settle. Without so much as a word, the others split into an unspoken formation around the entrance. I went to step forward with them, but Sterling, who had remained at my side, grabbed my shoulder. "You listen to everything I tell you. Do you understand? If I tell you to run and hide, you do exactly that. Remember what you have learned, and never hesitate. Trust your instincts, Kai." I nodded as I watched her immediately dismiss the concern that had started to seep through her cool exterior. We were already here. There was no use in being worried. Anxious energy began to roll off of her in anticipation, and I could tell she was ready for the fight.

Sterling gave the signal, and Roman opened the door. Everyone filed in, Sterling in front of me while Roman protected my back. The door closed behind the group soundlessly, plunging us into darkness.

A series of chatters and clicks that made my skin crawl echoed deeper inside the warehouse. I was startled as light flared around me. Various shades tinted blue, green, orange, and pure white were emitted in a circle that I found myself standing in the center of.

The others held their Agnis aloft, their backs to me as they faced outwards, searching for the source of the eerie sound. It began to grow closer and closer, though the pools of light revealed nothing around us. A metallic tang assaulted my sinuses. It was coppery and not unlike the scent of blood as it chilled. It was a scent so thick I could almost taste it. A shiver ran down my spine as I decided to chance a look at the ceiling.

Slowly, I raised my eyes to the rafters. Flashing on the edges of the orb's light, I glimpsed talons that came to a vicious point as they propelled grotesque bodies that were black as night along the ceiling. I tapped Roman, who was the closest to me, on the shoulder. Barely moving, I gestured with my chin at what I was looking at.

"Well, shit," was all he said as he aimed his light towards the ceiling. There were more than five hanging on to the rafters. They had milky white orbs for eyes, and three rows of jagged teeth that were set into an oblong skull. One let out a screech so loud it made my ears ring.

"SCRAMBLE!" Roman yelled, tucking me under his arm as he broke formation. We moved just in time. Where we had been standing just two seconds ago was now taken up by three *Epiales* that had dropped from above. They clambered over one another gracelessly, biting and screeching as they tried to disentangle themselves. Others fell from the ceiling soon after. I tried to count them as Roman drew his sword, pulling me behind him, and came up with twelve.

The others were in various places throughout the warehouse now, their Agni the only indicators of who was who in the darkness. I saw metal reflect light as weapons were drawn, and it was a matter of seconds before the squelching sound of steel and flesh filled the space. The metallic tinge in the air only grew more potent. As I looked around Roman's shoulder, I could see the demon he had cut down up close. It writhed on the floor, squealing, until the ichor that seeped out of it covered the area in which it lay. I may have been mistaken, but I thought I saw singe marks starting to form in the concrete.

Three more monsters descended on Roman and I once they noticed the demise of one of their own. "A little help here would be nice," he exclaimed as he took up his stance. But he wasn't talking to me. He was talking to the others, the ones who knew how to handle these situations. We took a couple steps backward, our backs coming up against a concrete wall.

Another grotesque scream sounded, and quicker than humanly possible, Sterling was at our sides. "You couldn't have killed the other two that were following you before you decided to come over here?" Roman chided. It was true. Sterling had been battling three at once, but only managed to overcome one, it seemed. The other two beasts followed her scent, adding to the small horde before us.

"I thought you could use more of a challenge, brother. Can't have you going soft on me." She was enjoying this. In the face of walking nightmares, Sterling and Roman were making jokes.

Roman's smile was feral. "It'll take more than this batch of bastards to challenge me."

They moved as one. Together, they fought back the five *Epiales*, even gaining some ground back. The gnashing of teeth was a sharp snapping sound. The powerful jaws of one off to Roman's right almost came down on his forearm. "Roman!" was all I could exclaim, but he pulled his arm back at the last second as Sterling brought her blade down, successfully decapitating the monster. Blood began to spray in my direction, and Sterling yanked me to the side.

"Their blood will burn you. If you aren't careful, you could go blind." She was breathless, but her eyes glowed a pale green thanks to the subtle golden hue as she watched our enemies advancing once again. "Do you see Mal over there?" I looked over to the right, across the warehouse, as Malachi effectively speared one of the two demons he fought.

"Yes I—Yes, I see him."

"When I tell you to, you are going to run to him, okay? Go as fast as you can and don't look back." I glanced back over to him, and suddenly the wide-open expanse of darkness seemed to separate us by miles.

"Kai, Roman needs me, and I can't help him finish off four of these things while I worry about you. Do you trust me?" I nodded. "Don't look back," she murmured before she turned back to Roman's side. She said something to him, and then the two of them began to slash wide arcs with their swords, giving us room to move away from the wall.

Over her shoulder, Sterling looked back at me quickly. "Now!" she exclaimed, and I took off at a dead sprint. I was aware of something following me, and I could hear it gaining on me. Fast. But I did what I was told and kept my eyes trained on Mal. I felt the creature's breath at the nape of my neck, teeth eager to close down on my throat, and I started to prepare for the end. Suddenly, I heard the shred of skin being torn apart by a blade, followed by the monster's screech into death. Heat bloomed along my left shoulder blade, but I paid it no mind. Within seconds, I had reached Mal.

He tucked me behind him, and I took in the fight from my new point of view. Roman and Sterling fought three demons now. I couldn't see the body, but I assumed one had broken off to chase me before it was met with one of Sterling's well-placed throwing knives.

Those two were on my left, and the twins were directly in front of us. They fought back-to-back, one *Epiales* already dead at their feet as they worked against two more. Eliza had a rip at the top of her thigh, blood brightly contrasted against her ivory skin in the Agni light. Callen's jacket had been lost somewhere in the darkness, and he fought in his plain black t-shirt. His hair had grown longer in the last few months, and now it was plastered to his forehead with a sheen of sweat.

I mentally started to count the screams I had heard, along with the demons still standing, just to be sure they added up to twelve. As I finished my count, two more squeals sounded simultaneously. Both Malachi and Eliza had dispatched their respective *Epiales*.

"*Epiales* use darkness and heat to find their way around." Mal turned to me. "I am going to find the switch to the lights. Hopefully, it will discombobulate them enough that we will make fast work of the rest. You stay here. When Callen is done, and the coast is clear, you go to him." Without waiting for my confirmation, he bolted for the steps, leaving me in darkness alone.

I watched as Eliza yelled something to Cal before sprinting into the distance, towards Roman and Sterling. Feeling useless, I started counting again.

Two dead at my feet. One that chased me and the first one Roman killed makes four. Sterling killed one before, as well as one with Roman. There's six. The twins killed two more, bringing the count to eight.

I reassessed the field before me.

Three still fighting back by the wall makes eleven.

I watched as Cal cut the legs off of his *Epiales* and was about to deliver the killing blow.

Twelve.

As he raised his sword, I saw the darkness ripple and shift.

Thirteen. "Shit," was all I could say. I grasped at my sides for one of my throwing knives. To the best of my abilities, I tried to aim for the creature in the darkness. My heart sank as the clang of metal sounded on the floor. I hadn't killed the beast, but I was able to distract it. Instead of coming for Callen, it had set its sights on me. I panicked, throwing three more knives with no aim or success. That's when I started to run through the dark.

"Kai, I'm coming!" I heard Cal yell. But the *Epiales* was already zeroing in on me. And then I tripped. I slid across the ground, my bones aching in protest of the impact. I rolled to my back as the smell of metal came closer.

"Pull your knife, Kai. Find a weapon and hang on!" Cal sounded too far away for it to be possible that he would reach me in time. But I drew another throwing knife, unable to get to the blade strapped to my back as the creature stood over me. I slashed wildly, blindly, as it repeatedly tried to lunge for my throat. It bit down on my knife, ripping it from my hand, and threw it off to the side with a shake of its lethal head. This was it.

My demise looked down at me with unseeing eyes. And, in turn, I refused to look away. It made clicking sounds as it slowly lowered its head. Despite the electricity now burning in my body, I didn't fight. I knew I was out of options. It was then that the clicking stopped. The *Epiales* pulled back, almost as if to take a proper look at me. Its head cocked imperceptibly, and time felt as if it stood still.

The only warning I got was the pool of light from Cal's orb as it encircled us, followed by a screech so loud I thought my ears would bleed. He had delivered a blow to the creature's leg, though it was not fully severed. The weight of the *Epiales* was swiftly off me as it turned towards Callen. He continued to try and lead it away from where I lay on the ground. He moved quickly, swinging his blade in wide arcs. One arc, however, lodged his sword deep into the side of a wooden pillar. I watched as he pulled repeatedly. Desperate for his weapon, he turned his back on the approaching demon so that he could use all of his strength to pull harder.

But it didn't budge.

"CALLEN," Eliza screamed, and my blood ran cold.

Callen turned as a long arm backhanded the upper right side of his body. He went flying to the side, and the *Epiales* was on him just as fast. I got to my feet and was moving towards the pair when I saw the glint of talons in the Agni light as they came down.

Callen screamed in agony.

Willing my legs to move faster, I came up beside him, but not before the sound of pain racked his body once more. The lights came on, and the beast thrashed its head from the sudden attack on its senses. It didn't see me coming before I had severed its head from its body.

I turned my attention to Callen as the sizzle in my veins dulled down to nothing. His breathing was fast and shallow, and he was barely holding on to consciousness. Three long talons had been slowly raked across his abdomen. In their wake, the monster had left jagged, deep lacerations running the entire surface of his stomach. Blood was flowing from the wounds and beginning to pool under Cal. I worked quickly to remove my jacket and hold pressure over the area. But it wasn't going to be nearly enough.

Mal had been right, the light had stunned the monsters, and the other three wasted no time finishing off the remaining *Epiales*. Soon, we were all gathered around Cal. Eliza's eyes were glassy as she held back tears when she reached her brother's side. She picked up his hand, and he gave hers a weak squeeze in return.

"It's going to be okay, Liza. I promise."

We used Roman's jacket, since it was the biggest, to continue to try and stop the bleeding. When we reapplied pressure, Callen screamed out. "It's going to hurt like hell to move him," I said, looking up at Sterling.

"Mal," she said, looking from him to Callen. He cleared his throat and nodded, knowing exactly what she meant. With what power he could muster, Malachi ran a gentle hand over Cal's eyes. As he did so, Cal's body relaxed some, falling into a deep sleep. Mal's fingers ran through Cal's hair, lingering for a moment, before he stood once again. It was a simple touch, yet I could've sworn we all looked away as if it were the most intimate of acts.

"Malachi and Eliza will take him home first. Summon the healers and get him settled. The rest of us will follow. We have to call this in, and I can't leave the scene until the report is finished."

Mal picked Callen up off the ground, and we all walked outside. We watched as he started to jog in the direction we had come from. The limp body of his friend in his arms did not seem to slow him down. Eliza followed along, periodically speaking to Cal softly, though none of us could hear the words spoken from this distance.

Once they were out of sight, Sterling called dispatch to give them a summary of what had happened. She paced as she explained that there would need to be a clean-up crew here before dawn to dispose of the demon bodies and mop up the gore. There were unheard questions coming from the other end of the call that suggested whoever was on the other end needed more details than what Sterling was capable of giving them. She raked a frustrated hand through her hair as she tried to ghetto off the phone with little success. Finally, something in her broke, the professional demeanor vacating her voice altogether. She promised there would be a more detailed report filed later in the week.

"But for now," she said curtly, "I need to prioritize the health of my friend." Then she hung up the phone.

I wanted to reach out to her, to say something. I wanted to do whatever I could to comfort her. But the cautious look that Roman gave me, a slight shake of his head barely perceptible, told me it would do no good now.

We ran back to the cathedral in silence. But Callen's screams haunted us the whole way there.

CHAPTER 19

Roman, Sterling, and I walked through the front door and stood in the entryway where, just hours before, we had all been gathered together. The sunny day had given way to a cloudy evening, promising a storm. Gray light filtered through the windows, painting the room in dreary colors to match the feeling in the air. It was the most somber and silent the house had been since I had arrived.

We sat down on the various couches and chairs in the living room. Sterling had not made eye contact with Roman or I since she had hung up the phone. I kept my eyes on the floor, not entirely sure what I was feeling at that moment. I had just seen real demons. I had killed one with my own two hands. I had watched as it almost killed one of the kindest men I had ever had the pleasure of calling my friend.

And I knew I was somewhat at fault.

My chest began to rise and fall rapidly. I couldn't catch my breath as the realization hit, and I heard myself starting to quietly gasp. The burning in my eyes warned me of the tears that had started to build, and I could feel the impending breakdown. Silently, Roman reached to wrap his strong arm around my shoulders, pulling me tightly to his side. I looked up at him, eyes blurring at the edges as I fought the tears from slipping. His dark almond eyes were soft, his face vulnerable, showing me that he, too, was worried about Callen and that it was okay to feel this way. Without saying a word, he took a deep breath in and let it out slowly. I could hear his voice in the training room as he reminded me that not all pain was physical.

I began to match him breath for breath. After a while, my eyes dried, and I could feel my respiratory rate return to normal without much effort on my part. I mouthed a silent thank you to him, and he gave me a tight smile while squeezing my shoulder. His arm stayed draped over my shoulders.

We sat in silence for what felt like hours, though it had probably been closer to forty-five minutes, until we heard light footsteps come down the stairs. Malachi stepped off the bottom step and joined us in the living room.

"He is in pain," he started hesitantly, "but I think he is going to be okay."

The breath we had all been holding was released in a collective sigh of relief. "The healer is upstairs now, mending what she can in order to expedite the healing process and decrease the infection risk. But she will not be able to heal him completely."

"No injury to any of his organs?" Sterling asked. She was thinking systematically, her tone robotic. It sounded like me when my patient had died all those months ago. She wasn't being harsh; she was doing the only thing she knew how to do in order to keep it together for Cal.

"No, thankfully. This *Epiales* was a sadistic one. It would have taken its time flaying him open before killing him. Luckily"—Mal looked to where I was sitting on the couch— "it didn't get the chance to take another swipe."

"It shouldn't have ever gotten the chance to begin with," I murmured quietly. Mal reached his hand out to me, and I took it, holding on tightly.

"These things happen, Kai. It is but a hazard of the occupation." Multiple sets of footsteps sounded on the stairs. We all stood when Eliza and a woman who must have been the healer appeared. They were talking in hushed tones and paid us no mind as Eliza opened the door.

"Thank you for your work. We are forever in your debt," she said, bowing her head as the woman left. Eliza shut the door behind her.

She turned to face us, her hands clenching and unclenching at her sides. Her lethality was more evident than it had ever been as she leveled her gaze at me.

"*You,*" she snarled. She strode into the room, and I shot to my feet. "I told all of you she shouldn't be here! She's a *liability,*" Eliza snapped. The last word dripped with malice. Her glare was razor sharp, the weight of it crushing, but I stood my ground. My shoulders set as I returned her gaze unflinchingly.

"Liza, had she not helped Callen—" Roman started to say calmly.

"Had *she* not been there at all, Callen wouldn't be hurt. She froze. She was unable to protect herself, and he went to her aid."

I could feel my emotions from earlier trying to make themselves known again. *Not here.* I shifted my feet ever so slightly, my stance faltering. It was enough to draw Eliza's attention. She was a predator, ready to strike at the first glimpse of weakness.

"Get a grip. You have no right to cry over his injuries." She raked her eyes up and down my frame. A cruel smirk ran across her lips. Look at her. Blood was spilled in her name, and she goes weak in the knees. She can barely even stomach the consequences of her inadequacies, of her *failures,*" she spat the words out like the taste disgusted her. Then she looked to the others, glancing at the boys before finally settling on Sterling, who was standing behind me now. "I told you she was weak. She doesn't know what this life would require her to witness. What she may have to do. War is hell, and the meek don't survive. The thought of her living to see the end of Metanoia is impossible. She will *never* be one of us." She looked me over once more, sizing me up, "You're all wasting your time."

Eliza turned to leave, dismissing whatever any of us might have had to say. It was then that I felt it. The electric wire thrumming under my skin stirred once more. It set my nerves on fire. The sensation was not like when the air shifted and time slowed in the training room. No, this feeling was erratic and volatile. A feeling deep within, like when I had dreamt about it weeks ago. Only this time, I felt some small semblance of control as it rose to the surface. Not thinking about my actions, I pulled the last remaining knife from my side.

"Weak?" I echoed Eliza, shrugging off Roman's arm. She didn't turn, only kept walking from the room. Without hesitating, I pulled my arm back and, before the others could move to stop me, I let the knife fly. Mal was at my side, reaching to secure my arm. But it was too late. It spun through the air, end over end. Time stopped as I watched the weapon rotate with precision.

Thud.

It found its mark.

The knife hilt waved back and forth as it struck true—right into the beam beside Eliza's head. It was so close to her, in fact, that a few strands of loose silvery hair were cut short and drifted soundlessly to the floor.

They might as well have been bombs.

Eliza whirled to look back at me. Her emerald eyes were saturated with deadly venom as she stormed back into the room to stand right in front of me. "What the hell was that?!" she growled.

"You think I can't stomach this? That I don't *belong?*" Eliza didn't answer. The tension was thick in the room, ready to break at any moment. No one dared to move as we faced each other. I pulled my arm away from Mal, the gesture rougher than I had intended.

"What happened to Callen is awful, and I feel terrible for the part that I played in it all. I really do, and I can't say enough how sorry I am. To *him*. But to sit here and say I can't stomach what happened, and that I cannot be one of you because of it, is as unfair as it is untrue." Eliza started to speak, but I held up a hand, cutting her off, "I have been covered in the blood of strangers. I have held them, adults and children alike, as they take their final breath. No family to be found. I have had to look a mother in the eyes as she told me she wasn't ready to bury her child," my voice caught, "I have lost the only family I have ever had.

"I may not have been trained to fight; I wasn't brought up to be a warrior. But I know what pain and suffering and loss and death look like. I am *very* well acquainted with them," I stepped toward her, realizing I was taller than she was now that we were close. "Callen is hurt, but he will live. Mal was much worse, and he is here now. And do you know *why* he is here, Eliza?" My voice was cold. With the static in my veins, I could feel the apprehension of everyone behind me. I'm almost sure that I felt Mal wince as I stepped into her space, now nearly nose to nose with the woman before me. "Because of *me*."

The rise and fall of her chest picked up. Behind those eyes, I could tell she was torn between wanting to throttle me and wanting to just hit me outright. I kept going, "Do not stand there and tell me I am unequipped to face this life of war and blood, Eliza. I was baptized into it long before *your* friends ended up at *my* door."

She snapped, pulling back to strike. If she hit me now, whatever happened after would be fair game. I prepared for the open palm of her hand to make contact with my cheek. My blood sang at the prospect of a fight, the way I wished it would have earlier this evening. But before she could touch me, a voice drew everyone's attention.

"Eliza. Stop." Callen appeared at the top of the stairs. His torso was wrapped several times to hold pressure on his abdomen. He looked paler than normal, though he stood tall with his shoulders squared. His voice was a command.

"Cal," Eliza dropped her hand, turning to face the stairs, "you should be resting."

"Hard to do that when you're out here causing chaos."

"Kai is to blame. She—"

"She saved my life. It was my fault that she needed help in the end. Kai could have done nothing, frozen by fear, and watched as the *Epiales* attacked me. She could have let me fend for myself and hoped for the best. But she didn't. She fought for me until the end. Very successfully, I might add," he gave a small nod in my direction.

Eliza's voice was softer as she addressed her twin, "She will ruin us all. The punishments that could come down are—"

"It seems you are the one hell bent on ruining us, sister," Callen murmured. "I think it'd be best if you left for a little bit. Cleared your head."

"Callen, don't be stupid. This is my house too. I have a right to be here. More of a right than some mere Child of Adam."

"You have been antagonizing the household for some time, and I have kept to myself how awful you have been as of late. I am speaking up now. Take some time away."

"Cal," she started to protest. Hurt seeped into her voice and, for a moment, I almost felt sorry for her. "I'll go to my room, but I—"

"Leave, Liza." Callen's voice was ice. "Now."

In that one word, Eliza's will seemed to break before our eyes. Her brother, her *twin*, was sending her away. He was choosing to defend me over her. Something she had promised me would *never* happen less than twenty-four hours before.

The silence was deafening.

"Fine," was all she said. Without another word, Eliza turned and walked out, slamming the front door as she went. I looked back to the top of the stairs. Callen used the railing to ease down to the floor. He pinched his nose between his two fingers as Mal and Roman moved to him, muttering about getting him back to his room. They helped lift him from the steps and disappeared down the hallways.

I turned to Sterling. Her face was vague, not giving anything away. Her eyes, however, bounced between the door and where Callen had previously stood. They trailed to the knife in the beam before finally landing on me. She had watched her family splinter, and I had been the starting fracture.

"Sterling, I'm so sorry. I didn't mean for it to escalate like that. I just felt so angry, and I couldn't think straight. I couldn't stand there and let her keep going. I'm sorry, I don't know what it was. I —"

Sterling held up a hand and said, "So, you do listen to Roman."

"I'm sorry?"

"That was a perfect throw."

Of all the things she could say about tonight, she wants to discuss my form? I stood there unable to find words, unsure of what she wanted me to say.

"Try not to splinter the wood when you remove the blade from the post." With that, she made her way upstairs.

I stood in the living room, alone, as the gray light faded into darkness. With no idea of what to do with myself, I went to my room.

I couldn't sleep.

The borrowed gear lay heaped together in the corner. When I had taken off the jacket, I had been surprised to find that a spot of sickly gray spread over one shoulder. I thought back and remembered the burning in my shoulder as I ran from the *Epiales* that Sterling had killed. That spot must have been where its blood had landed. I placed the remaining throwing knife on my nightstand, while the sword lay in the shower, its Damascus steel blade bloodied from the night's events. I would figure out what to do with it all in the morning.

As I lay there, I felt myself floating away. My mind was no longer anchored to anything. My sadness and anger had left me hours ago, and I was now left to navigate the new reality crashing down around me. I could no longer stand to be alone, feeling as if I were drifting away from the world. I threw my covers back and pulled on a pair of sweats. Grabbing a random sweatshirt from my closet, I walked out into the hall.

Not thinking much about what I was doing, I ventured down the hall to a door just across from the library, next to Roman's. I only stopped long enough to take a breath before I grabbed the doorknob. *If it's locked, then I'll go back to my room.*

I met no resistance as I twisted it.

My previous gentleness was replaced with haste as I quickly opened the door. I crossed the threshold and shut the door behind me, afraid that I would lose my nerve and leave if there wasn't something to stop me. I felt my nerves spike, and I silently cursed myself. I was here for answers, so why was I on edge? My heart rate started to pick up as I surveyed the room before me.

The floor was made from the same light gray planks as most of the rest of the house. The walls were pure white. A perfectly made bed was off to the right. A wardrobe and simple desk were to the left, pushed up against a wall. The walls were mostly bare, save for a few charcoal sketches that were tacked above the desk. A bookshelf faced my direction. It was up against the far wall just to the left of a window.

The window looked out over the expanse of grass in the front yard. The paneled glass was set into an alcove, and a bench similar to the one in my room rested beneath it. Sterling was lounging on the bench, a book in hand. She was bathed in moonlight, and her normally tanned skin absorbed the hues of silver. Her hair fell around her shoulders, still wet from a shower. She had on light gray joggers and a black sports bra. Leaning against the wall, her legs propped up on the bench, she looked like the picture of ease.

That is, until I came bursting through the door.

So quick I barely saw the movement, Sterling had a dagger in her hand, her book temporarily discarded at her side. She hadn't stood, but her posture had shifted, and she was ready to launch from her seat as her attention snapped to the door. The tension in her shoulders visibly receded when she saw it was just me.

"You know," she said, setting the dagger aside and reclaiming her book, "it's impolite to barge into someone's room. You have no idea what you might have stumbled upon during someone's private hours, with an entrance like that." The insinuation, vague as it was, sent a small thrill through me.

"Where did that dagger come from?" was all I managed to ask.

"I don't much like to be caught in the rain without an umbrella, let alone unarmed in a time of need. You will find that, throughout the house, especially, I am always quite prepared." She had resumed her position on the bench and started to scan her book again, only glancing out of the corner of her eye when I remained standing and silent. "Did you come here to tell me you ended up splintering the beam?"

"No."

"Then to what do I owe the pleasure of this late-night call?"

I had so many things I wanted to say, so many things that I needed to sort through on my own, but didn't know where to start. And the more time passed, the longer my list got. "How did you know that I took Roman's critiques?" It was not the least important question, but it was the easiest.

"You were having trouble with your blades connecting, aside from a few lucky throws, over the last week. Roman said that he had been trying to correct your form. And I watched as he told you to retime your release, keep your elbow up, and finish your follow-through." Her eyes did not leave the novel in her hands.

"You *watched*? I haven't seen you once since we discussed my starting to train. What do you mean you watched?"

"I meant it when I said you didn't have any idea about my part in your training. I have been in the background, providing my knowledge as best as I could." Sterling looked away from the book, an easy smirk on her face. "C'mon, Kai, do you think Roman is *that* good at teaching someone how to throw a blade?"

I know she was mostly joking, but still, I thought about when I had watched Sterling in the training room. How she had dispatched the demon tonight in near darkness. She was adept and lethal. And *so* magnificent.

I shook my head slightly, "I don't get it."

"I'm afraid that doesn't tell me much."

"I just want answers, Sterling."

"You and me both," she closed her book, the index finger of her left hand holding her place, "You have come into my room, late into the night, just to talk about the fact I complimented you? *That* is what you want to talk about? Honestly, Kai, after you accused me of being indirect, the least you can do is come out and ask what you really want to know. Don't be a hypocrite, it's unbecoming."

My skin heated in anger. "Callen almost had his insides flayed. Eliza and I almost killed each other in front of the entire house. I just saw and killed my first demon, and all you could do was mention the precision of the blade I threw at Eliza's head?"

"To be clear, you threw it *near* her head. And without that precision, it probably would have been a much more fateful and fatal evening."

"Are you serious?"

"You're not saying you *were*, in fact, aiming for her head, are you?"

"No, I just don't know why—"

"Then the comment still stands. It was a perfectly executed throw, and your lessons with Roman pay off when you listen to him. I'm just stating the facts." Sterling's feet were on the floor. One of her legs was bouncing restlessly, as if she were full of energy that needed to be released. Though we were not yelling, our tones were terse.

"Instead of stating the facts, why not address anything that happened? At all? *Ever*?"

"So, this isn't just about tonight?"

She was right. It wasn't, not completely. It was about everything. Because with each situation I thought I had put behind me, there was one common thread.

"You *never* address the elephant in the room. I have had open, meaningful conversations with the boys. Hell, even Eliza told me more than what I have gotten from you. With you, there is *never* an explanation for anything. Not since you told me about the Nephilim and Soteria that first night."

Sterling stood from her seat by the window, tossing the book aside. Her joggers were rolled, settling on her hips where the contours of her abdomen made a V-shape before disappearing under her waistband. She crossed her arms stubbornly over her chest. "That was way more of an explanation than you were entitled to, and look where it got us. In reality, anything I tell you will just doom us further. And what's more? I don't *owe* you anything, Kai."

"Is this how you treat everyone else? Do you just order your friends around and then expect them to follow you blindly? For God's sake, Sterling, just be honest for once about what is going through your fucking head."

"You want to know?" Her chest was starting to rise and fall faster. "You want me to tell you that every time one of them comes home with so much as a cut, I blame myself? You want to hear all of the ways my mind tells me it is *my fault* when someone gets hurt?" Her hands began gesturing wildly as she spoke, words tumbling out faster. "Do you want me to describe the dark feelings that nearly overcast my judgment when I saw Callen lying there, bleeding? Or tell you how much it hurts my soul to watch my family fracture apart? Because of my actions, nonetheless? That, when I thought that *Epiales* had you before Callen stepped in, I had never felt so helpless?"

"What could make *you* possibly feel helpless?" My voice was raised, tired from everything that had happened.

"Because it all became real, Kai!" she exclaimed. "I might as well be damned because I have watched as I destroyed the strict boundaries I have set for myself, all in the name of you, without hesitation. The second I kissed you in that library, my feelings for you couldn't *not* be acknowledged, no matter how hard I tried to fight it. And the moment I finally let myself realize what you meant to me, the weight of every decision, every consequence, involving you suddenly had the power to suffocate me."

She walked to the bed, sitting down at the end with her back to me. Sterling held her head in her hands like she had on the way home from the warehouse, her emotions showing in her posture more and more with each passing second. I took a few more steps into the room, but didn't dare to move closer, unsure of what I should do.

"Do you want me to say," her voice was coarse, her accent heavy as she stared at the floor, "that I have been observing every single lesson of yours in secret because, rather than train you myself, I am a coward who sent her friends to do it?"

"Why would you even think for a second that makes you a coward?" I asked, my voice softening.

"Because I feared that if I was solely the one to train you, and you failed, I wouldn't be able to live with myself. I brought you here. I put you in this position. If you died having only learned from me, then it would be as if I had killed you myself. And I didn't trust myself to be impartial in your tutelage because I knew I would be trying to find ways to save you the entire time, and you wouldn't have my full attention."

The sudden admission surprised me. Ever so slowly, I walked over to the bed where I sat next to her. Her face beheld both pain and natural beauty as she continued to speak without looking at me.

"I told myself I would let the people I hold in the highest esteem teach you, uninterrupted. I would only step in when the time came to assess if you were ready to face Metanoia. Then, I would help polish and fine-tune your skills.

"However, it proved to be very difficult for me to remain uninvolved. Not because I didn't trust the others, of course, I trust them with my life every day. No, it was because I found myself constantly thinking about how you were taking to the training. I spent my days wondering if you were learning quickly or struggling. I had sleepless nights where I worried that you may not be taking care of yourself or that they had been too rough on you. I was constantly warring with myself.

"It didn't go unnoticed by the rest of them, either. They all suggested that I be a sort of silent teacher. I'd observe and give them feedback on what I noticed was either helping or hindering your progress. Of course they were doing a phenomenal job, and my notes were minimal."

Sterling breathed a laugh and shook her head. A small smile crept over her face as she looked over at me. "You know, I was so desperate to contribute in some way the first few days that I all but fought Mal to let me deliver your food trays."

"You brought me the food?"

She nodded. "Mal thought it would help me compromise with myself. He knew my true feelings on why I struggled with the decision to have a hand in your training, though I am sure Roman and Cal had some idea, too. They know me well enough."

"You said you couldn't stay away," I said slowly, "but I didn't see you for over a month. Even though you didn't want to train me, you didn't have to avoid me altogether."

"I did, though."

"Why?"

"You said Eliza spoke to you. Did she tell you of our arrangement?'

I nodded.

"Then you will know that I had to stay away because, since I saw you at *Arcane*, I haven't stopped thinking about you. I left you at your house, and from the second that car put a mile between us, I felt like a piece of me stayed with you. I knew something was missing because whatever it was, it was tethered to me, and the line became tighter and more strained the further apart we got. That feeling didn't go away as the weeks went on.

"It terrified me, too. You were human, and I would never be selfish enough to have exposed you to the dangers of my life. Had it not been for Malachi, that is. It was then, with Mal on the verge of death, when I stepped onto your porch, I felt that piece slide back into place. Suddenly, I was whole again for the first time in a month. In a desperate act, whether out of gratitude and desperation, a hope for divine intervention, or something else entirely, I broke one of the most serious laws of my people.

"Then I proceeded to break more that night in the library. I couldn't stand wanting you then, and I couldn't bear the hurt I had caused you. I chalked it up to alcohol because I didn't want to admit the truth, but it didn't change the facts. There was something there, and I knew I needed to make myself scarce around you because of it."

"You were so cold towards me."

"And I hated myself every fucking second because of it, but I needed you to hate me too. Even if it was going to break my heart."

I couldn't deter the shiver that ran through me then, though neither of us acknowledged it.

"But do you know what's mad about the whole thing?"

I shook my head, processing all that she had told me as fast as my brain would allow.

"Despite the punishments that could follow, regardless of whatever domino effect I may have triggered with my decision to bring you here, I would do it all over again. I would sooner let Eliza burn the house down in a refusal to leave than never have had the chance to see you in it. My only regret in all of this is that I hurt you."

"Do you know what my regret is?"

Sadness and surprise blanketed her features as she waited for me to continue.

"That, in the time I have been here, I have only had glimpses of the Sterling I met that night. The one who, I believe, I have known you truly are this whole time. I regret the lost time, but nothing else."

Sterling's eyes lit up as she listened to me, having anticipated a much more severe response. "I'm not proud of who I have been in the past six weeks, nor of how I treated you. I swear to you that anything I said in anger was nothing more than some front in a failed attempt to keep me away from you. But, above all else, you belong here, Kai."

"Thank you," I said, "for all of it." A weight had begun to slowly dissipate from my body with each and every word she had spoken. Gently, I lay my head on her shoulder. We both tensed, only for a second, before she rested her head on mine. We sat there, enjoying comfortable silence for the first time in weeks. I sank into the moment, trying to memorize it in as much detail as possible. It felt as if it would never end had I not broken the silence with a yawn.

"It's late," I said, "We should probably get some rest." I stood with the intention of leaving.

"Would you like to stay?"

My heart almost stopped. *Is she asking—*

"Not in that way," she said hurriedly, her cheeks blushing a pale rose color in the moonlight, "I only meant that I haven't slept well for some time now, but your company brings me comfort. And, if you did not want to be alone after today's events..." Her thought trailed off, and she shrugged innocently. "I know I would like it very much if you chose to stay."

"Okay, Sterling, I'll stay." I smiled back at her, relishing the fact that she unknowingly had been holding a breath that she now released.

She pulled back the dark gray comforter to reveal silver satin sheets. We both lay back, remaining on our respective sides of the mattress. Even though she had laid all of the cards on the table, I was still hesitant to make any moves that might push her back behind that protective wall.

I didn't have to wonder for long if this was how we would stay before Sterling's hand crossed the middle of the bed and found mine. I rolled on my left side to face her. *God, she is beautiful.*

She took her hand back, moving her arm so that I could curl up to her side. I put my head on her chest while my other arm rested on her stomach. I breathed in deeply the smell of sandalwood and vanilla that I had long since come to associate with her, as she wrapped her arm around me and started tracing shapes along my spine. Warmth radiated from her bare skin, and I felt myself relax as I settled in next to her.

"You encountered your first demon today," Sterling said, "How do you feel?"

"Well, it confirmed that you weren't lying."

"Even with all of the training, did you doubt that I—that everyone here—was lying?"

"For all I knew, you were all just a house of mentally unstable people who liked to play with lethal weapons in their free time." I could feel the movement in her chest, suggesting her silent laughter. "I think that could still be said of Roman, demons or no."

The sweet sound of Sterling's laughter filled the air, and my heart squeezed. It was a sound I had rarely heard, and one I never wanted to be without again.

"Other than the undeniable proof that I'm not insane, how are you handling it all?"

"I don't think I have really had much time to process what happened yet. I was scared for Callen. At one point, I thought I was going to die, had it not been for your well-aimed throw."

"You could have chosen to yell for help, alert Callen, but you chose to take on that *Epiales* on your own. Why?"

"I knew there wasn't time. Malachi had gone to find the lights, and the three of you were too far, across the warehouse, dealing with a small host of your own. I knew I was the only option. If only I had been able to throw properly."

"What they haven't told you is that having a skill mastered is only the first step. When you throw adrenaline into the mix, you have to focus harder, be intentional all over again. It will come in time."

We lay there in silence. I stroked my thumb lightly over Sterling's side. Though her breathing was unchanged, I could hear her heart pick up speed. I smiled to myself.

"Can I ask you a question?" I asked, pulling my head up to look at her.

"Of course."

"That night in the library, when you went to leave, your eyes were a different color."

"Were they?" Her voice remained casual, but I could tell she wasn't too keen to answer.

"Yes. They were the lightest shade of brown, almost golden. It was as if the blue had burned away into honey. It happened in the warehouse tonight, too, but not as intense."

Her hand stilled momentarily on my back. "Oh, that."

"I had asked Mal about it, and he said that it was your story to tell and that I should ask you."

"It's a long story," she started to say, and I half-expected her to refuse to say more. But she surprised me when she asked, "Are you sure you would be able to stay awake for it?"

Excitement flooded me. "Absolutely."

She smiled down at me before looking back up to the ceiling. I moved my head back to where it had been, looking down at our feet and the room before us as Sterling's hand began to draw lazily once more. "Okay, let me think of where to start."

Sterling took a deep breath in and released it slowly. "My family history is a little unconventional," she said cautiously, "My parentage brought me many things—some a curse, while others have proven to be quite advantageous. What you saw that night was Heavenly Fire beginning to course through my veins."

She allowed me time to process. "Isn't that a power that only angels possess? I know Mal isn't even able to use Heavenly Fire without his wings."

"Yes, that is typically true. It is an angelic power, one that Nephilim do not have the ability to control. As you know, we can only control it by harnessing the flame in Agni orbs. Occasionally, it can be imbued into our weapon as well, but that's for a later time. In order to create the orbs, we need the help of an angel. Only once the flame has been encased in the glass, and blessed by an Archangel, can it be called upon by the Nephilim.

"However, my father isn't Nephilim. He is, in fact, part of the Heavenly Host. Because of his angelic blood, I have abilities that many, if not all, Nephilim do not possess."

"Wouldn't that ability have been passed along to descendants that are more directly related to angels?"

"Those bloodlines have long been mingled with the blood of Edenites and Nephilim alike. While some Nephilim become amazing warriors because they have closer, more direct ties to the angels, they do not carry any significant power that would obviously set them apart."

"You are twenty-six. Weren't the laws banning relations between Nephilim and Angels written *long* before that?"

"They were...and to this day I'm not entirely sure what the truth is behind my parents' complicated history. There is a lot of politics in this life, just as much as there is in your previous life. You see, my father is one of the Archangels."

I looked up to her face, my eyes wide. Half a smile crossed her face, and she nodded gravely.

"Tell me, what do you know of the Heavenly Host, Kai?"

"They are split into two factions. Angels are the general populace of Arcadia, as well as a line of defense between Eden and Hell, secondary to the Nephilim forces. Then there are the Archangels. What they say is law. While the Order of Nephi, our governing council, may be consulted when laws are written, ultimately, the Archangels have the final say. There are seven in total."

"Very good—Mal's lessons have taught you well. My mother was Nephilim, and my father is an Archangel. Because of this, I grew up stronger than my peers, both mentally and physically. I may be revered for my capabilities, but in all honesty, I wonder if it was worth it at the loss of growing up without the eyes of the world trained on me."

The change in tense was not lost on me.

"How did she die?" I asked quietly, my arm tightening around her subtly.

"As you know, we used to only live here part-time when I was younger. A majority of the time, we lived on a small island named Roavin. She was a strong woman. There was no family she could turn to; my father was rarely around. After we tried living here, when she told him that she refused to have me raised under such scrutiny, we left, and eventually, he no longer came around.

"It was illegal, their relationship. No matter where we went, talk of their affair followed, especially in the city of Soteria. That is why this house was built so far from any of the towns. She wanted to be away from the public eye. Even back home, in Roavin, she was never allowed to rest. Sure, there were fewer whispers, but they still plagued her." Sterling took another deep breath.

"I was eight when I woke up in an empty house. I looked through each and every room, though it was not nearly as big as the house we are in now. It was strange... I remember thinking that my mother never left me alone, despite my best efforts. Even if I was sick from school, she would make arrangements to be home with me. I went into the kitchen to make a bowl of cereal. I remember being worried but thinking 'nothing would get done on an empty stomach.'"

I thought back to the stashed cereal in the pantry, and I pictured a little Sterling walking into an empty kitchen as she cleared sleep from her eyes.

"I had settled into my seat, about to take a bite, when I saw it. There was a folded piece of paper on the table across from me, and it had my name on it. Curious, I pushed my bowl aside and read the letter. I read it probably three or four times before I barely registered what it meant. It meant she was gone," her voice wavered slightly, "She was gone, and she wasn't coming back."

"Sterling," I said softly, hugging her tighter, "I am so sorry."

"I still didn't fully accept it at first. I went into her closet, clutching the letter to my chest, where I curled into a ball on the floor. It was the closest thing to being with her I could think of, being surrounded by her clothes. I couldn't begin to guess how long I cried for until I finally fell asleep.

"I woke up disoriented. I was pretty sure it was dark, and I realized I was cold and alone, unsure of what to do with myself, when someone threw the closet door open. A bright light erupted from somewhere, and it hurt my eyes. I covered them, and a small cry broke from my chest. The light disappeared, and a deep voice—one I had not heard in years—spoke." She dropped her voice a few octaves and said, "'Look at me, child,' he commanded. His tone was harsh, but I couldn't ignore him. I obeyed.

"He stood in the doorway, larger than life to my childlike eyes. His wings were pure as snow, and they spread wide behind him. His face didn't move an inch when he looked upon me, a child destroyed and lost. There was no emotion in his eyes. He simply folded his arms and stared at me. 'Stand up.' Another command I followed without hesitation. He looked me over before he grabbed my arm. 'This place is no longer your home,' was all he said before we were off.

"I was brought to this house, where I had nothing to do but fill my time with training. Most of the time, it was on my own; occasionally, my father would stop in to see what adjustments needed to be made and ruthlessly made sure I corrected my flaws. Once I was ready, he sent me to the school here, in Soteria, where I progressed rapidly until I was moved to work with the boys. You know the rest from there.

"It turns out that light had not come from him, but from me as I shuddered, scared on the floor. My body reached for Heavenly Fire, shrouding me in protection when I could not protect myself. On the rare occasion I did see my father, his visits usually included grueling lessons in controlling this power."

"I can't imagine how hard that must have been."

Sterling shrugged beneath me. "I think I became numb to everything before it had a chance to fully sink in. I lost control of myself once when I was ten, after I started working with the boys. We were playing games outdoors when a group of them took my jacket and put it in a tree I couldn't reach. I was tired of being picked on at this point, and it was before I had met Cal. I ended up losing control of the Fire for a split second, and they saw it in my eyes. From then on, the rumors that once followed my mother now followed me. The Bastard Child of Gabriel."

"Your father is Gabriel?" I was shocked. He and Michael were the most powerful of the seven.

"That he is. And because of that, I had to work harder. I was held to a higher standard by my teachers and targeted by my peers."

I remembered Mal mentioning Sterling having to adhere to the rules more strictly than others had to. "They want an excuse to make an example of you, don't they?"

"I wouldn't put it past them to try, given the right opportunity. My mother is gone, my father is untouchable even where the angels are concerned. I exist to serve as a reminder of the laws the two of them broke, and I am the only one who can be punished for their transgressions."

"That isn't fair. You didn't break the law. Their choices shouldn't haunt you for the rest of your life."

"I wish it were that simple, Kai. I really do. But the best way I have learned how to survive this life is to be the best at what I can, and to follow the law to the letter."

I was angry for her. This selfless woman beside me, who cared for those around her so fiercely, was condemned the moment she came into this world. However, I decided not to push the issue. She didn't need my anger, too. "I'm sorry," was all I could manage.

"Don't be. It has brought me strength in some parts of my life, believe it or not. In others, I'm grateful for where it put me. When I found out my mother had left the house to me when I turned eighteen, and my father signed his half over without a thought, I was able to fill this place with my closest friends. I learned what family really was. I was tested by those closest to me, and it allowed me to face my personal demons. It allowed me to find you." She pressed a gentle kiss into my hair, and I felt my stomach somersault.

I snuggled closer to her, draping my right leg over one of hers so that our limbs intertwined. I counted her breaths, trying to match my own to hers. She was still running her hand up and down my spine.

"Sterling?"

"Mhmm?" She sounded content, despite the heaviness of her past.

"Do you think I can do this?"

Her hand stopped near my shoulders. "I believe that this is the life you were always meant to live, Kai. You are only just now being allowed to live it. And I think it suits you."

Then I said that which I hadn't divulged to anyone over the last month and a half.

"I'm scared."

Sterling wrapped both of her arms around me then, holding me tight. "Fear can be healthy; it keeps you on edge and alert. Don't worry, Kai." She kissed my head again. "We still have time."

Though she sounded as if she were trying to convince herself of this fact, too, I let myself sink into the moment, surrounded by the warmth of her body. She released me and sat up, but as I went to protest, she only pulled the sheets around us before lying back down. I began counting the beats of her heart until I felt myself slowly lose consciousness.

She's right. We still have time.

CHAPTER 20

I surfaced into the waking world slowly. It started with minor movements at first—the wiggling of my toes, the small stretch of my fingers. I barely opened my eyes when I felt soft skin underneath my fingertips. My hand was resting on Sterling's bare stomach. Her waistband sat so low on her hips that the haze of sleep blanketing my mind was replaced by something much less innocent. For the moment, I savored the feeling of being tucked into her side. She radiated a warmth that was so familiar it felt as if we had been this way our entire lives. I let my eyes slowly drift over the length of her body, drinking in the details.

The rise and fall of Sterling's chest was even. Her free arm—the one not wrapped around me—was laying at her side. The muscles there were defined despite being at rest. She was the picture of ease, the tension that was ever present in the set of her jaw erased, and it allowed me to see her in her most vulnerable state. Warm rays of light danced across her golden skin, highlighting a silvery-white strand of skin along her collarbone. I realized it was a scar—the one from when Malachi had saved them all. With a feather-light touch, I traced the raised area, giving silent thanks to whoever would listen that this was all she took away from that night.

I snuggled in closer to her and let out a contented sigh. It wasn't long after that when I felt Sterling stir underneath me. She rolled to encircle me in both arms, kissing the temple of my head.

"Good morning," she said, her voice raspy with sleep.

"Shhh," I whispered, "If we acknowledge the new day, we have to face the problems that come with it." I felt her silently laugh against my side.

"I could use a break from problems for one day."

We wrapped ourselves around one another, and I was hanging in the balance between dreaming and reality when I heard the door open. Sterling sat up quickly, a blade in her hand, by the time I had opened my eyes. *She really* does *have a weapon everywhere.*

"Sterling, I hate to wake you, but—" Mal's voice followed him into the room. "Oh, my apologies," he said when he saw the two of us, Sterling half-dressed, in bed together. He looked to the opposite corner of the wall.

"Nothing happened," I blurted out immediately. Sterling gave me an amused smile, not offended by the outburst.

"She speaks the truth, my friend. Sleep wasn't able to find either of us last night, it seemed, so we got to talking until it did."

"More people would believe that story if you hadn't jumped apart as though you were teenage lovers who were surprised by a parent coming home early," Mal said sarcastically. It only served to broaden Sterling's smile.

The happy atmosphere didn't last long, though, as his tone returned to one of seriousness. "Merik is here."

Sterling was out of bed faster than humanly possible. "What do you mean, 'Merik is *here*?'" She pulled on the first shirt she came across, a white one that had been discarded on the floor.

"He is approaching down the lane from town. There was no warning of his arrival; they never sent word that we were to expect him. Had it not been for Roman being out early this morning, I would not have had the chance to give you even this much notice." Something akin to fear clouded Mal's expression, looking out of place on his beautiful visage. A new sense of urgency started to emanate from him, and I could feel something begin to coil in my stomach.

Sterling yanked on a pair of black jeans, deft fingers moving quickly to button them. "You don't think—?"

"I wish I could say. I wouldn't believe it, however," he put his hands out to the side and shrugged. The gesture was full of sadness for reasons lost on me.

"Fuck," Sterling cursed, running distressed hands through her hair.

"I'm sorry," I said quietly, "who is Merik?"

Sterling swung her gaze back to me, not acknowledging my question. "Other than clothing in the wardrobe, is there *anything* else that would indicate you have been staying here?"

"I...I... The weapons and clothes. One is in the shower, the knife is on my nightstand, and the clothes are in a pile in the corner."

Sterling looked at Mal, and he nodded back, understanding some unspoken command. He turned to exit the room, but Sterling called, "Malachi." Her tone was soft. At that moment, behind the eyes of a commander, she was a girl who needed her friend.

He softened. "One moment at a time, Sterling. We will do all we can." She nodded, and he left the room, closing the door behind him.

Sterling stood by the bench seat I had found her lounging on last night. She allowed herself a moment or two, trying to work through the sudden distress brought on by the announcement of a new arrival, before she rolled her shoulders back. Standing tall, she became the leader I had seen last night as we entered the warehouse.

"Sterling?"

She walked over to the window, still not acknowledging me. When she saw no one walking up the path towards the house, she began to pace back and forth. Her hands were behind her back, and her body was tense. It was as if I hadn't spoken at all. I got out of bed and went to her. Grabbing her shoulders, I spun her around to face me.

"Sterling, who *is* Merik?"

"He is the last person we want in this house right now." Her tone was grave. She sighed, shaking her head. "He is a representative of The Order, basically a second in command. And there is only one reason he would be here."

"Me," I mutter, not needing her to say it.

She nodded. "I don't know why he would decide to pay a visit now. Maybe a debrief and to check in on Callen? But even then, those aren't usually points of interest for his position. As much as I want to believe it's a mere coincidence, I don't think we are that lucky. No, the universe is too cruel. Someone reported us."

It clicked into place then. Sterling's unfinished question, Mal's sad response. *They think Eliza sold us out.*

"What do we do?"

Her hands came up to cover mine where they rested on her shoulders. "Mal is sweeping your room, wiping it clear of any trace that you have stayed there. You will remain up here, hidden. I typically have wards placed on my room anyways; it won't pique too much interest. Hide if you must. Under the bed, in the wardrobe, wherever you can, should you hear us come this way," she said all of this rapidly, glancing to the window. "We will do everything we can to keep you safe, Kai."

Her lips pressed into my hair as she pulled me into her. I hugged her back, but the moment was too short. Sterling separated us, the cold mask slipping back into place. Without another word, she left the room. The door seemed to momentarily shimmer in gold— I assumed this was what it looked like when wards were set—before her footsteps disappeared in the hallway.

Moments after Sterling's departure, voices started to float up faintly through the small opening in the window.

"Merik." Sterling was curt. "To what do we owe the displeasure?"

"Well, well, well," The man's voice was raspy and deep, "long time no see, Valkyre. How is the Bastard of Angels fairing these days?"

"I feel it's best if we skip the pleasantries. For both our sake."

"Very well, then. I was sent because the rumor mill has been turning as of late, and The Order needed proof before it could squash them for good. Naturally, no one believes that *any* trouble could come from the great Sterling Valkyre, daughter of Gabriel. However, the tip was on good authority."

"And they sent you to check on a little rumor?" the bass of Roman's voice boomed. "What, Merik? They don't give you any *real* jobs to do there? Open schedule?"

"Oh, quite the opposite, actually. You see, I volunteered," his tone sent a shiver through my spine, "Won't you invite me in?"

It was silent until the front door was closed with more force than anyone here would have used. Merik was inside the house. I strained my ears trying to hear what was being said to no avail. Curiosity threatened to get the best of me, and I considered moving into the hallway, but I knew it was better not to risk it.

The wait was agony. It felt like hours before I heard footsteps up the stairs, voices coming closer and closer.

"If we have visitors, they stay in this room," Sterling said as they passed by me. I heard the faint sound of my door opening at the end of the hall. The voices stopped, and I pictured the faceless man inspecting every inch of it for any sign of my existence.

Apparently, he found no trace of me, because the door closed.

"What of the rest of these rooms?"

"A few are closets," Sterling said. "On this side, you'll find a closet, my room, the library, Roman's room, and an empty guest suite. Down the other hall, the armory, Callen, Malachi, and Eliza's rooms, more storage, and the stairs to our training room. Care to look up there?"

"After I check your room, along with everyone else's."

"Can't get a girl to let you into their room, so you have to hound Sterling, huh?" Roman shot at him.

"Not all of us need to sleep our way through life to feel accomplished," Merik retorted, and I could imagine the eye roll Roman didn't try to hide. "Open the door, Valkyre."

I tried to keep the panic at bay as I dove under the bed, concealing myself underneath it seconds before they stepped into the room. Merik wore heavy leather boots, and his feet were followed by those of Roman, Sterling, and Mal. He walked in large, slow circles around the room, and I was afraid he would hear the sound of my heart pounding against my ribs. He opened the bathroom door. He checked the wardrobe and even pulled the sheets back on the bed.

"On to the next," was all he said as his boots turned towards the door.

It was only now, lying on the floor in the daylight, that I noticed Sterling's room was not as clean as I had thought. She had articles of clothing in various places on the floor. I scanned the room and froze. *Oh shit.*

Merik's boots stopped mid-step at that same moment. *He saw it too.*

"Sterling, I didn't know you were such a fan of education in Eden. So much so, in fact"—he reached for a sweatshirt— "that you decided to *buy* something from a university." I watched in horror as his hand grasped the article of clothing—he held the sweatshirt I had lent to Sterling the night she had brought Malachi to my house.

"What can I say," Sterling said coolly, "a girl needs her hobbies."

"Where is she?" Merik demanded, ice lacing his words.

"Who?"

"You know damn well who, Valkyre. Where is the Edenite who has been hiding out here with you idiots?"

"I have no idea what you are talking about, Merik." Sterling gave no signs that she would cave.

"So be it." Merik's voice was venomous. "You're under arrest and are to be subjected to further questioning by The Order."

There was an eruption of voices, and I could mentally picture the boys trying to protect Sterling as Merick advanced towards her. I heard steel as three blades left their sheaths.

"Don't be fools," Merik sneered, "If you take up weapons against me, I will have every right to kill you. Something I would have *zero* issues with. And are your lives really worth losing over *her*?" He spat the last word as if the idea of Sterling's existence disgusted him.

"The real question whether you ever actually improved your skills with a sword. Tell us, did you cheat your way through the physical test for The Order like you did the written portion?" Roman snarled, "Guess we will find out."

"Stop!"

I couldn't sit idly by and watch as weapons were drawn. I couldn't allow my friends to commit further treason on my behalf. Scrambling from my hiding spot, I stood before the group.

Three pairs of eyes looked at me with devastation, while one looked at me with vengeful delight.

"Hello, Daughter of Adam," Merik sneered.

"I have a name," I said as I brought myself to my full height, "though I don't believe you deserve to know it."

"Oh, it makes no difference to me what your name is. All that matters is what runs through your veins. According to Eliza Hale"—my friends flinched at the confirmed source of betrayal— "you have been living here for some time now. They have been breaking laws, teaching you everything we hold sacred. A blasphemous thing to do, considering you're of Adam's blood."

I took in the man before me. He had cropped brown hair and cold, unforgiving eyes. He was muscled, though smaller than Roman, and dressed in all black. A leather jacket matched his boots. The sight of him made my hair on the back of my neck stand on end. Merik looked between Sterling and I, a cruel smile curving his lips.

He turned to Sterling. "You fucked her, didn't you? Wanted a little taste of the forbidden fruit?" His laugh was sadistic as Sterling's hands clenched and unclenched at her sides. "Like father, like daughter, I suppose."

"The Order," Mal ground out, "reports directly to the Archangels. You'd best mind your tongue, lest Gabriel hear the disrespect that you spew in his name."

"Last time I checked, you had been cast out from Heaven. Fallen just like that whore sister of yours—"

"*SHUT UP.*" Mal's anger flared up around us. The room became several degrees warmer as his chest rose and fell rapidly, his hand gripping the small blade tighter.

Merik sheathed his sword and raised his hands up as if he were innocent, though his smirk gave him away. "Easy, Swordson. Wouldn't want you to waste what little power you have on parlor tricks. Last I heard, you couldn't summon Heavenly Fire if your life depended on it. Now, if you boys will excuse me, I need to take Sterling in. Someone will be here to deal with this," he scanned me up and down, disgusted, "*liability* later." My blood boiled at the insult—at that word being used synonymously for me yet again. He walked over to Sterling and grabbed her forcefully by her upper arm. She jerked away, which only evoked a bigger smile from him as he gestured out the door. The defeat in her eyes was unseen to Merik, but to us, it was crystal clear. "Oh, and if you try to run," he said, looking back at me, "the punishments for the Bastard Blonde, and the rest of the house, will increase tenfold."

We followed him and Sterling out of the room and watched as they started down the stairs. The boys shouted behind me, but it was all a cacophony of indistinguishable sound. I was too busy desperately trying to figure out what I could do or say to stop him from taking her. There was something that was missing... It was then that I felt the pull under my skin, the kiss of electricity, as Merik opened the front door.

"I'm not mortal," I said confidently. The room went silent, all eyes on me.

"I'm sorry?" Merik looked as if I had told him the biggest joke in the world. Sterling looked as if I had ripped her heart in two.

"Whatever is in my veins, it is not the blood of Adam. I never knew my parents. But I do know that I can drink *caelacrimae*. I know that I am susceptible to the effects of an elixir, something that Children of Adam are not."

"Even if that is true, it's not enough to prove anything."

"But it's enough to have brought me here. It's enough to grant me a chance. Which is exactly what I wanted. Despite the protests of those present in this house, I demanded they train me in order to prepare for Metanoia."

Merik broke into laughter. "Is this true? Because if not, it is one hell of a last-ditch effort to save your lover. And not one that is in your best interest, I might add. Tell me, do you value your life? Because if you tell me this is true, you're gambling with it. Heavily."

"It's true. I sought them out and forced this on them. In the last few months, they have remained well within the law."

"You expect me to believe that Eliza Hale came *running* to The Order with a report of a punishable offense that was entirely kosher? A report that included her twin brother? Why would she do something like that?" My stomach flipped, and I was suddenly happy that Callen wasn't present. But I needed to play along. I rolled my eyes and scoffed.

"Eliza and I didn't quite get off on the right foot..." I let my eyes coyly drift to Sterling, "if you know what I mean."

Merik made a sound of disgust in the back of his throat. "Your people's fascination with her is unfathomable."

"I want to face Metanoia," I repeated, not acknowledging what he said.

He shook his head incredulously. "Fine, have it your way then," he stepped around Sterling, leaving her with us, "You get two days to prepare."

"Only two?!" Roman exclaimed, "Merik, be fair. Give the girl a chance."

"The only reason she is even getting two is because of the time it will take to summon the appropriate parties that must be present. If I had it my way, she would have hours. Consider it mercy." He looked at Sterling, "Because she admitted to seeking you all out, she just absolved you and this house of your crimes. Count yourself lucky, Valkyre." He stepped over the threshold, only to turn back around once more. "If I were you, I'd use the last of that luck to try and get her into bed, seeing as how her time is limited. I bet she's an even better lay now, knowing her clock is ticking."

The resounding smack echoed through the house.

Sterling's handprint was highlighted in an angry red on the side of Merik's face. He was visibly angry, but thought better of moving against her as Roman and Mal flanked her on either side. "I think it's time you see yourself off my property, Merik."

He turned on his heels and stepped off the porch, walking down the pathway into the front yard. "See you in two days' time," he threw over his shoulder. We watched as he walked past the gate and into the distance before heading back inside.

"I hate that prick," Roman said sullenly.

"You and a majority of the Nephilim people," Mal replied.

"He was an ass even in school. Constantly trying to go after Sterling, blaming her..." Roman paused, looking for the right word. "Her *heritage* on why she was so superior to him. Never could accept that the real problem was the fact that he is a talentless douchebag."

"Merik is the least of our issues now," Sterling muttered. She pinched the bridge of her nose between her finger and thumb. "Why did Eliza have to go and do this?"

"Do what?" We were all startled by the sound of Callen's voice from the top of the stairs. He sounded stronger than yesterday, though he was still shirtless and bandaged as he leaned against the wall for support.

"Oh, shit." Roman ran his hand guiltily through his hair. "Who wants to fill him in?"

CHAPTER 21

We sat around the kitchen table in silence. Malachi had made a plate of sandwiches that now sat untouched in the center of the table. The empty chair at the end of the table silently mocked us as we all tried to wrap our heads around what Eliza had done.

Callen raked his hands through his jet-black hair. The others had filled him in on everything that had happened, and I was able to learn what was said once they stepped into the foyer, though it was mostly insults launched from Merik that made my blood boil.

"I know he is the least of our issues right now," I began to say, "but what the hell is this guy's problem?"

"Merik Malificar," Callen shook his head, "He always had a big mouth in school."

"Still does," Mal replied. I stared at my friend and briefly thought back to what Merik had said to him. *Mal has a sister.*

"He liked to talk shit, make people feel lesser than they really were," Roman went on.

"He's a bully," Sterling said without feeling.

"That he is," Roman agreed, "and no one ever stood up to him. Not until Sterling came along."

I looked at the woman who sat across from me. Her arms were crossed over her chest as she slumped in her chair. She shrugged. "I wasn't going to endure years of torment from that worm, nor was I going to let him give Callen shit just because he got paired with me."

"Merik didn't like that a girl was coming into our ranks," Roman said. "He tried to intimidate and threaten Sterling until one day she told him to get a life."

"Did you have to fight him?"

"No," Roman answered for Sterling, "she stood up to him, something he wasn't used to people doing. She told him he needed to mind his business and that her existence wasn't hurting anyone. Sterling told him that he was the only one insecure enough to be making any real noise about her being there. Merik didn't like that... He's always had a temper; he hauled off and punched her. He hit her repeatedly after that."

"You didn't defend yourself?"

"I did enough to protect myself from any serious injuries, but in order to win a war, you can't always play the physical side. Mental warfare is just as important, if not more so at times."

At my confused look, Cal explained, "They were on school grounds, not in any sanctioned sparring areas. Fighting on school grounds is frowned upon. Something that may be seen as a vicious attack on another student is prohibited and has severe consequences. A professor came around the corner and saw the scene. He pulled them apart and, with a single glance at Sterling's bloodied face and bruises, Merik was suspended. He was forced to work on controlling his anger and attend mandated sessions where they would evaluate his progress."

"Clearly, he never made much progress," Roman laughed without humor. "He was prohibited from working in the field like us. You see, Merik wants what Sterling has. A group to lead, talent, and the loyalty of his peers. Because he was deemed mentally unfit, he must always work under someone's supervision. He will always be second in command."

"So, he is unfit to lead a small group in battle, but he was allowed a position in The Order? Over the entirety of the Nephilim?" I asked incredulously. "That doesn't make sense."

"That's what we all said," Sterling muttered.

"They believed that if he was talented enough to pass the physical portion of the entrance test, and levelheaded enough to pass the written leadership portion, he would be safe to work under the authority of others in The Order," Callen explained.

"But we all know he cheated his way through the leadership test," Roman exclaimed, "Probably paid someone off to pass his physical, too. And if that isn't enough, he went and told the whole world about how Sterling was—"

"Roman!" Both Malachi and Callen hissed at the man beside me. He seemed to realize that he was starting to say something he shouldn't.

"She already knows." Sterling shrugged, exhaustion starting to cloud her eyes. "I told her everything."

There was silence for a minute before Roman nodded and continued, "Once he was settled into The Order, Merik went to anyone he could find and told them about Sterling being Gabriel's daughter. It went from rumor to fact for everyone. At one time or another, there had been chatter. Like other rumors, though, it subsided over the years, leaving only those in The Order who needed to know privy to the truth. But after Merik...well, now everyone knows."

"It made my life hell," Sterling was staring blankly at the table.

"Merik wanted to ensure that Sterling would never rise to be his superior," Callen said.

"Not that I would ever take the position, even if there was a chance it would have been offered to me. I don't want to lead the Nephilim body."

My hate for Merik grew with every word spoken. I started to feel the static within me rise to the surface, and I had to temper the fire within. Whatever this was, it was growing stronger by the day. I needed to figure it out, and soon. *Just add that to the ever-growing list of uncertainties.*

"Circling back to the more pressing issues," Malachi said softly, turning to Cal, "do you know where Eliza is?"

He sighed heavily. "I don't. She hasn't responded to any messages this morning."

"Do you think she would go home?" Roman asked.

"Not likely," Cal responded, deep in thought, "She hasn't spoken to our parents in some time. I doubt that even *this* would make her consider asking for their help."

"We can deal with Eliza another time," Sterling spoke, shifting to place her clasped hands on the table. "The damage is done. Now we have to plan our next steps. She told The Order that Kai was an Edenite. She didn't mention her training, her being with us on the call, or anything that would so much as hint at the possibility that she is also Nephilim.

"Kai also took full responsibility for her being here. The option of her testing hadn't even crossed Merik's mind because he was salivating at the chance to arrest me. Kai's admission saved us all, but it also cost her time. They expect her to appear in two days," she looked out at the golden light streaming onto the patio, "which, after all the excitement, might as well be one day. We need to figure out how to maximize the time we have left. I need everyone to take the evening to reassess their training plans, pull the most essential pieces from it, and be prepared to get to work bright and early."

They all nodded and stood to part ways, leaving Sterling and I alone at the dining table. We stared at each other, the distant sound of the ocean filtering in through an open window. Sadness crept over her face, and she didn't bother to hide it as she broke the silence. "You didn't have to do that," she said quietly.

"Do what?"

"Tell Merik that you had come here for a legitimate shot at the Metanoia. If you had let him take me, they would have taken your memory of this place, and you would have been allowed to go back to your normal life. You would have been safe."

"I couldn't live a life not ever knowing any of you, Sterling. I couldn't live with you being punished so harshly."

"I could have. I'd have happily served my sentence if it meant knowing you were alright. But now...now you face something very dangerous, with far less prep time than we had anticipated."

I reached my hands out across the table, and she placed hers in mine. Despite the small scars that dotted her skin, her hands were soft, the calluses on her palms barely noticeable. I gave them a gentle squeeze.

"You asked me once to give you a shot to show me that this world was real, that you weren't a liar. You asked me to take a chance on you. And I said I would open my mind to the possibility that maybe you weren't crazy." She laughed a little. "You only asked that I stay in order to believe you. You convinced me, Sterling. I chose to stay afterwards. I chose to continue and pursue this path. Regardless of the outcome, it was a choice I decided to make. Now I have to take a chance and believe what I know is real within *myself*."

Sterling stood and walked behind my chair. I leaned against the backing as she placed her hands on my shoulders. She leaned her head down so that her lips were at my ear. "Spoken like a true Nephilim." Her tone was quiet, and the breath of her words tickled my ear, sending a small chill along my spine.

I leaned my head back, eyes closed, and sighed. "That's the goal."

She laughed lightly and kissed the side of my head. "I need to go and check on Callen. On top of his physical injuries, I need to make sure he is handling this as best as possible. Are you going to be okay?"

I nodded as I stood. I noticed Mal went out onto the porch, and I needed to speak with him alone. "I'm sure I can manage on my own for now." She gave me a smile that made my heart swell.

"I will find you later tonight, then." We parted ways as she went upstairs, and I turned to head out the back door.

I stepped outside into the warmth of the evening sun. Seated at the table that Sterling and I had once sat at, what feels like a lifetime ago, was Mal. He was staring into the distance, and whether he had heard me or not, he didn't acknowledge me as I took the seat across from him.

"You were quiet in there earlier," I said softly.

"I wasn't in school with them," his tone was clipped, "I had no insight into the events that transpired between them and Merik." He all but spat the name. I had never seen this side of Mal before. He was angry, terse. I let the silence hang between us. He sighed, rubbing his eyes with both hands.

"I'm sorry," he said, softer now. The tan shirt he wore, fitted to his muscled chest and arms, brought out the honey streaks in his eyes. It was a color similar to Sterling's when she was filled with Heavenly Fire, and it made me wonder if all angels had golden eyes like his. They glistened in the light, and I thought he might be on the verge of tears.

"Are you okay?"

"There are very few things I have struggled with in this life. Those that have caused me strife are never easy to face, no matter how long ago it may have been."

"I didn't know you had a sister."

"Very few people do, though I assume more know now, since I have Fallen. People love to gossip, especially about an outcast," he shook his head once, "Even the angels are not above such childish things."

"Do you want to talk about it?"

Mal looked at me then, his posture softening at my willingness to listen, "It was a long time ago. The short version is that she chose to leave. We fought because I was angry with her decisions, and we never saw each other again. I lived with the rumors about where she was and what she was doing. In time, though, the whispers were left to the wind, and only the miserable had something to say.

"When tensions were rising between me and the others, before they took my wings, my past was dredged up, and the drama began to churn once again. Remarks were made about how my sister was a traitor and a monster. They called her the disgrace of Arcadia. Our bloodline was tainted, they claimed, and I was doomed to end up just as vile as she was. Once they took my wings..." He paused, looking out to the sea. "Well, let's just say those miserable gossips suddenly feel they have a leg to stand on now."

"I'm sorry." I hesitated. "Were you close with her?"

"At one point, yes, we were very close. I am her younger brother, though we trained together as equals. She taught me everything she could. We fought side by side together, laughed together, grew up together. I'd be lying if I said I saw the fallout between us coming."

"You miss her, don't you?" I asked after a beat.

"I miss what we used to have. Who *she* used to be. But she started to change. Slowly at first, and then rapidly. Whatever remained of her, it has been consumed by something else entirely. She is someone that I no longer know."

The salt was carried on the breeze. The reds and oranges of evening light set the sea aflame. Spray from the waves as they crashed against the rocks flew into the air, refracting light in hundreds of fiery gems. They hung, suspended briefly, before dropping back into the controlled chaos below.

"You know, I love the ocean, and I never get tired of it," I told him. "But I have a newfound appreciation for it, now that everything is about to change."

We sat together, watching the sun as it began to dip behind the horizon. Any other day, its descent would be so slow, its progress imperceptible to the eye. Tonight, with time no longer on my side, it seemed to set as if on a time-lapse. I blinked, and the oranges had faded to violets and blues as another day came to a close. The water below, previously a sparkling jewel, had now turned to a dark, stormy gray. I couldn't help but take it as a sign that something ominous was about to happen.

As the air cooled, Mal squeezed my hand tighter. "Care for a bowl of cereal?"

I smiled back at him. "I would love nothing more."

"Good, because Sterling bought a new box of the good stuff."

We took up our places on the island as we took turns loading up the bowls Mal pulled out of the cabinets. I sat in the chair while he leaned against the marble counter directly across from me, and I couldn't help but smile at how much things had changed since that first night.

"How are *you* feeling after today?"

"I don't know," I told him honestly. "I don't think it has fully sunk in yet."

He nodded thoughtfully. "If I had any doubts, I would have already had you and everyone in this house hidden somewhere far from the reach of The Order. You know that, right? I believe in you, Kai. I think fate brought you here, to us, for a significant reason."

"You only think that because the 'reason' was likely that I ended up saving your life," I teased, pointing my spoon at him.

Malachi laughed his low, warm laugh, but shook his head. "I think we have yet to see what your true purpose here is. The story is only just beginning."

"I wish I had your confidence in me."

"You will find it, but for now, take heart in knowing that we are all behind you."

"I appreciate that."

I looked into my bowl, stirring the remaining milk with my spoon. Now was as good a time as any to ask my next question.

"Do other Nephilim have the power to control Heavenly Fire, or any other special abilities? Outside of Sterling?"

"Not that I have seen in my lifetime, nor in any recorded history that I have ever read. Why do you ask?"

"I have felt this...I don't know, call it a sensation, over the last month of training. And moments leading up to it, I have felt the air around me *shift*, I guess you could say."

"What do you mean?"

"It feels like electricity under my skin. It feels powerful, makes *me* feel powerful. Last time I felt it, it was like the entire essence of my being wanted to respond to a call to fight. Every fiber in me was itching for it."

"When have you felt like this?" Mal's gaze was intent on me.

"Initially, it had happened in a dream, but then it happened last night when the *Epiales* was standing over me, as well as when Eliza was going off. It was right before I threw the knife into the beam. I think it was *why* I threw it, actually." I silently recalled how my brain had felt as if it were two steps behind my movements.

"Has this ever happened before?"

"Aside from the dream? No, last night was the first time. Although the night I had talked to Sterling about training, she had thrown a knife near my head to test me, I assumed. When I didn't flinch, she agreed to the plan. However, when she threw the blade, it was as if everything stilled, or at least slowed down. I could see everything happen in slow motion. It was the only reason why I didn't flinch."

Mal watched me for a moment and then shook his head. "It seems to me that this has happened in times of stress. Almost like a heightened fight or flight response. I haven't heard of Nephilim possessing anything like that," he repeated, "but I will look into some literature and see what I might find."

I thanked him for his help, but something still weighed on me. Clearly, it was written on my face because Malachi asked, "Is there something else?"

"It's crazy, " I said, "but I feel like the *Epiales* looked at me like it recognized me somehow."

"Why do you say that?"

"It hesitated. It had every opportunity to end me, and I really thought it was going to. I should have been dead before Callen got to me, but it hesitated, turning its head like it knew me or was intrigued by me. I don't know why that would be, and it has troubled me more than I had realized, I suppose."

"Perhaps you have more luck than you realize," he said with a soft smile. "What did Sterling say about this?"

"I haven't mentioned it to her—or anyone. You are the first person I have brought it up to."

"I'm honored," he laughed lightly. "I will investigate further, but for now, you just focus on the next few days, okay? One step at a time, you will get through this."

"Thank you, Mal."

He reached over and squeezed my hand, the gesture warm and comforting.

"I hate to break up a Hallmark moment"—Roman sauntered into the room— "but we need Angel Boy here so that we can figure out the best plan for tomorrow." His hair was a tangled mane around his face, and he had opted for a loose-fitting blue shirt and black shorts. Roman would have been the poster child of relaxation, were it not for the concern he attempted to hide.

"He's all yours," I grabbed both of the bowls from the island, "I have no arguments against you guys getting things in order on my behalf." I walked over to the sink and began rinsing the dishes. When I felt their eyes on my back, I turned over my shoulder, giving them an encouraging nod. "Get out of here, I'll be okay." Roman gave me half a wave as they turned and ascended the stairs.

Once I was sure their footsteps had faded out of earshot, I braced my hands on either side of me. Leaning against the sink, I dropped my head as I let out a heavy breath. It was going to be a long night. The last twelve hours started to swarm my mind, and I didn't stop them. Yes, this had been the plan, but not this soon. Despite Mal's comforting words, I was still not convinced that I was ready. Judging by the worry in Roman's eyes, I bet they were all worried as well.

What the hell am I doing here?

If it weren't for the fact that this was the only way to absolve my friends, I don't know that I would face this. But that is the thing about adversity. We often don't have a choice when it comes to call, and the timing is always shit.

I took a couple of deep breaths to steady myself as I worked to neatly pack away the panic that was promising to set in. If the others were working this hard to give me a fighting chance, then I would work to help myself, too.

Now, what can I do?

I looked at the clock on the wall. It read 8:30. Before I could start to question where the time went, I wandered up the stairs, eventually making my way into the training room. It was empty, which was perfect. I found the stash of throwing knives that were set to the side and piled them at my feet. I started to throw them one after another. While a few more stuck in the wall than during previous lessons, I still had an underwhelming success rate. What few did make contact were farther from the center of the target than I would have liked to admit. I threw every single one before I let myself stop.

I collected each blade and returned to my spot. Before I started again, I cleared my mind. I pulled to the surface memories of the night before. I searched for the fear and anger I felt as I faced down the demons and Eliza. Sinking into those feelings, I began to feel the tingle run under my skin. It started in my fingertips and worked its way lightly up my arms and down my spine. It was a gentle caress.

I settled into the feeling and pulled new memories to the surface. Anytime I had felt threatened or alone or angry came in through a flood gate that I had thrown wide open. Every wound was on display.

My skin started to glow faintly. The caress turned into something more volatile and demanding. Somehow, all of my chaos, as if it swirled in my veins, felt as if it were something palpable that I could control. I was all too eager to pick up the next blade that lay closest to my foot.

I felt a speed in my movements I had never felt before. I released each knife, one after the other, with a force that I had not expected. With each release, I grew stronger and continued to surprise myself. Of the 10 blades I threw, only 3 did not find their mark. Those that did were almost dead center.

I let out a cry of anguish and relief. Maybe I would be able to channel this after all. Even if only a little, then I may have a fighting chance at surviving what was to come. I only needed to learn to regulate it.

The next few hours were spent trying to master just that. I stuffed the memories back into the box where they belonged. Slowly, I picked smaller moments to relive. I experimented with certain combinations that allowed me to feel the hum of whatever it was flow through me. It was a comforting feeling to have nearby. It made me feel focused and surer of myself than I had been in the last few months.

I longed to call on it in its entirety, but I worried I wouldn't be able to keep it contained, and I did not want the others to have any reason to ask questions. I suspected that if Mal was unsure of what was going on, it was best to keep it between us until we knew more. No, I would wait and, for now, would use the minimum power that was necessary in order to survive.

With sweat running down my back, my arms aching from constant use, I made my way down the stairs into the main hall. The house was still, and I wondered if everyone had turned in for the night in order to prepare for the early morning. I was about to walk to my room when I heard the sound of music in the air.

Somewhere, piano notes filled the silence. They were haunted and sad. And so, so beautiful. I walked downstairs until I stood before the door concealing the music. When I stepped into the room, I found a piano in the center of the floor. Moonlight streamed in as if it were meant to spotlight the instrument and its pianist. On the bench was

Sterling. She played as if the piano were an extension of her soul, emotion filtering from her into the keys.

I walked quietly over to where she sat. She must have felt my presence, despite having closed eyes, because she slid over a little, allowing room for me next to her. I sat down, and she started to remove her hand from the keys, the melody stopping momentarily.

"Don't stop on my account," I said, gently laying one of my hands on hers, coaxing them back to the piano, "please, finish."

Sterling, eyes on where our hands met, smiled but nodded as she took up her position once again. Her long, delicate fingers moved confidently. Each note was perfect as she struck the chords with just enough pressure to elicit the desired tone. Some notes came out soft while others had more weight to them. I watched as the movement in her hands triggered the fine muscles in her forearms. At that moment, I couldn't help but wonder how someone could be so lethal yet so delicate.

A warrior and an artist.

The song came to a close, and Sterling rested her hands in her lap.

"That was beautiful," I said in awe. The room felt heavy in its silence as the remnants of the last hollow notes faded into nothingness. "I had no idea you could play."

"I spent a lot of time alone. Even though I trained most of the time, I still needed a hobby," she raised a cocky eyebrow, "I told you I'm full of surprises, Kai."

"That you did." I laughed lightly at the reminder.

"I didn't wake you, did I? The music can carry more than I realize sometimes."

"No, I was still up. I was trying to find things to busy myself with while everyone else was occupied with their assigned tasks."

"I see," she loosed a breath and looked down at her hands resting in her lap, "I have to apologize for not considering the fact you may have wanted to be a part of that meeting." Her words came out hushed and severe. "My initial thought was that it would be more anxiety-inducing, if anything, to hear what we had not yet been able to teach you. What we do not have the luxury of teaching you."

"It's okay, I—"

"No, it was wrong of me." Sterling looked at me, her ice blue eyes clear and honest. "I have had too many decisions made for me behind the doors of rooms in which I was not allowed. It is a practice I do not wish to perpetuate. So, again, please let me apologize for my actions and any additional strife it may have caused you."

I let her words sink in, deciding the best way to word my response.

"I appreciate the apology, but it is far from necessary." She started to protest, but I held up a hand to stop her. "I say that because it did not cause me any anxiety. Normally, the idea of others making decisions involving my survival, on my behalf, *would* concern me. However," I reached slowly for her hand. She instantly took mine in both of hers. Something in my chest relaxed as I continued, "I think that the reason I don't care is because of *who* was in the room."

Steely blue eyes drifted from where our hands sat, her thumb tracing absent-minded shapes on my skin, and locked with my own. "Oh?"

I nodded almost imperceptibly. "I have been on my own for so long, I can't remember a time I wasn't making decisions for myself. Watching my patients with their families, the idea of having to allow someone to make important choices on my behalf... It was daunting. After my aunt passed, I don't know that I fully ever thought I would trust someone to do that for me.

"But…" I took a moment to clear my throat, my voice catching after mentioning Erica. "You all have only ever done right by me. I have been protected at the expense of all of you."

I dropped my gaze, watching as her gentle touch looped across my skin, up over my wrist, and back again. "Sterling, this is the most secure I have felt in years. It didn't cause me distress because I would trust each one of you with my life. I *have* trusted you all with my life. And it was probably the best decision I have ever made."

Sterling's hand stalled momentarily as the last of my words clicked into place. I searched her face for signs of a reaction. The changes were minuscule. Had I been someone who was less enamored by every single reaction of hers, I would not have noticed them. There was a small tension that had been released from her shoulders. Her eyes had warmed, and a small smile tugged at the corners of her mouth discreetly. I was surprised to note that her breathing subtly changed. The rise and fall of her chest was quicker than normal, as was the pulse barely visible in the hollow of her throat.

"You know," she started to say after a moment of silence, "I questioned bringing you here mere moments after we arrived that first night. In my soul, I knew it was for purely selfish reasons that I decided to do it. And yet, no matter how many times I told myself I had acted out of self-interest, I could never bring myself to admit that I would have chosen any differently. Because I have no doubt that I would choose you every time."

My breath caught in my chest with the admission. Before I could respond, before I could start to breathe again, Sterling released my hand. The calluses on her palms gently caught against my skin as she gripped both sides of my face, closing the distance between us. There was a moment of hesitation as her eyes searched my face, and she tucked a stray strand of hair behind my ear. Whatever Sterling had been looking for, she had found her answer in that whisper of a moment.

She kissed me deeply. Her lips were softer than I remembered as they captured mine. Her tongue traced the outline of my bottom lip. No longer in shock, I granted her further access as I reached a hand behind her head, weaving my fingers in her hair.

I kissed her back.

Her teeth gently caught my bottom lip, and she pulled away slightly. I met her tongue stroke for stroke. Our rhythm started to pick up, and I needed more. I turned to face her on the bench, sitting up on both my knees. From this position, I was a head taller than she was. Using her hair, I tugged just enough to tilt her chin up, deepening the kiss further.

I couldn't contain the sigh of pleasure that escaped as Sterling's hands moved from my face. They worked their way down my sides and rested at my lower back, as she too straddled the bench. The hem of my shirt came up slightly, the fabric tangling in her grip as it tightened.

Sterling pulled away. Her eyes burned with desire, her chest rising and falling as she worked to catch her breath. I felt my stomach drop as I allowed myself to revel in the fact that she looked this way because of *me*. The thought was intoxicating.

"I guess I lost myself in the moment," she said as color darkened her cheeks.

"You guess?" I echoed humorously.

"I wasn't sure if this," she looked between us, "was what you wanted."

Every fiber of my being wanted this, wanted *her*, in whatever ways I was allowed. Still, part of me knew who sat before me. The woman who would sacrifice every need of her own in order to adhere to the rules. Rules that, if broken, would bring even more trouble down on herself and those she loved.

And they had just barely dodged a bullet with Merik today.

Sterling was giving me a chance to be the one who saved us from ourselves. Saved her from her desires. But I wasn't her. I couldn't stop the selfish need burning through every fiber of my being, begging to finally be acknowledged.

"I have wanted you since the night we met, Sterling," I said honestly, "I want everything you are willing to give me." Hesitation rolled off her, and options warred behind her eyes as she debated her next move. I sat back on my heels. The distance between us was small, but with how close we had just been, it felt as if a canyon separated us. I couldn't stand it.

"I don't want to regret missing anything. Just in case..." I let my voice trail off, my implications clear, "I especially don't want to miss a single moment with you." I let the desperation I had been trying to hide today seep into my voice as I begged. "Sterling, please."

It was a single word, but it was enough. I watched as her resolve shattered. "To hell with the law."

We crashed into each other.

I was running my hands through the golden waves of her hair. I sucked her lower lip between both of mine, hard, and she groaned softly into my mouth. Her hands gripped my hips viciously, trying to pull me closer.

When the space between us was still too great, Sterling grabbed underneath both of my legs, just below my ass. In one fast movement, she pulled me into her lap so that I was straddling her. The contours of our bodies fit perfectly together. Despite Sterling's grip holding me firmly against her, I needed to be closer to her.

I broke the kiss again, breathing hard. My hands dropped from her hair as I tried to find the hem of her shirt. Not breaking her rhythm, Sterling's mouth moved to the left side of my neck, where she kissed hungrily down to my collarbone. My head fell to the side, allowing her better access, as a soft sound of pleasure fell from my lips. "I need you, Sterling," I said breathlessly.

She pulled back to look at me, her blue eyes glazed over. "Stand up," she said as she started to release me.

"Wait," I reached for her wrists before she could completely pull away, disappointment slowly clouding my features.

Sterling raised an eyebrow, and an amused smile spread across her face. "I was just thinking that this is a rather inconvenient place for what I had in mind. And besides," she leaned in close, the whisper of her words tickling my ear, "if I'm going to see you naked, it should be in *my* bed where I can take my time with you."

A chill ran down my spine, and I shuddered against her. She kissed me once more, emphasizing her words.

I practically jumped off the bench.

We grabbed hands and made our way through the hall and up the stairs, staying deathly silent until we reached her bedroom door. She opened it, and I stepped in after her. Sterling closed the door, pinning me against it with her body. She resumed her place at the hollow of my throat, sucking harder when I pulled her tighter against me.

Using the door as leverage, Sterling lifted me up by my legs, which I wrapped tightly around her waist. She looked at me with a devious smile before we started to move. The kissing continued, and in four strides, we were at the edge of her bed, still unmade from the night before.

She set me down gently, guiding me backwards to the center of the mattress. I leaned back on my elbows and slowly inched back. Sterling followed my movement, never leaving my lips. We reached the middle, and before I could lie back on the pillows, Sterling pulled me to a sitting position. She quickly slid my shirt over my head, discarding it on the floor. Her fingers brushed under the band of my sports bra, but lingered. It was an unspoken question. She was waiting for permission. I nodded, my lips feathering a kiss on hers. It joined my shirt on the floor within seconds.

She hesitated as her eyes scanned down my torso. "You know it's only fair to level the playing field," I teased, tugging lightly at the hem of her shirt.

She chuckled but nodded, "As you wish." Her arms crossed in front of her, grabbing opposite sides of her shirt. In a smooth movement, she took off everything from the waist up and discarded it all to the floor. Her tan skin glowed in the moonlight. I ran my hands over the muscled contours of her abdomen, feeling them flex instinctively under my touch. I continued reaching up her body, over to her sides. My thumbs caressed the sides of her breasts before moving to cup them both completely. I squeezed gently, and heat coursed through me as Sterling's eye fluttered shut. Her hands came up to cover both of mine, encouraging me, begging me to be less gentle with her.

I was more than willing to oblige.

My grip tightened, one hand reaching around her side to her back, pulling us together. As I clung to her, Sterling lowered us to the bed. Her lips found mine, while my hands continued to explore every inch of her. She kissed me slowly, working her way down my jawline and to my neck. As she continued down my chest, her kisses became more aggressive and promised to leave reminders in the morning. My hands tangled in the curtain of blonde hair that fell around us as she took my nipple into her mouth. Her left hand gripped my side, while her right held my other breast. Her thumb circled slowly and torturously, matching her tongue on the other side stroke for stroke.

Sterling mirrored her movements on the other side of my body before continuing to kiss down my sternum and over my abdomen. Teasingly, she ran her tongue just above my waistband before placing a kiss over where my hip met my stomach. I arched my back, silently asking for more. Sterling pulled away, amused.

"What do you want, Kai?" My name fell off her lips seductively. When I didn't respond, Sterling sat up so that she could pull off my pants, leaving my underwear in place. She grazed her nose, then chin, lightly up my center. The thin fabric that stood between us served to create friction with her movements, and I felt my eyes roll back.

"For fuck's sake, Sterling," I hissed.

Sterling laughed against the inside of my thigh as she kissed it. "Your body has no issues telling me what you want," she brought her mouth to my ear, her breath warm, "I don't see why you should deny it." Teasingly, she ran her fingers between us, up along where her face had just been.

"Don't stop touching me," I whispered against her skin.

"Closer," she murmured against my neck. The pressure from her hand increased slightly as she lazily drew circles. "Still not quite what I had in mind, though."

My core ached. I was no longer able to resist. If she wanted me to beg, I would. If Sterling wanted me to sell my soul for her, I would.

"For the love of God," I sighed, dizzy from her teasing touch. "Fuck me, Sterling. *Please,*" I begged, not for the first time tonight.

Her eyes sparkled as she looked down at me. Without breaking eye contact, she pulled my underwear to the side. Slowly, she ran two fingers over me before sliding them inside. Our moans of pleasure were simultaneous. Her eyes fluttered closed in ecstasy as she felt how much I wanted her. I arched my back, rocking my hips to the rhythm as she stroked me.

"You feel *so* good, Kai," she said against my lips before she kissed me once again. The weight of her hips pinned her hand inside me as she positioned herself between my legs. She moved them with the movement of her hand, allowing space for her to almost completely remove her fingers, before sliding into me once more. Sterling set the pace, slow and steady, but deep. I couldn't breathe between her touch and her kiss. I needed more. I raked my nails along her back, and she didn't need words to know what I was asking for.

Our rhythm quickened, and I moaned into her mouth, her name lost on my lips. I wrapped one leg around her waist as she kissed the hollow of my throat.

"Don't stop," I said breathlessly. I was so close to the tipping point, everything in me was ready to shatter. Sterling knew this was the case, too.

Because she stopped.

A frustrated sound broke from my chest, but Sterling ignored it. Instead, she worked my underwear down my legs until they were completely off. "You didn't think I was going to let you get off that easy?" Her smile was wicked as she slowly kissed down my body, letting me catch my breath.

"I have wanted this for too long, Kai. I have to drag it out as long as I can." Her body moved lower against mine, first her stomach, then her breasts, trailed against the endless nerves that craved her touch. She stopped here, leaning in to kiss my hip, as the cold metal of her silver chain made me shiver. Then she settled her head between my legs.

Sterling kissed everywhere but where I needed her most. I felt as if I was going to explode. However, just when I was about to plead, I felt her tongue drag slowly over me. I wrapped my hands in her hair as she started slow and gentle. But before long, her movements became desperate as she devoured me.

"Sterling," I moaned repeatedly as if her name was the only word I knew.

It *was* the only word I knew.

I glanced down at her. Her hands braced my hips on either side, taking away any control I could have possibly had. Her glacial eyes, now starting to burn brighter with molten gold as she pushed me to my breaking point, locked with mine as she watched my every reaction to her touch. It was almost too much to bear.

My head fell back on the pillow once more. One hand knotted tighter in her hair as the other ran along her shoulder, trying to pull her closer. Sterling moaned against my body. I felt everything that I was as it wound up tighter and tighter.

"Please, Sterling, don't stop," I whimpered. And this time, she didn't. She continued to kiss and nip and run her tongue over me, tasting every last bit.

I shattered beneath her.

I had said her name until I could no longer speak; all that was left were sounds of ecstasy as I hurtled over the edge. My legs shook out of my control as Sterling continued, not giving me a chance to relax. I had to push her head away, only to receive a coy smile.

"Everything okay up there?" I could only give her a thumbs up, which received one of her beautiful laughs. She moved over me once more to kiss me on the forehead. As she settled to the side of my body, I began to reach for her waistband, only to have my hand gently guided away. "Tonight was about you, Kai."

I started to protest, but she silenced me with a kiss. "We will have all the time in the world for you to return the favor. Tonight, I wanted to worship you."

I smiled and kissed her once more before snuggling into her, resting my head on her bare chest. We lay together in silence, Sterling falling into her contented habit of tracing patterns on my skin.

"What was that you said earlier about' taking your time with me'?" I teased.

"You kept saying my name, and it was driving me crazy. After you begged me not to stop the second time, I couldn't help myself. I could have gotten there myself just by hearing you alone."

A thrill ran through me. "You are very good at what you do," I said, running my finger along her lips, "It should get the appropriate amount of appreciation."

Sterling buried a kiss in my hair. "We should get some sleep. We have to be awake early."

I glanced at the clock on her nightstand. "In about five hours, if I'm not mistaken."

She smiled, "Go to sleep, Kai." Her arms tightened around me as I scooted closer. Her body heat warmed me while the comforting smell of sandalwood and vanilla surrounded me. My eyes grew heavy, and I sighed in contentment.

"Thank you, Sterling."

"For what?"

"For caring enough to bring me here."

CHAPTER 22

The morning came with a vengeance. As gently as she could, Sterling stirred me to wakefulness. The sky was cold and gray, mirrored in the sea below, as the sun slowly made its appearance for the day. I squinted as my eyes adjusted to the morning light, only to immediately throw the covers over my head. A shiver racked my body as goosebumps covered my arms. "Do you always leave your windows open?" I complained, sleep still evident in my voice.

Sterling tugged the blankets down to my neck. She looked like she was glowing in contrast to the grayscale scene outside. Her hair was tousled from where my hands had been, and somehow, she still looked immaculate. To my dismay, a loose gray t-shirt hung off one of her shoulders.

"In my defense, I rarely have a beautiful, naked woman in my bed." She kissed my forehead. "And besides, the weather is rarely ever this cold."

"You seem to be perfectly content with the cold." A strong breeze came in through the window, and I immediately pulled the blanket over my face again. Sterling laughed softly. I felt her weight on the bed disappear, followed by the sound of the window latching.

"Is that better?"

I peeked my head out, showing only my forehead and eyes. "It's a start," I said hesitantly. In a flash of material, something hit my face. I freed my hands and unwrapped the balled-up clothes, holding up a powder blue hoodie and a pair of light gray joggers. I looked at Sterling out of the corner of my eye. She circled her hands, one over the other, as if to say, 'let's get moving.'

I stood up from the bed, the sheet falling in a pile around my ankles. Sterling's mouth opened slightly. Her eyes were the size of saucers. Seconds passed before she cleared her throat and finally blinked. I smirked at her as I quickly pulled on the clothes I had been given.

"Some would say it's rude to stare, Valkyre," I teased.

She took a step towards me, dropping her chin in order to meet my eyes. "Are any of those people in this room?"

"Not a chance," I murmured, kissing her quickly.

"Glad to hear it," she smiled, "but the others are expecting us. By the smell of it, Malachi has already started breakfast and has coffee brewing."

She was right. I could smell the delicious scent of roasted coffee beans wafting up from the kitchen. If it were any other day, it would have been especially sweet. The stormy weather outside mixed with the cozy smell of Mal's breakfast promised a relaxed fall day. However, there would be no relaxing. There was work to be done.

We left the room, Sterling trailing behind me as we walked down the hallway. When I no longer heard her footsteps, I stopped and turned to look at her. She was leaning against one of the door frames, her arms casually crossed. She had pulled her hair up on top of her head before leaving the room, not wanting to deal with the hassle of brushing through it. A soft smile danced on her lips.

"What?" I asked with a small laugh.

"I just," she hesitated, "I really love seeing you in this house." Her eyes roamed slowly over my body, taking in every inch, "*Especially* when you are wearing my clothes."

I felt heat rise in my cheeks. Despite everything that had happened between us, this single comment did not fail to knot my stomach. It was then that a thought occurred to me. "Everyone will know if I go down there dressed like this, won't they?" I started to walk back down the hall, planning to change into something of my own.

Sterling pushed off the wall and put both of her hands on my shoulders. "What are you doing?"

"Going to change."

"Why would you do such a thing?"

"If we're going to keep this to ourselves, then—"

"I have worked hard to keep my personal life to myself in the past—this is true. But I have zero desire to keep you hidden, Kai." She leaned in close, the whisper of her words sending shivers down my spine, "I want everyone to know that I am the lucky soul that gets to occupy your bed."

All I could do was nod up at her. Sterling stepped back, fist raised to the door in front of her. "We just have to survive Roman's comments for the duration of breakfast."

She pounded on the door twice, and a groan sounded from within. "Breakfast in ten, sleeping beauty."

We made our way to the kitchen, but before we cleared the last step, Sterling reached for my hand. We crossed the threshold of the kitchen, where Mal and Callen stood across from each other at the island. Mal leaned to peer around Callen and gave us a nod that was subtle but approving. Happiness radiated from his eyes.

Cal noticed that Malachi was no longer paying attention to whatever they had been talking about and turned in his seat. His eyes widened slightly as he took us both in, reading between the lines. The lopsided grin I had come to love spread across his face.

Sterling pulled out the chair next to Callen and gestured for me to sit while she poured two cups of coffee.

"Good morning, you two," Callen said cheerfully. The color had returned to his face, and he was already moving more easily. If I hadn't been able to see the extra bulk that the bandage added to his torso, it would have been easy to believe that he was completely healed.

My heart swelled with gratitude. Without thinking about it, I placed my hand on his shoulder. "It's good to see you are doing well, Cal."

"No arguments there," he said, squeezing my hand gently. "Though it seems I'm not the only one doing *impossibly* well this morning." He arched a suspicious eyebrow at me. I intentionally glanced at Sterling, who was leaning against the counter, sipping her coffee and watching the exchange with amusement.

"What can I say?" I squeezed his hand in return. "I got a great night of sleep."

"You were able to sleep last night?" Roman drawled as he shuffled into the room. He was still plagued by sleep, and it was evident in his gait. "I could barely fall asleep, damn turtles came up to the beach trying to procreate."

Sterling choked on her coffee, caught off guard by her own laughter. Beside me, Callen started to shake his head. Though his back was to me, I could see the slight movement in Mal's shoulders as he said, "Turtles mate in the spring, Roman."

"You know, my flightless, feathered friend, you're right. I was just trying to spare Kai here the embarrassment of being compared outright to a sea creature. But since you decided to fact-check me, the ruse is up." He shrugged as he bumped Sterling out of the way and poured himself a cup of coffee.

"Bastard," I said, feigning offense.

"Randy reptile." He raised his cup before drinking deeply.

Despite the exchange being goodhearted, Sterling had bristled at his side. Her instant defensiveness warmed my chest.

"Easy, Roman," Callen warned. "Sterling looks like she's about ready to kick your ass."

"It's okay," I reassured. "He's just jealous no one has ever been able to accuse him of pleasuring a woman to the point of keeping the house awake."

Laughter erupted from the group, drowning out Roman as he exclaimed, "That is *not* what I said!"

"Breakfast is ready, everyone," Mal said as he walked a plate of pancakes to the table.

We each took our respective seats as Roman continued to mumble something about bedroom etiquette when everyone had an early morning. Sterling patted his shoulder and gave him a third pancake, as if it were an olive branch. He shook his head but began cutting into his food, accepting the offer easily. "What is it about potential near-death situations that makes people so horny, anyways?"

The joke fell short. The air in the dining room snapped taut as we all tensed. Cal and Malachi glanced at each other, their shoulders both sagging under the weight of the elephant in the room. Sterling's knuckles turned white as she gripped her silverware tighter. I was almost sure she was about to wedge the butter knife into the table.

Roman realized seconds after the words left his lips what he had just said. He dropped his eyes to the table, shame covering him like a blanket. Shaking his head almost imperceptibly, he murmured, "Kai, I'm so sorry. I didn't mean anything by it. It was a poorly timed joke."

"Maybe you should learn when to *stop* joking, Roman," Sterling ground out through clenched teeth. Anger, fueled by worry, threaded her tone.

"I..." Roman searched for words but came up empty. The rest of them were waiting for my response, I realized. No one so much as moved as they studied every inch of my face—waiting for me to break.

I cleared my throat and gave him a small smile. "It's okay, really. It was a valid statement, and the humor of it wasn't lost on me." I was telling the truth. It was funny, the whole exchange had been. For all of the danger I would soon face, it wasn't what was sitting at the forefront of my mind.

It was being able to sit here laughing with all of them each morning. Being able to spend nights wrapped in Sterling's arms. It was the promise of a perfect life with days as simple as this, being laid out in front of me, and the possibility that it would be taken away before I had a chance to start truly living it, that haunted my thoughts.

Silence stretched before us, save for the sound of utensils pushing food around uselessly on plates. I chanced a glance at Sterling. She was staring at a point just in front of her plate. So much time seemed to pass since she blinked last, I couldn't help but wonder if her eyes had completely dried out yet.

We all snapped to attention as Mal's voice sounded through the room, gentle yet firm. "There is nothing to mourn, nor will there *be* anything to mourn," he reached across the table to grab my hand, lending me his confidence, "Let us not waste perfectly good time dreading the unknown."

From there, the day progressed quickly. We pored over strategy, drilled techniques with multiple different weapons, and recited demonology until nightfall.

We were all gathered in the library. I was in and out of consciousness as I sat in one of the plush chairs. One by one, the boys slowly trickled out. Each one stopped beside me, offering their own form of brotherly comfort before departing. I didn't have the energy to wake up enough to acknowledge them, but I made a mental note to thank them in the morning.

I felt strong, warm, arms encircling me. Gently, Sterling picked me up and carried me down the hall. When she sat me on the bed, I knew it was mine. It was softer than the mattress in her room. I was prepared to wake up, if only to ask her to stay, but it wasn't necessary. She tucked me under the covers before taking her place beside me.

I felt her press a kiss to my forehead before pulling me close to her. "You have to survive this, Kai," Sterling whispered into my hair, "Not just for me, but for the others. I don't know that this is a loss any of us could walk away from without losing a piece of ourselves. We love you," she buried her face into my hair and paused before speaking again, "Just survive."

I was on the precipice of unconsciousness, though I was sure Sterling thought I was already deeply asleep. I fought to stay awake, to see if she would say anything more. However, it was not long before her breathing evened out and the tension in her body receded. Sterling was asleep.

I snuggled in closer to her and finally let my mind rest, too tired to worry about what the morning would hold.

There was no coffee brewing in the morning. The sweet smells of Mal's cooking were absent as apprehension blanketed every surface. It was as if the house itself waited in silence, holding its breath, as we met in the entryway. The five of us stood facing one another. Three of us were dressed to hold court with The Order, while two were dressed to remain at home.

Before we had parted ways last night, it had been decided that it would be best for Callen and Malachi to remain here. Though they both had legitimate arguments as to why they should also attend, it didn't change the facts. Mal was an angel who had been cast out and left for dead. His attendance would likely only hurt whatever case I could manage to build for myself.

Callen, though not detrimental to my case, needn't be there either. He was still healing from an injury that I was, in part, to blame. Roman suggested this might only add more doubt to The Order's belief that I was Nephilim. There was also the fact of his sister. Eliza had not been seen or heard from, and none of us wanted to subject Cal to a reunion in front of a crowd. Especially at an event such as this.

Ultimately, they conceded, agreeing to stay home for my sake. Nonetheless, I appreciated them fighting so hard to be by my side.

Roman and Sterling excused themselves. They said their good-byes and stepped onto the porch, allowing me time to say my own farewells. I approached Callen. The dark-haired boy who had been on my doorstep months ago with worry etched in his brow stood before me. He was no longer a stranger, though a ghost of that worry touched his emerald eyes now.

"I'm sorry," he started to say, "If it hadn't been for my sister, we wouldn't be here today, and I wouldn't have to say goodbye."

I hugged him before I could think twice. If it hurt, he didn't show any signs of it. Instead, his arms wrapped around my shoulders, squeezing me tighter still. As we parted from one another, I looked up to him. "This was always the plan, remember? It's just on an accelerated timeline now. But I refuse to say goodbye to you, Callen. I only just got here, and I don't plan to leave you guys anytime soon."

He nodded, "Good, because I have enjoyed watching you antagonize Roman. It has made things much more fun around here. Take care of yourself, Kai." We hugged once more before Callen ascended to his room, leaving Mal and I alone.

Neither one of us moved at first. I was afraid that if I hugged him now, I would finally break. Malachi had been my first friend here. He had welcomed me, comforted me, and I had confided in him. Of all of my farewells, this would likely be the hardest.

"Breathe," he exhaled, and I did too. "You are ready, Kiara. Of that I have no doubts."

"What doubts do you have?"

"Nothing that is within your realm of control, love." He smiled and opened his arms, "Come here."

I cleared the distance in two steps, allowing him to envelope me in a warmth that was exclusive to him. Another shaky breath left my chest, causing my shoulders to shudder ever so slightly. But nothing got past Mal.

"You don't get to fall apart. Not yet. If you crumble now, they will have won before you have had a chance to begin. Channel your emotions, Kai. Use them. Anxiety and a will to survive are tools just as powerful as strength and skill with a blade, if not more so."

I held on to him tighter. "Thank you, Malachi."

"Don't thank me yet. Save it for when you are home and I can say 'I told you so.'"

I took a step back from him. His golden eyes searched my face, looking for any cracks in my resolve. He found none. Satisfied, he nodded. "They will ward you inside the terrain. No one can get in, and you will only be allowed out once the task is complete. They will see every move you make. Have you talked to anyone about your question from earlier? About other Nephilim controlling Heavenly Fire?"

I shook my head, "No one."

"Good. If you feel so much as a hint of that power starts to surface, best to snuff it out. Especially since you have no idea how to harness it. Now is not the time to arouse more questions with zero answers available on your part."

"But how do I stop it?"

"You said it comes with moments of stress, correct?" I nodded. "Then you control your emotions. Breathe and think through the situation. When you focus and rein in your feelings, so too will the power dim." I looked down at the space between our feet, only to have Mal lift my chin so that I met his golden eyes.

"Trust yourself. In there, that will be the only thing you *can* trust." He thumbed the pendant of St. Michael that hung from the chain on my neck before tucking it under the collar of my shirt. "Show them who you are."

"I will see you soon. Watch after Callen."

"Always do."

We exchanged smiles with each other, but I knew I could not bear another hug. Malachi knew it too. He reached behind me to open the door, and I walked across the porch and into the front yard with the others. We began walking down the path towards town, but I stopped just outside the gate. I turned to look back at the house that had become a home and made a promise.

I will survive this, and I will come home.

Chapter 23

We walked to town in silence. The trip from the heart of Soteria to its outskirts was not much different as we waited for our train to arrive. Sterling sat close to me, the pressure from a reassuring shoulder pressed against mine kept me grounded. I fidgeted with a stray string hanging off the cuff of my sleeve. The fighting gear was new and fit perfectly down to the boots. I had woken to find everything on a hanger outside the wardrobe. Attached to it was a note.

Tradition dictates that new gear is presented to a Nephilim when they are tested.

I figured since you too will soon be a tried-and-true Nephilim, traditions should most definitely apply to you as well.

We all know how talented you already are, and now you have the clothes to match. Kick ass today, Kai. I'll be waiting for you on the other side.

-S

Every article was black. The leather jacket draped across my lap was adorned with silver zippers that matched the zippers and buckles along the pockets of my pants. I wore a weapons belt, seated low on my hips, though it held nothing. My throwing knives were hidden in two sets of four, tucked into specially made spaces on each thigh. Two more were

337

secured to the insides of my boot, one on each side. As a group, we had decided it would be best if I carried the knives alone since I was both comfortable with them and they were lightweight. There was no need to bog myself down with a heavy broadsword that I was incapable of wielding skillfully.

As I plucked the stray string from my sleeve, the train came to an abrupt stop. We all looked up simultaneously. Sterling tensed at my side, and I could've sworn that I watched the color in Roman's face drain.

"We're here," he murmured, as if there were any doubts as to our destination. None of us moved to stand. The doors opened, impatiently insisting on our departure. Sterling stood, offering her hand to me. Grateful, I took it as I stood. I squared my shoulders and led the way out of the doors and into the bright sunlight.

I had to squint against the light until my eyes were able to adjust. What I saw stopped me in my tracks, my jaw going slack for an instant.

A beautiful, white marble arena stood in the distance. Massive pillars were spaced out evenly along the perimeter, helping support the glass dome that provided protection to whatever lay inside. Dresses and tunics of golds, creams, and whites flooded the steps. While some were dressed in Nephilim fighting gear, much like ourselves, though most of the crowd was dressed in fine linen, separating themselves from the warriors who would prefer gear to traditional garb any day of the week.

"There are so many people here," I muttered more to myself than the others.

"It has been nearly 200 years since someone willingly opted to face Metanoia," Sterling responded. "It is a once-in-a-lifetime event, it seems."

"I bet it's been even longer since someone chose to attempt the Metanoia over letting their kidnappers face punishment," Roman said. We both shot him a look. "What?" he asked innocently. "I'm just saying your case isn't exactly textbook. Not to mention it has the name of Gabriel's bastard tied to it." Roman sighed, "And let's face it," he shrugged, "be it angel, Nephilim, or Child of Adam, rarely are there those who will turn away from the suffering of others."

"Very bleak, Roman. Thanks for that." I punched him in the arm, but he acted as though he didn't feel it. He only shrugged again.

"They have come to watch me fail, haven't they?"

"No," Sterling placed a hand on my shoulder, "they have come to watch *me* fail. Unfortunately, that just means their eyes will be fixed on you. This is nothing personal against you, you're just the middleman."

Though I could see the sentiment, her words did not make me feel better. I was going to be made into a spectacle for hundreds of strangers. My death was something to be wished for, perhaps even gambled on, because of others' dislike for Sterling. It was ridiculous.

We stepped off the platform and began to walk towards the arena when we were stopped by two fully armed Nephilim wearing matching gray gear. One stopped us, holding a hand up, while the other stepped forward. "Kiara Novak?" he asked.

"Yes?"

"We are to place you in shackles and escort you to Sloane." He went to place the cuffs on my wrists, but Sterling stepped between us.

"I can assure you those won't be necessary."

"Merik requested it."

"Well, Merik can go to hell," Roman thundered as he stepped up to Sterling's side. The second guard, large but still smaller than Roman, placed his hand on the hilt of his blade.

"She is here voluntarily," Sterling said sternly, "She isn't going to flee."

The smaller one spoke again, "She is here because she got caught, Valkyre. As far as The Order is concerned, Kiara Novak is a prisoner and will be treated as such. Now step out of my way." He placed a callused hand on Sterling's shoulder, ready to shove her if needed. I saw a flash of steel as Roman slapped the flat side of his blade against the back of the guard's hand.

"I'd take that back over there with you, my friend, lest you want to end up mighty lonely at night." They were locked in a staring match. The second guard had drawn his sword but was unsure of what to do next. It was clear he was not in charge.

"If you so much as *nick* me, I will arrest all of you."

"If *you* so much as touch Kai with those damned things, you both will cease to exist." I had never seen Roman so menacing before. All traces of my friend, the sarcastic giant, had been replaced by this cold-hearted soldier. "Remove. Your. Hand."

"Now, now," crooned a silky voice from a corner behind us. "Do we not wish to have minimal bloodshed today? Roman, I insist you stow your blade."

Suddenly, everyone stepped back. Roman did as he was told, while the guard dropped his hand from Sterling's shoulder. A sickly-sweet scent filled my nose as a man stepped into the center of our two groups.

He was tall—equal to, if not taller than, Roman. Though he was dressed in white and gold finery, his arms were bare and rippled with muscle covered by tanned skin. He had a head of curly, rich brown hair. His face was that of someone in their early twenties. Flawless and beautiful. I followed the chiseled line of his jaw up to where his eyes were. They were eyes of molten gold. He stretched, and behind him, massive wings of white splayed out, before tucking back in once more.

"Fuck," Roman hissed as he dipped his head, taking a knee. The two guards also kneeled to the ground, and only Sterling and I were left standing. Tension rolled off of her. While I looked at the scene before me, confused, Sterling did not drop her gaze from the being before us. If anything, she tilted her chin up in response to the unspoken challenge in his eyes.

"Hello, Sterling."

"Hello, father," she ground out, as she finally bowed her head. *Gabriel.*

"Still haven't learned to play well with others, I see. These men are only doing their job."

Sterling raised her eyes once more, anger peppering her face. "Please, these men are on the same power trip as Merik. The only reason they are so insistent on her being shackled is because that is the closest they will ever get to putting a woman in cuffs for fun. If she wanted to run, she would have by now. So let her preserve some dignity."

"My daughter makes a fair point. Those won't be necessary. Run along."

"But sir, Merik insisted that we shackle and bring her to Sloane," the first guard stammered out.

"I will see to it that they end up in the proper place. Or am I to be under the impression that Merik's orders trump my own?" The threat in his tone was menacing.

"Not at all, sir. We will be on our way now." Before Gabriel could say anything else, the two guards were jogging towards the arena. He chuckled as he watched them go, and Sterling narrowed her eyes at him.

"What are you doing here anyways? You aren't *actually* overseeing this, are you?"

"Unfortunately, no. Ramiel will be standing with Sloane and Merik today. I am simply here to enjoy the show." He locked eyes with me and winked. "She is quite pretty, Sterling. Well done."

She ignored him. "Aren't the affairs of Nephilim below you?"

"What can I say? Centuries have passed since someone last faced Metanoia, and my interest was piqued. Especially when I heard my daughter was involved. I thought it was time for a reunion of sorts. I do hope you'll sit with me, daughter. You may bring your," he paused, throwing a dirty look at Roman, "brute of a friend too. Provided he promises to be on his best behavior."

Roman muttered something derogatory under his breath, but was interrupted by an elbow in his side from Sterling. "Just show us where we need to go."

"Right this way."

We walked in silence, heading into the arena. Though people gave us a wide berth, all eyes were on us. Groups whispered as we passed, most with their gazes locked on Sterling. No one made an attempt to hide that they were talking about her, yet she held her head high. I saw a cruel smirk run along Gabriel's lips as we made our way out of the crowd and into an empty corridor.

Gray stone steps that paled in comparison to the marble surrounding the stairwell circled their way upward. We followed what felt like four flights worth of stairs before coming to a landing. The hall only allowed us to go in one direction and eventually returned us to the sunlight. We stepped out onto a balcony that overlooked the arena. Where a railing would be on any other balcony, there was nothing but the ledge that dropped straight into whatever may be waiting below.

Four lush chairs sat raised on a dais pushed back from the ledge, though three of them were already occupied. I recognized Merik, sitting in the chair farthest to the right. He seemed tense, his cocky demeanor from the other day nonexistent. I wondered if it had any-thing to do with the company he was in.

Gabriel pushed his way through us and onto the balcony, his wing brushing my arm as he passed. The soft down of feathers, mixed with lethal muscle, combined to form a paradox that was something of deadly beauty. The other three rose from their seats at his approach. Merik and the other Nephilim—Sloane, I assumed—bowed. The third had his own set of wings, and he inclined his head. "Nice to see you, brother," he said.

Gabriel grasped the other Archangel's hand in his own briefly be-fore turning back to us. "Children, this is Ramiel."

I studied the Archangel closely. Like all of the beings of Heaven I had met, he was magnificent. He had long white hair that flowed to his shoulders like silk. His skin was lighter than Gabriel's but flawless nonetheless. When he spoke, though his voice was deep, it was as if each word was its own melody, creating a complex symphony with every sentence.

"Ah, yes. I am familiar with them. Roman Hallowell and your daughter. Though I must say the third one I have never seen before. You must be the Daughter of Adam."

"Useless Daughter of Adam," Merik muttered under his breath.

Ramiel shot him an annoyed look that silenced him instantly. Bringing his eyes back to me, the Archangel studied me intently. They were silver, a stark contrast to both Gabriel's and Malachi's, and I wondered if it made him different from the others. "You seem to have caused quite a stir in Soteria, child."

"Something we shall hopefully remedy today," Sloane said. He was tall and lanky. He had dark hair and a well-trimmed beard to match, though silver peppered his temples. His body language commanded respect from those around him, and it was then that I realized he had not introduced himself. I had a feeling he hadn't needed an introduction in a very long time.

"I couldn't agree more, sir." I squared my shoulders, looking him in the eyes. "I am tired of being treated like a felon when I have committed no crimes."

"Don't be so sure about that," Merik spat in response. Though he was talking to me, he was staring at Sterling. She stepped in front of me slightly, her hand a breadth away from the small blade in her belt.

Gabriel looked between the two, saw how Sterling had shielded me, and a cruel smile broke across his face. "Play nicely, daughter. We just discussed this, did we not?" Her hand relaxed at her side, but she did not move from her place. She held Merik's gaze as he sneered back. From the side, I was barely able to glimpse it as Sterling's eyes flashed golden, Heavenly Fire swallowing the blue of her irises. Merik's face dropped as he took an involuntary step back. Sterling's eyes returned to a glacial blue. She had won, and the knowing smirk on her face said as much.

"Fucking freak," Merik huffed. Roman bristled, ready to jump to his friend's defense.

"*Enough,*" Sloane said sternly. The one word commanded us all, save for the Archangels. "It is time to proceed with the trial. Say your goodbyes, Daughter of Adam."

I turned towards Roman as he picked me up in a vice-like hug. "Kick some ass, Ace." He kissed my temple and set me back on my feet, expertly sliding a single gorgeous dagger into my belt in the process. It was one he always carried with him.

In an attempt to give us privacy, Roman stepped in front of Sterling and I, facing the others while giving us as much space as possible.

Worry was etched into Sterling's face as I spun to face her. Even nervous, she was insanely beautiful. I brushed a strand of hair out of her face, cupping her cheek briefly. "It will be okay, you said so yourself, remember?"

She nodded, "I know it will be. I just haven't had to feel like this in such a long time."

"Feel what?"

"Like one of the few good things in this life could be taken from me at any given second." I hugged her tightly, relishing the feel of her arms wrapped around my waist. "Kai," she started, "I'm in—"

"Don't," I cut her off, pressing my hand to her mouth. Hurt flashed behind her eyes, but was gone in an instant. "That's not what I meant," I tried to remedy quickly. I removed my hand but remained in her embrace. "Whatever it is, not here and not now. When you say those words, I don't want it under threat of punishment or with people like Merik around." Her body relaxed as she processed what I was saying. I grasped the back of her head, pulling gently so that I could kiss her forehead. "I'm not going anywhere."

With that, I disentangled myself from her. I was a few steps away from those who would judge my fate when I turned once more. "Sterling," I worked to not let my voice break, "me too." Ecstasy and longing fought to break through, but for everyone there, she remained a blank canvas.

I turned to the three men. "What comes next?"

Sloane stared down his nose at me. "You will be placed in the arena below. Both the terrain and whatever beings live down there will remain unknown to you until the task begins. Your goal is to find the Agni hidden in the terrain. It is larger than most, encased in moonstone rather than glass, and emitting pale blue Heavenly Fire.

"While searching, your job will be to outlast and outsmart whatever dwells there. Should you find the stone, or slay the demons below, the wards will fall and reveal the stairway out. The outside world will not be visible to you, but all will be able to see you. And I assure you, Daughter of Adam, we see *everything*. Tricks from you or your friends will not help you here."

"I don't intend to try and cheat the system, sir," was all I could manage to say. He seemed satisfied enough with the answer.

My eyes strayed from the men in front of me. I turned my back on them as I swept my gaze around the arena set before the dais. Swells of white and gold and silver and black moved in the seats surrounding the ominous pit below. My vision tunneled as the vastness of the crowd became the only thing that I could focus on. People must have started to notice my presence on the platform because the wave of bodies rippled. It started from the middle, directly in front of the ledge I was perched on. They rose to their feet. Those seated on either side of them followed suit, creating a nauseating illusion of a torrential surf. The roar of voices, some cheering some booing, followed their movement assaulting my ears until it was all that was left. I felt my heart as it tried to claw its way out of my chest with every new, rapid beat. The others were forgotten behind me as my breaths came in quick, small gasps. I felt the adrenaline building up, the sizzle of electricity in my veins swiftly following. My skin felt hot. I wanted to vomit as the severity of the next few moments washed over me. But I'd be damned if I showed them any sign of weakness.

I was so focused on composing myself that I barely heard Sloane's words. "Very well. Ramiel, take her into the arena below."

There was no warning as the Archangel picked me up before stepping over the side of the ledge. His wings snapped out effortlessly, suspending us in the air. The scent of overly sweet flowers burned my nose, though it was not nearly as pungent as when Gabriel had appeared.

Ramiel guided us lower into the pit. The majority of the arena was shaded in dark black shadows, save for a small square of packed soil in the center. That was where we landed.

I stepped away from Ramiel to look at the shadows that formed something akin to walls. I reached out to run my hand through the darkness, and ripples of gray and silver appeared where my hand caused disruption.

"It is cloaked from all sides, as Sloane said it would be," Ramiel explained, "It will lift when we are ready to begin, and the crowd will be allowed to see in."

"There won't be anything ready to attack me the second that it lifts, will there?"

"It is unlikely. In my three thousand years of life, I have only seen it happen once."

"That's almost reassuring."

The Archangel stepped closer to me, his arm outstretched as he offered whatever he held in his hand. His fingers unfurled revealing an Agni orb. Its glass was frosted. Specks of gold were dotted along the surface and, etched in gold, was Michael's sigil. The orb flared in Ramiel's palm, silver flames, dancing brilliantly within.

"For you, Daughter of Mystery." I gingerly took it and the flame went cold.

"Why call me that? Why not 'Daughter of Adam,' like the rest?"

"We have yet to discover your truth, child. And I do not like to assume."

I nodded as I thumbed the smooth glass. "I have never tried to use one of these."

"Perhaps there is no time like the present to learn."

"How do I...?"

"It will come to you, should fate decide this is the course of your life."

"I hope fate is on my side, then. It seems like this is the only course I have to follow."

Ramiel stared at me, curiosity now plain and obvious behind his eyes.

"This is where I leave you. I pray there is a touch of angelic blood in your veins, Kiara Novak. Good luck." He shot into the air, leaving me to face the unknown alone.

I stood in the square for what seemed like an eternity, trying to tame the fluttering in my chest. Without warning, the shadows evaporated, an expansive forest stood before me.

I had all of five seconds to appreciate the view before a set of razor-sharp teeth started gnashing in my face.

CHAPTER 24

The force of sheer muscle was enough to knock the wind out of me, even before we fell to the ground in a tangled mess. I rounded my back, allowing the momentum to roll us backwards so that the creature wouldn't end up coming out of the skirmish on top of me. I scrambled to my feet, trying to get a head of the monster. I needed to clear my head of the initial shock, which was hard to do through the growling-screech that erupted from behind me. I chanced a look backward. The heap of mottled grey skin writhed on the ground, looking for purchase to find its feet. A head resembling a human skull—save for the elongated teeth and jaw—twisted towards me with a sickening crack. Deep set eyes with red irises, ringed by black circles, locked onto me. It twisted its body, popping and cracking its way to its feet. It tore its long, taloned fingers out of the earth as it commenced chasing me. There was no mistaking the nightmare.

Daemoni.

For something so ungraceful, the demon was fast. In no time at all it had covered half the distance I had put between us. The smell of rotting flesh and metal was getting closer and closer. I knew I couldn't keep this up for long—I needed to stand my ground. I dug deep inside, and sprinted to the point of my lungs giving out. The regret was almost immediate, but I needed the advantage of the extra space. When I knew I couldn't gain anymore ground I turned and planted my feet, bracing for the fight.

The *Daemoni* charged again as I drew two of my throwing knives, letting one fly almost instantly. It missed the mark, nicking the humanoid-like demon in the shoulder. In its fury, the *Daemoni* snarled as it clawed blindly at me. I wasn't able to take another shot with my blade. My forearms took the barrage of the monster's blows, blocking it from getting close to my core and while narrowly avoiding its talons.

I was given a moment of relief, and I attempted to go on the offensive. I swung out and was only met with air. The mistake made me lose my balance, and I took a stumbling step forward. The loss of my guard costs me. I feel the clammy backhand across my cheek before it sends me reeling. Stars blocked my vision and, on instinct, I reach for my face. I felt the heat building on the side of my face as the bruise started to form. My head began to swim and my training from the last few months drifted from my thoughts.

I was disoriented, my body not moving the way I desperately needed it to if I was going to survive this. The light was too bright, the putrid smell of my attacker was too strong. I spun around and put my fist up instinctively. I connected with the demon's head. I let my adrenaline loose, landing punches where I could. My confidence increased. I felt that I was gaining ground, tiring him out.

I was wrong.

One key thing to know about *Daemoni* was their adept ability to learn the fighting style of its prey. And once they learned something, they never forgot it. An ancient *Daemoni*'s knowledge of combat could be that of several hundred warriors combined. That was why most Nephilim were unable to fight off more than one at a time.

Its head came down, slamming its skull into my nose and rocking my head back. It didn't break, but I still lost the ability to see as my eyes began to water. There was a brief pause as I tried to get my sight back, panic setting in.

The pain at my side lit me up like a live wire.

I screamed in agony, swiping my small blade out blindly. It made contact just beneath the demon's ribcage and bought me some time. I put as much distance between myself and the *Daemoni* as I could before I dropped to my knees and pulled my hand away from the warm, wet wound at my side. Dark red blood covered my hand. The burning was enough that my body begged for a reprieve. But the stirring of the creature not far from me spurred me on.

I knew I couldn't outrun it on my best day, let alone in this shape. I also knew I wasn't going to win this fight head on.

I stumbled my way into the foliage, hoping to find coverage in the shrubbery. Luckily, there was an expanse of undergrowth that would be able to fully conceal me. As an afterthought, I allowed some of my blood to seep onto the path before I tucked myself away. I slowed my breathing, despite the pain, desperate to not give my position away. I needed to be silent for this to work.

The *Daemoni* wasn't far behind me. It appeared where I had just been standing, hungrily sniffing the fresh blood on the ground. A low growl emitted from the back of its throat as it stood to its full height. It sniffed the air, looking to catch a scent of me on the wind. I drew another small blade and took a deep breath. Another.

I struck out hard and fast.

The nightmarish creature shrieked as I severed both of its Achilles.

It fell to the ground, no longer able to support itself. It's screams continued, the bloodlust forgotten by its sudden affliction. I threw myself on top of the *Daemoni* and, with all my strength, drove my blade directly into its heart.

There was silence.

I avoided its blood touching my bare skin, leaving my blade embedded in the monster's chest, as I stood. The talon marks that raked my side and over a part of my stomach smarted with the sudden movement. I needed to find something to staunch the bleeding. But I had nothing. I groaned, sweeping my eyes around the area for anything. I was just about to give up until my eyes landed on a big-leafed bush. It looked as though it has been caught in a rainstorm, liquid dripping from the ends. But the rest of the surrounding plants were visibly dry.

Relief flooded me as I recognized shrub for what it was—*Thromvi*.

It was a medicinal plant used by Nephilim healers in medicinal remedies. The leaves carried both antiseptic and painkilling abilities. In normal circumstances, the leaves were crushed to create a salve that was used before the healers applied sutures. In a pinch, it would numb the pain and help slow the bleeding. I tore several leaves off, layering them over the area. The coolness provided some relief as the stickiness of the fronds gently adhered to my skin. I rolled more leaves up and tucked them into my pocket in case I needed to change out the bandage later. Understanding that this was the best I could do, I surveyed my surroundings.

Now that there wasn't a demon chasing me, I could see how beautiful the forest was. A grove of tall dark trees stretched onward. The forest floor was lush with various types of foliage. There was a light shroud of mist hung in the tree line and, for a moment, I was taken back to my childhood as memories of my aunt and I driving through coastal greenery in search of the ocean flooded my mind.

I shook my head as if the thoughts would fall out onto the ground. I needed to find the orb before anything too lethal found me. Moonstone could be found in rivers, and it was said that Nephi was wading through water in the dark when he called an angel down to ask for light. The angel gifted him the first Agni, the original encased in moonstone, because it had been the material most accessible to Nephi at the time. The angel promised that it would provide light for him and his people for eternity. If Metanoia was testing my knowledge of history, the best bet was to find a river and go from there.

While I had studied intensely, nowhere was basic survival in the woods mentioned. I had no idea what to look for. All I knew was that I was in the dead center of the pit. Without reason, I began walking to the right.

The forest was eerily quiet. No birds flew between the trees. There was no croak of frogs or hum of insects to break up the silence. It felt unnatural. To distract myself, I began racking my brain, trying to think of the demons that may be lurking in the foliage. Outside of Imps, I was drawing a blank, my mind feeling more sluggish with every passing second.

"Kai?"

I jumped at the sound of my name, barely containing a scream of my own.

"Kai?!" the female voice called out again, more urgent this time. "Where are you?" That voice was so familiar, but I couldn't place it.

"Hello? Is someone out there?"

"*KAI!!*" the woman exclaimed in terror. Without a second thought, I broke into a dead sprint, running in the direction I had just come from, ignoring the protest of my side. I stumbled over tree roots and shrubs. I stood with new scratches on my palms each time, but paid them no mind. The familiar voice was in trouble—I needed to help h er.

I wasn't sure that there were many rules for Metanoia. Could they bring in others against their will? What if this woman was innocent and a creature of the night had cornered her? I wouldn't allow anyone else to suffer harm on my behalf. I drew Roman's blade as I burst through an overgrown bush.

"Kai!" the woman crashed into me, wrapping her arms around my neck. "I'm so glad you found me." She pulled away, caramel brown hair tumbling out of the bun she had had on top of her head. I couldn't believe my eyes.

"*Lainey?* What the hell are you doing here?"

"I hadn't heard from you. I mean, I know we don't talk like we used to, but usually when I reach out, I hear from you in a few days. Anyways, I went to your house to check on you, but when I knocked on the door, a man answered. He told me you had stepped out but would be back soon. So, I went inside to wait—clearly not my smartest idea. Next thing I know, I woke up here, wherever that is. I was scared, and the first person I thought of was you. Did he take you, too?"

"Kind of. I guess you could say that," I stammered. I had no idea where to start, and I wasn't sure there was even time to explain all that had happened to her.

"Oh my God, Kai. You're *bleeding*! Are you okay?"

"I'm fine," I reassured her as I absentmindedly touched my side. The leaves were still in place. "We have got—"

"What the hell is going on?"

"I know it's a lot but—"

"One moment I was visiting my friend and the next I wake up in the woods, and you've been mauled by some animal."

"I know, and I am so sorry you got dragged into this. But listen, Lane, it's a long, *long* story. But I know how we can get out of here, and when we do, I will tell you everything. Do you trust me?"

"Always. What do we need to do?"

"There is a stone that contains fire inside. It burns extremely bright. All we have to do is find it. I think the best place would be by water somewhere."

"I saw a river when I was looking for you! I can lead you back the way I came from."

The sudden potential that we might find the Agni sooner rather than later sent my heart racing. "Lead the way!" Lainey turned to walk towards what would be the southwestern quadrant of the arena, but stopped short. She took a long look at me, taking in my poorly bandaged wound and the way I stood with Roman's blade in my hand. The steel of the hilt was ornately twisted together with sapphires embedded up the middle. Her eyes were sad.

"Oh, Kai, what did you get yourself into?" She didn't wait for an answer, only turned and started to hike in search of the river.

We must have been walking for two hours with no signs of water. Though I was anxious to be out of here, I had to admit that having my best friend by my side made this much more manageable. Now that I wasn't alone, I was able to relax. But I had changed my leaves twice now and I was almost out of them. I needed to find the Agni.

"I went on wandering, looking for you for a long time," Lainey explained, "I'm positive we are still on the right course, though."

I nodded. The arena must have been a lot bigger than I thought, since we had yet to find its outer edges. The pain slowly ebbed away, and my mind started to wander as other thoughts found me.

How long can I go one like this, without a healer? How did this look to everyone watching? More importantly, what kind of monster *would drop my mortal best friend into a pit of demons?*

"Hey Lane, I'm sorry you've been dragged into this. I never thought—"

"Aw, what is this adorable little guy?" I swiveled around, afraid to see what she had stumbled across. "Look, Kai! Isn't he just the cutest thing?"

"Lainey put that down, now," I said, my voice quiet but stern. In the palm of her right hand sat a blue-skinned creature. It had eyes of obsidian, disproportionately big compared to its head. Its pink nose matched the pink membranes that fanned across long, floppy ears. It swung its feet back and forth, as if it were a child sitting in a high-top chair, cocking its head to one side, then the other, as it studied Lainey.

"He's harmless, Kai." She poked its stomach, but it hardly noticed. It had fixated on the diamond set into her wedding ring. Its eyes got bigger, if that were possible. In one quick motion, the Imp hooked its extra-long fingers under the prongs of the band and popped the diamond out of the setting. Satisfied with its treasure, it skittered off her hand and onto the ground below.

"Hey!" Lainey squealed, "Give that back!" She took off after the Imp, swiping at leaves and bushes as it sprinted through the forest.

"Lainey, you have to let it go!" I called after her, but it was too late. Reluctantly, I chased after them. I nearly took Lainey out. She had stopped dead in her tracks, causing me to crash into her. "What the hell, Lane," I started to complain as I regained my balance. When I looked at where she pointed, I froze. Behind the Imp we had been pursuing was a hundred more. These ones were full-grown, about twice the size of the diamond thief. And they were furious.

"Walk slowly backwards. Don't make any sudden movements." Lainey only whimpered in response.

"I want my diamond back."

"If you don't want them to claw the fillings out of your teeth, you'll let the damned diamond go."

"Screw that!" she exclaimed, lunging for the jewel. But the Imps were faster. They charged, climbing up her legs and arms. They bit her in various places, pulled her hair, and scratched wherever they could find purchase. Lainey screamed.

I drew one of my smaller blades and began to swipe precisely, commanding my friend to stand still. When the majority had been removed, I yelled, "Run!"

Lainey swiftly obeyed, and we were able to get far enough away for a small reprieve. But I knew we wouldn't be able to outrun them for long. They were tireless. I tried my hardest to think of what to do, my mind working slower than I needed it to. Lainey was beginning to slow down, stumbling over practically everything she came across.

Finally, I thought of something that might have bought us some time. "Give me your earrings."

Lainey was appalled. "Absolutely not!"

"It's the only plan I've got, and since you didn't listen to me before, I *really* think you should listen to me now," I panted.

"Fine," she whined. We stopped, and she plucked a pair of studs and a pair of silver dangly discs from each ear. As the Imps drew closer, I started to throw the jewelry in different directions. The light caught the objects as they flew through the air, gleaming and glittering enough to catch the horde's attention. Distracted, they broke off into groups, running four separate ways.

Once each of the groups reached their designated item, they began to retreat back to where we had come from. "What are they doing?" Lainey asked.

"When Imps find something of value, they take it back to their home for safekeeping. They value shiny objects above all else."

"So, we are just going to let them leave? What if they come looking for us again?"

"I don't know that they will," I said, but there was hesitation in my voice, and Lainey sensed it.

"Do you know how to kill them?"

"I do but—"

"So then why don't you? Clearly, they are a threat to us."

The thought had crossed my mind, but I was resistant to the idea.

"They didn't do anything out of their nature, Lane. If you hadn't picked the little one up, if you hadn't chased it, they wouldn't have attacked us. I won't kill something for reacting when I was the reason it felt threatened. It's needless," my tone was stern, "Especially now that they have gone off on their own. We leave them alone, and if they come for us, then I will take care of it. In the meantime, take this," I handed her one of my throwing knives, "try to keep yourself alive for a minute."

Her eyes were huge as I turned my back to her and began to pace. In our years of friendship, I don't think I had ever spoken to her that way before. Some part of me felt bad, and maybe I would apologize later, but I was no closer to finding the Agni, and now we were completely turned around.

I thumbed my pendant of St. Michael nervously. Despair slowly blanketed my shoulders as I tried to figure out another way to find the river. Lainey insisted she recognized the outcropping of rocks nearby and started to jog towards them. I followed behind her, too mentally exhausted to think of another solution.

She had returned to her bubbly self, despite me snapping at her earlier. Lainey began to reminisce about our time together in school, but I was only partially listening. My head began to ache, the sun suddenly too bright despite the tree coverage. I fell behind, but she was unaware as she rambled on.

Without warning, a mixture of smoke and amber assaulted my nose. My mind felt as if it was about to cleave in two, causing me to grab my skull in anguish. And then, just as quickly as it set in, the pain was gone.

Left in its wake was a swirl of violet smoke and shadows. Something that felt familiar to me yet alien altogether.

"For the love of all that is holy or otherwise, shut her up, would you?"

I jumped at the voice, spinning around to ensure that it was only Lainey a few paces ahead and me. No one else was around. The burn in my side erupted and I hissed at its sudden return.

"Of course, no one is here, darling. This is what you would call a solo adventure. And don't move to quickly, you'll need your strength and that blood you keep losing sooner than you think." The voice...It was the one from my dream all those months ago. Androgynous and...bored, it seemed.

"I'm not *alone. Lainey is with me. Clearly, you can hear her too."*

"Ahh," it sighed, *"are you positive about that?"*

"I don't know who or what you are, but you need to get the hell out of my head."

"I can assure you, darling, that that is the last *thing you want me to do."*

"This is just some trick of the arena."

"Is that so? Look around, and I mean really look. Does anything look familiar?"

"It's a damned forest; it all looks the same," I thought exasperatedly as I trudged behind Lainey.

"Stop arguing and try," the voice commanded. I listened and began scanning the area around me. Slowly, as if a haze were lifting from my vision, I noticed what I had not seen before. Two pairs of shoe prints were visible in the dirt, only they walked in several different directions.

The voice spoke again, more gently this time: *"She has been leading you in circles."*

"No, Lainey would never do that, not intentionally."

"Think about it, love. You stumble across your best friend in this God forsaken wood, and she leads you the direct opposite *way from which you came. You are observant. You've noticed the fog that has settled in your mind, correct? I bet it's why you didn't notice you walked around this very piece of land several times over. I'll ask you, only once more. Are you sure that that is the friend you know?"*

"Yes," I was defiant in my answer. The voice only sighed in response.

"—that blonde?" Lainey had been yammering on.

"What did you say?" I asked aloud, something catching in my mind.

"I asked if you ever talked to that blonde you met at the club. The one you said you couldn't stop dreaming about."

I stopped in my tracks. Her voice sounded off. It had undertones of nails grinding over a chalkboard. The brown in her was no longer rich and voluminous, but flat and mousy.

The voice spoke again, *"You really should make sure you know what company you are in before you go handing out weapons."* I ignored it as I responded to Lainey.

"Lane," I said hesitantly, "I never told you about that."

She stopped then, an inhuman cackle racking her body. As she turned, the illusion fractured. I glimpsed the face of something terrifying before it returned into a barely passable version of my friend's lovely face. "Seems, I've slipped."

"What are you?" I asked, fear slowly turning my veins to ice.

"I suppose the jig is up," the creature shrugged. In a flourish of movements, the disguise dropped. Gruesome sounds of pops and snaps as ligaments and muscles tore assaulted my ears. Bones elongated while others shrank. In the aftermath of the twisted transition, the true form of the creature stood before me. He was tall, at least seven feet, with the muscled body of a man, save for his head. On his shoulders sat what looked to be the head of a deer. He had twelve-point antlers and a beard. The entirety of his body appeared as if it had been carved from a tree but was combined grotesquely with layers of flesh.

I stumbled back at the sight of him, earning a manic laugh as he flipped the blade I had given him in the air. "So sorry to frighten you. Is this form more palatable for you?" In the blink of an eye, Sterling stood before me, a cruel gleam in eyes that were too blue. Mottled flesh and bone fragments surrounded her feet, as if every time the monster shifted, it was shedding a snake's skin.

"You do not wish to talk to your lover in front of a crowd? Fair enough! Perhaps this, then," he crooned. The sickening sounds as the creature morphed permeated the air a third time, and I felt bile rise in the back of my throat. Now, a thin woman with auburn hair stood where Sterling had been. Freckles dotted her face, but the kind smile did not reach her green eyes.

Not like how my aunt's used to. Somewhere in my mind, I heard a snarl of anger, but there was no time to pay attention to that.

"I almost had you, girl. And you made it so easy."

"Who are you?"

"I am Leshy, the protector of the woods, a demon of the earth." He transformed back into his normal form, though shorter now. "I wondered how long I could get you to wander before you caught on. I almost got you back to my home for dinner."

I realized he was gesturing to the mouth of a cave that was at my back. Off to the side, the embers of a fire burned and crackled. A pot sat nestled in the heated coals. "I'm afraid I'm not hungry."

"Just as well." Leshy shrugged. "I had not thought to set a plate for you anyways. It's a shame, though. I had really wished not to eat on the run."

"I'm sorry?"

"*RUN!*" the voice in my head exclaimed.

I did as it commanded, turning and running into the mouth of the cave. The darkness swallowed me whole. I continued forward on a straight path as long as I could, keeping my hands up until they came in contact with the cool stone of the cave wall. My breathing sped up as the fear of succumbing to the darkness surrounded me as Leshy's manically laughter bounced off the walls. He was taking his time with th is.

"*Use the Agni in your pocket.*"

"*I can't. I don't know how.*"

"*Pick up the orb, child.*" I reached into my pocket, but hesitated making contact with the orb. If I couldn't call on the Heavenly Fire, then I was doomed.

"*Do it. Now.*" I shook my head doubtfully but listened all the same. "*Good girl. Now, focus. Reach for something that makes you feel warm, something that makes you feel happy. Not the best day of your life, just a compilation of simple pleasures.*"

I lifted the lid to my box of emotions. I pulled out gently things that reminded me of why life was good. Days on the coast. The first spring

day after a long winter. The first time Sterling's hand brushed against min
e.

"Okay that is quite enough of that. The orb is going to warm in your hand. It is a conduit, used to channel your power to call on the Fire. You need to push that happiness into the orb. Ask Arcadia to light your way the same way the memories have lit your life in the past."

I closed my eyes and focused, trying to do as the voice instructed. I held my breath, nervously waiting, until I finally felt the smallest of changes. Warmth whispered at my fingertips, and I latched on to the feeling, determined to maximize it. I tentatively opened my eyes and was flooded with relief when the orb was alight with its silver flame.

"Oh, thank God," I murmured.

"He has nothing to do with that specific orb, actually. But that's for a different time. Get the hell out of there."

I spun around the cave and froze. Littered on the sides of the floor were bones. Human bones. I started to retch at the site of the remains but knew there wasn't time to waste. Collecting myself, I picked a tunnel and wove my way through the passages that followed, looking for any sign of an exit.

"Hello, child." Leshy's voice sent a chill down my spine. I heard him before he came into view. He lounged on a makeshift chair, a bone in his hand that he had been using to pick his teeth with. "Happy to see you were able to use the Agni. There must be a whiff of divine heritage in you after all. Too bad you won't live to reap the benefits." His deranged laughter filled the cavern and made my skin crawl. "I'll tell you what, lost child of angels, it has been ages since I have encountered one of your kind and I am having far too much fun. So as not to end our little game early, I will give you a head start to get out of my home. And here's a hint—there is but only one way out. Ready? Go."

I whirled around and sprinted back the way I had come. The voice in my head whispered hurried directions, reminding me of when to turn left or right. It was only moments later that I heard the pounding of feet closing in behind me. I pushed my legs to their limit as I increased my speed and stride.

The light of wood shown directly in front of me and I pushed myself harder still. I felt new warmth at my side as blood started to seep out from my wound. But there was no time to address that now as I barreled out of the cave. I kept running until suddenly I felt something snare my ankles together. I crashed to the ground and looked down in horror at the thick vine wrapping my legs tightly. Two small boulders were tied on either end of the vine, serving as a makeshift bolas.

And Leshy was standing a few feet away.

"You gave it a solid attempt, I will say. I did not expect you to make it out of the cave. Well done. But, alas, I am afraid that I no longer wish to prolong my dinner. It was fun while it lasted."

I rolled onto my stomach attempting to crawl away. I distantly realized how pathetic this would look to the crowd, but I no longer cared. I felt Leshy as he gripped my shoulder to roll me over. At the last second, I noticed the pot sitting over the coals. Ignoring the burning in my hands, I grabbed a fistful of coals in one hand and the pot in the other. I threw the charred remains into Leshy's eyes. He howled in pain, temporary blinded as I swung the pot. It connected with his large head, temporarily stunning him long enough that I was able to cut myself free.

I ran into the forest.

I didn't hear footsteps behind me, but I wasn't about to turn back and look, either. With enough distance between Leshy and I, I decided to scale a tree. I kept climbing until the ground below looked minuscule.

Leshy appeared in the clearing, singing to himself, *"Angels watch while the demons play. They sent this girl, Heaven's stray. From her path, she doth roam. Now trapped with Leshy, under this dome."*

The limb I stood on snapped under me, and I fell to the ground. I cried out in pain as my left wrist cracked on impact. Leshy wasted no time and soon stood above me. He smiled, displaying razor-sharp teeth. "Time is up, child." He straddled my hips, locking me in place with his weight. "Don't worry, I'll make it quick."

Fear coursed through me. I was not going to get out of this, not this time.

Sterling is going to watch me die.

I was no longer concerned with concealing the power that coursed through me. I would be dead soon, and it would no longer matter. Leshy spun my small knife around in his hand, grasping my shoulder with the other.

"Draw your blade."

"In case you haven't noticed, I can't."

"He will give you an opportunity. When I give you the signal, you will do so."

"I doubt he is going to—"

"NOW!"

Leshy's weight shifted as he raised both of his arms to plunge the knife into my heart. It allowed just enough space for me to draw the blade that Roman had given me and drive it into Leshy's chest.

He sucked in air, surprised to see the dagger protruding from his chest. My throwing knife fell from his hands as he fell, almost completely on top of me. He used one hand and what little strength he had left to prop himself up. I inhaled a breath of shock as I saw a flash of turquoise light reflected in his gaze.

Leshy's eyes grew wide momentarily. He placed his mouth near my ear and, barely able to whisper, murmured, "Thank you for sparing my Imps." And then he collapsed. With all my strength, I rolled the demon's corpse off, careful to mind my wrist that was surely broken. I was shaking from the adrenaline and pain. As I took a deep, trembling breath, I felt the tears threaten to spill from my eyes.

"Not here," the voice commanded, "Remember, they are still watching you. Find the Agni and be done with this."

I stood on shaky legs and began to search for the square that I started on. Luckily, it was not too far from where I had fallen out of the tree. Leshy had confirmed that he had led me in the complete opposite direction of the orb. I decided that the best course of action was to follow my original path before he had intervened.

The familiar sound of birds started to fill the air, as if the demise of Leshy called for a choir. Their soft harmonies were somehow both bright and melancholy. The world above glowed a lively emerald as the sunlight pushed through the canopy above. Slowly, the natural hum of the forest joined the birds in a symphony of sadness. I slowed my steps, in awe of the organized song. Something in my chest ached as I let the sound consume me. I knew it had been my life or his, but I suddenly felt the loss as if it were my own. The forest had lost its guardian, and all its inhabitants were mourning.

I ambled through the forest, savoring the warmth that kissed my cheeks through the spaces in the trees. In time, the song ended, and life proceeded as normal for the creatures in the wood. As the noise died down, I heard the faint babble of running water. My pace quickened, and soon, I stumbled upon a stream that was ankle deep. In the middle of the current, a pool of brilliant light refracted magnificent colors from within. I reached down and withdrew an Agni the size of a large egg.

There was a flicker overhead, and the wards fell, revealing a cheering crowd above me. Steps appeared, leading up to the balcony where the two Archangels and the Nephilim leaders sat. Gabriel looked bored. Ramiel and Sloane wore no discernible expressions, but Merik was seething. I moved to step on the first stair when Merik stood.

"You are not finished."

"I'm sorry? I did as I was told. I found the orb. I faced a *Daemoni*, the Imps, and Leshy. I called to Heavenly Fire using an Agni of my own *successfully*. I fail to see in what way I haven't completed your trial."

Gabriel sat forward now, eager to watch the drama unfold. Sloane glowered down from his seat. "You left the horde of Imps alive, despite their attack on you and your perceived friend."

"It wasn't specified that I had to kill everything in the forest *and* find the Agni." I could feel my blood heating. My heart began to beat faster and faster. *They are going to deny me on a* technicality?

"They assaulted you and someone you thought was *human*. We are supposed to protect Edenites from these monsters," Merik said, his tone dripping with disgust as he took his seat once more, "not show some twisted, weak compassion for them. A *true* Nephilim would have known what was expected of them."

"I *am* a true Nephilim." I could hear my voice shake as the words left my mouth. It only made me more upset.

"Prove it, Daughter of Adam," Merik spat in retort. My skin was on fire, every nerve begging to release whatever it was that was building inside of me.

"Kiara, turn around now. Do not look them in the eyes until you get it together. Rein in your emotions, or they will bring ruin upon you."

I turned, not completely sure why I was still listening to this voice in my head. It dawned on me then that it might look as if I was crying.

I decided to play it up, rubbing at unshed tears, until I felt my heart rate even out once more.

"Better. Now, respond to that bastard."

I pulled three knives from my right thigh, flinging one after the other. They sank into Merik's chair. One was placed perfectly on each side of his head. The third was between his thighs, promising that I could castrate him should he move another inch. He was white as a sheet as the crowd fell silent.

"I am not a Daughter of Adam. I am Nephilim. I have angelic blood in my veins. And I have proven myself enough today. I am not here to *entertain* you."

Sloane cleared his throat, "Ramiel, you have the final say at the end of the day."

The Archangel stood, his hair rustled by the breeze. "Ms. Novak showed mercy in a time when she did not have to. More often than not, I feel that mercy is often perceived as a weakness in your ranks, rather than the ultimate demonstration of strength it is," he shot a pointed look at Merik, who was still focused on the blade seated near his crotch. "Being able to know you are strong enough to defend yourself, but aware enough to know when you are not in danger of needing excess force, is how balance is maintained. I do not believe this call showed any lapse of judgment on this young woman's part.

"The *Daemoni* proved to be a lethal opponent, yet Kiara persevered, resourceful despite her injuries. She was able to outsmart the Imps. She saw through Leshy's facade and bested him to ensure her own survival. The Fire responded to her call, something it does not do for anyone wielding an orb. And she returned the Agni as requested. Not to mention," he paused, a smirk appearing on his lips, "she appears quite formidable with a throwing blade.

"I acquiesce."

"I'm sorry?" I couldn't grasp what I was hearing.

"Yes, Ms. Novak, you have achieved Metanoia. Welcome to the ranks of the Nephilim."

Sterling met me at the top of the stairs. She picked me up, spinning us around as she did. It wasn't long before Roman was there too. He pulled both of us into a hug. I yelped, having forgotten about my injuries in my excitement. They immediately stepped away, worried eyes running over every inch of my body, taking in the multiple options that could be the source of my pain. I could only imagine what I looked like to them. My clothing had various tears from the Imp attack. I was acutely aware of the small cuts and dirt and grime that covered my face and neck. My jacket had protected me from the worst of it. But that was nothing compared to the damage done by the *Daemoni*. Blood had started to seep through the leaves, their numbing effects no longer effective. The drainage outlined the three vicious talon marks that had opened my flesh. The fabric surrounding the area a wetter, darker shade of black. My wrist had started to swell and was turning a mean shade of red as heat radiated from around it.

"I think it's broken," I said sheepishly.

"Time to work on your falling, kid," Roman teased.

"We will have a healer meet us at the house," Sterling reassured me. I nodded as Gabriel made his way over to us, the others having already departed.

"Good show, child. Well done indeed. I expect you will be around Sterling and her lot often, then?" he inquired, his eyes drifting to Sterling, who refused to look at him.

"I'm not going anywhere anytime soon," I promised.

"Lovely. It'll be a pleasure getting to know you. Until next time." He tilted his head before launching into the air.

"So that's your father, huh?" I said playfully to Sterling. "He seems like—"

"A downright prick?" Roman offered. We all laughed.

"There is a lot to unpack there, I'm afraid," Sterling sighed.

"Luckily, we have a lot of time to learn about one another." I kissed her quickly, and Roman feigned a gagging noise.

Sterling smiled that dazzling smile of hers. "Let's go home, everyone."

CHAPTER 25

We came walking up the lane. Sterling had her arm draped over my shoulders, both in affection and to help support my weary body, while Roman marched ahead of us. His singing announced our arrival to the whole house, but it wasn't necessary. Callen and Mal were seated on the porch steps. The tension that drained from both of them when they saw me was evident before we even crossed into the front lawn.

Callen gave me a hug, careful to avoid my injuries. His bandage was no longer in place. "Minimal scarring, I guess." He shrugged as if the news disappointed him, which only made me laugh.

"I can only hope to be so lucky," I teased.

"What did you in?"

"A *Daemoni*."

"Nasty things, aren't they?" He chuckled. "The healer arrived moments before you did. She is waiting upstairs."

"Thank you, Cal."

Before I could walk into the house, Mal came up to me, happiness radiating from his golden eyes. "I told you so." I laughed, hugging him tightly, ignoring the pain in my side.

"I have never been happier to have been proven wrong."

"I'm glad you didn't die," he said genuinely.

"The feeling is mutual," I laughed at the repeated conversation he and I had had so long ago.

I went into the house and was met by the healer. Her work was quick and efficient. She was kind, too and it briefly took me back to thoughts of my own job. So much had changed since the last time I had cared for a patient. She gingerly peeled the *Thromvi* back and exposed three deep lacerations that were about 4 inches long. They ran from the lower left part of my abdomen and ended on my side. The healer grimaced. "This is likely to scar, I'm afraid."

"It's a scar worth remembering."

She smiled and continued her work. When her sutures were finished, and my wrist was set and wrapped, she started to work on the smaller injuries. Salves were applied to the small abrasions. Bites were cleaned properly. I was exhausted by the end of it all, but I felt infinitely better all the same.

I thanked the healer for her help and kindness as I walked her out the door. The others were all still outside where we had left them. They expressed their gratitude as she departed. We remained on porch watching long after she left, and I recalled the events from my perspective for Malachi and Cal. I was sure to leave out the mystery voice that had coached me through the majority of the trial Sterling and Roman added commentary here and there, which mostly consisted of detailed descriptions of how pissed off Merik became the more successful I had been.

The sun began to set as the stories died down. Oranges and pinks painted the sky, reminding us all just how beautiful this world could be, and how lucky we all were to exist in it together. I stepped over to the side and watched the sun slip slowly down behind the horizon.

I felt someone come up behind me before the smell of vanilla, sandalwood, and ocean water filled my senses. I turned to Sterling and smiled. There was no longer tension in her shoulders, at least not like there had been this morning.

"I guess you guys are stuck with me now," I sighed dramatically.

She beamed with joy. "I don't know how we will ever manage." She lifted my chin and kissed me deeply despite the pairs of eyes that watched us. We didn't care and, deep down, we knew they didn't either.

"I don't know about the rest of you, but after all this doom and gloom, I need a drink," Roman said, interrupting the peace. "Who is ready to hit the bar?"

Sterling and I both went to raise our hands but stopped short at the distraught expression on Callen's face.

"We aren't quite out of the woods yet," he muttered. He ran a hand through his jet-black hair, and it was the first time I noticed how truly disheveled it was. As if he had been anxiously messing with it all evening.

"What are you talking about?" Sterling asked. "Did something happen while we were gone?"

"Show them, Mal," Callen said. Malachi handed a piece of paper to Sterling, who began to read, the lines in her forehead deepening with every word.

"Before you guys got back," Mal explained, "Gabriel flew in to drop this off. He asked that Cal make sure it got to me."

"What does it say?" I watched as Roman took the letter next. Sterling stared at Mal, sorrow evident on her face. "It's an unofficial letter stating that Malachi is to appear."

"Appear where?"

"Arcadia. They plan to indict me for treason, and I will soon receive an official summons that will state I am to report and be tried for my crimes. Formally, this time," he added, no emotion in his tone. "There is no hint as to when they will call me back."

"What are we going to do?" Roman looked around, hoping someone already had a plan in motion. But he was met with silence.

"We will figure it out," Sterling started to say, "we always—"

Thunder cracked in the cloudless sky. We all turned to look into the yard as smoke began to gather and swirl. Shadows of night and hues of violet mixed together, coming together to create the silhouette of a figure. The smell of smoke and amber filled the air, and I froze in place.

Just like in my dream. And the arena.

Sterling, Cal, and Roman drew their weapons as a second crack of thunder erupted, equipped with a bolt of lightning that scorched the earth where the figure now stood. Only this time, instead of a silhouette, a female appeared. She had long black hair, highlighted with touches of red throughout. Tattoos snaked along warm brown skin, peaking out of her leather top sporadically. Her eyes were deep brown, with honied centers just around her pupils. And behind her, splayed wide, was a pair of ebony wings.

"Mazikeen," Mal said stiffly, signaling the others to lower their weapons.

"Hello, baby brother," she crooned.

Brother?

Callen and Roman looked back and forth between Malachi and the stranger, Mazikeen, who stood before us. Clearly, they were not expecting to meet our friend's estranged sister either.

As she spoke, there was no denying it. Her voice may have been decidedly female now, but there was no mistaking it. This was who had been in my head earlier this afternoon in the arena.

"You shouldn't be here, Maze," Mal insisted.

"That's no way to greet someone who is here to help you, Malachi," she pretended to be offended.

"You? Help?" Sterling scoffed, "Spare me." She did not show a hint of surprise the way the others did. It was as if she had already met this woman once before. If her attitude was any indication, it didn't go well.

"Believe it or not, I've become quite the philanthropist. In fact, I've already saved one of your wretched souls today—at no cost, might I add." Mazikeen looked in my direction, winking smoothly. Sterling took an intentional step in front of me, her gaze attempting to burn a hole through Mal's sister.

"How sweet." Mazikeen looked her up and down slowly and smirked, unfazed by what she saw. "But that is beside the point. I'm here to help Malachi now."

"And just how do you plan on doing that?" Mal asked.

"Unlike you and the Archangel's bastard here, I am not bound by laws and etiquette." Maze looked bored now. She stood examining her nails, speaking as if she were explaining something to a child, "I have no limitations."

"No morals is more like it," Sterling snarled.

Mazikeen's eyes sparkled as she looked up. A lethal smile parted her lips, showing perfect, white teeth. "Precisely," she purred. "Now tell me...who is the bastard Angel that took my brother's wings?"

ACKNOWLEDGMENTS

This book has been a passion project for the last two years, and it would not have the life that it does were it not for the amazing team of people who supported me through every twist and turn. I don't know that I will ever be able to properly thank them, but I'll start trying now.

To the beta readers who read the first version of Kai's story—thank you for everything. You spent time on the roughest version of this story and stuck with me despite the growth that this story would inevitably require. For this kid with a dream of being an author, you were my first audience, and I will always have a special place in my heart for you.

To the authors who have come before me—I'd be lost without you. The path to indie publishing is long and scary and there are so many uncertainties that you were all able to help me navigate. A special thank you to Sarah A. Bailey, Emily M. Syn, Courtney Whims, and Jalen Noel who dealt with me constantly sliding into their inboxes with question after question. You saved this baby author more than o nce.

To Charlie, the best editor I could have asked for—without your insight and talent, this story would still be in crude shape. Thank you for doing right by my characters while also helping me to do right by others. Working with you has been nothing shy of amazing and, from the gang in Soteria and myself, we thank you for your time and effort.

To my family who did not know I had written this story until right before the ARCs went out—I love you all and I never doubted your support. Mom, you have always raised me to believe in myself and know that I can do anything I want to do. It is because of you that this was even possible. To my aunt, thank you for encouraging my dream and sharing your experiences in the world of writing with me. One day, I hope to see your name on another amazing novel.

To the best friends anyone could ask for—I'm not sure how I ever deserved you guys. Thank you for cheering me on through this crazy adventure. Every soft moment of friendship in this story was inspired by you all. Katie—you heard this crazy coworker of yours was writing a book and you jumped in feet first with encouragement and marketing ideas. Carlee—Thank you for the random texts of encouragement telling me how proud you are and never failing to show up for me. You have no idea how much motivation these things gave me in times where it all felt impossible. Jen—I've said it before, and I will say it again; This would not have been possible without you. From the day I called you up with a story idea to my incessant yapping about these characters, to the cover art, and everything in between, you have been there for it all. Thank you for being my day one as both an alpha reader and a friend.

Lastly, to my wife—thank you for supporting the dream of a kid who found solace in books. You suffered hours of me being glued to a screen chasing this goal without complaint. You are the best part of this life, and I am so grateful for your love and support. Without you, none of this would have been possible. I love you more than words can express.

About the Author

 Originally from Southern Oregon, Cora grew up constantly having a book in her hand. At a young age she dreamed of being an author. Despite life taking a different route, she finds herself finally achieving that goal. Determined to contribute to the visibility of sapphic relationships in the adult book community, Cora sat down to write in 2023. What started as a desire for more inclusivity, ultimately lead to a passion project that resulted in her debut novel, The Sparks of Saints.

Cora lives in Salt Lake City with her wife and four fur babies. By day (okay okay she's nocturnal) she works as an ER/Trauma nurse. In her free time, you can find her camping, hammocking, and always sipping on an iced coffee.